THE VAMPIRE JACK TOWNSON

FAME HAS ITS PRICE

THE VAMPIRE JACK TOWNSON
BOOK ONE

JACK TOWNSON

To my cherished Fangfam community, to my Tiktok compatriots and kindred spirits, to my Vampyre comrades and graceful swans, and to the love of my life, Shayne. I extend my heartfelt gratitude. Your collective inspiration has propelled me to breathe life into the chronicles of Jack.

Before you enjoy your reading experience of *The Vampire Jack Townson, Fame Has Its Price,* please be aware of the following trigger warnings:

- Rape
- Moments of Discrimination
- Graphic Violence
- Grooming

"As someone who has had their power taken from them, I believe in the importance of consent in all things. However, to shy away from these topics is to not make them go away, but to be blind to them."

Jack Townson

FOREWORD

Allow me to regale you with a tale— for three years, this character has resided within the recesses of my mind. I wove his narrative through countless roleplaying odysseys, cast him as the nom de plume for my alternative modeling endeavors, and serenaded the world with verses from his perspective, ultimately giving rise to a literary opus of its own.

From the TikTok web series, adored by the Fangfam community, to the pages that Shayne fervently impelled me to compose, this journey unfolds. She once declared that I possessed the soul of an author, a truth I had yet to embrace, and her words now ring resoundingly true. I am brimming with anticipation for the voyage we embark upon, a testament to the shared odyssey that has brought us to this juncture. We have triumphed together, and my affection for each of you knows no bounds. Let us raise our glasses to the forthcoming chapters, to our roles as creators, and to the eventual *Part Two*.

PROLOGUE

"The setting sun always marks the close of mankind's day: parents tenderly putting their children to bed, ensuring their little heads find solace on soft pillows; people hurrying home from work amid the bustling evening traffic. The mundane world shuts its weary eyes, mirroring the fading ball of flame as it gracefully dances out of existence, soon replaced by a better one.

"Finally, they could lay their heads down, savoring a moment when their ordinary lives temporarily cease to exist—drifting away even for those few hours in which they are dead to the world.

"However, *we* are always dead to the world. While their lives pause within that brief window, our realm stirs with some semblance of life. Vampires, Darklings, Werewolves, Witches, and terrors beyond imagination—we prepare to commence our enigmatic dance, donning our masks of life, despite many of us being quite literally... *dead*.

"We thrive in darkness, tormented by the sun's detestable rays that deny us true coexistence (although some attempt and tragically fail). Nevertheless, we scurry about our supernatural lives while the mortal realm slumbers. And those who dare to play with monsters soon learn the rules of our world: finding their truest fears come to fruition whenever that floating piss-stain vanishes beyond the horizon.

"We aren't entirely different from you—not completely. We, too, endure tediously mundane jobs, attempt and stumble in relationships, pay homage to our kings and queens, or defy them by hurling flaming bottles through their windows, and fighting wars in the streets and even across oceans. We share similarities, you and I, and I always yearn to bridge the gap between mortal and monster—to understand you, to be one with you, even as my world burns.

"I extend my clawed talon to grasp at any frail human hand that dares reach out to mine, though they often meet gruesome ends, whether by my doing or... others. Still, I try and continue to try.

"But this story isn't about the present. As you have expressed your curiosity, it delves into the past, when I became what I am. When I was taken... when I leaped away from the brilliant, blazing rays of light and allowed darkness to embrace me like a newborn babe.

"When *he* found me.

"So, shall we commence? Or shall we linger here, gazing at each other from opposite ends of this fireplace, rain pouring outside as I swirl my favorite... *apple juice*... in my chalice while you savor your wine?

The gentleman across the way gestures for Jack to continue.

"That's what I thought. Growls can wait. It's story time now.

"I believe the best way to embark is always at the beginning. If I approach you from the middle, you won't grasp the chaotic whirlwind that has been my undead existence or how I arrived at this mystical place where I now rest my crown. We shall commence from my conception— the day I was born into darkness.

"The year was 2012. Surprised? I'm not some ancient unholy creature sent by a dark goddess to conquer the world. At that time, I was merely a young man, striving to find my path in a world that had failed me as much as I had failed it. I was human, like many others, yet I never felt like I belonged with them. Always the outcast or the pariah in a society that deemed my talents pointless and foolish. So, I buried them deep within, diverting my focus from my aspirations to fulfill the one thing that mattered to me more than my art: taking care of my dear little sister, Chloe."

CHAPTER ONE
LAST DAY ALIVE

"Wake up, Jamey, it's time for another day," my sister's melodious voice sang, rousing me from my deep sleep. Her choppy black hair concealed smiling green eyes as piercing rays burst through the bedroom window.

Items I had spent my life collecting sparkled in the mid-morning gleam, like treasures from a sunken pirate wreck. There were my dice, used in the games I played with my few friends, their ten to twenty-sided faces ready for the thrilling combat rounds we enjoyed during our long evening hours. There was the loose cash and coins earned from my job at a local restaurant, where my acting aspirations made me a true cliche. And then there was the silver pendant—a gift from my late mother—adorned with twin dragons embracing a garnet heart, offering eternal comfort and love.

"Songbird... are we seriously doing this?" I groaned, too familiar with my sister's habit of pulling me from my sheets like a cartoon princess coaxing small animals to join her crusade of disrupting my peaceful rest.

Her slender fingers danced their way to my forehead, and

with one cruel motion, she abruptly ended all of my comfort, as if she were suddenly an evil villain instead...

Flick.

"CHLOE!" I snapped, not realizing my loss of composure would cause damage. "Fuck." I cursed under my breath, regretting my outburst at once.

Those tears of my little Songbird were an instant downer. She could have held an entire building hostage, destroyed my beloved journal, or smashed my guitar against the wall, and her tears would still win any battle they faced. She was like a miniature nuclear weapon, unstoppable by any regime.

Taking a deep breath, I closed my eyes and prepared myself to apologize. "Chloe," I started, "thank you for waking me. I should probably start the day—"

I began to free myself from the prison of fabric, stretching both arms toward her. She allowed me to pull her into a firm embrace, burying her face in my chest, and muffling her short cries so that only I could hear them.

My poor Songbird, my vulnerable sister. She acted more like a child than an adult, easily upset by the smallest of things.

She had experienced so much pain, and it was my duty to shield her from as much as I could. Most of the time, she remained strong in the face of adversity, but with me, she broke down the hardest. Leaning forward, I pressed my forehead against hers before releasing her just enough to see the damage I had caused.

Her disheveled hair and red, puffy eyes revealed the aftermath of her tears, and her sniffles persisted. It pained me to see her like this, especially knowing I was the reason for it.

"James—" she started.

"Chloe, I'm sorry. I'll get out of bed—" I interrupted, beginning to lift myself from the mattress.

"James!" she repeated, her tone firmer than usual.

"What?" I stopped short.

The small girl raised her hand and pointed at the clock. "Your shift started three hours ago. You overslept!"

My heart leaped from my chest as I jolted out of bed.

"Shit—shit—shit—*horse ass*—" I vomited a string of curses while rushing to gather my things, my honey-colored gaze falling across the phone I coveted. One in the afternoon. "Shit!"

I never took day shifts. It was a code—an oath I proclaimed to myself when I became a server. Evening hours were when most tips were dished, when the more interesting and affluent patrons frequented, and the whole restaurant was much less... dead.

However, I had recently agreed to an extra shift out of desperation. Money was tight; my father had lost his job and was on disability, my brother was a selfish drug dealer, and my sister... her skills lie elsewhere. No excuses— I was on thin ice and risked so much when I agreed to take that shift. Obviously, I wasn't the best at time management, but I tried. Thank God for Chloe.

Uniform? Check.

Wallet? Check.

Phone? Check.

No time to shower. No time to wave at my father. Just out, out, *OUT*!

I ran to the door, my feet skittering on the tiled floor as my work shoes struggled to find traction. I almost careened into the hallway wall from panic.

Just as I was about to clear the opening and leap from the porch steps, a hand grabbed my wrist.

"James!" Chloe's voice came again.

Before I could wrench free from her grip, she embraced me with her little arms, bestowing upon me the warmest hug I might ever receive.

"Good luck!"

I barely looked back, and even now I wish I had stopped and taken my time—absorbed every last ounce of warmth and human emotion from her. It would be one of the last times I would ever feel such a sensation again. Oh, how I wish I drowned in those eyes, enveloped the girl in a tight hug, and lavished her with the praise she so desperately needed.

Alas, I was tunnel-visioned. Even so, I had the right to be absent-minded then. Life truly was difficult.

At twenty-six years old, I was running on foot through the suburbs because I was late to a dead-end job that I hated. I was without transportation because my brother had totaled the only family car. I was living in my parent's house as the sole financial provider. And most tragically, I was forced to ignore my talents and dreams.

On wheels, the trip to the restaurant would have taken five minutes, but by foot? Forget it. Twenty-five minutes later, I arrived at the doors of my employment—the job I desperately needed and was on my last legs of keeping.

Fuck.

I cursed and prayed in my mind that I wouldn't find Bryant working the day shift. I had forgotten to check who would be on the floor with me when I agreed to this schedule. Sure as shit, as the doors opened, Bryant stood on the blue and gold carpet looking smug. The swinging glass door caught me at the back and knocked me forward, closer to the doom I couldn't escape.

Not today, anyway.

Please, let me keep this job, I begged in the sanctum of my mind, the one place I found true comfort from the tyranny of the world.

"Donovan. Are you *fucking* kidding me?" Bryant's eyes drooped halfway, as though I were a blinding ray of brilliance, but let's be honest... it was the glaring light of my failures searing into his retinas instead.

Just another blunder added to my list.

Bryant encircled me, and I braced myself for a scolding, but this time, he only placed a hand on my shoulder.

"You know, I should be furious with you for leaving me alone with all these tables, but I secretly wanted you to mess up just so I could see what happens." His words stung, his sharp tongue stabbing behind his wicked simper. "Thanks for the show."

Oh no. Oh god. What did that mean?

My mind raced with possibilities. Was there a camera recording this? Would my late arrival be shown to my manager? Or worse...

As I entered the moderately busy restaurant, my abject terror materialized in the form of *Shelly*, the owner, waiting for me near the kitchen. Her arms were folded. Her eyes were daggers.

She had held a grudge against me ever since she made inappropriate advances toward me during the Christmas party. Of course, I had politely turned her down because she simply wasn't my type. Since then, she had been eagerly waiting for me to fail at every turn, as I usually did.

I shuffled further into the restaurant and there it was—the smile. She never smiled at me. At that moment, I knew. My legs turned to jelly as the distance closed.

"Jimmy," she sighed.

I despised it when she called me that, her cheeks bouncing around her apple-shaped face as she prepared to scold me with apparent delight. "Let's go to the back. We need to have a conversation, you and I."

Once we were within her office—a safe distance away from customers—her tirade rained hell upon my shoulders. It included everything under the sun while she attempted to maintain a work-appropriate tone.

I pleaded. I begged. I mentioned how I was the sole legitimate breadwinner in my family. I even brought up my father's poor condition. None of it could assuage Shelly from the torrent of anger and bitterness she unleashed, as if she had bottled it up since that Christmas party. When her words finally burst from her, it felt like a bomb exploding near my head, the piercing whistle ringing in my ears.

Another lost job to add to the pile. My world crumbled.

"Didn't you hear me? You're fired. Leave. We expect you to return your uniform within the week, or we'll bill you for it."

Shelly smiled through her rage. She relished this. Of course, she did. Another man had rejected her advances, but this time she had the power to punish him. Yet, even in my dismay, I couldn't deny the truth... I *was* frequently late and often uncooperative. Damn it. What could I do? I had no car. Instead of working the shift, I had desperately pleaded for, I was condemned to walk all the way back home, my pride crushed as my blistered feet still throbbed from the first trek.

Upon returning to the small house, I glanced at the clock: Ten minutes til three. I had wasted the entire day running to the restaurant and dejectedly walking back. Not only had I slept away the day and lost my job, but I also squandered the rest of my time drowning in self-loathing.

As the day rapidly faded, I made the only choice available to me—I plunged my face into the large pillow resting at the head of my bed.

I was a failure.

I needed to find another job; wait tables at a different restaurant, or take up another meaningless labor position. Hell, I could even go back to working with Brad and become the muscle for his damn drug deals—not that I wanted to—just saying that I could. Nevertheless, I knew deep down that *still*, I would fail. There was only one thing I excelled at...

Lying completely prone against the weighty comforter that provided me solace in that house, a place I no longer desired to be, I stretched out my hand to retrieve my oldest and dearest companion—my leather-bound journal.

With nimble fingers, I flipped open the pages, each corner caressing the pads where my unique fingerprints gave away my identity. I turned to my favorite poem:

A world Away

In time and space I find you
Floating, untouched, imperfect
A symbol of chaos and tranquility
In this place we see one another
And I am forever changed
In this place you found me
Shattered, discarded, perfection
A symbol of bliss and mystery
In this place we are blind
To the world and what pain it brings
Here we are equal
Here we are trapped
A place between expectations
Where dreams go to die
And here is where I keep you.
Here is where you know me.
Beyond is meaningless,
This is all that matters.

I remembered writing it in a fit of passion, without a face or name in my mind's eye. The idea was to love someone so deeply that we could transcend space and time, finding each other in our own isolated plane that we created. Just imagine having the power to create something out of nothing and to bring the person you love most to live out eternity away from those who wished to harm you. What an incredible idea. What a captivating fantasy.

What a joke.

Such a reality didn't exist. I wrote these romantic poems about eternal love, but deep down, I knew I would never find it. No matter where I looked, the outcome was always the same: Failure.

I had made attempts to love, going on dates on and off for years, taking on the trauma of others, and even enduring painful experiences with certain individuals who shall remain unnamed. But still, regardless of the pain and the way my experiences unfolded, I wrote with fervor, like a demon on helium, cackling away as the fumes of my own flames filled the room with a unique smoke that only belonged to me.

It didn't matter if others might never read my poems. They were mine.

Chloe had always tried to persuade me to publish or find someone who would appreciate my art for what it was, but my preferred career choice was acting. Poetry simply flowed from me every time I closed my eyes. I wanted to strive for excellence in something, rather than just throwing words on a page and hoping they would resonate.

Or maybe I was simply a snob. Yes, that was it. I arrogantly disregarded everyone's advice, including even my own.

I buried my face in my journal, and before I knew it, I had fallen into a deep sleep. Back in the darkness where I felt most at home, there was no dreadful father, no unsatisfactory boss, not even my doting sister. Just me. Alone. My nose in a book, my body returning to the stillness of death where I belonged.

CHAPTER TWO
FAMILY MATTERS

"You slept the entire day away, again?" The voice erupted over me like a looming specter, a menacing presence that had come to snatch me from my bed and drag me away—and that was exactly how I reacted, jolting upright at once.

"What? What time is it?" I mumbled, my arm instinctively reaching toward my mouth to wipe away the drool that had gathered above my chin.

The shadowy figure stood in the darkness of my room, just big enough to cast a shadow over the light streaming in from the hallway. It moved closer, growing in size.

"Your sister let it slip that you were late for work again, and by the looks of it, you must've been fired if you're fast asleep at five o'clock."

Two more hours of the day had slipped by, lost to the world with little excuse. I sat up, facing the formidable foe with a raised eyebrow, feeling the venom build at the back of my throat.

"Yeah, you got it right... you really know how to kick 'em

when they're down, don't you?" I spat out, bracing myself for impact.

His palm struck like a thunderclap, my head recoiling from the force.

"You live in *my* house rent-free. You're going to treat me with more respect than that. Watch your damn mouth!"

The acrid stench of alcohol sprayed from between his sparse, yellowed teeth as my father prepared to strafe me with another onslaught of insults and slaps. Clearly, he was drunk, as usual. It was the only way he could cope with losing his own job, drowning his life away while his mind deteriorated. The alcohol did him no favors, of course. In fact, it only exacerbated his belligerent outbursts.

"So..." I started, my fingertips grazing over the place on my cheek where his meaty palm left its mark. "I guess you conveniently forgot that I'm the only one with a job around here. Or at least I *was*, and that your sorry ass depends on me to get you the things you so desperately need...or claim to need." I continued, struggling to contain my anger. "You know. Booze, porn, cigars, that new television you bought by pocketing my money, that phone sex line that keeps you company at night—those things that are apparently crucial to the survival of our household." I had to bite my tongue to restrain my anger. "Maybe try not to abuse the only person in my *mother's* house who actually makes an honest dollar."

His hand clenched into a fist, and my stomach lurched. Though I had endured my fair share of fights and had been beaten up throughout my upbringing—whether by friends, family, or just the occasional bully—I never wanted to willingly take a blow from this man. He simply didn't hold back. I locked focus with his beady, rodent-like eyes, refusing to show an ounce of fear. His hand exploded forward.

"Dad, what the fuck—" the voice came from behind where my father stood.

The other male member of the Donovan household appeared. Brad.

It was a rare occasion that the entire family was home. Maybe I missed some important date or holiday. I truly must have been lost— to not even realize if it was a special occasion or not.

Before I could wrestle with another rambling thought, Bradly wrapped his arm around my father's to stop another blow from being fired toward my rugged mug.

"He's just being a prick," he croaked as he struggled to hold him back, "you know that." With another labored grunt, Bradley eased his arm back down and clasped our father's hunched shoulders. "Come on, Dad. Leave him alone. Come out to the kitchen. Chloe's just started making dinner."

I glowered after his words. *Of course.* Heaven help the Donovan men from learning how to cook in the wake of their matriarch's demise. Just force the small, emotionally-broken girl to do it all; cook, clean, and wash in between their cracks. The usual.

With my father practically being pulled from the room, Bradley and I shared a fleeting glance. At that moment, I could tell my disgust was not lost on him. He looked sorry. Blood between brothers held no significance when you're only one was a lowlife. Even worse, his repugnant actions tarnished the minds and bodies of the people he claimed to love.

After Mom died, I vowed to protect Chloe from harm, and so did ...Bradley. But only one of us upheld that promise. His impulse to protect me tonight changed nothing.

Once they were gone, I extricated myself from the sheets once more and ambled into the hallway. Keeping my weary gaze to the floor, I was determined not to lay eyes on any of them.

Today was lost. Night was descending fast, and I knew I had to make up for lost time.

"Anywhere but here," I muttered to myself. "I just want to be anywhere but here."

I genuinely yearned for something to take me away—to a place where I could truly be seen, loved, and valued. A place where I could live a life entirely my own, free from the shackles of my pathetic existence, free from the broken fragments of the life that had been thrust upon me; A place where my mother hadn't succumbed to cancer, where my father wasn't a drunken victim of frontal lobe dementia, where my brother hadn't become a drug dealer and ensnared our beloved sister in the grips of heroin. Anywhere but here.

Through the bedroom door and down the hall, the carpet clung to my work shoes as I hadn't bothered changing out of my uniform—I had even slept in it. Returning the uniform would be a hassle; I did appreciate a nice suit, especially when it came for free. I knew my newly unemployed status would leave me without suitable attire for the forthcoming rounds of interviews I faced.

I hastened my pace through the hall, avoiding memories of the past that scattered like shards of a broken mirror I refused to gaze into, fearing the distorted reflection that would greet me. Grief and shame would be the only things looking back.

A framed photograph of my mother and father holding each other in joy hung over my head. In their arms, a newborn bundle was swaddled—my baby sister—her smile illuminating her flushed cheeks, my brother's face aglow with happiness, and my own youthful countenance mirroring theirs... that innocent face that would never wear a genuine smile again once she was gone.

Despite everything that had transpired, we left this capture on display, the sole remnant of what our family once was, haunting me every time I stumbled out of my room. An entire lifetime of seeing my mother's face, as if her ghost hovered in our hallways, forever trapped in that frozen image. It was like staring death in the eyes and deliberately ignoring his existence, pretending as if the cold-hearted reaper hadn't snatched her away from us all.

For me, there was no moving forward.

She was my entire world. Every boy may claim that his mom is his everything, but she truly was. I can still vividly recall her hands caressing my face when I was five years old, the delicate scent of her rose perfume, the way her red curls bounced around her eyes as she laughed, and the bouquets of wildflowers I would thoughtfully pick for her. As her battle with cancer progressed, I did everything I could to remain her beacon of hope. Even my older brother had lost faith in the possibility of her survival. I will never forget her final words to me—

"James, keep dancing. I love watching you dance," she whispered, her hand tenderly brushing my tear-streaked cheeks. "Keep smiling, my dear. Your smile is the most beautiful thing. Keep singing, your voice is music to my ears." Her voice faltered momentarily, a harsh cough interrupting the air. "And James?" She struggled to speak.

I gazed at her picture in the hallway, imagining her presence as if she were still there, lying in that hospital bed, fighting to sit up straight and lock eyes with me. Even at such a young age, I understood that it would be our final moment together.

She whispered, "Keep your little sister safe. I love you."

I failed her. I failed myself. And this family decayed from within like a discarded apple left in the trash, unworthy even of the lowliest maggots.

Torn away from the memory of my mother's angelic smile, I continued trudging down the hallway, my hand grasping the wall to maintain balance as I entered the kitchen. The usual suspects were there: Bradley engrossed in a show on his phone, my father smoking a cigarette in the corner, and Chloe toiling away over the stove, preparing dinner.

I un-slumped myself, doing my best to look bigger, casting a venomous glare at both men while this young girl worked tirelessly.

"Chloe, can I help you?" I inquired, my voice softening, pulled back to the weight of the promise I had made to my mother that day. *Keep your little sister safe.*

Chloe turned, her voice barely above a whisper. "Silly, I've got it under control. Are you eating?" She studied me intently, clearly concerned, her motherly instincts surfacing as she noticed the work uniform I still donned. It was wrinkled now. I shrugged lightly, my hand rising to rake through dark tresses that rained down to my shoulders.

"No, maybe later. I need to get some fresh air."

The truth was, I couldn't bear to be there. Not with them. Not with her. Not even with myself. If only I could find some forsaken gutter to lie in for a few moments and forget about the torment that consumed my life.

Nevertheless, she smiled. "Jamey, just remember to eat something, or I swear... I'll be so mad at you," she playfully threatened, her hand pulling the ladle from the pot she was stirring.

I watched as her fingers trembled with the itch she could never fully scratch, waxy sweat beading across her face. It was getting to be that time again. My heart sank. This small girl possessed our mother's spirit in abundance, unaware of her own spark or memories she had been far too young to recall.

"I'll be back soon, alright? Then we can have something to eat later. How about one more hug before I go?" I leaned forward, wrapping my arms around her tiny waist and lifting her away from the boiling water and the blazing burners. I swung the little girl around as my father and brother watched with disdain.

"If you're going out, try filling out some job applications. The bills are due next week, and we're running low on funds," my father grumbled from his chair, attempting to dampen our moment of joy.

But our happiness prevailed, and I continued to swing Chloe around like the princess she was. Bradley remained silent, his face bitter. As I gently placed her back on the floor, she beamed up at me, ignoring the dinner she had worked so hard to prepare. Those emerald eyes bore into my soul, and I found myself captured within their depths. I failed her. Knowing so made my bones feel hollow.

A frown creased my face as a new painful memory surfaced. The moment I found her frail form strung out in one of the many houses Bradley was connected to. I remembered how I toiled relentlessly to afford her rehabilitation, desperately trying to restore her incredible voice that had fallen silent.

My songbird.

It almost felt like an ironic nickname, once meant for the melodious tunes that used to grace my ears, now shattered by the loss of hope.

My failure. She was never the same. I wasn't sure she ever would be.

I placed both hands on her shoulders and leaned in, planting a tender kiss on her forehead. Her little eyes squinted, framed by long black lashes also inherited from our mother.

"Good luck out there, and please be safe," she chirped, the concern etched on her face despite the vacancy that never seemed to leave. I turned away from her, heading towards the door.

As my feet slid against the tiled floor, the old man croaked his usual displeasure from his soggy seat at the table. "If you're

going to live in this house as a twenty-six-year-old man, it's
time to start paying rent."

I rolled my eyes back and squeezed as hard as possible. I had
lost the energy and will to retort. My fingers gripped the doorknob, urging me to turn and twist, to grant me freedom and the
sticky evening air.

"Sure," I muttered, my voice lacking conviction as though I
hadn't been paying all the bills for years. *Dementia,* I reminded
myself, *don't forget he's sick.* "I'll take a look around."

The old man chuckled at my refusal to argue or put up a
fight, his satisfaction evident in his twisted, corpulent face. He
had succeeded in crushing my spirit, leaving me devoid of any
will to defend myself or even care about my own well-being.

*Well done, old man. Well done. You've done an excellent job of
destroying the morale and fighting spirit of your only decent son.
Mom would be so proud.*

These bitter thoughts reverberated in my mind, amplifying
the weight of defeat that settled upon me. With trembling
fingers, I finally mustered the strength to turn the doorknob,
allowing the entry to swing open before me. I squeezed my
muscular frame through the narrow gap, slithering like a snake
desperate to find shelter from a predator. Freedom awaited on
the other side.

CHAPTER THREE
A CITY WITHOUT SLEEP

As I left the small shamble of the home I called mine, dusk began to take hold. The golden sphere tucked behind the clouds and into its slumber. The walk to Main Street would take me about a half hour. I deliberated, kicking a cursory pebble. I wasn't feeling the local hub. Not tonight. I needed something new. Something more... alive.

Manhattan—

An atmosphere of electricity and light, buildings taller than castles, and the angriest, yet most creative people in the world gather to the metropolis looming over my backyard.

I could be biased. We New Yorkers truly do carry our ego on our shoulders, especially when it comes to pride for our loud and obnoxious city.

A simple walk wouldn't cut it tonight. I needed to get some real space. I called myself a car with what money I had left on my debit card. There wasn't much after monthly bills, but it was enough.

Forty minutes later, and after the most boring conversation ever with the driver about the failing of crypto-currencies that I barely understood, I was in the city. The bastard had been wafting cigarette smoke in my face the entire time, and as I stumbled from the back seat, my lungs ached for the balmy air.

Every step down the filthy tar-speckled pavement clashed with the polish of my work shoes. There was no doubt Manhattan was disgusting. Alleys were littered with trash and the fluids of vagrants, yet its boroughs still held a sort of magic somehow. They say if you could make it in New York, you could make it anywhere— but I think if a person looked hard enough, opportunity could be lurking around any of its seedy corners.

It was a melting pot of people, a place of supreme justice yet steeped in crime, of both the lucky and the downtrodden, of starving artists and inflated businessmen. What a place. It was dangerous, of course. Every corner hid some sort of secret as if at any moment some masked mugger could spring from the darkness and claim your life.

As I made my way through Midtown, my attention was drawn to the flashing lights of a solitary police car. Its tires hugged the curb as it blocked off a narrow alley and a portion of the sidewalk. The car shielded onlookers from... something. I edged a bit closer.

Two officers stood over a fallen figure— a young man sprawled in a heap on the filthy blacktop just beyond the walk-way. Intrigued, I paused and observed. Others soon joined me, forming a crowd that eagerly pressed up on their toes to better witness the disturbing scene.

Blood.

It stained the side of a small Fajita place, like a vicious wound on its cheek. The body on the ground was drenched in its own crimson pool, the result of the angry end of what was undoubtedly a blade.

Paramedics started to arrive.

In stunned silence, I listened to the conversations of those gathered around me.

"Could it have been a mugger? Maybe a drug deal gone wrong?" muttered one onlooker.

"He probably had it coming. Look at all those tattoos!" croaked an older woman.

"I'm just glad it wasn't me," whimpered a man in his early twenties.

"Who cares? Get out of the way! You're blocking the sidewalk," snapped a man in a suit.

More exchanges like these bubbled up from the crowd, the energy about the street buzzing with more and more chaos. I stood there, feeling nothing. No horror at the sight of the blood pouring from an open gut, no contempt for the callousness of those around me, and no sorrow for the family that would grieve this unfortunate soul.

Nothing.

I was numb. What did that say about me?

A heavy sigh escaped my throat and dissipated into the smog-filled air. I watched a bit longer as EMTs attempted to lift this man from where he lie, scarlet staining their hands. The same deadness radiated through my cold bones, and I realized it was time to go.

I started on again, considering how often something like that happened here.

Just another body in the sea of countless others, another extinguished candle in the mausoleum of life. What was happening to me? Had I become so joyless, so shattered, that not even death could rattle me or evoke the slightest emotional response? Had the weight of my own burdens crushed me to the point where, instead of *feeling*, I simply observed?

Fuck.

Perhaps my own apathy and self-pity had finally sucked me under and drowned me.

As I hurried down the slicked city block, neon lights above me seemed to dance in the dark atmosphere. Despite being so filled with light, Manhattan exuded overwhelming darkness. Maybe I shouldn't even go home. Maybe this was the place for me— a forest of skyscrapers devoid of emotion, yet with streaks of color only some would appreciate—a place so empty yet so full. My insides cast outward.

A crack of thunder echoed through the sky, and lightning slashed across the overcast heavens, disrupting my melancholy idea. The sky grew darker yet brighter simultaneously. I opened my mouth to curse when the air filled with marble-sized rain-drops, soaking my now-useless work attire.

Panicking, I ran. Not out of fear of a potential mugger or the presence of a lifeless body on the street, nor from the suffocating claustrophobia of the crowded sidewalk. No, I ran from another bill, the idea of having to pay for these damn shoes.

Each step I took scattered the rain, splashing my work clothes with murky water. As my shoes filled with the vile liquid, I noted the soggy squish added to each stride. I needed cover, so I darted under the awning of the first coffee shop I spotted.

I pressed my palms against the closed glass door and pushed, but it didn't budge. I pushed harder, frustration build-ing, as I clenched my teeth. Knocking on the glass, I hoped one of the patrons would open it for me.

That was when she appeared—a beautiful young woman with strawberry hair. I felt a surge of excitement as I stumbled back from her beauty. She was coming to my aid. But to my surprise, she pushed the door open in my direction, pointing out the obvious sign indicating that I should have pulled it.

"Pull, not push," she said, her finger gesturing towards the sign.

I flushed with embarrassment. There went my chance. As I entered the coffee shop, I expected her to retreat to her coffee and forget about me. However, she stood there for a moment, observing.

"Rainy day, isn't it?" she remarked, her hand assisting me in holding the door open. A small smile played at her eyes.

I was stunned—amazed that this beautiful woman was taking the time to talk to me, even about something as mundane as the weather. I cleared my throat, trying to maintain composure as my heart raced. "Yeah, it's... it's crazy out there. I swore I saw a cat hit the pavement, but then I remembered we're in New York, so it was a rat...more likely."

I started to sweat, but my attempt at a joke worked, eliciting a delightful burst of laughter from her. Her smile was captivating, and I wouldn't mind being consumed by it.

"They do get pretty big here, I've noticed," she continued to laugh. "Be careful out there..."

Our eyes met again briefly, and in that fleeting moment, something passed between us. But then, her expression shifted, as if she had remembered something important. She offered me another smile, one that was a bit flatter than the first, before her feet carried her away. Reaching her table, she glanced back at me, her freckled cheeks pulling up once more as she seemed to deliberate.

Maybe I wasn't as lost as I initially believed. I returned her gesture, watching as she turned to a man who had been sitting there waiting—a companion, I presumed.

He was slightly shorter than me and appeared uncomfortable, casting a dagger-like glare at the redhead. His gaze then shifted to me, and I could sense his immediate aggression. His beady eyes bore into mine from beneath his shaven head, until her hand rose to his cheek in a calming manner, just above his carefully maintained five o'clock shadow. Was he trying to appear rugged? What a tool.

As I continued deeper into the coffee shop, my mind still preoccupied with the missed opportunity, I swiftly moved right over a puddle on the tile. Suddenly, everything seemed to spin, and I braced myself for the impending embarrassment of falling flat on the floor. I imagined the laughter that would follow such a calamity. After all, it had been that kind of day. But instead, arms wrapped around me from behind, catching me before I could make a complete fool of myself.

"Woah, careful there," a voice came from behind, securely holding me against a broad frame as my feet desperately sought traction.

I let out a sigh of relief, realizing that at least I wouldn't ruin this suit just yet.

"James?" the voice inquired with a hint of recognition. "James!" The voice behind me roared with confidence, and a peal of booming laughter ensued as my savior celebrated. "Holy shit! It's been what... six years? Still falling all over yourself, I see."

With the help of the mysterious stranger, I regained an upright position, my gaze shifting to the side to see if the beautiful redhead had noticed. But by then, the man she was with had taken a stance, blocking her view of me. Idiot. With another heavy sigh, I turned to express my gratitude to the... *stranger*.

"Hey, thanks. It's been a lousy day, and it would've gotten way, *way* worse if you hadn't..." I paused mid-sentence as I turned fully to face my rescuer. "*Chris?*" I exclaimed, my eyes wide with disbelief.

There he stood, blond hair, blue eyes, looking like he came straight out of a eugenics program—my old friend from my hometown. We had been inseparable—best friends bound at the hip since childhood. I stared at his more professional appearance, my gaze falling across his built form under his gray dinner jacket and pressed slacks.

"Seriously, has it been that long? You're looking at me like I died and came back to life. I just moved to the city," he chuckled, while I remained fixed on him as if he was a guardian angel or a specter come back to haunt me. "Come on," he hummed, gripping my arm firmly. "You look like you could use a coffee."

I muttered an affirmative under my breath and agreed. Coffee sounded like an amazing idea, and I had nowhere else to be... or *wanted* to be. I followed, studying his elevated appearance as he led the way. It felt odd being in the presence of the man whom I had trusted more than anyone else, the one with whom I confided every secret and dark desire. It seemed like fate brought him back to me during this most consequential moment. I believed he was there to save me, but little did I know...

Sliding into a booth, our rain-soaked suits clinging to the laminate, mine a representation of an impoverished life and his a symbol of fortune and success. My curls stuck tightly to my face, resembling octopus arms attempting to drown an old pirate ship, while his hair was golden and slicked back, perfectly suited for the weather.

"So..." His blue eyes locked onto mine, causing my heart to skip a beat. "How is home life? Are you still taking care of the riffraff in your family, or have you finally managed to get out of that situation?"

I exhaled, memories of our past conversations flooding back —the tear-filled venting sessions on the steps of the dirty village coffeehouse, where I poured out my heart to him.

"It's the same. Everything is the same. Don't let the bargain bin suit fool you. I'm still in the same shitty situation you left me in," I said, my smile laced with defeat.

The truth was, Chris had abandoned me—left me in the place he once promised we would escape together.

His responding smile was cursory and didn't reach his eyes. "Looks good on you, nonetheless. And how about your sister? Bradley? Is your old man still around?"

What should have been a casual catch-up between friends felt more like a conversation with an absent parent. I barely contained my spite as I responded, "You know, they're all just as shitty as usual... And what about you? Living the dream, huh? I mean... fuck, you're glowing like a goddamn angel in this miserable place," I snorted. "Nice suit, by the way."

Even my venomous words seemed to barely scratch the surface of his composure. "Thanks, it's an Alejandro. Costs a bit more, but I—" He paused, his face momentarily dropping, and then leaned in closer. "I actually have this amazing job now, and the pay is just..." He whistled, speaking to me as if he was about to sell me a car.

"Must be nice," I groaned, slumping back into the booth and folding my arms.

"Listen," he started, his tone softening. "I know we said we were going to get out of there together, but sometimes life doesn't work out that way. It's not so simple. I can't be responsible for another grown man, you know? We were friends, not in a relationship. So... I hope maybe we can start fresh. It's been six years, and I just..." He exhaled deeply. "It's been a lonely time out here. I'm really happy I bumped into you."

His confession made me feel like an ass. He had valid points. I couldn't expect him to literally carry me on his back and take me along on his journey to success. Maybe I had been too expectant.

"Fine. Fine. You're right. I'm being... Fuck, I'm sorry," I fumbled, remorse flooding my gut. "My day has been a nightmare. I woke up late, had to deal with my dad threatening me, got fired from my job, and... it's been a shitty time."

Chris's eyes filled with sympathy as he watched me. "Damn, man. I had no idea things were—alright, listen..." He leaned closer, assuming his former drug dealer pose. "You're still acting, right? Or modeling, at least? Look at you, no matter where you are in life, you always look like a damn statue from a Roman coliseum. Why not... *bank* on that? Get some work in that field?"

I returned, "I've tried, it just never works out. I can't remember the lines, or... I'm just too exotic for what they're looking for. Nothing ever seems to stick."

His blue eyes left me at the table for a moment, scanning the surroundings as if his next words were some sort of secret. "Have you ever heard of Alexander La Mont?"

My amber eyes squinted at the name. It did ring a bell. "Yeah, actually... Can't place where I've heard the name, but it does sound familiar," I answered cautiously.

Leaning even closer across the table, his face just inches from mine, I couldn't help but match his proximity. Two grown men leaning into one another during a thunderstorm in the city —probably looked a little romantic. Not that I found the idea uncomfortable.

"If you've ever seen any big-budget films, from Hollywood or otherwise, La Mont's most likely had a hand in it. He's a savant—a genius. He has an incredible eye for talent and knows just who to cast and where. I kind of...rub elbows with people in the industry. I know him. Sort of. Not directly. Know what I mean?"

My interest piqued, renewed hope replacing the pain bouncing around my hollow ribs. "Are you saying you can set something up for me... to meet this guy?"

Chris shook his head with vigor. "No, but I can get you an

audition! There's this big project he's working on, and he's looking for actors. I don't know the details, but it could be a major opportunity—lots of money, fame, fortune, *women*."

The word "*freedom*" slipped from my lips, carried by a fading exhale, and Chris nodded in agreement.

"Exactly. No more dead-end jobs. No more asshole father or brother. Just success and hard work," he explained.

I couldn't contain my excitement, bouncing in my seat slightly. "Alright! I'll audition. Just point me in the right direction!"

A wry smile graced Chris's chiseled features. "Yeah? Perfect! He has a venue a few blocks up called the Prepotent. Let me send a few texts... and we'll get you a spot."

I nearly leaped from my seat. "How soon?"

"Tonight, I'm sure. I know he's been in a rush to fill the role," Chris mumbled, his fingers flying across the small device in his palm.

But then, a certain promise I had made surfaced in my memory. "Wait. I have dinner with my sister. I promised Chloe I'd be back to—" I was cut off as Chris abruptly stopped his rapid tapping.

"Hey. James." Chris sighed through his words as he glared pointedly at me. His blonde brows furrowed. He cleared his throat. "I know it's been a long time and everything, but this is a once-in-a-lifetime opportunity. You've taken care of your sister the entire time I've known you, and—"

"And?" I snapped, confused by why that made me so defensive.

"And... it's time for you to choose yourself, bud," Chris continued. "You've done everything you can. The question is pretty simple: Is it worth risking a massive opportunity just for the ten-thousandth dinner with your little sister? I mean..."

At that moment, I realized how much time I had spent

taking care of everyone else and neglecting myself. Was it really so bleak? Had I chosen a life of mediocrity just to keep my sister happy while putting my own happiness on hold?

"Could I... could I have a moment? I just need to step outside."

"Take your time. I'll come out when I get some answers," Chris said.

I left the small booth, where the two of us had forgotten to order any coffee at all, and made my way to the glass door. In my nervousness, I pushed instead of pulled but managed to slip out nonetheless. As I stepped outside, a lumbering figure collided with me without warning. Despite his shorter stature, he nearly knocked me to the ground as he pushed past. The redheaded girl from earlier rushed along behind him.

"I am so sorry. Are you okay?" she halted, offering a hand down to me, her small mouth pulling to the side in concern.

I gave the girl a swift nod. "I'm fine. Don't worry."

I offered her a reassuring smile before collecting myself on the sidewalk, my hands finding leverage on the wall to keep myself from tasting the wet asphalt beneath me. As I regained my composure, my eyes drifted to her partner who casually left her behind as he entered the crosswalk.

"He seems lovely," I blurted out. I couldn't help it.

The girl released a labored breath. "He can be difficult some-times. I really am so sorry—" she began, but I interjected a bit too loudly than I should have.

"James! My name is James."

The girl's cheeks grew rosier, and her hands raised to hide her smile. "It was nice meeting you, *James*. My name is—"

"Annie! Hurry the fuck up!" Her angry partner's voice boomed in the distance.

The girl visibly flinched as if struck by a lightning bolt. "I have to go. It was *really* nice meeting you!" she called, her pale hand reaching to push back her flaming curls behind her ear. "I am so sorry, just—"

And there she went, away from the door and off the sidewalk, following her miserable jailer into the rainy labyrinth of concrete and chaos.

I looked after the girl with the flaming hair, watching her figure fade. It was a pleasure even to watch her disappear into the distance. The rain subsided.

Wonderful. I had been on time to get drenched, stuck in this soppy, pathetic suit for what was potentially the biggest audition of my life.

My fingers trembled as the phone rested in my palm. I knew how upset Chloe would be, and I wished that somehow I could be in two places at once. If only there were more of me. Choosing the contact with the adorable picture of my apple-faced sister, a deep sense of dread washed over me.

"This is Chloe Donovan. I can't come to the phone right now. Please leave your message after the beep," her voicemail greeted me.

"Hey, Songbird. So, I've got good and bad news. The *good* news is that I've got this huge opportunity—an audition that could actually change everything for us. The bad news is that I won't be able to make it home for dinner with you. I know things have been crazy lately, and I've been in a funk, but I promise everything is going to get better. I miss you, Chloe. Love you, little sister." As the beep of the disconnected call sounded, the door behind me opened once more. Chris, with a wide smile on his face, offered me an umbrella in the rain.

"I've got a time slot. Ready for the biggest night of your life?" he asked.

CHAPTER FOUR
THE "AUDITION"

A four-block walk brought us past sixteen homeless people, a jazz player, a living statue, four pissed-off dogs, a rat dragging a pizza slice, and a cab that almost ran us over in the crosswalk, but we *did* make it to our destination: *The Prepotent.*

This mysterious building seemed older than the city itself, modernized with flashing lights and a digital sign across the front, yet it boasted an air of antiquity. It stood tall with stone pillars and gargoyles perched high above, casting their watchful gazes down at denizens below. Old stone carvings with Latin inscriptions adorned its exterior. It was a sight that belonged in either the darkest nightmare or the grandest fantasy, depending on the time of day.

As I stared at this architectural marvel, I couldn't recall ever noticing it here before. I frequented the city. I knew the blocks—the alleys. It felt like a Mandela effect, making me question if this place had sprung from the ground like a cursed tree. I was horrified to enter and meet the person who claimed this kingdom as his domain.

"Alright," Chris chuckled hurriedly. "Get your ass up to the top floor. Tell them Chris Cornton sent you for a private audition, and they'll get you to Alexander's personal office." He turned to me, smoothing down his lapel.

I gaped stupidly at him. "Wait, you never mentioned that I was auditioning *with* the owner himself. That's not how this usually works!"

It felt like showing up for an audition for *E.T.* and finding Steven Spielberg waiting for you in the casting office. My stomach flipped and my knees turned to putty.

Chris grabbed my shoulders and pulled me into what could only be described as a *bro huddle*. "Hey! Knock that shit off. You've got this. Do you want to be stuck in that broken town forever, waiting tables, and being your dad's whipping boy?"

I shook my head.

"Then get the fuck up there, kick down the door, and impress the hell out of this guy with your talent and charisma, okay?"

Chris may have left me behind—he may have found success while I tripped over failure, but he was a true friend. He always had been, and I was starting to remember why I once felt so connected to him.

"Alright. You're right," I exhaled, hyping myself up. "I've got this."

"Damn right, you do! Now stop wasting time and get up there!"

Chris gave me one last slap on the arm and a shove in the right direction. My shoes nearly slipped as I struggled to catch myself from the force.

Inside, the massive, marble lobby was overwhelming as I scoured the various corridors and entries in search of the right way to go. An older man seated at the front desk waved me over. He had very little to say, glancing down at some list on a clipboard. I supposed he'd already been informed of my arrival. How efficient Chris was.

The paunchy-gutted guard guided me toward the elevator, punching a button for me. "Up you go, Mr. Donovan. Break...a leg."

I scrambled inside. His wrinkled sausage-like fingers pressed the button for the top floor, the light illuminating the fleshy pink just above his nail. Then his fingers retreated, finding the hat he wore, and gave it a reassuring tug in my direction. A creased smile appeared, causing his lips to pull broader under his mustache.

Up I went, the elevator screeching its way to the top floors of the old stone building in a straight vertical ascent. Once I reached the sixth floor, it lurched to a stop. I exited the cage and was greeted by something unexpected—

Confusion washed over me as I took in the sixth floor. The area was a departure from the grand venue below. It was a tight space flooded with red neon light, almost resembling a nightclub—but one that would have felt very intimate.

An island bar stood against the back wall, offering a view of the city through plated glass that stretched around to the right. I cautiously explored the empty place, my shoes awash in the flashing blue lights along the floor that trailed the bar's base. The dance floor was not far from the surrounding tables, but what caught my attention was a hidden room tucked away in the back, past a set of very curious-looking stairs.

Ignoring the red velvet stairway, I made my way toward the room, which was partially obscured by sheer, rose-embroidered curtains.

As I approached, I could make out the shape of what appeared to be a throne inside. It seemed out of place—a gothic piece of furniture that stood as a symbol of power and authority there in a seedy nighttime establishment. I wondered who would have the audacity to sit on that throne there in that club. Perhaps it was a perk for fancy bottle service... or maybe for patrons who requested a lap dance.

Just as I reached to touch it, a voice boomed from behind me, startling me.

"James, right?"

I turned to face the source of the resonant tone, my heart nearly leaping out of my chest. I thought I had been totally alone in that room.

Before me, stood a stocky man, likely in his thirties or forties, gazing at me with concern. He had dark salt and pepper hair, a thick beard, glassy blue eyes, and heavy brows. He grumbled, his hands resting on his wide hips.

"You okay, buddy?" he asked in a surly southern drawl.

My eyelids fluttered rapidly before I nodded in acknowledgment. My bones gave a shiver under my damp work suit.

"Just looking for where my audition is supposed to be. I got lost. This isn't the top floor?" I asked, the whipping motion of my soaked black curls threatening to slap me in the face.

The stranger chuckled before running broad fingers through his beard. "Actually, this *is* technically the top floor. See, the elevator doesn't go any higher. It stops here, and then you've got to rely on your feet to go the rest of the way." He indicated the velvet stairs. As I turned toward the bar, he offered, "Just up the staircase and to the right. Don't go any further than that, or we'll have to call security. Understand?"

I nodded quickly. I didn't want to jeopardize this opportunity any more than I already almost had.

"Not a problem." I swallowed hard. "I understand. I'll mind myself." I practically choked out the words.

The man's pale features scrunched as a single ashy eyebrow lifted in skepticism. Muttering something indecipherable, he continued ambling toward the bar as I made my departure.

I could hear his grumbles fading as I ascended, gripping the gold-trimmed railing so tight my knuckles turned white. Nerves made the climb feel like scaling the side of a mountain, pulse thundering in my chest.

Finally, I reached the top, gaining a clearer view of the hallway stretching out before me. Paintings, large enough to climb into lined the walls. Their images seemed from a time long forgotten, unfamiliar faces glaring back at me.

At the end of the hall, a dark wooden door with golden letters sat in reticence: *A. Lamont.*

I came face to face with the entry, my hand trembling as it hovered just above the large *O* in front of me. This was it, a massive opportunity to change my life—a chance at a dream that could lead to stardom and fame. I was ready—ready for this chance to become more.

But I hesitated another moment.

Something held me back even still. Was it the image of my little sister with her infectious smile and attempts to take care of me? Or was it the memory of the mother I had lost, the pain still fresh despite the passing years? Perhaps it was the fear of a life-altering transformation—the idea of breaking free from the complacency I had forced upon myself. Was it normal to fear freedom and independence?

"Come inside," A voice like hand-spun silk, urged me through the entry. My hand instinctively gripped the doorknob, and with a twist and push, I found myself inside without fully realizing how my feet had carried me. My gaze fixated on the owner of the establishment, sitting in an expensive-looking leather chair before a large, oak desk.

"Please... do not fear. I don't bite," he said, his jeweled hand sweeping at his front, inviting me to take a seat before him.

"R-right," I stammered, momentarily forgetting about the audition.

My focus remained locked on Alexander La Mont, unable to shake the image of his face from my mind. The room and its surroundings were suddenly inconsequential; The gothic fixtures, gaudy paintings, mural overhead, and the long, blackout curtains mildly drawn aside—they all faded into the background, overshadowed by the man's captivating visage.

His eyes were of the deepest purple—an unnatural color, akin to a field of lavender with the saturation dialed up to the maximum. They pierced my soul and tainted it with their hue. His hair resembled a golden lion's mane, radiating an impossible luster and shine. It cascaded across his chiseled jaw and cheek, reaching his shoulder before spilling onto his chest. His brows were furrowed, giving him a perpetual scowl, like a predator on the hunt, ready to tear its prey limb from limb in the darkness of night.

But his voice... *that* voice. It was like a siren whispering words of damnation to a sailor lost at sea, simultaneously shaking my courage and drawing me in.

I couldn't help but notice his outfit as well—a partially open black mesh button-down that revealed the contours of his firm and muscular chest—the tight curvature of his nipples.

"Um, I—" I shook myself out of the trance induced by his presence, realizing that I had forgotten basic protocol.

I still hadn't given my slate: my name, age, and where I was from. I took a moment to collect myself and provided the necessary information, my voice cracking terribly in the process.

"James Donovan, twenty-six years of age, from—"

Alexander sat up straighter in his chair, his voice curling out from between his pale lips like he breathed smoke. *"James...* peculiar. I would have taken you for something a bit more exciting."

I blinked, unsure of whether or not his words were meant as an insult or a compliment.

My voice quivered as words tumbled out, "It's the name I was born with, sir."

The man shook his head defiantly. "No, no. That won't do."

"I'm sorry, sir, I don't... understand," I stammered, panic bubbling in my gut. My hands grew clammy, and my breathing came more rapidly as my heart raced in my chest. Had my very *name* somehow ruined this opportunity?

Leaning forward, the man tapped his chin with manicured fingers. "You're far too dashing for such a name. James is so common... so bland." His head tilted against his hand, and a realization seemed to strike him. "How about..." A slender finger rose to his lower lip. "*Jack.*" He leaned back in his seat, flicking his wrist to send waves of golden hair scattering from his face. "Has a certain...electricity. Don't you think? That would suit you much better."

This audition was more than strange. Here was a man I had just met, suggesting I change my name as if the one given to me by my deceased mother was no longer sufficient. The thought fluttered briefly across my mind. How far was I willing to go for success? Even so, I felt unable to resist the mesmerizing gaze of his violet eyes. They drew me in and drowned me like a hapless victim in a bathtub.

"Should I... c-continue with my slate?" I managed to ask, my words catching in my throat as I struggled to maintain composure.

The sight of him left me disoriented, my inhibitions slipping away.

His voice was as intoxicating as rose perfume as it filled the room, enveloping me completely. "Tell me about yourself, Jack," he commanded, effortlessly adopting the new name like I'd worn it forever.

I couldn't deny the allure of his presence. Not because he

was gorgeous, but because— *what was I thinking*? I tried to regain my focus.

"I'm not really very interesting," I began, but he raised a hand to interrupt me, the rings on his fingers gleaming in the sultry light.

"Please. Everyone has something interesting about them —some hidden secret, some delicious little dream or goal. You must have something you can share with me... something forbidden that no one else knows. Something... *unique*," he prompted, his words slicing through the stillness in the air.

Then, I remembered my most coveted journal.

I had always considered myself unremarkable— a failed actor, a failed brother, and son, a failed worker. But there was one thing I cherished, something I had kept hidden within the depths of my soul and the stillness of my room back home.

I was a poet.

"Actually," I began, hesitant but unable to resist his probing gaze, "I enjoy writing. Particularly poetry. I love the arts— singing, dancing, performing—but I haven't found the right platform to showcase these talents. They've sort of been... in limbo. But writing is something that I've kept close to me my whole life."

Alexander beamed, his eyes seeming to glow in the darkness. "A *writer*, you say? Is that so?"

"Yes, sir... I'm a poet." The words stumbled out of my mouth and onto the polished marble floor.

As Alexander expressed his interest, head tilted to the side, a new question emerged from his lips. "Do you have any of these poems on you by chance?"

My heart raced as I nodded fervently. "Of course!" I always carried my poems with me, kept within the sanctuary of my phone.

"Share one with me?" he requested, leaning against his desk with his hands stacked, his chin resting upon his knuckles.

I was taken aback. How did an acting audition with the biggest producer in New York turn into a poetry reading? Nevertheless, I had little choice but to comply with his request.

I pulled my phone from my pocket.

Feeling the weight of his gaze upon me, I selected a poem that I believed captured the essence of the evening. With trembling hands, I began to recite the words aloud, offering a glimpse into the depths of my soul, surrendering to the lion that stood before me, hoping my words would satiate his hunger, lest I become his next meal.

I cleared my throat and started to read aloud...

> **"Beautiful Agony**
> *In glass entwined*
> *She sits*
> *Aching beautiful agony*
> *Sweet sinister lips*
> *My mirrored soul*
> *She sits*
> *Love, sweet love*
> *Burning twisted pleasure*
> *Tainted by my touch*
> *I call her mine, forever*
> *She sits*
> *Waiting*
> *Writhing*
> *The reflection of a goddess*
> *I saved them for her*
> *Pages burned and tattered*
> *Mended with mangled claw*
> *Scribbled phantom words of wolf*

Written lions roar
She ignites me, this twisted thing
Sets my love aflame
Rakes my soul across the coals
Then makes me whole again
Through the flames she takes firm grasp
My heart pulsing in her palm
A decision she could make, any time
To smother or to calm?
Would she,
she could and even that would be enough
No
The twisted thing, scorched and changed
She holds the lump softly still
Cares for it, molds it
Until...
What once was broken stands renewed."

Silence lingered in the room as my recitation came to a close. A wave of panic threatened to drown me. Had I failed to impress him? Was my poem not good enough? His expression was so unreadable, I wondered if my poetry had insulted him.

"Should I continue my slate, sir?" My words fumbled across my tongue. I felt the panic rise again, my heart throbbing in my chest at the fear that I had somehow destroyed this new opportunity. *What a stupid idea*, I thought to myself, *reading my poetry to some famous savant like some love struck fool in a romance novel, how moronic.* I emotionally battered myself as I awaited my fate, my self esteem plummeting off of the edge.

"No. Don't bother." His protest stabbed me like the bluntest blade from the rustiest dagger, I had truly failed.

I hung my head, my nerves wilting in my skin as I could feel nothing but numbness take me, "Well then, thank you for everything." Hanging my head in defeat, I got up to leave.

Suddenly, Alexander's voice broke the quiet. "Don't you dare!" he exclaimed, his voice filled with urgency and determination.

The sudden change in his demeanor shocked me. It seemed that he had been deeply moved by my poem, despite his initial silence.

Confusion and doubt clouded my thoughts as I hesitated, unsure of what to do, but Alexander's words reeled me back into my seat.

"You have the job. *Please*...don't go," he uttered simply.

"What?"

"I said..." He stood to his feet, palms pressed firmly to the desk. "You have...the job."

I couldn't believe my ears. It was a sudden turn of events. A surge of hope and excitement coursed through my veins. It was hard to breathe. Alexander's presence filled the room, his energy weighty and overwhelming. He possessed an undeniable magnetism, and my heart leaped into my throat with a mixture of anticipation and uncertainty. His words echoed in my mind, his praise igniting a spark of confidence within me I thought had been snuffed out forever.

My eyes widened in confusion. Heat blossomed in my cheeks as I watched the man round his desk and stalk towards me, his arms wrapped behind his back like some aristocrat. I obsessed over his every step. It wasn't like me to be so taken so quickly, and especially never before with a man.

"That was the most beautiful thing I have ever heard," Alexander mewed. "Clumsy, a bit unrestrained, but the heart and passion in it make me yearn for my younger years—something so few have been able to do. You are so much more special than you realize." He paused, seeming to deliberate over something. The corners of his eyes strained. "Perhaps even like me. Perhaps... destined for greatness."

As he approached me, his eyes filled with admiration, his hand left his side to rest upon my bicep. His touch fixed me in place and I was unable to move, unable to speak.

I had the job. The audition was successful.

Successful.

I wasn't used to the word. The notion rolled around heavy and strange in my brain. I wouldn't live my life as a failure after all.

I mustered up a meek *"Thank you,"* unable to fully articulate my gratitude and surprise. My focus narrowed in again on his hand perched against the muscle beneath the wet fabric of my sleeve. The weight of his words finally began to sink in, and I struggled to comprehend the magnitude of everything.

Alexander spoke again, his voice softer this time.

"Now, of course, we'll have to speak about your lodgings and fetch someone for your things," Alexander mumbled as his hand on my arm stayed in place...constricting even. His other hand tapped upon his cleft chin.

"Excuse me?" I blurted, breaking the hold that his glorious presence had on me. "Did you just say I was going to be *living* here?"

His tapered eyebrows lifted high on his forehead. "Did your friend not explain it to you in full? The position here is to be my *protégé*, my ward, my... apprentice. You will learn everything I know; every skill, every tool, every trade. And have every contact of mine at your disposal. It is truly..." He raised his index finger. "...a once-in-a-lifetime opportunity."

I doubled back at his words. "Mister La Mont—"

"Please. Just Alexander—"

"Right. Alexander, I need to think this through. I have a sister back home that I care for. I have to make sure she's alright

—that my family doesn't go hungry. I have... I have fam —family—"

As I spoke, Alexander's soft pads left my arm to find their way to my lips in an attempt to silence my fear.

"Poor boy. Please... no anxiety, no worry. I would not let your family go without compensation. You are more than welcome to share what you make here with your dear sister to keep her comfortable."

His words didn't help, but that finger... oh it was sending euphoric, little zaps through my skull.

"I have an idea! You come with me—see my world, embrace all that this life has to offer, and you make a decision when the night is at its climax. Do we have a deal?" Alexander brought his finger to dance down my chin and tap over my clavicle.

My mind spun violently. "Just tonight...?"

His responding chuckle was a drug. "Just tonight. And then, if you don't enjoy it, you may return home without a second thought, and I will think of you from time to time as the one who got away."

I inhaled deeply, holding that breath at the base of my throat before giving him one, fateful nod. I agreed to venture into his world for just *one* night, knowing that my next decision would have a profound impact on my life.

"What's the danger in a single night?" I whispered...but only barely. "Show me your world, Alexander."

CHAPTER FIVE

LAST NIGHT ALIVE

The city post-audition was a different world altogether. Soggy dumpsters and pizza-stealing rodents gave way to a version of New York that was opulent under a sea of stars. Our foray into the night was a whirlwind of euphoria, and excitement ran like liquid fire through my veins.

Nothing was off-limits.

Alexander and I began our night at a small dive bar. The location seemed like nothing of worth at first, but then, the owner came to greet us. He and Alexander seemed to be old friends as they chattered about life over broad grins, the man's speckled by caps of gold.

"Come to the back, Alex. Come, come..."

He gestured with arms sleeved in tattoos and we followed. There, we were treated to the most incredible show—twin dancers coiling their bodies like snakes beneath the glitter of a disco ball. Two tight black braids whipped and swayed at the backs of each head, more tattoos spiraling up their legs and across each set of ribs.

It was an intimate exhibition, only for us. These identical

vixens writhed against one another, showing us sights that should have been forbidden. Normally, it wasn't my sort of thing, but Alexander's boyish smile and commentary made it seem like this display was his favorite and rarest treat.

A server came to our private booth, offering a strange green liquid. *Absinthe*, he called it, and we both drank deeply as the world seemed to slip away. Anything left of my inhibitions melted, the fear-riddled boy of the past replaced by a daring demon who yearned to share in Alexander La Mont's devious glee.

The world began to formlessly shift and change, faces melting into one another and the twin dancers at our front colliding again and again until two became one. It was horrifying. Yet with Alexander at my side, I felt safe. There was no danger.

My hand found his leg as I watched, my fingers digging into the muscle as he released an encouraging laugh. His palm slipped over mine. We locked eyes, and in my moment of inebriation, his lavender orbs seemed aglow, as if he was somehow inhuman. Something in my heart gave a knowing tug, but I couldn't place it.

We spent the better part of an hour there before leaving. And that was only the first stop of the evening....

From there, we galavanted toward the Metropolitan Opera House, where a poor fool like me could have ever only dreamed to go—a place where the greatest sang upon a glittering stage, telling stories of romance, death, and despair.

At first, I panicked. It was instinct. I had no money, no tickets. Too quickly, I forgot who my companion was for the evening. Alexander grasped my hand and led me into the champagne-colored lobby. He waved to a familiar face before walking me up a few sets of stairs to a particular box overlooking the stage from above. I had always dreamt of seeing a Broadway show, but the opera... I could have never even imagined. Alexander slithered through plushy red seats and practically pulled me on top of him.

The house was vast, a rolling sea of red and champaign opulence. Below, the orchestra was nearly half filled with patrons. To our left, the mezzanine was also filling up quickly, excitable chatter sweeping through the space. Everyone in attendance was dressed to the nines except for me, but the funny thing was, I didn't care so much anymore. The fear of the past was swept away and replaced by his boldness. All Alexander and I could do was giggle into one another's faces, like two drunk lemmings.

Soon, the lights dimmed, and the show began.

It was beautiful to behold—the opera, of course. I could hardly focus with Alexander's pokes and prods. It seemed to be some strange story about a large-bellied man who wished to kill his enemy and bed his wife. It was... odd... bizarre... *magnificent!*

I had never heard such rich tones with my own ears. For the first time in years, my heart was full, and I was inspired to sing myself. A considerable amount of time had passed since I tried. I, like my Songbird, had lost my love for music when Mom passed, but *oh*... the opera. It dragged the yearning out of me kicking and screaming.

The show lasted about three hours, but it captivated me so much that time was barely a concept. It ended with a grand finale, red ribbons strewn about the stage, simulating the last strike to the man's neck as blood-painted tissue paper rained from the scaffolding and down onto the audience and the cast. They bowed. Then, *we* bowed, giggling like children in a fit. Those nearby stared at us in confusion.

On we went, two fireballs filling the sky with the cinders of jubilant chaos. Alexander ushered me to yet another stage, this one more similar to the first.

It was another strange, small operation. After the absinthe and the Met, another cramped space made me claustrophobic and even a little nauseous. This time, it was a piano bar, the neon karaoke sign buzzing above a narrow platform. The solitary microphone stared daggers in my direction. My devilish companion gestured to the stage and I realized exactly what he intended.

"No—n-no... I don't think so..." I protested furiously, my hands lifting near my face, yet he began pushing me toward the platform.

"Come on, Jack," he cooed. "Forget about anyone else in the room. Sing to *me*."

The room grew darker. Even though I had only counted about fifty people, all their eyes were on me. An eager quiet fell across the space. Muddled whispers and a stale cough from the far corner made my stomach flip. Nerves made my hands tremble and before I could step away from the microphone and abandon the mission, I felt my mouth open.

Strangers stared with mouths agape as I sang for the first time in years. Alexander pressed his palm to his mouth. Was it awful? Spectacular? I was so eager to show him my potential.

The melody flowing from my lips was sorrowful as my voice reverberated against the walls. A woman standing near the front mirrored Alexander's gesture as tears filled her eyes.

It was my favorite song, an old lullaby from childhood that my mom would sing to me. No matter what stage of life I found myself traversing, it seemed to resonate perfectly.

Nature Boy by Nat King Cole. I used to sing my dear Chloe to sleep with it when the nights became particularly hard.

Alexander beamed and his smile was infectious. As I sang, I couldn't tear my eyes away from the man who had given me the courage to stand upon a stage and show myself to the world, even just a little.

"*Bravo!*" He cried when I concluded.

The crowd exploded to applause, a feeling so new to me. *Applause*, not angry screams, nor disapproving grunts, but the cheers of an audience. It was beautiful. The numbness from earlier had vanished. Tears flooded my eyes. It was a great release, my soul bursting from iron chains at last.

Alexander tugged my arm, pulling me from the stage, through the crowd, until I was able to gulp down cooler city air again.

"Why didn't you mention there was such a songbird inside of you, Jack? What a gift!"

He gave a wolfish smile down at me, and even while I tried to revel in this high, his words reminded me of Chloe waiting back home. I couldn't help but wilt a bit.

"Jack," he breathed, catching my weary gaze. "Whatever is the matter? Aren't you having fun? You should be so proud of yourself! Look!" He grasped my hands and showed them to me. "You've stopped shaking, my friend."

He was right. The tremors of the moment had gone, my nerves becoming as strong as steel even with the shockwaves of anxiety and exhilaration.

"How? How did I work up the nerve to do that?" I fumbled. The midnight breeze was sobering and I closed my eyes, letting it wash over my skin, sticky with perspiration.

"No magic, no tricks. It was you! *You* did this. You stood on that stage and wooed that audience. You showed them the depth of your soul, and you are... *so* incredible." His musical voice circled my head and made my bones warm.

My focus returned to his as he squeezed my hands tighter. Were these emotions really mine? I never thought I'd feel anything this deep so suddenly for anyone, let alone another man.

"Jack." His muscular jaw clenched. "You are so special. Do

you know that? Beyond what you could have ever dreamt—a diamond in a sea of quartz. Whoever made you feel like you weren't enough... they were *wrong*."

Heat blossomed in my face. With all my strength, I tried to wrench my gaze from his, but it was a useless effort. It was all I could do just to keep breathing as his eyes swallowed me down into a violet abyss. Hypnotic.

"Come along. The night is still young, and so many adventures await!" Alexander was off yet again, his feet gliding across the pavement.

We were like two children basking in the glory of the city that never slept. We drank down pools of moonlight as it poured from cracks in the weighty clouds. I had never felt more alive, however, feeling as if I had died and was living out the fantasies of the life I had always wished for.

Alexander was everything I always wanted to be. I followed every step, mirrored every grin—every laugh to a friend or acquaintance whose name I'd forget almost instantly, and every pirouette upon those urban streets. He made this place feel like a mysterious wonderland, and not some trash-covered waste pile. Every stop was a new mystery, a new chance to watch him work his magic.

And every affair made me fall even deeper into the love that was blossoming under my sternum and tossing my mind with confusion.

"Jack?" he asked, wrenching me out of my inner monologue.

His hand reached for mine, elongated nails pointing daringly in my direction as if ready to rip me to pieces.

"Ready for what's next?"

I continued with him, my hand clutching his as we ran to the next location, a boutique I had never heard of. The sign was illuminated with red and gold light, a rose wilting over cursive letters, which spelled out, *The Gilded Rose*. Its windows displayed high-fashion styles and the fanciest clothing I had ever seen.

How strange that a clothing boutique would be open at two in the morning.

Alexander dragged me through the double doors, down an aisle, passing the mannequins styled with fashions meant for the runway. They adorned mostly gaudy French designs I wasn't fond of, myself. We then approached the clerk's desk.

A young girl sat in a swivel chair chewing a wad of bubblegum, her rose-tinted, bottle cap glasses pointed down at the gossip magazine she was reading.

'*Monsters among us? Body Found Drained of Blood, Horror Show in the Big Apple*' the headline screamed in bright yellow. The words were splashed over a darker picture I could barely make out.

What an idea. There were no such things as monsters. Just people—horrible and broken people—doing monstrous things. Tabloids would do anything to sell a story, though.

Alexander shoved me at the store clerk, my suit tie flopping about and nearly slapping the woman in the face.

"Holy. shit," she cawed, seemingly recognizing my companion. Her cheeks drained of color—or what color was left of it. Her complexion was a striking sort of pale....

"Claudia, this is my dear friend and possible protégé, the incredible *Jack*! He seems to be suffering from an illness I like to call... tedium. Symptoms? A horrid lack of style." He smiled playfully. "We can fix that, yes?"

He wasn't wrong. My work uniform was indeed very dull. Glancing down at myself, I found my jacket stained and crumpled from the rain and the festivities we both delighted in. Not to mention it was steeped in the scents of the city. The store was freezing, the air permeating my still-damp shirt and hitting my bones. I was for sure going to get pneumonia.

The girl stared with little emotion at Alexander, a heavy exhale causing the gum she chewed to fill with air until... *POP!*

"I'll get her, though I doubt she wants to talk to *you* right now."

I wondered what she meant by that.

Claudia stood from her seat and disappeared behind a back curtain. The girl had sass. I watched the sway of her narrow hips as she retreated. A few silent moments passed, my companion examining his talons before a shrill cry resounded from the mysterious foundries of the store.

"ALEXANDER!" A woman's angry scream practically rattled the windows. My body tensed as the shrillness of it took me by surprise.

In seconds, the curtain was shoved to the side, skinny digits gripping the cloth. There, with possibly the most infuriated snarl I had ever seen, was a tall, Amazon of a woman. Her cherry-red hair was pulled into a loose bun, eyes of fiery green staring passed me and burning holes right into Alexander's soul.

"You have some damn nerve showing your face here, you little *himbo*!"

Her red stilettos clacked across the tile as she approached. The tight dress she wore left very little to the imagination as it hugged every curve of her pale body.

"Ah, still angry, I see..." Alexander grinned, his expression hardly changing in the wake of her apparent rage.

As she grew closer, both her hands slammed onto the surface of the counter, her exposed cleavage struggling within the restrictive outfit. She stared daggers at La Mont.

"You're damn right I am! Six of my girls. SIX! How could you?" Her tantrum was cut short suddenly by the man's cold and precise tongue—

"Annabelle!" he snapped but corrected himself at once. "We have a guest. Mind yourself, my dear."

At that moment, I thought nothing could have calmed this femme fatale from her assault. Yet, at the sound of his voice, her face softened, eyes of brilliant emerald widening before landing upon me.

She sighed, her shoulders easing down from her earlobes. "Right then. Who do we have here?"

Her voice faltered, eyes glazing as she leaned in close across that desk, a slight flush to her cheeks. Our eyes locked and I felt my heart drum in my chest, her pouting ruby lips pressed together as metaphorical hearts seemed to fill her pupils.

"You're... *beautiful*. Alex, who is this? Your friend?" She turned from me to aim the question at Alexander.

He simply smiled with a nod, his hand raising to flick more strands from his narrow face. "This is Jack, my... protégé if he decides to be. We've been having an incredible evening out on the town. He's been learning about our world..." His tone dissolved to something of a whisper. "You know... in the *industry*." He gave her a cheeky wink and a sudden feeling emerged that I was not in on the joke.

She nodded, eyes never fully leaving me.

"So," she started. "You're obviously here for a reason, and..."

There it was. Her glare finally fell over my suit. I cringed.

"Oh, sweetheart. What the fuck are you wearing?" she groaned, her hand leaving the counter to run down the length of my tie.

With a hard swallow, I finally mustered the courage to say words. "It's... just a work outfit." The statement came out more like a squeak. "I was fired today."

The woman shrieked, her lacquered talons pulling me closer. "And you never thought to take it off?"

I shrugged. Her glare finally released me, returning to Alexander. "Oh, Alex, he's so beautiful. But not very bright."

I relinquished a hard sigh.

"Well!" She clapped her hands together as she stood to her full height, which I was surprised to find was the same as my own. "I have a very high-end store, as you can see. I'm sure everything is far beyond your budget, but seeing as Alexander always foots the bill..." She shot him a dark look and he nodded. "Pick out anything your heart desires. And make it count."

La Mont simpered at me, one talon hooked beneath his lower lip. "You heard the harpy—anything you want. Have fun."

Scouring the displays around me, my heart swelled. Perhaps the only reason I had never cared for designer fashion was simply because I knew I couldn't afford it. But oh, the colors! The fabrics, the quality. All of the zippers! It was more than my secret, inner-fashionista's heart could manage.

As I practically danced my way through the various aisles, I overheard Alex and Annabelle's heated conversation. They kept their voices low, but whatever happened must have been pretty horrible. I snuck behind a wrack of coats and leaned forward on my toes to get a better view.

From the side, I could see Annabelle reaching a hand to her face, her red makeup must have smeared from a flurry of tears, for there was no other way to explain the bold red splotch stretching across her cheek as she attempted to wipe it away. Perhaps from her eye shadow?

"Jack?" Alexander called and I startled, ducking behind the heavy wall of clothes.

I wasn't completely used to my new name yet, but his voice breaking through the quiet was enough.

"How goes the hunt, darling boy?"

There was too much to look at and so much to try on!

"Uh...uh...still looking!" My voice broke on the last word. Did he know I was eavesdropping?

I spent the better end of thirty minutes trying on every outfit possible. My destroyed work suit lay crumpled on the dressing room floor. Legend has it, it's still crumpled there to this day. Instead, I endeavored to replace it with tail coats, mesh shirts, leather or lace—I couldn't decide. I was completely absorbed in it all.

And then...

A very specific item demanded my gaze and gripped it tight. Harsh, alternative zippers wrapped around the front, a hood large enough to hide my long hair and face, and sleeves I could easily roll up to my elbows. A bold, red hoodie.

It was perfect—the marriage of my mundane life and the potential of this new, gallant one. An homage to the old while welcoming in the new.

After finding some black, leather pants with almost as many zippers, I found them both still bickering back at the counter. I stood before them, like a child in elementary school ready for picture day, my face beaming. Annabelle tilted her head, her eyebrow perking. I cringed, readying myself for some harsh critique. Instead, she responded with a bright smile.

"How..." She left the desk to encircle me, her hand landing upon the material at my chest, tracing a small pattern. "...bohemian. How expressionist. I love it when high fashion goes a bit urban. And the color's an obvious favorite of mine." Her hand left me to tap upon her lip. "Perhaps, Jack, there really is more to you than meets the eye."

I was shocked. My first attempt at being fashionable had been approved by the shop owner herself. My mind was made up.

"This one, please." I beamed at Alexander.

"I love it! You look marvelous. Breathtaking! *Fringant, auda-*

64

JACK TOWNSON

cieux, incroyable!" The words dripped from his lips like liquid silk, my heart fluttering as the praise fell across my skin.

Annabelle simply rolled her eyes before returning to Alexander, closing in on him. "Remember what I said. If you ever pull that stunt again, we *will* have a problem. I don't care who you are. I will make it count," the vixen hissed through her teeth.

The jubilant mood of the moment was slashed through by her intensity, the energy about the store becoming still and awkward.

Alexander simply grinned in return, the perfect picture of calm.

"Noted," he whispered over a wink.

The woman then turned to me once more, brushing off a speck of dust from my hoodie and fixed my rain-slicked hair.

She sighed. "Listen good, you. If he gives you any issues, you come to me. And if you need any new clothes, they're yours." Her stare tugged at me. Everything else in the room grew fuzzy around her sharp face. *Beautiful.* "Memorize it. Annabelle Cross. *Gilded Rose.* I know it's probably pretty hard to retain information with a head as pretty as that, but just try to remember... alright?"

I nodded, yet I couldn't help but linger, our gazes colliding like the forest on the edge of spring, the greens and bright browns dancing in spite of the waning winter wind.

We left Annabelle's boutique and made our way through the streets, my mind swimming with the delights of the evening, hardly remembering how it all began: the horror of the body on the street, the embarrassing moments in the coffee shop, the loss of the job I hardly cared about. Even my sister's small face as she wished me well on my journey seemed hazy now. It was as if my old life slipped away shred by shred with every new experience, replaced by this incredible adventure into the night.

It came upon four in the morning. We returned to the Prepotent, though the place seemed so different to me now. When I first laid eyes on the theater, I was terrified of the audition to come. But now, mere hours later, I felt like I had been baptized into this new, more confident existence by the one, the only, Alexander La Mont.

Up the elevator, through the empty club, and toward the office where we had originally met, Alexander stopped me before the door which displayed his name in heavy golden letters.

"This is where it ends if you so choose, dear Jack."

I noted the lump forming in my throat.

"Our night has been incredible—adventure and joy I haven't experienced in... quite a long time. If you choose to stay the evening with me, then you accept my offer. If not, I will gladly see to it that you're returned to your home, and compensated for your time here."

My mouth fell open at once to protest—to decry my previous home and my dismal life. How could I ever return to such a dim existence now? But as a strange, frantic sound blurted from my throat, a sharp finger quickly thrust against my lips to silence it.

"*If* you stay, Jack," he began again slowly, "then you are my protégé. Mine. With that comes a very weighty responsibility. I need you to understand that. A new path of fame and intrigue will be yours, and people will say, *'Jack is the most celebrated artist in the known world'.*"

I stood over weak legs, my dear songbird singing in my mind as her last words resounded within my head...

"Good luck out there, and be safe... please."

Inside my mind, a war raged. Responsibility or glory? Fortune or the familiar?

"Alexander..." I started, his violet glare resting upon me. My lips trembled, the hands at my sides clammy as I squeezed them in fear. Then, the finite words slipped from my mouth. "Show me your world," I begged. I staggered toward him. I couldn't help it. "Take me with you. Teach me everything." I practically moaned the request.

In an instant, his hand was in mine.

"*Everything?*" he questioned, his voice only a breath but somehow drowned out the sounds of the whole world.

"Everything."

CHAPTER SIX
THE DEVIL AND I

With our fingers entwined, Alexander La Mont pulled me away from the office door and down the corridor I was not allowed to enter earlier that night. The broad man at the bar warned me that if I trespassed, I would have to answer to security. This time, Alexander and I both rushed through it with haste.

Double doors revealed an impossible space hidden away at the back of the building. This was no doubt his room.

The space was opulent and baroque. Everything was polished and crisp and it didn't seem all too lived in.

It was a massive bedroom, the walls alight with old, gothic fixtures. A king bed sat flush against the back wall. Drapes lined in red velvet bubbled down the frame and to the floor. The space was sumptuous. A familiar mural stretched across the ceiling, one that I recognized from my Catholic upbringing. Art of the winged Lucifer, the fallen angel, was splayed across the makeshift sky in gorgeous detail, those furious tears forever welling within his eyes.

"Breathtaking," I murmured.

It was all I could say before Alexander spun me towards the balcony to our left, out another set of double doors and through more silk curtains. The view overlooked most of the Upper East Side and Central Park. It was something I had never seen before — the lights of Manhattan glimmering impossibly like a sea of fallen stars.

At this time of night, if we'd been anywhere else in the world, the streets would be quiet and the citizens would be slumbering. But not here. Never here.

Onto the landing we danced, Alexander's blonde hair bouncing as he brought me closer to the railing, edging dangerously near a fatal fall. All it would take was a wrong step or playful push to seal our fates.

"Jack. I have to tell you something," he began softly. "I have not been entirely truthful, you see. There is something more I need to show you." His voice was barely a whisper, his eyes falling to the stone beneath us.

I couldn't imagine what he was about to divulge. My thoughts wheeled over possibilities like the mafia, or perhaps he was something of a Russian spy. My pulse thumped violently in my chest, the anticipation making my sternum ache.

"Alexander?" I matched his thoughtful tone, placing my hand over his on the railing. "Whatever it is... I'm here. I'm not leaving. You've shown me so much magic in a single night. How much more unbelievable could this possibly get?"

He smirked darkly, as if some great secret lived there beyond his violet stare. "Don't be afraid. Close your eyes." He instructed and so I did.

I heard the slight shuffle of heeled shoes and the metallic tapping that followed. The railing vibrated under my hands and fear was the very thing that forced my eyes open.

"*Alexander!*"

There he stood upon the metal bar, the wind whipping about his ethereal hair and the dark mesh of his shirt.

I reached for him in my panic. "Are you *insane*? Get down from there!"

My stomach lurched, my fingertips splayed as I tried to grasp the hem of his pants and then... I failed.

My gut shot up to the roof of my mouth as I watched Alexander La Mont spiral off of the edge and down... down... *down*. His screaming voice vanished as so, too, did his body.

"*Holy shit!*" I shrieked. "He killed himself. He fucking killed himself! What the fuck!"

But before I could spiral any further and get sick all over the balcony floor, the most peculiar thing happened. A voice. A tiny whisper of a thing beckoned to me.

"Jack. Jack, look down."

His voice called to me from the side of the building. It was impossible. He was surely dead. This had to have been some sort of trick. Was I losing my mind from the trauma of watching this man splatter on the pavement far below? Wait. *Did* I actually see him hit the pavement? I leaned over the railing, my raven curls interrupting my view of the streets below as wind swirled them about my face.

There he was.

Standing on the wall, staring up at me, feet pressed against the brick and completely disregarding gravity, was my mentor. He stood there as effortlessly as some arachnid-themed superhero, the lights of the city shining behind his head creating an almost angelic halo about his blond curls.

The world spun rapidly as I white-knuckled the banister. What was happening? Perhaps it was still the absinthe playing tricks on me. Yes. Perhaps *all* of my drinks had been spiked that evening. There was no other way to explain it. This had to be the product of some intense hallucinogenic.

"No. You weren't drugged," he stated simply. "What you are seeing is very real, and I imagine very confusing. I had to show you. I needed you to believe me. There was no other way."

"Alexander!" I screamed, my eyes welling up with tears, watching them rain down over where he stood. "Please, please come back up! This is unnatural!"

He shook his head in protest. "No, no. How about *you* come down *here*." He laughed, twirling in his spot with his arms outstretched to demonstrate he was truly not affected by the earth's gravitational pull.

I hugged the railing, my hand gripping the metal bar tightly as fear turned my blood to ice. "N-no! I can't!"

He cried up at me, "You've been telling yourself '*no*' for so long! You've restricted yourself to a mediocre life, when so much more awaits you! Stop living in fear! Release yourself! Be free! Come to me! *Now!*" His hand outstretched towards me. Lightning cracked overhead.

I exhaled sharply, my fingers twitching in fear as I brought one leg over the ledge. I squeezed my eyes shut, focused on remembering how to breathe. Then came the other leg until I stood on the dangerous side of the railing, gripping to the metal and what might have been the last moments of my life.

"Jump, dear Jack," he laughed.

"I can't! I'll fall!"

Terror gripped me to my core and reduced me to a little boy again. My heart lodged itself in my throat. The world beneath me spun in vicious circles as all the lights started to blur like watercolor. If I didn't step down, I would surely fall forward with the vertigo. Few options were left now.

"I will catch you! I will keep you safe, if you only trust me!" Alexander promised over the rush of the wind, his smile flashing across his beautiful face.

His velvet words coaxed me enough at last, and down the lip

I went. For a moment, time froze, the city fixed in place as my life flashed before my eyes. My mother, Bradley, Dad, Chloe—all happy and awash in sunlight. What if this was all truly a hallucination? What if I just hurled myself into my doom? Time resumed as I tumbled, arms flailing, the world about me smeared in violent color. Everything I had ever known was both literally and figuratively flipped upside down.

At last, arms wrapped about my body, holding me in place. Alexander hardly moved as he caught me against his chest with inhuman strength, his tight body acting like a bed for mine. He grinned up at me, our forms finally closing the distance that had plagued me all evening. I could feel my heartbeat slamming against him, yet his didn't respond. There was nothing there.

"What... are you?"

He grinned, his lavender eyes sparkling as they beamed through the darkness into mine. "I am what rules the night. A master of the starlight, a fiend of flesh, both angel and demon as one. I am walking history—legend and myth, and you've known it in your heart all along."

His tongue was held steady with the weight of truth. From the moment I saw those unnatural purple eyes, I knew that there was no way this man could be human. All night, it had been so clear. I had simply refused to see it.

"Dance with me?" he boyishly mewed, his tone vibrating through my ribs as I hung on for dear life.

Clinging to him, I buried my face in his chest and begged the question, "How?"

Squeezing me tighter, he began to spin us upon the vertical surface, careful to keep me from falling, waltzing as we tempted fate and laughed at the gods who wished for us both to plummet to our demise.

"What are you, Alexander?" I moaned into his chest as he danced me about, a rag-doll in his embrace.

He slowed into a gentle sway, focusing on my question. His response was soft and sultry. "It's simple. I am Vampyr, Nosferatu, Strigoi."

I blinked up at him, confounded, though I knew it was true.

"I am a Vampire... and I've chosen you to waltz through eternity with me, never to be afraid again, never to feel the sting of embarrassment, never to know a life of failure previously so unavoidable."

A vampire. A beautiful monster. A divine paradox. It all made sense, now. His charm, his grace, his style, the way he moved, talked, and tempted. He was the thing of the darkness, and there I was...*with* him. He had chosen me where every other human being in my life had tossed me aside.

Alexander *chose* me. I was his.

He walked me back up to the ledge, his hands clasped around my back, his impossible body moving mine like a lift. Both of his legs bent for a moment, and before I could make another sound, we were airborne, floating through space. Terror replaced elation. My eyes never left his. Back down to safety we traveled, the two of us gliding back to the balcony as if Alexander had been enchanted by pixie dust.

As our feet touched down, more questions riffled through my brain. "Show me," I begged.

A large smile overtook Alexander's features, and I saw them. Twin fangs clearly visible, their length impossible to miss, yet somehow they hadn't captured my attention before this moment. He must have kept them hidden from me somehow.

"How? Am I going crazy? Tell me this isn't the absinthe."

He smirked. "Darling, no. We utilize something called the *glamour*. Humans will never see us unless we choose to reveal ourselves. Most of the time, they can't see past their own noses. How would they perceive the fangs, poised to strike at their throats, just beyond their eyes?"

I chuckled nervously at such a dark statement. I had been like all the others—just as oblivious, just as nearsighted. Never again. The horror had passed, and now there was this sort of comfort in knowing I wasn't crazy. This was real. The famous Alexander La Mont was a vampire. He was *my* vampire.

"Wait!" I blurted. "Does this mean you're going to make me like you?"

The query was met with a bubbling laughter that erupted from the base of his throat. "If you would like to be. It must be your decision, though, dear one. You must want this for yourself. I can't force it on you... my darling Jack."

What a concept. The end of my human life. The end of everything I knew. The end of my pain... to become beautiful and eternal, like him.

A soft, nostalgic sadness crawled up my spine and clutched my heart. My *life*. My family. Everyone I had ever known. Making this choice would imprison them in my past.

A feeling began to overtake me, the agony I kept hidden unraveling. "You'll never leave me?" Tears streamed down my face. I thought of my mother again, her lifeless eyes as she stared at me from her hospital bed. "You'll never grow sickly and die?" My breath caught in my throat and my lip trembled. I was no less vulnerable than a child.

Alexander's face grew soft and compassionate as he watched my wave of emotion take hold. He pushed the hair from my face. "No, Jack. I'm not like the ones you've loved and lost. You will have me... for eternity... if you so choose."

In his arms, I stared up at the taller man, my heart so full of love and foolish whimsy, my head spinning with the romance of it all—with the idea of never having to lose the man I was falling in love with.

"Yes," the word left my mouth and my heart gave a great jolt at the finite sound of the word. "Yes, Alexander. Make me like you. I choose this. I choose you."

In an instant, he was upon me, his arms holding me tightly against his muscular form, blonde rivets wrapping in my inky coils. His lips pressed against my neck as my eyes fluttered shut. I could feel my arousal pushing against the material of my new pants.

"Make me like you," I whimpered.

There was an eruption of cold pain, the worst I had ever felt. Two icepicks plunged into the side of my soft throat as my teeth clenched down over a silent scream.

And then it was gone...

Instead, the pain was replaced by incredible bliss I never could have imagined in all of my years. I moaned his name over and over as he drank down my warmth. I felt my own vitality, hot and slick as it pooled over my collarbone.

"*Alex...*" I gasped, my hands clutching desperately to his muscular upper arms.

His lips broke the connection against my neck, his face rising to allow me full view of his visage. His complexion was now ashy and pallid, purple veins scattering across his face like the streaks of lightning that crashed above us. Those violet eyes burned holes into me as blood masked his lips and chin. It was true. He was a monster. *My* monster, and I finally had a moment of acceptance—of truth and revelation.

I was in love with him.

Before I knew it, my lips found his, my teeth biting down upon his lower lip hard enough to draw, the taste of his blood and mine filling my mouth as our first embrace took us both like a hurricane. Under that weeping, moonlit sky, Alexander and I kissed and pressed our bodies together lewdly, and I was afraid of nothing. He was the first man I ever kissed, and the first shred of happiness I'd had in years.

He returned to my neck, quickly lapping up gulps of my fluid as if I were a bottle of his favorite wine, drinking me down until the sky began to swim above me. I felt my legs become frail, my body slumping against his. Not before long, Alexander was carrying me through the doors and back to his room, his arms swept beneath as he cradled me through the threshold like a bride. La Mont leaned down to rest my body over his wide bed, the black silk sheets enwrapping my cold body as I shivered from blood loss.

"You will die this evening," he purred. "But know that your life will be returned to you in a way you couldn't possibly imagine. This night marks the end of the man you were—of the boring and pathetic James Donovan. The Vampire Jack is born."

Fingers danced across his shirt with ferocity, releasing the last buttons before he tossed it to the side. His body snaked over mine in the bed.

"Give me everything," I begged, moaned, cried through my lack of lucidity.

His smirk darkened his features, his slender hand brushing the hair from my eyes. "I intend to."

Both fists pinned me to the sheets, my body heaving in my near-death as I struggled to keep breathing. Even still, I was aware of everything. Hands like a vice wrapped about my throat, his thumb and forefinger cradling my jawline to keep my neck wrenched back against the pillows, his erotic grip nearly suffocating me as I was held down in place.

"Alex-Alexander—" I choked out, not used to such force.

It was a hard truth. My sexual experience wasn't vast. When I did have relationships, I focused solely on romance and love and emotion. This, however, was something much different. Primal. Obsessive. Like a man possessed by an ancient deity offering my soul up to sacrifice, and just like Eve in the garden, I sank my teeth deep into that apple and didn't look back.

Alexander's body writhed on top of mine forcing me to react in ways I never experienced before. I gasped, my hands struggling to grip the bedclothes, my fingers grappling, instead, for his face, desperation taking me. My nails found purchase over his forehead, digging into his cold flesh as streaks of crimson appeared over snowy white. Alexander hardly reacted, scarlet ribbons trickling down his brow and into a single purple eye before dripping onto his lip.

"Still so much fight in you," he breathlessly laughed, pushing harder against my throat.

My mentor left me for the briefest of moments, his left hand fumbling with his trousers, the belt slipping away before it met the ground with a clatter. Once his pants were removed, he went to work on mine as well, pulling them off with swiftness and tossing them away in similar fashion.

"Jack, you are so strong. Even now..." He leaned down, his words falling over my cheeks with his sweet, flowery scent. He exhaled into my mouth. "Death knocks upon your door and waits to call you briefly home, yet you fight for life. You battle me even now. A powerful undead you will be."

My body clenched as I felt it against me—a hard, monstrous thing waiting to devour my soul like the kiss of a fallen angel. I winced, terrified even in my euphoria with the knowledge that this would be painful.

"Alex..." I moaned, and he hesitated. "This is new to me. You're my first... man." My words fumbled out of my mouth and splayed across my chest, his purple eyes barreling into me as his head tilted with a sneer.

"I'll be gentle. Just... for... you."

There was nothing that could have prepared me for the sheer mass entering my body as he thrusted forward, his bare chest pressing over mine. My sweat-slicked skin coasted against his cold form, our nipples brushing against one another's as he pushed further and further inside of me.

"Alex—holy fuck—"

I bit down too hard on my lower lip, blood spurting down my chin. In barely a moment, he was there to meet it, his tongue lashing out to taste the fluid and lap it up. Eventually, he drew my lip into his waiting maw to suck upon it and take what little was left.

"Hush, sweet Jack. Breathe as much as you can with what breaths you have left. Let the pain consume you. It is mind over matter. A perspective. Pain is not some angel sent to punish you, but instead a demon tempting you to pleasures you could hardly imagine."

Another hard thrust, his hips gyrating as they clashed against mine. My own thick shaft was pushed to the side as his body violently rubbed against it with his motions, like nothing I had ever experienced. We were entangled in our furious lust, twisted in carnality and lost to the desires I once thought were forbidden to me.

As my half-dead mind wandered, my brain flooding with the intoxication of dreams, all sorts of shapes formed in my imagination. I stared upwards upon that mural. Lucifer's glare weighing down upon me, each thrust causing new images to appear. As I watched the images shift and change, one thought stood apart from the others—

Was this man who had taken me, who was breaking me down to the core of my being, the devil? Or had this lechery lived inside of me all along? Had this always been me?

The image of Chris came to mind; his blonde hair and blue eyes, his tight and muscular body as I watched him walk away at the coffee house, our long, heartfelt chats on those broken steps pulling at my heartstrings as I felt his pain so deeply. Did I feel so deeply simply because I was his friend? Is that why I had rushed to those steps every day, and why I mourned his leaving and resented his absence? Or was it because I secretly, even unbeknownst to me, *loved* him?

Perhaps it had always been more complicated than simple friendship. Maybe this had lived within me all along, and it took a vampire fucking me to death to force me to realize it. The irony was that instead of out of the closet and into the light, Alexander's clawed hand pulled this revelation into the darkness where I could dance with the devil. Finally free.

"Tell me," he cooed, his eyes rolling to the back of his head, hips bucking as he rocked my half-dead body against the sheets. His thick member swelled inside of me as I grit my teeth with both pain and pleasure. "Are you ready to die for me?"

My body tensed, and the realization of what he intended to do came all too quickly. I panicked.

"Alexander... no. Please. Don't kill me," I begged through the winces of his destructive force and his unbridled rhythm.

My protests hardly quelled his lust. Instead, he brought his hand back to my throat, pushing harder this time as my world began to dissolve into an inky void.

"It's too late, Jack. You've decided," he growled against my ear.

As his body pushed harder into mine, I sensed he was growing close to climax. My hand found his this time, struggling to fight him off—to push his hands away from my neck.

"Alexander... please... wait..."

Then, something strange happened. I was barely conscious, but I swore I felt his fingers meld into my skin. I felt them inside my throat before he brought them back, the skin reforming over the place his claws breached. In my moment of deliriousness, it was impossible to ask what he'd done to me, all my remaining strength spent on my fight for my survival. I gave everything I had left to delay my moment of death.

Alexander towered above me, his fangs digging deep into his lip, spraying blood into the air, splashes of it cascading onto my face and bare torso. I tried with all of my might to wriggle free. Down he came, pinning me with even more force as his lips crushed my own, the bitter taste of his vitae flooding my mouth. It danced across my tongue like fire. I attempted to break free, to spit it out, but it was useless. There was nothing to do except swallow. I took in heavy swigs of his bleeding lip. It was like drinking battery acid. I could feel it filling me with its strange, toxic magic.

He released me with a laugh. "Don't fight it. This is what you chose. Submit. Submit to me." Both hands took their place around my throat again, clenching tightly as if trying to remove my head from my shoulders in fear that I may attempt to escape again.

I reached to his hips, digging my fingernails into his flesh to distract him, but nothing worked. His purple eyes rolled like they had before as he remembered his ecstasy. His pelvis rolled back against me as I could feel my member rubbing fiercely against his skin. I had staved my moment of death, if anything for a final moment of desire.

"Jack, why are you fighting?" He slammed into me harshly, my blood covered mouth drawing open as my body tensed. He continued, breaking me as I clung to him for dear life. "You agreed to this. You said forever. This is how it happens," he snarled.

I felt the tension in my hands ease, my nails still deep in his skin as small wells of red began to pool beneath them. "I'm... I'm scared," I admitted, the hands around my throat growing limp, allowing small breaths into my lungs again.

"Is that all? You haven't changed your mind? You're just scared?" The man's face grew more sympathetic, a hand leaving my throat to gently play with the curls spread across the dark pillowcase, then to caress my cheekbone with the back of his knuckles. "Let me make you more comfortable. I didn't realize... Such emotions escape me sometimes. I forget them..." His eyes burned brightly as just above him I could view Lucifer's woeful grimace.

Alexander's thrusts became softer. The intensity of the moment passed as he brought me closer to my own ending. My body shuttered at every touch, his member hitting deep as I felt my muscles convulse and shake, my toes curling as my legs spread wider to the edges of the bed. He tapped away, knocking on the door to the last shreds of my innocence, and all it took was his gentle begging for invitation. I felt myself erupt against us both, my mouth hanging open as sounds that could only be described as animalistic ripped from my core. It was pleasure beyond pleasure, our bodies a sticky mess as he coaxed the last bit of what I had out and onto my stomach.

"Alex... Alex, oh... oh fuck," I moaned hard.

All the fight left within me dissipated, every memory of my earlier panic fluttering away like the ruffled feathers of angel wings.

"It's time," he growled, his lips pushing against my own for a moment before his hands took their place back against my windpipe once more.

The world froze yet again, the room around me losing its color as the voices of my friends and family echoed in my subconscious. Everyone I had known. Everything I had done. It was all about to end to bring in this new life. I was going to die without even saying goodbye to my sister. The fight returned for a moment, but he had milked the cobra of its venom.

"Alexander," I begged, "No..."

Chloe's image came to my mind's eye as breath began to slip from me, her smile twisted and changed until it matched the small impish grin of the mother I had lost, her face branding the inside of my skull in my last moments.

This was the end.

"Jack!" He grew closer to his release. I could feel it, his body heaving as everything grew tighter around him. He panted cold breaths onto my face, his thrusts deranged as I felt him slapping against wet flesh. There was nothing more to do, no hope, no reason. Everything began to become a vortex of black and blue, fuzzy white stars on the edge of my vision. What was I fighting for? It was hopeless, and I was in love. Promises of a new life, of dreams fulfilled, of seeing my name in red lights. Of never being alone again.

"Do it..." I muttered.

Hands around my throat gripped tighter, the light from my eyes giving way to darkness as the world above spun into oblivion. That painting of Lucifer screamed down at me. It was the last sight I would ever see as a human man—those horrible, piercing eyes of the fallen angel claiming my soul for eternity.

A last gasp. The monster erupted inside of me, his fluids filling my tight unclaimed sin, and the world simply fell away into the inky black of the abyss. Gone. I was gone. Numb. Dead. Never again to be the man I was before.

It seemed like the void lasted far too long. Was I still breathing? Would I ever awaken? Had the process failed from my struggles and now I was exiled to permanent darkness?

And then, seemingly from nowhere, a tiny voice surfaced from that endless sea of nothing...

"Wake up, Jamey. Time for another day."

CHAPTER SEVEN
AWAKENING

Some time later, the void dissolved. The darkness parted, and it was almost like the reds and golds of the room from the previous night were painted before my eyes by an old master. Death fizzled away. My last and first image waiting to greet me was the glory of the Lucifer mural stretched above my naked body.

The chill of doom evaporated from my skin before my body wrenched, frantic for breath. Yet not a trace of air flowed into my lungs as it swept through my parted lips. I was breathing, but the feeling was cold and hollow. My lungs were like stone. Instead, the air flooded into my numb chest cavity. I was alive... however...*not*. The strange realization caused panic to press against the back of my eyes.

I was dead.

Shrill anxiety drilled into the top-rung of my spine, jolting my body forward and wrenching me from the ebon sheets. A yelp erupted from the base of my throat. I couldn't help it. Every extremity felt like a fusion of ice and electricity.

Extremities. Hands. *Claws*.

My nails were now tapered into claws.

They tore into the silk bedclothes, ripping through them like cheese cloth. It was then I realized my new potential. I had been strong all my life. My physicality was nothing to sniff at—an avid fitness fanatic and backstreet brawler—but now, a new kind of strength buzzed under my fingertips unlike anything I ever felt before.

Tossing aside the tattered sheets, I stared at my hands. Vibrant blue veins ran under the surface of pale flesh, like tiny slivers of frost. Turning over my left wrist, I marveled as I clenched and unclenched my fist, seeing every tiny muscle fiber go to work. Impossible. Living art.

My perception was beyond human. In fact, every thread, every divot, every particle of dust was dialed up to maximum now. The fabric of space was not only obvious, it was blaring. My eyes drank in every detail—every fractal of light.

Light.

The long black curtains had been drawn shut. I had no doubt the intention was to shut out any trace of sunlight, though I remained unsure of what time of day it was. When I realized there was no sign of Alexander anywhere, my heart gave a mighty tug. I needed him. I wanted to feel him there next to me—comforting me, holding me. Perhaps I could find him. He couldn't have been too far.

I launched out of the sheets and into the air without effort. My body felt nearly weightless as I flung myself from the bed and almost slammed into one of the posts holding up the frame. I landed like a cat, my bare feet sliding past the black furred rug. Glancing over my shoulder and back to the bed, I realized the distance was an easy thirty feet away. Remarkable. I wondered what else I could do—what other possibilities were in store for me?

The desire to explore pulled at my toes. I wanted to see the club at the very least. Were the other people who worked there also vampires? The bartender? The lovely woman from the boutique? The front desk guard? I wondered how much magic *really* teemed under the noses of mundane people. A hundred more questions buzzed around my head like a swarm of angry hornets.

I retrieved the red hoodie and the leather pants from the floor, sliding into the sleeves and hardly zipping it in the front. Alexander's evocative appearance from the night before inspired me. I left the zipper half-open, my chiseled pectorals on full display as his had been. Thinking back to the way Annabelle had admired me, I remembered how much I reveled in the attention.

Not so far away, the door beckoned—tempted—dared. In an instant, my hand gripped the knob and the realization hit me like a punch to the back of the head. It seemed like I had blinked myself from one side of the room to the other, my body traveling faster than the thought it took to work my legs. My mind raced. Was I still dreaming or was *inhuman speed* part of my new arsenal of abilities?

Lost in the thought of it, I gently caressed the door's wooden surface. It was then I noticed the ecstasy of *touch*. I fingered every indent, as if it were a lover from the past, every motion sensual even without such an intention. The subtle changes in the mahogany sent lovely little zaps of pleasure through my system and I pulled my hand away.

I was different—changed. It was so very clear. This was all too real. Alexander was divine. And I was undead.

As I went to leave, something sleek and white in my periphery caught my attention. A small letter had been left for me on the dresser, propped against the wall to the right of the door. My new name whispered across the white paper in elegant cursive.

I opened the crisp envelope, careful not to move too fast and accidentally tear the note to shreds.

> *Dear Jack,*
>
> *I know it will be difficult to control yourself in these early moments—to tame your overwhelming, new senses, but I ask you to please remain in this room.*
>
> *There are a few matters I must attend to, and if these things are not addressed I fear the dangers you may face beyond this threshold. Ignore the thirst drying your throat and the hunger in your belly. We will ensure you are well fed and taken care of.*
>
> *One more thing, my beloved...*
>
> *If you leave the sanctity of my room without permission, which you very well may attempt to do, beware a man in a black suit with a red dress shirt. He is no enemy, but it is best I make the necessary introductions when I return.*
>
> *Soon. So soon, my darling.*
>
> *Yours always and into eternity,*
> *Alexander*

Curious. A man in a black suit and a red dress shirt didn't sound ominous at all—not one bit.

Okay, it was time to think logically. If there were others I had to be wary of, maybe I should heed Alexander's advice. Perhaps it would have been best to return to the comfortable sheets and close my eyes, though I wasn't sure if sleep was something I could do anymore—

Then, like a cannon blast to the gut, it hit me.

My nostrils pulled false breath inward, but the oxygen found nothing to stick to. That didn't stop the scents beyond the door from capturing me. It was like nothing I had ever experienced—the aroma of a thousand summers, of every feast known to man, of every favorite food and drink, of paradise, and warmth, and sex, and sumptuousness. Nothing compared. It was impossible to give a truly worthy depiction.

A new beast roared up from my depths. It wasn't just my stomach. It was the very foundation of my essence roaring in defiance at Alexander's request that I stay still.

Hunger. Hunger. Hungerrrr.

My new talons found the knob again.

SLAM. The door was sent against the wall of the corridor, the paintings swinging from the force I wasn't accustomed to yet. One of them swung straight off its nail and crashed to the floor, scattering glass everywhere.

"Shit," I mumbled to myself. I had to be careful.

I crept down the hallway, every old and weary face within the canvases watching me. Now, I felt they stared less mockingly and more with a sort of silent approval.

Reaching the end of the hallway, I caught a glimpse of my reflection in one of the paintings housed in glass. I halted at once. There, in the reflection, was a man I'd never met. Taking a few steps back, I tried harder to catch the stranger's gaze in the reflection. Horror struck me. This was no mirage nor trick of the light. This was *me*.

My long black curls were still there, but under them was a firm and unforgiving brow, a tighter jaw, higher cheekbones, and those eyes— menacing red eyes—not like Alexander's purple hues whatsoever. I looked like a demon straight from the depths of hell.

Panic set in, my fingertips tracing the face that was no longer mine. Who was this? Never mind who, but *how*? *How* did my face change entirely, as if someone had given me plastic surgery overnight? Everything about me was more defined. Straighter. Sharper. More severe. Even my lips were fuller. The red eyes would have been a ghoulish sight if I hadn't looked like I belonged on a runway.

Memories from the night before scrambled through my mind as I stumbled back from the sight, my mouth agape in a silent scream. What happened to James? James. Sweet, sensitive, clumsy James. No one would ever see him again.

James Donovan was dead.

As I fell back, though with my gaze still locked to this new face, I realized something more had been added to the visage— something glinting just below the upper lip.

Holding my breath, I leaned forward once again, my fingers diving into my mouth and curling my lips back. Twin fangs had replaced my normal, flatter canines.

I cried out and fell against the wall behind me, both palms flying to cover my mouth. In my shock, however, I accidentally bit down on the inside of my cheek. Blood filled my maw and ecstasy flooded every single sense I had left.

"MMMMPPPHHH!" I tried to keep quiet, blood dripping between my fingers and spilling onto the carpet, my hand a sticky mess.

Sweet. Succulent. My mind swam and the room faded for the briefest of moments. It was all I could do to collect myself and lick the fingers clean. My new red gaze darted from the coveted drops to take one last look at this new version of myself in the reflection of the glass. My mind formed one, singular word: *Monster.*

I turned to leave the sight, attempting to shake off the idea of someone violating me in such a personal and terrifying way —to replace my face with something new—to instead focus on the scents and sounds coming from down the carpeted stairs.

Down I went, my steps becoming more hasty as I reached the familiar sixth floor. The curtains here were open. It was black outside, well past sunset. I was unsure if I had lost only a single day or if I had been dead longer.

The last few times I found myself in the club it had been mostly empty, so I expected much of the same. This time, however, it wasn't as vacant as I had hoped.

There, just past the dance floor, beyond the tables and chairs, a man sat at the bar, facing the tender. Two men, instead of just the one I had met the night prior.

It was rather embarrassing to pad through the club bare-foot, but I was freshly undead. What did it matter? What did anything matter anymore? I continued toward the bar, trying to swallow down the knot stirring in my belly. It was hard to parse whether it was nerves or the lingering hunger.

"Well, well, well... look at you!" the bartender from earlier moved to greet me at the corner closest to me, his thick, hairy hands wiping down a glass of something the other man had just finished. "You decided to stay for good, huh? Got yourself the gig."

As the bartender croaked at me with a wry smile, the man leaning into the bar raised one dark eyebrow, his fingers drumming against the bar top with a definitive *click-clack*. His claws were sharp and left mild indents. Another vampire.

The mysterious patron cleared his throat, his glare locked onto the tender. He snapped his fingers and the friendly, gray man sidled back to the front of the sharper one, sharing in a whispered conversation. I strained to hear what they were saying, but it was no use. The room might as well have been silent. Realization set in. Supernatural hearing must have also come with supernatural quiet, which was frustrating. I knew their exchange was about me.

The pointy man's fist slammed into the bar, the wood cracking beneath the pressure. I caught a glimpse of his fangs just behind the quickness of his snarl.

"He. Did. What?"

CHAPTER EIGHT
THE MAN IN THE SUIT

The strange, lithe man curled in on himself, eyeing me sharply from over one shoulder.

"Claude," the man started again, "When was I going to hear about this?" he asked. His voice was smooth and steeped in a crisp English accent.

One piece of the mystery was solved. The scruffy bartender's name was Claude. Though I was still missing much more important details about why my presence there was seemingly so vexing.

Setting the glass down, Claude leaned closer to the stranger. "Hey, listen. It was a need to know sort of thing. Only people on the inside had any knowledge about La Mont's intentions last night. Myself. A few scouts. That's about it."

The man's hand shot forward like a bullet from a gun, fist gripping a handful of Claude's salt and pepper tufts. He wrenched him closer to the mysterious face so that they could stare eye to eye with one another.

"You filthy, little shit," he snarled. "I *am* the inside. Who the fuck do you think you're talking to? I am *not* one of Alexander's c-list fuck boys! I am the fucking hound, do you understand?" As his words spewed out in violent, quiet rage, the man jostled Claude's head with the beat of every consonant. "The eye in the shadow that takes what needs to be taken, breaks what needs to be broken, and destroys any snag in it's path. If *he* is the alpha, then *I* am the omega, you insolent fuck."

At last, the stranger released Claude with a hard flick of his wrist, the bartender stumbling back into the drink table behind him. Glasses and bottles tumbled to the floor and shattered.

"Holy fuck, man," Claude growled, doing his best to right himself. He massaged the spot on his head where the stranger had almost ripped out his hair. "I was just saying...you know... you've been away from the city. How would you have known?"

The aggressor stood to his full height, and that was when I saw it. He wore a black suit, a red dress shirt, and a tie. This was the one Alexander wanted me to avoid. It was clear why. I could sense it better than ever before—something uncanny, supernatural, and dark. Waves of power flowed from this man. He didn't *look* like a hard fight by his appearance alone; A clean suit, slicked back hair the color of mud, a five o'clock shadow, and the same piercing red eyes as my own. It was his presence that sent my gut into a frenzy. Every instinct in my body screamed one word...

Run.

However, despite that conscience that usually ruled me from my shoulder, I stood firm. In fact, there was a new daring feeling that vibrated just beneath my ribs that I couldn't explain. It was a fire. It was courage. Or perhaps, because I had already experienced death, it was simple, stupid arrogance.

"I don't know what your problem is..." The words tumbled from my mouth before I could stop them. "...but I would suggest you stop being a prick. If you want to talk to me, I'm right here."

That was enough to send him into a fury. His hands found

the material of my hoodie and raised me in the air, my bare feet dangling over the floor. Eyes of crimson rage pierced what was left of my soul as he held me there for a moment, fangs bared in full ferocity. My first official night as a vampire, and I had already involved myself in a bar brawl with a powerful member of the undead. Perfect.

"Who do you think you are?" He glanced back to Claude. "This little piss ant was dubbed worthy of my sire's kiss?" His wolf's focus shifted back to me. "To accept the dark gift so eagerly, gobbling it up like larva? How long did it take for him to turn this one? A month? A *week*?" He quite literally spat the words into my face.

My hands gripped his wrists to keep myself steady, knowing that he could easily destroy my new favorite piece of clothing, or better yet...*me*. Still, that new, flippant, little voice in my head couldn't shut the fuck up. I sniffed the word down at him: "A day."

His fists wound tighter in the fabric. I felt it pull more snuggly against my skin. The stranger's narrow glare widened with some other emotion. Shock was there, but there was something else. Was it pain? His thin lips around those sharp teeth trembled.

"Did you say..." he started, his feet guiding me away from the bar and closer to the dance floor. "A. *FUCKING*. DAY?" He screamed out before violently launching me into the air, my body landing on the wood and sliding toward the other side of the room in a crumpled heap.

Surprisingly, there was no pain, but I could tell something definitely broke even without my nerves firing. The bone jostled loosely near my stale lungs.

"Alexander is *mine*, and mine alone," the stranger continued, stalking me like a wild cat. "Don't you dare think for even a moment that you hold any sort of claim over him. Especially

after a *fucking* day. Not after all I've been through! Not after all
the trials, all the pain, and torment. Everything *I've* sacrificed,
and he adopts you after a single fucking escapade like you're
ORPHAN FUCKING ANNIE!"

He was upon me again, his arm stabbing downwards to take
hold of my ankle. A twist of his hip and a pivot of his heel sent
my body spiraling through the air and against the staircase.
Something else *crunched* in my back. I didn't even have time to
blink. He was instantly over me once more. Shit. I wondered just
how old and strong he was, the power scaling of vampires not
being something I understood yet. I saw the Hollywood movies.
I knew the folklore, but there was still a lot to learn about what
was real and what was fantasy. I mean, I *did* have a reflection,
after all. For all I knew, this guy had a good few hundred years
on me.

Hands clasped my throat—a familiar feeling from my time
with Alexander, and I couldn't help but grin up at the stranger.
He was jealous. That much I *did* understand.

"You're nothing, aren't you?" He sneered into my face, his
cold breath sliding across my lips. "Insignificant. A toy for
Alexander's pleasure and nothing more, I'm sure. Replaceable,"
he threatened. "I can show you, if you prefer."

The stranger growled and gnashed his teeth in my face, his
hold constricting—tighter and tighter, as if to crush my voice
box.

I pushed myself to speak anyway. "It didn't... work... the way
you wanted..."

His eyes twitched, hands releasing only slightly.

"What? What do you mean?" That British tone had started
off so cool, but at that point, I started to wonder how La Mont
dealt with how nasally it sounded day in and day out.

I began again. "That... orphan Annie line..." I sputtered. "The
way it was worded... made it sound like Annie was into fucking

orphans. Which, honestly, I don't know what movie you saw but that's not how I remember—"

My words were cut off as the first strike came, blinding me from the world as fist after fist slammed into my brand new face. I saw stars. Splashes of blood sprayed against my cheeks from my nose and onto the carpet under my shoulders.

There was no way to defend myself from such a powerful foe, but I couldn't give him the satisfaction of winning either. I did what came naturally. It was the way I unnerved every opponent and bully from my past—the way I always managed to win even when I had lost.

I laughed.

I laughed to my heart's content as haymaker after haymaker landed against my jaw. I imagined the bloody scene was like something from fight club with Brad Pitt and Edward Norton. He stopped for a moment, his fists splattered with scarlet as he stared down at my mangled face.

"What the fuck is wrong with you?" he whispered, a look of complete bewilderment taking his features before he was suddenly gone from sight.

Abrupt, frustrated growls resonated, drifting further away from me accompanied what sounded like a different physical struggle. I pushed into a sitting position against the stairs, struggling to open my swollen eyes in time to see my first *real* vampire fight.

Claude had taken hold of the man's jacket, pulling with all of his might and sending him hurtling backwards. Both vampires toppled over one another before scrambling to their feet to come face to face.

"Aiden!" Claude roared.

Another piece of information was gained. The man in the suit, the furious Brit, the jealous boy—his name was Aiden, and he was fucking pissed.

Claude continued, "I don't want to hurt you. I know I don't stand a chance at defeating you, but I'll tell you something... I *can* cause some damage that will put you out of work for a week. And Alexander won't take too kindly to that. You got it?"

I could almost see the smoke erupting from the suit's ears. It didn't take much to set off this *Aiden* guy. He was as relentless as a rabid animal.

Aiden fired a vicious jab at Claude's face, barely telegraphing. It landed with the same force as a speeding truck, knocking Claude back on his ass. I froze.

Aiden had barely moved his hip—a trick of perception—the sign of a man who truly knew how to fight. A move like that made it impossible for Claude to have seen where the punch was coming from. This suit wasn't just reckless. He was dangerous.

Coming up, I had experienced my fair share of fights. My adolescence produced many adversaries well-versed in the language of street combat. One needed to know how to defend themselves in the underworld. My time with Brad had taught me that quickly. Drug dealers came equipped with guns, knives —all sorts of nasty tools. All I ever needed was my fists. In all of my years, there was only ever one man that used the same technique Aiden had just employed, and that man was the only one who ever put me on the ground.

Claude seemed proficient enough as well, however. He was already squared up and ready to go, but as he went to block another attack, he miscalculated the speed and took the punch straight to his mouth. A trickle of blood added a streak of red to his salt and pepper whiskers.

"Oh, look. Silly me... I seemed to have struck you too hard. Shall I pick you up a tampon for that pussy of yours?" Aiden threw his head back, allowing a shrill cackle to pervade the open air.

I couldn't help but watch in a mixture of horror and admiration. This man was insane, but he was skilled. I couldn't stop myself from wondering, beyond the fact he was a badass vampire, *who the fuck was this guy?*

Claude snarled, his guard hand coming down to check the stream of red as it dribbled onto the floor. "Nice shot," he grumbled before sending two follow-up punches in retaliation: A jab and a cross, both casually parried by the suited man. It was like a pit bull playing with a puppy.

Claude threw more shots in his direction. Aiden's head simply bobbed from side to side. "This is adorable. Truly. But I haven't even activated my *gifts*. Do you really want this to be the day I land you at Cadavers?"

Aiden evaded another punch, but Claude closed the distance. His body sailed between both of Claude's arms as his forehead slammed hard into Aiden's. The attack caused his skin to erupt at last, exposing his skill, sending more blood into the air and down his face.

"Gotcha fucker," Claude snarled before firing a brutal shot at Aiden's side.

The vampire hardly budged. And then another three, four, five—followed by a kick to Aiden's stomach. As the onslaught came, the suit whipped his claws sideways, slashing deep into the raw area above Claude's eye. A waterfall of blood interrupted the bartender's vision and he fell back. He squeezed his soaked lids shut, trying to keep his guard up and ready.

But Aiden was already in position.

"I'm bored," he sniffed. "You're boring me. This ends now, mongrel."

What happened next made me wonder if I was hallucinating. Aiden's arms became a blur as each shot landed faster than a hummingbird's wings against Claude's chest and sides, the sound of the raid like machine gun fire. This must have been the *gift* Aiden referred to. Blood splashed from Claude's mouth and out onto the suit of his attacker, but I was amazed to find the burly tender wasn't ready to give up just yet.

As Aiden's punches continued, Claude closed his eyes. The area of the assault began to sound less like soggy meat and more like concrete. Aiden paused to witness the damage. Staring down at his hands, Aiden's knuckles were covered not just in Claude's blood, but now his own, the skin ripped and torn exposing raw muscle and bone beneath.

"Impressive," he grumbled, seeming to know what Claude had done. My mind still felt mortally slow, and hardly able to grasp anything I was witnessing.

Before Claude could go on the offensive again, Aiden vanished. The weary salt and pepper vampire scanned the empty club before looking at me.

"Where did he go—" *WHAM*!

A blow to the back of the head sent Claude to a knee. *WHAM*! Another to the side of the head. Aiden appeared and disappeared as his target fell, his palms against the floor. Weary blue eyes left their downward cast to find me again with a look of apology.

"I tried."

Aiden appeared at Claude's front. His right arm wrenched upwards as those broken and bloody knuckles caught just beneath my defender's chin with a crunch. The force was enough to send him through the air from his knelt position, his body flipping unsettlingly through the club before landing with crushing impact onto one of the tables. Broken, beaten, and unmoving.

Aiden stood back to his full height, a grimace cast upon his face as he began to shake out the pain that must have been left by the fight. He snarled, cracking his knuckle. Flexing his joints forced him to wince.

"You're so fucking lucky I don't kill you for even making me try," he said to the still-motionless Claude.

Aiden adjusted his lapel and smoothed his jacket with both bloody hands, though he still appeared a frazzled mess. Fancy dress shoes clomped against the hard wood surface, flecks of fresh blood splashed against the polished floor as the skilled combatant made his way towards Claude again.

"If you know what's good for you, you'll stay where you are long enough to think about how silly of a mistake you made. Now..." He turned back to me. "Where were we?"

To his surprise, however, I was already right behind him. I hadn't meant to. I fully intended to just stay on those steps, a broken mess. But something in me stirred—a fire awakened and a core tenant had been triggered. I fucking hated bullies.

Without hesitating, my balled fist met the man's face with fury, knuckles shattering against his jaw as the bone shredded through skin. His face contorted from the new strength I mustered as his head whipped, his neck cracking with a snap. That fancy suit flipped open as his body lifted through the air and into one of the chairs just beyond the dance floor.

The legs of the chair skittered against the ground with a screech, his body slumped against it. Genuine shock took us both as we stared at one another from the distance. My chest heaved. One of my ribs was definitely still broken, the edge of the bone pressing against my soft flesh. One wrong move, and it would rip right through. Aiden growled as composure took him again.

"Who the fuck *are* you?" he howled, less of a question and more of a violent scream of desperation.

"I don't know yet, but I'm not going to stand by while some fucking lowlife in a cheap suit takes his jealousy out on people who don't give a shit," I shouted back, my fists falling to my sides. A growl erupted from my chest and it was unlike any sound I had ever made before. I reminded myself of a bear...or a wolf. Or a lion. "Try having a civil conversation instead of acting like a jilted twelve year old."

Aiden raised himself from the chair and started to hobble in my direction, his lip busted, his eye bleeding, knuckles bloody and shattered. The once fancy suit was now covered in the combination of everybody's vital fluids, but like the villain in a classic horror movie, he still kept coming.

"*BOYS!*"

We both stopped in our tracks as the familiar voice shattered through the heat in the room. At once, our attention snapped to our maker as he entered from the elevator.

One thing was certain. Alexander La Mont did not look pleased.

CHAPTER NINE
MASTER'S PET

Alexander sauntered deeper into the room. Behind him, the elevator door rattled as it closed. He wasn't happy. That much was clear. His angular glare slid from one broken table, to the bloody floor, to the staircase, and then to me.

He was dressed quite differently now. A crisp white coat fell past his knees, a button down shirt adorned with silver roses on black, white pants and black dress shoes made up the rest of his ensemble. It was much less laid back than he had appeared the night before.

"Master," Aiden croaked, falling to a knee like some pathetic little incel.

My sire passed his guard dog and came straight for me. I sighed in relief. *Finally.* My knight in shining armor, blazing in white, trailed by the flames of the gods. My love. My hero. My—

CRACK!

I felt my world spin for a moment, my ears ringing horribly as everything turned into a blend of color and sound. It was impossible to reconcile with what had just happened. I tried to compose myself as much as I could. My legs wobbled as I was hardly able to keep myself standing. As everything slowed I brought my hand to my face to feel a far more raw spot smart under my palm. He had struck me. Hard. My skin was damaged and split at the force of the backhand.

My love, the one I died for... hit me.

"I told you to wait for me," he hissed into my face. "You directly disobeyed my direction after I've bestowed you with such a gift—"

"Alexander, he's a monster!" I cried before he could continue, adrenaline spiking to the top of my skull. "He tried to kill me—to kill *us*!" I barked, indicating Claude who was still knocked out.

As I rushed to explain, Alex's fingers clasped around my jaw to muzzle me like his pet. "And you did nothing to provoke him. Is that right?" He released my face roughly before gesturing to his establishment. "Look around you!" he snapped, angrier than before.

Even while Alexander was furious, the octave of his voice still seeped with honey and dripped into my brain. Trying my best to shake the way his very presence intoxicated me, I scoured the club in its current state. It was a mess. Blood everywhere, several chairs destroyed, the bar cracked and bottles shattered. A single table lay crumpled with the bartender's body wedged between its two halves. I cringed.

"If you had stayed within your room, did as I said, I would have had time to speak with him." His clawed finger stabbed toward the still-kneeling guard dog. "He is my first, you see. Your brother. He's been with me for many years, loyally at my side."

As he finished, I went to protest, "Alex, he started everything!"

The taller vampire reached, wrapping his fingers within my curls, and tugged me toward him.

"Jack," he breathed. "Aiden is hot tempered. He has been my charge for a hundred years and has never strayed—never stepped a single toe out of place." My heart dropped. "Imagine how *he* must feel." Alexander continued to grip my hair, keeping me in place like some errant pet.

As he explained, Aiden refused to glance up from his downward glare. His cheek twitched and his eyes hardened. I stared at him, wondering. Was he just as in love as I was? A hundred years, and he was seemingly replaced in a day. No wonder he was so sour. I sighed.

"You're right," I exhaled. "I should have stayed in the room. I was... I was just so excited," I explained. "You were gone and I... *missed* you. Why did you leave me alone?" I whimpered, pathetically overcome by him, even with all that had just transpired.

My sire released me at last to instead rake the back of his knuckles across the cheek he had marred. "I have my dealings, Jack. My business... both with the living world and to ours. It is very difficult for me to stay in one place. Your transformation took evening into day, and by the time I awoke, you still had some time left. I didn't wish to leave you confused and lonely. That is why my note was there. I only wish you heeded my words." His purple eyes shifted to Aiden then. "And I knew that my eldest progeny would be returning from his... *work*... this evening. I hoped to spare him the pain of learning this himself, to comfort him, and reassure his fears."

Alexander sauntered over to where Aiden remained on his knees. A single blood tear rolled from the corner of his sharp eye to the point of his chin as he continued to glare at the floor. I watched in envy as Alex ran his palm across the top of Aiden's head in the tenderest of ways.

My dead heart felt like a led brick in my stomach. There was no other option. Time to make peace.

"Aiden." I looked down at the kneeling form—the Hound, as he called himself. "I'm sorry. Can we... fuck. Can we start over? I mean, we're brothers, sort of. Right?"

Alexander offered Aiden his hand. He took it at once, pulling to his feet, his face only slightly softer. The two older vampires stared at one another for a weighty, silent moment. La Mont brushed off a few droplets of crimson from Aiden's cheek. My throat constricted as I waited for them to kiss, but released a breath when that didn't happen.

"Sire. I don't want a... *brother*. I only want you." He whined in the same manner a dog would as its owner gave affection to the new puppy brought in from the rain.

"My dear, Jack is wonderful. You will come to love him as I have, and then we will be a marvelous family. The three of us... *together*. Imagine it."

And then it happened. Alex leaned forward, placing a gentle kiss onto Aiden's lips. Every muscle in his body seized and then melted. I watched his eyes flutter even a moment after the kiss broke. Bitter jealousy permeated my bones and turned them to ice. Just like before, I felt compelled to tear the Hound's head away from his body.

"Fine," Aiden breathed. "I'll make an attempt. If only for you, my sire."

Alexander responded with a large smile. "I know you will. That's my good boy." Then, he bounced away from Aiden to attend to Claude. "Hm..." I heard Alex mutter from the distance. "Might have to give a call to Cadaver's."

Aiden turned to me and my stomach twisted into a tight knot.

"Hey, Jacko?" he muttered.

I clenched my jaw.

"I don't care where this path leads, but know this..." he started, leaning closer until his nose was merely inches from my own.

"I will never, *ever*, accept you."

The admission stung. It was true that I'd just met this man, and he did a terrific job of spilling my blood all over Alexander's hearth, but his words stung worse than any blow ever could. They brought back the feelings of the past. Rejection from people who were supposed to be family surfaced from the deepest parts of my mind. Suddenly, a dozen faces manifested before me—those who had once tossed me to the side. I thought myself impervious to traumas from my life now that I was a vampire, but I learned too quickly that even death couldn't heal that sort of pain. Everything still hurt the same.

Aiden ambled away from me, joining Alexander at his side. They pulled Claude off the table and brought him to a room beyond my view. Blood smeared a trail across the ground as they dragged him.

"Is he going to be okay?" I called to them.

I knew Claude was immortal, but I was still genuinely concerned for my new friend. If he hadn't jumped to defend me, it was terrifying to consider how Aiden might have ripped me to pieces.

"He'll be fine. We have resources for situations like this. He will be as good as new within the evening," Alex answered before they dipped behind the wall and vanished from sight.

Cadaver's. I recalled the word. I wondered if that was the resource Alexander meant. What other parts of this dark world had I yet to learn about?

A weird stillness blanketed the room. The riot was done. Everything was silent. A heaviness filled my heart.

"I guess... I guess I'll just go wait in the room." Nobody answered. "Cool."

I ascended back up those familiar stairs and down that same hallway. I re-entered Alexander's bedroom and collapsed over the nest of silk sheets. They gently cradled my wounded body. But what about my wounded pride? Eyes heavy, I drifted off, the scent of blood filling what dreams came for the short time I would embrace them. Anything was good enough to take my mind off the first failure of my unlife.

My first failure... even as a vampire.

CHAPTER TEN
A NEW WORLD AWAITS

My undead dreams were strange—much different than when I was... alive. Instead of being a scrambled mess, they were quite lucid. In the past, I might've dreamt of a cat driving a toaster for example. These dreams, now, were different.

Instead of an abomination of discord and confusion, Alexander swam through my layers of consciousness, his hand outstretched, purple eyes drawing me in. Yet, the more I reached for him, the further he drifted. So desperately I wanted to touch my fingertips to his, but when I finally did, he was gone. I called for him, begged and screamed, but there was no more evidence of him in the black void.

I awoke with a start, gasping and shivering at the horror of losing Alexander. I struggled to catch my breath, pushing up on my arms, and digging the heels of my hands into the hollows of my eyes. It took a moment to remember that I didn't actually need to breathe anymore—therefore, I could calm my own pulse and stop hyperventilating.

Something moved at the darkest, farthest corner of the

room then. Unlike my awakening, this time I wasn't alone. There he was, emerging through heavy shadow to lean against the dresser at the other side of Alexander's domicile. *Aiden*, the vampire who had beaten me and Claude within an inch of our unlives. I didn't dare shift my focus as he flipped a small dagger in his hand, catching it at the handle in steady rhythm.

"Jacko," he hissed, the blade stopping to land perfectly between his fore and middle fingers.

I prepared for another barrage, throwing the sheets away from my corpse, remembering that I hadn't tucked myself in. Someone must have done it for me. How unsettling. Slowly, I swiveled off the mattress and stood to my feet.

"Aiden..." I muttered hesitantly. "Are we... we good?" If I wasn't deceased, I would most certainly be sweating. "Where's Alexander?" I asked.

Aiden rolled a pair of eyes that looked just like mine and tilted his head to one side. His smirk was smug and knowing. "He had to take Claude to the shop." He said it like Claude was a '57 Chevy. "Fixed you first... of course. He'll be back any moment."

Alarmed by his admission, I inspected my own flesh that had been broken and bruised not too long before. I was surprised to find not even a scratch remained. There was no blood—no protruding rib from the break I had suffered. Nothing rattled when I dared to draw a breath.

"How did he... *fix* me?" I asked, my hands gliding over the areas that were still a bit sore.

Aiden gave a shake of his swarthy head before slipping his dagger within the breast of his jacket and out of sight.

"You were fast asleep. He gave his blood. Nothing's more powerful than the source, you see. Your wounds were a quick fix... hardly an inconvenience."

I couldn't help but wonder why Alex hadn't done the same

for Claude, but before I could ask, Aiden answered the question, as if he was somehow inside of my mind.

"Claude isn't family. He is just a pet of the master. He would benefit from Alexander's blood, sure, but it wouldn't do all it needed to do. Which is why Cadaver's is so important."

So many more questions hung on the edge of my tongue, but before I could ask for Aiden to elaborate, a silhouette breached the doorway. Alexander returned, a blood-stained cloth dangling from his hand.

"Boys... Lovely to see you getting along," he cooed, a playful, little laugh bubbling up from his throat the way champaign bubbled in a glass flute.

I sat back down on the edge of the mattress, enamored and weak in the knees.

"Aiden, have you informed Jack about anything yet?" he asked.

His other progeny simply shook his head in response, eyes landing on him for a moment before shifting back to me with more intensity. I wondered what Alexander meant.

"Very well. That is good, I suppose. Very... good." He made his way to the bed, his tight, supple ass plopping down beside me. "So!" he started, his voice containing some mysterious sort of glee. "I had this *wonderful* little idea. You need the experience, darling, and some understanding about how our world works. I am a busy man—so many bibs and bobs and overseeing all my ventures and this and that—and Aiden has just returned from some... *business*." When La Mont's gaze shifted up to Aiden, his eyes glittered.

Oh no, oh no. Please, oh fuck no. I knew exactly what was coming.

"I figured..."

Claws sinking into the side of the bed, I nearly fell off the edge and onto the floor.

"Aiden could fill in for me—give you a sort of... *tour*."

Fear formed a new lump at the base of my esophagus then and suffocated me. I opened my mouth to protest, but—

"I know it's usually the sire's job to lead their progeny through the night, but we will have our time together, I promise." Alex tapped the point of my nose with his index finger. "Aiden can teach you as much as you need to know about your new abilities... other important details..."

"Care for a *ride-along*, Jacko?" Aiden chuckled.

"Precisely! A ride-along." La Mont clapped his hands under his chin in excitement. "Aiden will give you the full tour of the other side of the city, or, as we call it, the *Undercity*. He will make sure you are well-educated regarding all of our rules, pertinent locations, as well as the many different families and Guilds of the city."

I felt myself die inside even more than when La Mont had his hands around my throat. I wanted him. I wanted him next to me—to take the night the way we had when we met. Aiden's very presence was more sour than old socks and I couldn't imagine how I was going to stomach being alone with him for longer than ten minutes.

"Alright," I said and forced a smile. I feigned my excitement, doing my best to mask my fear. "Let's get to it."

I straightened up and pulled on my shoes.

Alexander led us away from the room and back down to the bottom floor. The large clock in the lobby hung ominously over the elevator. 11:20 PM. I wondered if that was early or late in terms of vampire hours.

Even in my hesitation, I still followed the two like a golden retriever, my tail wagging even while I tried to fight away the fear that clung to my heart. As we exited, I gave a wave to the front desk man. The large smile on his wrinkled face was infectious as we passed on our way out the door.

Once onto the city street, I felt a wave of energy slam into my chest. Anxiety quickly washed away with the scents, the sights, the lights of the city. I'd experienced these things a million times, but it all seemed so new now, taking me into its loving embrace and coddling me like a lost child on a winter night. Manhattan wanted my soul, so I offered it up as quickly as I could.

This city made sense for vampires. At that moment, I understood. It was sensory overload to a degree that almost seemed comforting. The constant sounds and vibrations made the stillness of death less... noticeable. If we could no longer have a pulse of our own, New York would beat *for* us.

Before, the smell of city pizza was the most appetizing thing in the world, but now it was the human passersby who shuffled past us unbeknownst to the monsters lurking at their sides. Every artery throbbed. It was so easy to notice now—the pulsing veins nestled shallowly beneath thin layers of skin. One bite was all it would take, like piercing the flesh of an apple and sucking down the juices. My mouth watered, the new sensation strangling my mind from any other thought to only focus on one: *Blood*.

The instincts of a predator overtook me. In an instant, I had forgotten about everything I had ever cared about—every shred of morality and justice—and replaced it with the crave to kill everything that moved around me.

"Jack!" Alexander snapped, pulling me back to the present. His voice was enough to recapture my focus.

I realized then that I had stopped in my place to stare at every stranger, my red eyes stabbing at them with my fangs bared. But the glamor was still a thing. To them, I probably just looked like some pervert or head-case.

"I know this must be overwhelming now, but it will become much easier with time." His firm grip on my shoulder centered me. "You will learn to control these impulses, I promise. Now, don't dawdle."

Down the street we went. As we walked, I absorbed each sign, each face, each bouquet, and every other detail. I could hear every conversation, feel every emotion, follow visible lines of energy to see where they had traveled from and who they belonged to. Vampirism felt like a video game—one that would make leveling up easy if I was only willing to snuff out a life.

My body craved the hunt, and I hoped—*God*, I hoped—that Aiden was taking me to do that first. The thirst was impossible to ignore. However, disappointment bloomed in my hungry stomach as they led me instead into the waiting mouth of a nearby parking garage. There, La Mont showed us the car we would be taking for the evening. A sleek black thing, like it was more ready for a racetrack than the street.

"This is just one of many," he indicated with pride. "I own six within this lot alone, but this is one of my favorites. Be careful with it, Aiden," Alexander warned as he tossed the other vampire a silver set of keys.

Aiden smiled impishly and nodded. "You know how my tastes match yours. You treat me oh so well, *Alexander*."

Ugh. The way he spoke his name made my skin crawl, and I could feel the heat beneath my collar building once again as jealous swelled where the thirst lived.

"Well then, Mongrel. Pop in and keep the drool off of the seats, would you?" he sneered.

I realized the moisture at my chin. Furious, I reached to wipe away the abundance of saliva that came with the idea of fresh throats in my maw.

Alexander shot Aiden a lofty brow of disapproval, but Aiden only responded with a snigger. He slid into the driver's side to wrap his fingers around the steering wheel, his head craning to meet Alexander's glower. He sighed.

"Fine, I'll be nice" he croaked, his other hand reaching to wave me into the car. "Come on. We've got things to do and places to see. Don't keep me waiting."

I popped into the passenger side, buckling my seatbelt out of habit. Aiden didn't, of course. I didn't need to question why. It was quite obvious, but I still wasn't taking any chances, especially with this maniac behind the wheel.

With the push of a button, the engine of the sports car roared to life. Aiden flashed me a large, fanged grin, as if he was ready to rip my world right open... or my flesh. Alexander tapped his knuckles against my window, and I pressed the button on the door, allowing my maker to push his head through, his blonde mane falling over me and practically into my lap. He smelled like jasmine and wine.

"Now, Jack. Listen. Our world is very different from the one you remember. What you see may not make sense at first, but it is a necessity that you become versed in the language of our lands and know how to survive. Good luck, my love." He pressed a gentle kiss against my lips, my lids fluttering closed, matching the sudden feeling in my stomach.

BEEP.

Aiden laid on the horn, interrupting our lovely exchange, and my soul momentarily left my body. I turned to stare at him.

He simply shrugged, brows raising high on his forehead as if he was innocent.

Motherfucker.

Alexander simply laughed and reached in to push my curls behind my ear. "See you soon, *mon cheri.*"

Off we drove, out of the garage and into the night, La Mont shrinking into the distance before disappearing into the blackness.

CHAPTER ELEVEN

THE UNDERCITY

Through the city we went, the car sputtering down derelict streets flooded with fluorescent light. Normally, I would have been exhausted by the sights and sounds of denizens wasting their little lives away, but now every colorful detail was a kiss to my senses. I drank it all down with the anticipation of what sort of pleasures awaited me when I would come face to face with my first victim.

My mind was different—sharp and ready. The moment I was given the opportunity, I would prove to myself just how different I really was.

The inside of Alexander's sleek sports car was mostly silent save for the smooth hum of the engine. Some snide joke played at Aiden's features, turning up the corners of his lips, but I wasn't in on it. He kept the Mercedes steady through the lanes, and in a matter of ten minutes, we sailed our way to our first destination.

Central Park.

Aiden effortlessly sidled the car up against a curb. Worried thoughts flared in my mind. What if we were dealt a parking ticket? I was fairly certain we were not supposed to park there, and yet Aiden didn't seem bothered. He simply waved a flippant hand and assured me that everything would be fine, that we had nothing to be worried about.

"Jacko, here's something you're going to learn very quickly. This isn't the world you left behind. You're no longer at the bottom of the food chain. Those laws don't apply anymore. We own the police. I could park in the middle of the fucking street. And that car?" He extended his talon at its sleek, angry nose. "It would end up right back at Alexander's garage with a notice on where it was found."

I blinked stupidly at him. Vampirism felt more and more like some secret society, and it seemed to come with some heavy duty perks.

"Keep up," he continued, walking ahead of me at a faster pace. "Things are about to get weird, but we've got to make sure you're introduced properly. You've got to have a good under- standing about how all of this works and I won't be responsible for you if you fail. I don't tolerate anything less than perfection," he muttered as a warm, evening breeze rushed all of my hair into my face.

As much as this man terrified me, I knew I should stay as close to him as possible. Our amble through the park was simple. Uneventful. Over the years, I had heard so many stories about not going there after dark. It was proper knowledge that gangs and drug dealers called the place their domain, and that a night stroll could be the forfeit of your life, but as my undead gaze fell across every bush and tree, I found nothing to be scary. At least... no more scary than Aiden and me.

After a few moments traversing the leafy walks, we came upon an entrance that looked to be some sort of service hatch— maybe for maintenance. I went to question it but before I could speak, Aiden's hand found the handle and shoved it into a downward position. The push was strong enough to move it but with enough grace not to snap it completely off its base. With a second tug, the hatch opened and milky moonlight flowed downward over a portion of stairs. The rest of the way ahead was dark enough to blind even my new vampire eyes from seeing anything beyond it.

Aiden led the way, his dress shoes clacking against the stone stairs as he began to descend. My hesitation must have been louder than the city sounds about us, because Aiden stopped on the fourth step and glanced over his shoulder at me.

"Come along, Jacko," he growled up at me.

Reluctantly, I followed. There wasn't any other choice. Something came to mind then. The small cellphone where I kept my poetry should have weighed down my pocket. I reached down to retrieve it in hopes of using the flashlight, but there was nothing there. I scrambled to the other pocket. Still nothing. I began to panic.

"Aiden, hey... uh... my phone's missing. I must have dropped it." I continued riffling stupidly through my clothes, hoping it would magically appear somewhere.

He spun at me. "Quit your babbling, you buffoon! Alexander took your phone, no doubt."

He reached into his jacket pocket and threw a small flashlight at my chest. I fumbled, nearly dropping it, my fingers juggling the marker-shaped device. Clicking the button at the top, a broad yellow cone of light illuminated the tunnel ahead. I wondered why my new undead eyes couldn't pierce this darkness on their own.

"Why would he take it?" I prodded. "I have important things on there—" The train of thought stopped and I remembered the most important thing, far more sentimental than my writings. "Holy shit! My sister! What if she tried to call! I never told her when I'd be back. She must be so worried..." I wilted with guilt.

Aiden turned to interrupt my anxious rambling, one tapered eyebrow cocked. "You don't know?"

"Know what?" I muttered. "Why don't you fill me in?"

Aiden *harrumphed* and continued our walk through what now appeared to be a pipeline. Our shoes tracked through shallow, murky water and somewhere in the distance, rat claws scraped against metal.

"Listen to me, and listen well," he began. "Your phone was taken by Alexander because your old life is over '*Jack*'. Those people in that phone—your friends, your family, your *darling* little sister—they don't belong in our world and you don't belong in theirs. Our sire may not say this to you as bluntly, but I'll spare you all the sugar. If they become involved in any way, if you try to see them, or even tell them what you are..." He dragged his forefinger across the radius of his neck.

"Don't you *dare!*" I snapped. I clawed his suit jacket and tugged him around to face me. This time, he didn't fight me. He simply leered at me through the heavy darkness.

"I know. Hard truth—it truly is—but the last thing you want to do is learn the hard way... like some of us. There's no reason for me to touch a hair on your humans' heads, but there *is* law. There is order. I am just a small fish compared to some others out there that would come for their throats if you even so much as blink in their direction. Consider this bit of information my welcome gift. You've been warned...*Jacko.*"

I released him, frustration expelling past my lips. I wondered why Aiden seemed... softer about this subject, as if he'd seen it happen before. Maybe he'd even experienced it.

Down... down... down we went. Into the bowels of Central Park, through every winding passage until we finally came to a wider birth. It took thirty minutes for us to find our way there. Ahead of us was an immense, circular door, the tunnel opening up to a pocket that allowed for twenty feet of space vertically.

The damp place smelled overwhelmingly of moss and decay. The door's surface had started to rust, several nails protruding from the metal. If I had traversed that labyrinth alone, I would have walked right past it, for it was innocuous enough to appear as just another wall. I figured that was by design.

"Alright," Aiden grumbled. "Here we go."

His knocking vibrated up the door, heavy enough to make steel sound like tin.

"Thanatos!" He cried out, his voice echoing back up the tunnel behind us.

The word seemed familiar but I couldn't recall where I'd heard it before. Some sort of code, I was sure. Within moments, the two halves of the large entry began to shift. The two of us took a step back as the ceiling above scraped with a raucous shriek.

A low, gravelly voice came just beyond the crack. "Who approaches?"

"We're here to see Marcus. Is he present?" Aiden asked firmly, folding his hands in front of himself.

The voice responded with surprise. "Aiden Pierce. You are not here on work duty... right?" it inquired.

"Not at all," he chuckled darkly. It was obvious he loved the effect he had on others. He moved through space like he had the biggest cock in the world. "There is fresh blood amongst the *Sanguineous*. I'd like to introduce him. Alexander sent us."

The door opened a crack, and beyond it stood the tallest man I had ever seen. Easily eight feet in height, his face was adorned with tribal tattoos, scaled ridges jutting out from his cheekbones and eyebrows, his skin reminiscent of a crocodile's. His clothes were ragged and torn. Any mundane would guess he was a homeless man who took a dive face first into toxic waste and came out victorious.

Claws as large as my head gripped the rusted metal and

pushed the door the rest of the way with tremendous strength. It bid us entry into the most impossible place I'd ever seen. The Undercity.

Through the dented archway, we emerged into a massive cavern almost the size of Times Square. Mouth agape, I stood marveling. Shuffling monstrosities paid us no mind as their silhouettes moved through the haze and they continued on with their tasks. Promptly, I clicked the flashlight off. Fixtures in the shape of demonic faces were placed evenly across wide, stone walls. Water rushed from their mouths, cascading into a narrow mote that snaked around the cavern's circumference.

Most of the Undercut's denizens looked similar in kind to the one who had opened the door, yet none of them were nearly as massive. Perhaps my toxic waste theory wasn't too far fetched after all.

Overwhelmed and excited, I staggered forward a few more steps only to trip over a ledge far too difficult to notice in the grotto haze. Missing the large, stone staircase to my side, I tumbled freely, just as I had done before on the balcony, but this time with no Alexander to catch me. I could hear Aiden laughing from above, even catching a glimpse of his ghoulish grin as I rag-dolled for what felt like an entire minute. Out of instinct, and even a twinge of fear, I thrust my hands forward to brace for impact. As I did, I could sense something change. The air began to shimmer and shift around me, my body slowing before hovering through mid-air and sailing downwards and towards the landing.

"Holy shit," I breathed before losing myself to hysterics. "I can fly. I CAN *FLY!*"

Many creatures on the surface below stopped to blink up at me, confused.

Aiden's voice called from the last dozen stairs. In my chaotic descent, I hadn't noticed him passing me, his body moving in a blur. He stood there, his fingers drumming against the copper railing at the end.

"No, you moron," he groaned as I floated downwards. His red eyes rolled about that narrow skull of his. "We can glide, however. Consider it falling with style, but do keep your attention!" He pointed to the ground below, making me aware that I had lost my focus.

"Oh? OH!" I began to kick my legs and flail my arms, trying desperately to swim through the air, yet my *Mary Poppins* moment ended when my body dropped like a stone. My deviated attention caused me to crash down into a pile of crates. Lucky for me, they were empty, though the splintered wood wasn't the best for a gentle landing.

Several pairs of glowing eyes gawked at my arms and legs sprawled about, splinters sticking up through my clothes, yet only one thing worried me: "Is my hoodie ripped?"

Aiden grumbled as he finished his last few steps and approached to offer his hand, yanking me from the pile of splinters.

"Careful," he simpered. "You're lucky one of those shards didn't puncture your gaudy, little shirt."

I still didn't know much about La Mont's guard dog. Aiden having a moment of concern seemed oddly uncharacteristic, though. Perhaps there was a side of him I wasn't seeing—something hidden beneath the surface. But as my mind wandered through the possible inner machinations of Aiden Pierce, another thought sparked.

"Wait a second!" I cawed as I dusted myself off. "The wooden stake thing. Is it real?"

The British vampire shook his head. "Not exactly," he explained. "Puncturing the heart with a wooden item won't kill us, but it will paralyze us until it is removed. A tactic the higher ups use when they need to drag us in for questioning... or worse. Execution."

Higher ups? Execution? I'd have to ask about that later.

Two shadowy figures proceeded toward us. One of the taller forms raised crooked fingers to tug at a shroud wrapped about its face. A series of grumbles and grunts echoed as a dirty mug emerged into the light.

Heterochromatic eyes stabbed at me through the shadows as I felt something invisible grip my throat tightly. I also began to realize I might have developed a new kink, because all of this choking evoked thoughts of Alexander at once. One eye a blazing orange and another cool blue eye left me to land gently on Aiden's pointed visage.

"Hey, kid." The monster said.

A second one stopped at his shoulder, cornering me, and making sure there was nowhere I could escape.

"Sylas..." Aiden snarled, his lip quivering from the very sound of the name. "We're here to see your maker. Care to escort?"

This *Sylas* creature nodded, his large brows knitting together in unison, their ridges gleaming in the dim light like the scales of a lizard.

"You know it. Come on. Marcus is doing his usual."

As Sylas and the others turned to begin our journey to meet the mysterious '*Marcus*' Aiden intentionally caught my eye, his head nudging me to come along and follow silently.

My thoughts returned to our earlier conversation about how he refused to have whatever my would-be failures reflect on him. I hurried along, a nervous lump in my throat, flicking lingering splinters away from my shoulder with a brush of my hand.

CHAPTER TWELVE
MARCUS

The Undercity's chasms were an impossible and stark contrast from the modern city buzzing above us. I was a new vampire, and compared to the others, I was still clumsy. Every step was a question. Every corner revealed a revelation that I hadn't fathomed could ever be real. Turns out the conspiracy theories about alligators in the sewer systems of New York were right... except they got one detail wrong....

There were no *actual* alligators, but there were certainly members of the undead who resembled them. Lizard people were a thing.

Aiden navigated me through the subterranean tunnels as if I were a lost child. I practically clung to the hems of his dinner jacket as we went, wide-eyed as we passed more stony pockets of scaly people going on about their *un*lives.

There were others, too....

Amidst the alligator men, there were goblins, gray-skinned fiends, wispy specters floating between the stalagmites, and of course, other vampires. An interesting detail, was that each of them had different hues of glowing eyes that pierced through the darkness. It all reminded me of a Guillermo Del Toro fantasy —every new being seemingly ripped straight from his imagination. In my living days, I had been a bit of a cinefile. I couldn't deny that. Latching onto those familiar comparisons was the only way I could rationalize what I saw.

As we ventured through the stony slums of the city, we came upon an opening that was broader than the others, and therefore, seemingly more important. Two creatures, similar in height to the first, stood vigilant at either side of the cavernous mouth.

"Here's your stop," Sylas croaked, a clawed hand welcoming us into darker depths. "Oh, and uh... kid?" This time, the address was aimed at me. "Just do yourself a favor. If you want to get out of here quickly, don't engage too much. Just make with the introductions and let the greaseball do the talking."

I swallowed hard. The ruler of this place sounded like a hard ass, possibly with a sharp tongue and an even sharper personality. I would take this lizard man's advice and mind my words. Without waiting for me, Aiden had already disappeared through the entryway. I hurried to fall into step with him.

We breached a small hallway that was much like the others —craggy, covered in moss, and, well... it was a sewer. The air was pungent and like trying to swim through spoiled soup. Yet, as we got further, a brilliant light shined far beyond where we were and illuminated the dismal greens and grays, ushering in more startling yellows. Portrait after portrait of hideous monsters lined the walls, their gilded frames seemingly misplaced among the crudeness of it all.

At the end of this corridor was a red velvet curtain. Old-fashioned music leaked beyond its edges to reach our ears. The songs were what my grandparents used to listen to. The record player's needle scratched a few times as the music played. I didn't miss the way Aiden's expression hardened, his glare narrowing. He was not looking forward to this, that was obvious. I would almost immediately learn why.

We pushed through, entering into warm, golden light. The room very similar to the rest of the Undercity—stone walls, dank floors, exposed pipes, the ceiling dripping with what was most likely hazardous sewage water.

Pieces from an old Hollywood set were erected in the far corner. New questions begged. It seemed to be from some pirate ship, retrofitted with a little desk and a double bed covered in a red comforter with matching pillows. Upon the desk, there was an old oil lamp and a journal left open for anyone to read. I had to admit, I was extremely tempted to.

"Marcus!" Aiden barked.

Clearly, Aiden was neither intimidated nor afraid of this man. My curiosity piqued at exactly why my dangerous blood brother seemed so reluctant to stand face to face with the lord of this pit.

"Well, well, well. Alexander has sent me his progeny, and a new brother he has so expeditiously decided to create. Come. Let me get a good look at the new boy."

The voice sounded like it came from the mouth of a *Shar Pei* —all jowls and gums and nothing more. I took a few steps forward from Aiden to introduce myself.

"Sir," I started, my voice cracking. "My name is... *Jack*." It was the first time I'd said that out loud. "I'm Alexander's protégé. Or... that's what he called me. It's very nice to meet you."

I heard Aiden give an irritated sigh behind me.

Still, I couldn't detect where the new voice came from. There was no towering lizard man before me—no hideous sewer beast. I scoured the room, but landed on nothing.

And then, from behind a tall pirate ship wall, I realized why I had missed him entirely: Small shoes tapped against the stone floor as a small, crooked creature emerged into the light. He was fitted with the smallest red velvet suit I had ever seen, topped by the most intriguing little top hat which he wore slightly askew. It was a tad too small, even for him, barely fitting his balding head. The being couldn't have been more than three feet tall, his face like a pug. His bottom lip protruded under his scrunched up little countenance, his left eye permanently shut, and his right massive and tinted yellow from some eternal disease, no doubt.

He came hobbling towards me with outstretched arms and what I could only imagine was his version of a smile.

"Don't be so far away. Come, come. Let me look at you. Let me..." He smacked his large lip. "...drink you in, you tall glass of water."

A strange tingling buzzed under my cheek but the usual heat I was used to did not bloom with the sensation of blushing. I was dead, I recalled. Vampires couldn't blush.

I approached, Aiden giving another *harrumph* behind me. I then began to understand; this being was nothing but jubilant and kind. Those characteristics probably didn't sit well with someone like Aiden.

The man's little hands tugged at my hoodie, forcing me down to stare nose to nose with him, his good eye scanning my features. "My boy, you are lovely to behold—a classic vision of a vampire. I am so glad you are a fan of the same colors I am. Your house is very fond of them, and I am very fond of the styles of your house." The man indicated his suit with a broad stroke of his hand.

"Sir." I thought for a moment. I could almost feel Aiden's sniper stare barreling into the back of my head. "What do you mean by *house*?"

It became clear. I was Alice. This was some very fucked up version of Wonderland.

"Alexander hasn't told you? How very carless, but I'm sure

he's busy. Come, sit with me. We'll have a nice conversation and then you'll be on your way."

His little underbite made a few of those lisped words come out more comical than they should have been, but I swallowed down my snicker and followed him back toward his desk. Aiden just stood there with the most vexed look I'd seen him have yet.

Marcus crept passed me, his wrinkled little hands searching the bookshelves near his desk for something less apparent—a large book, older than the journal that rested open, was far more decrepit looking.

"Let's see here... where shall we begin, young one?" His voice was weathered with time and I enjoyed the way it crackled through the air. Tiny claws fingered the pages with care. "Ah, here. Let us start at the one you have been sired into. House *Epine*, the guild of Alexander La Mont and his roses. Formerly known as House Valentine, Alexander's sire was Bartholomew Ward. *His* sire, Tiberius Valentius, re-established the House in the early 12th century. Before that and preceding him was the great sire Ain Mostafa, the founder of the original house. She had first called it *Nymphaea*, for the magical Blue Lotus plant that grows along the Nile river. Now called *The House of the Thorn* in English, Alexander has made his adjustments within the last few hundred years and restructured his guild more towards style, expressionism, and the arts. Your numbers have dwindled immensely over the years, however. Alexander is *very* selective about his progenies. At this moment, the Epine are only Alexander, the guard dog..." He lifted his eyebrows, indicating Aiden, "and, well, *you.*

"A particularly vapid bloodline but not without its reasons, focused not only on honing their talents but their personal power as well," he continued to ramble, staring down his nose at the page. "Most known for their exquisite sense of fashion— my own outfit is inspired by *your* house." He ran his palms down his lapel once again in show of his support for what I learned was the *Epine*, or the Thorns.

"There are only three of us?" I could hardly believe it. "Why so few?" I blurted out as though Marcus were a familiar old friend, forgetting myself and my place before this master of the undead.

"Your maker wanted to covet the great power within his veins, and so he chose to keep your house more concentrated. Your bloodline being small is not a bad thing, my boy, it's a sign of stronger roots—an easier flow from the magic your blood calls upon. It makes your guild very unique And very powerful." A smile crept across his wretchedly adorable face. "Think of it this way, with each transformation unto undeath—with each newly-created undead, there becomes less and less power to draw from." His fingers traced the words across the page as he whispered, "Remarkable. It's why Alexander La Mont is so respected and also so very rightfully feared. It takes immense self control not to give in to the calling to spread your blood across the world. Ain may have been the pioneer, but she learned too early when her original children staged an uprising against her and she was forced to slay them all. With their betrayal she chose to create a new rule: To only have one progeny at a time. That was when she created Valentius. That tradition carried on through your house...until now."

Marcus's good eye flicked up to Aiden before sliding over to land on my face.

"Now," he continued. "This rule is seemingly... broken."

Broken.

Turning me had broken the code put into place by the originator of an entire vampiric faction, and now Aiden wasn't alone. No wonder he was so upset. Glancing over my shoulder, I found him to appear more sour than ever. Alexander destroyed a millennia-old code put into place for protection.

I reeled with the gravity of the idea. In that moment I felt more love than ever for Alex. He trusted me. He thought I was important enough to shatter a law. Silently, I vowed to never betray the maker who trusted me with his very essence—to never have him feel what Ain felt when her children turned on her.

Thwap. A tiny hand struck my leg, bringing me back to the present.

"Sadly, my boy, I believe it is time for you all to depart. There is still much to learn, but let us save that lesson for another evening."

The two of us turned toward Aiden who was leaning languidly against the wall, his palm cradling his face to hide an expression of complete agony.

"Well!" Marcus began, clapping his claws together in front of his face. "You've got a schedule to keep, I assume you have been to see the king already and introductions have been made?"

King? New York had a king? This was the first moment I had heard mention of any sort of vampiric royalty. I shook my head in response. The smaller Vampire turned to Aiden at last, glaring pointedly at him.

"Does Carver know?" There was an air of judgement hanging off the end of Marcus's question. The suit left his perch to walk his dress shoes against soggy stone. Dim light through the top of the dwelling poured over him like warm cider in autumn.

Pierce scoffed, the corners of his mouth turning down in a dangerous scowl. "What do you think, Marcus? Do you believe my sire to be one bound to such constraints?"

Marcus snapped back. "Boy! This is *serious*. Did he seek permission from Carver to create this new progeny or not?"

A flippant hand arose and fell as Aiden played coy. "I don't enjoy your tone, Marcus, but I'll humor you even so. Alexander has nearly twice the years on Carver and is much more dangerous. Why should someone like him need to bow to some illegitimate authority?"

Marcus slammed the book shut and approached Aiden, his heels clicking against the floor as he broadened stance. "Of course. I am nowhere near surprised at this development. Your sire *would* be this brash and reckless. Does Jack even understand the significance of such a decision?"

Aiden gave an arrogant shrug and shook his head. The only sound in the room was the exasperated sigh of the one called Sylas. I watched his large claw cover his frustrated face. Confusion gripped me as it often did over those past few nights. Clearly, there were many details about this life I was not yet privy to. Marcus turned toward me again. I could feel the blood thin in my veins, afraid of what he might say next.

"My boy, Carver is the patriarch of this city. He has one rule above all else: Those who are to be granted the gift of unlife shall be approved by him first and foremost to avoid any possible recklessness and exposure to the mortal world. If he deems you unworthy...well..."

My blood ran cold.

"It is possible you could face oblivion tonight."

CHAPTER THIRTEEN
A DANGEROUS GAME

My last night alive could have possibly lead to my last night *unalive*. The thought sat in my cranium like a grenade with the pin freshly pulled. I could hardly focus on the argument unraveling before me now as Aiden and Marcus launched verbal assaults at each other across the cavernous room dressed in Hollywood props. I slumped against the wall to stabilize myself in my moment of panic. To my surprise, a hand landed on my shoulder in gentle support.

Sylas had drawn closer. With this proximity, I could see in better detail his mismatched eyes of blue and orange as they locked onto mine.

"Hey kid," he rasped. "Stay calm. We're gonna figure this out and you'll be right as rain. First time out's usually a bitch... especially with a maker like yours."

I pushed all the stale air from my lungs and allowed the calming words of the scaled man to keep me from spiraling.

"Is this sort of thing... *common* for Alexander?"

If I had physically still been capable of breaking into a sweat, I would have. Sylas gave a firm nod before raising a finger to his mouth and gestured to the two vampires still verbally sparring. I supposed that meant he would fill me in another time.

"Alexander has no reason nor rhyme to answer to that dog! He's nothing but a figure piece—a charlatan in a cheap suit with a tinfoil hat as a crown!" Aiden's rasped as he bent to yell into Marcus's face, that thick British accent growing higher in pitch, replacing the soft velvet tones with a sound more like a hyena laughing.

Marcus stretched up on his legs, trying his best to stand chest to chest with Aiden, a clawed finger stabbing up at his face. His volume raised to match.

"Carver Wellington may not be as old as your sire, nor may he be as skilled, but he is still the ruling body of this city and you will do your damnedest to remember that!" Marcus pressed both thumb and middle claw together to produce a large snap. "If he wished for it, he could snap his fingers and have an army at Alexander's doorstep. Do not forget it! The only reason I am not completely outraged and calling him myself is because I love your guild and the legacy it holds, but this must be accounted for. The boy must be attuned!"

Marcus's little hands shook with anger, his face as red as his coat. It was incredible to see how the educational spirit of the evening unraveled into a much more explosive atmosphere. This was serious.

He continued, "This poor boy—this new fledgling now has to fear for the rest of his journey into this strange new world and neither of you thought to keep him safe! A dangerous game, indeed!"

The crisp suit pushed hard toward the red velvet as Aiden closed what little distance there already was. "Careful, Marcus," he hissed like a viper ready to strike, those crimson eyes growing as unstable as they had been back at the bar.

As I watched the confrontation, I noticed Sylas had already left my side and mystically appeared near my blood-brother's heels, his form crouched low, ready to defend his leader.

"Aiden, you'd be a damn fool to lose your cool in a place like this." I noticed Marcus's focus give a knowing shift to the near-invisible monster. "Best to remember that with whatever you plan to do next, pup."

The Brit's hand had already found its way into the breast pocket of his jacket. I wondered what weapon he meant to retrieve. Aiden must have realized Sylas's proximity as well, because his jaw muscles clenched over another smart response, no doubt. The two stared daggers at one another as everything froze. No words, no putrid blasts of air careening down the subterranean tunnels, not even the sounds of mice skittering about in the darkness. There were only two enraged vampires ready to rip one another to pieces, and my presence was the catalyst.

My dead stomach twisted.

What I had once imagined as this romantic transformation —this beautiful, dark gift bestowed upon me by my great love of all loves—was a mistake in the eyes of my peers.

But then a new thought made my heart flutter.

Alexander bypassing the law made the idea even more... forbidden. My dark angel, whose eternal kiss stole me from the day for an unending night, did it all in spite of the ruling of a king. In secret. In love.

Fuck it, I thought. *Can't get much more romantic than that.*

Marcus gave a harsh grumble, thick phlegm bubbling up his throat in deep upset. With a twist of his hips, he moved away from Aiden and back to me. His fragile-looking, little claw found its way to the saturated reds of my shirt, tugging.

"My boy," he wheezed, his good eye bulging. "Do yourself a favor. No matter what happens next, find it within yourself to confide in us when need be. Your... *elders*... are playing a fool's game and would see you suffer in this new world if it meant dirtying their hands in order to protect you." He sighed, crusted lips meeting to produce another wet smack. "When you go to Carver's palace on the West Side," he added with a cautious tone to his graveled voice. "Tell him *we* vouch for you—that you are aware of the rules and the inner workings and will strive to be a beneficial piece to his menagerie. Do you understand?"

The question lingered in the air for a moment. Silence held me—not out of an unwillingness to cooperate, but from the overwhelming fear wrapping around my undead organs like a parasite. For more than one reason, my mouth went dry.

"Boy!" Marcus snapped. "I need to hear that you understand."

"I understand," I muttered, embarrassed by the way my voice cracked.

With a forceful exhale, Marcus hobbled back to his desk to continue whatever he had been doing prior to our arrival. My focus dropped to my hands, seeing how my knuckles clenched turning whiter than even death could produce. My mind raced with thoughts. *Could this be the end of my journey already?* Panic caused my airways to constrict.

"Hey, kid."

The shrouded being returned to me, revealing his solid body through a plume of shadow. His mismatched eyes materialized first, like the Cheshire Cat from an old nursery tale. While my name might not have been Alice, it was starting to feel like some truly fucked up version of Wonderland. Sylas placed a large, nodulous claw upon my shoulder. Now, I could easily view the patches of scales and warts dancing up his fingers and escaping into his sleeves. The tapered points of his talons seemed to be tinted a muddled yellow while his fingers were adorned with rings made from wire and metal scraps—things that had been left in the city's gutters, no doubt.

"I'm going to come with you, alright? I'll be right behind you every step of the way. I figure that might be what Alexander had in mind when he sent you two knuckleheads down here—a little bit of security and our reputation to ensure you don't lose your head." His hooded face craned to the side, scowling in Aiden's direction. "Isn't that right, Hound?"

Aiden gave another roll of his unholy eyes, fang digging into his bottom lip in irritation. "I wouldn't go that far, Sylasss."

Every time my blood-brother spoke the name of the sewer-dweller, he drew out the last half of the name in a singsong manner. I wondered what history there was between these two that they reacted to each other in such a way.

Sylas gave my shoulder another hard pat before lumbering over to Marcus who was already seated at his desk and pressing on with his work. He licked his thumb before his little hands searched through more documents and old books to land upon yet another revelation.

"Sire?" Sylas started. His protruding bottom jaw made him appear like some sort of puppet whenever he spoke.

Marcus simply glanced upwards with that singular tennis ball for an eye and gave him a large nod. More intensity filled the air, rivaling the miasma of humidity in the underground dwelling. As I stood in wait, I wondered if panic attacks still occurred in members of the undead. Those moments shared with Aiden and Marcus made me certain they were, even though my heart had mostly stopped beating forever. Even so, my leg began to bounce.

"We haven't got all evening," Aiden blurted. "I have places to show young *Jacko,* and you're keeping us from finishing our trip. So whatever you want to do with this, speak up or get out of our way." Aiden's hand left the inside of his jacket to slick back stray hairs over his head.

"Go on. You know what to do," Marcus grumbled dismally, allowing a single claw to wave in Sylas's direction.

"Come on," the scaled man said to me. "We've got a king to meet first. Then, I'll help Aiden show you the rest of the city and it's important parts."

My stomach eased a bit as a new flicker of excitement sparked in my chest. Something about Sylas felt safe, and I was glad to finally learn what was needed and to start this journey off right. I had confidence I would now, but meeting Carver still cast a heavy sense of dread over my shoulders.

As the two elder vampires started out of the small dwelling, warm light leaving their ghoulish forms, the gravely, little voice came as my back turned.

"Jack." Marcus's small smile returned to his cheeks, his crinkled hands cradling something close to his chest. It was a satchel filled with papers and books—the thing to give him pause just a few moments earlier.

"What are these?" I asked, my own hands reaching to take the satchel from him.

The elder chuckled softly. "Information I fear you will not receive from the one who sired you," he whispered. "Jack, keep them safe. Study them keenly. This world has just as many rules as your previous one, but the consequences of breaking ours are even steeper," he warned. "If for any reason—any at all—you need help, Sylas and myself will be your guides and your allies. You can always count on the shadows to protect you in a moment of need."

I nodded, giving my silent thanks before turning to leave.

"Oh, and Jack?"

I hesitated.

"Good luck. Please be safe out there."

Be safe.

Chloe's last words to me danced in my head again. I had nearly forgotten her until that moment. My Songbird, my sister, my—

The thought ceased and a new one arose in its stead: Would I ever see her again? Was what Aiden said true? Was there no place in the underworld for the living?

Why would Alexander lie to me?

So many questions buzzed around my mind, yet I was afraid to learn the answers. I wouldn't be able to avoid the truth for very much longer, though. That much I knew. Truths were often ugly, and I would never be the same.

CHAPTER FOURTEEN
BEING A MONSTER

Through the subterranean tunnels, out through the service hatch, and back up to Central Park we went. There was nothing remarkable about our trek through sludge-filled corridors and slime-slicked walkways. Similar to the way we entered the Undercity, we dodged denizens of the darkness with ease.

The large undead from earlier shut the massive door behind us with a thunderous boom. Retracing our steps happened mostly in silence. The tension between Aiden and Sylas remained uncomfortable. The two had very little to say to one another, as if they were jilted lovers forced to work together. Were they? The new question begged. It seemed unlikely, but the more I learned about vampire society, the more incestuous it seemed to be. By the time the door to the service hatch closed, I decided to sate my curiosity.

"So. You two don't like each other much, do you?" The words toppled out of my mouth in the same way my feet fumbled to catch up to them.

The two greater undead shot vexed glances between one another before turning to blink at me.

Aiden started, "He's a know it all."

Sylas finished, "He's a putz."

Without any further delineation, the two continued leading me back to the car. It wasn't enough for me, though. I had to understand. Perhaps it was my need to know them better in order to belong or simply my hyper fixation sputtering out of control, but I knew there had to be more of a reason they seemed so annoyed with one another.

I skipped over my heels, gaining enough speed to wedge between them. "So, you just hate each other to hate each other? That can't be it," I pressed.

Aiden raised his hands to his face, pulling down the skin under his eyes in frustration. Sylas grimaced.

"Listen, kid," Sylas began, "Aiden and I have similar positions in our guilds, alright?"

I nodded in rapid motion, waiting for more. Halting in my tracks, I may as well have dug my heels into the earth, because I was not moving until they elaborated. My curious fledgling mind needed to be sated.

Aiden released an exasperated noise and continued for Sylas, his hands leaving his face to rest upon his narrow hips. "While Sylas and I have similar rankings, our methods and expertise are quite different. It creates many opportunities for... disagreements." A fire ignited behind his eyes as he spoke the last word.

"Good enough," Sylas concluded.

The two began walking again. My legs itched to get in front of them, but I settled for simply cramming myself directly in-between the suit and rags.

"Why is that a bad thing?" I prodded. "We all have our differences—each and every one of us."

As I tried to play therapist to the undead, Sylas interrupted with a vicious bark. "He's a fucking murderer, Jack. Yeah, we used to get along, even ran a few jobs together. Security detail... repossession..." he rattled on. "But, that was before I took notice of how many bodies were left in his wake at the end of each job. Not to mention his *side* work."

"Murderer? I know Aiden is rough but, I mean, we're *vampires*."

As I attempted to make light and foolishly defend my brother, a sickening laugh arose from within Aiden's throat, his silky voice shredding through past his flesh as it entered the open air.

"He's right, Jacko," Aiden started with an almost psychotic smile, his face contorting into a monstrous grin. "I *relish* it. Every kill is a chance to understand the inner workings of the mortal mind—to unlock the depths of fear your target feels just before they taste their last moments. It's divine."

Sylas growled. "It's sickening. I know we're vampires, kid. Bloodlust is our nature, but the bastard takes pleasure in the pain he causes. It's vile."

Aiden's smile faltered for a moment. He moved ahead of us at a faster pace.

"You're a hypocrite, Sylas," he said in that same singsongy way. "And you're no angel, either. You'll never get away from what you are or what you've done."

Sylas kept stride with me as Aiden took the lead. The size of his ego became very apparent. It seemed impossible for him to swallow Sylas' very understandable distaste for his cruelty.

"Fuckin' sadist," Sylas barked as the suit took larger strides out of the park.

Aiden leaped over the sidewalk before breaking into a light jog the rest of the distance, reaching the Mercedes at last. We both watched as Aiden pulled open the driver's door and slid into the front seat. The engine revved angrily as the vehicle jumped to life.

I lowered my voice, hoping Pierce wouldn't overhear. "So he's just always been this way?" I asked in earnest.

My gloomy companion grumbled in his displeasure. "Yeah, always. But I feel like he's on his bullshit more than usual since his vampire papa adopted a new puppy. You're in a difficult position, kid." One of Sylas's brows arched high on his forehead before those unsettling eyes found me once again. "You're quite the predicament, know that?"

I stopped walking again, feeling a new fire flare in my belly. "Am I really such an issue? I didn't know about Aiden, or this world, or *anything* really. Look. Alexander gave me an offer, and I took it." The words dripped venomous from my mouth. I was tired of being seen as such a burden. I thought all of that would have ended when I drew my last breaths as James Donovan. "I wish everyone would stop speaking to me as though any of this were my fault."

The taller vampire craned his neck back to drink in the moonlight above. It gave me the feeling he hadn't been topside in a while. He exhaled before looping an arm around my shoulder, hugging me closer to his body, his muted blacks and my saturated reds marrying one another in a side-hug. I could feel the form beneath his shroud then; protruding ribs and sharp edges that dared to suggest what lived beneath the obsidian rag was only skin and bones—a living halloween decoration.

"Jack," he began again. I realized it was the first time he used my name. "How long did Alexander wait before turning you?"

A lump formed in my throat as I recalled my first evening with Alexander La Mont.

Reluctantly, I mumbled, "A day."

This grand, romantic event had begun to seem far less beautiful than I originally thought. The more I recalled the haste of it all, the more unusual it felt.

"Shit! A *day*? That's... not really how we do things, buddy. Usually, an intended progeny is allotted a period to learn about our world and see if they're the right fit, you know? Prove themselves. This is also a time for our makers to prove themselves as well. I mean, that's just generally speaking. Of course, there are special cases with the sick or dying, but when you're chosen, it's supposed to be a process!"

I could feel my stomach drop, a slow, unforgiving nausea taking hold.

Sylas continued under his breath, "So, they sent me a fresh one. No wonder Aiden's so fucking angry." Eyes of sun and moon shifted to scan me up and down like I had just committed a felony just for existing. "You know you have lingering magic on your face, right?" he stated flatly.

He stabbed one of his talons at my cheek. I reached to feel the new curvature of my transformed appearance—the new face I had seen in the mirror. I wanted to believe it was a trick of the light or a symptom of lingering death, but this was all starting to make sense.

"I had a feeling something happened," I admitted. "When I woke up, I saw my reflection and realized I was almost a completely different person. I figured it was just the change into being a vampire, but... are you saying someone actually did this to me?"

Distant bass vibrated under our shoes. We both looked to the car again, seeing the silhouette of Aiden's head bobbing to some music we couldn't quite hear beyond the military-thick windows.

"Yeah," Sylas murmured. "That's what I'm saying. Your maker decided to fuck with your face for some odd reason.

You're in a different world now. Magic is real, and real damn scary."

It was a hard truth to accept—the idea that someone had molded my flesh to change my appearance for their own preference. I shuddered. That someone was the very same man I had died for. How does one process such enormous things while also making your way through a crowded city to a vampire king who could possibly snap his fingers and order your demise? My mind swam my stream of emotions behind the barricade of my clenched jaw.

Why?

The notion that Alexander did not love me for me was horrible and sinking.

Sylas gave the matte handle of the passenger side a firm yank, allowing entry into the sultry vehicle. Pulsating house music poured out from the cab. Aiden cringed at Sylas's filthy shroud as it slid over the fresh leather. Stale fecal matter from the sewers clung to the torn cloth as he settled in. I slipped into the back seat. Aiden gave a frustrated grunt, obviously uncomfortable with this seating arrangement. The weighty tension returned.

Our drive through the avenues was silent for the most part, aside from the teeming that continued right outside the polished windows. The city that never slept remained awake and thriving.

Aiden and Sylas kept their supernatural vision fixed on the road ahead, once in a while, shifting to humans on the street. I knew why. Each of their scents wafted through the channels of the car's air vents. If I had been out there, refraining from chomping down over someone's throat would have been impossible.

In fact, as the night pressed on, my hunger became more and more unbearable. It ripped with needle claws at the walls of my belly, roaring for a meal I had never truly tasted, yet damn did I want it worse than anything I could ever imagine.

It was torture. Everything in my mind screamed to ask about feeding, but I remembered how important our current errand was. Despite the ache in my gums and the burning in my throat, instead I sat back against the seat, drawing in counterfeit breaths, focus fixed on the roof of the car. If I didn't *look* at the people, perhaps refraining from lunging through the window would be easier. Their aroma was impossible to escape, so I resigned myself to simply fantasize about the kill to come.

What would it be like? Would it consist of everything from those vampire movies I had seen from Hollywood? I pictured a billowing cape behind me as I outstretched my arm and coaxed a young virgin to place her neck gently against my mouth. The image played over and over in my mind. Surely it wasn't so simple. Would we hunt and how did that work? My mind was abuzz as I continued to drink in the scents of the city and the potential victims on every block.

The tires screeched to a halt and my body lurched forward. I didn't wear a seatbelt, because I was undead after all, and wanted to be cool like my older brother, but that proved to be a mistake.

My face careened forward to slam against the back of Aiden's headrest. If I were still alive, my nose would have most certainly broken. Regret plagued me.

"Jacko, are you fucking serious? Did you fall asleep back there?" Aiden adjusted his rearview mirror in order to glare at me.

Sylas gargled over some broken laughter—a horrifying sound. With a shake of his head and a sigh, Aiden cut off the engine and stepped out into the night once more, fluorescent light pouring into the driver's side seat.

A hand found my shoulder with a hard slap, jolting my

deadened nerves. Apparently, they hadn't died quite to the degree I thought they would.

"We're here, kid," Sylas grumbled before joining Aiden in the stark light.

Out I clambered until my feet touched down on cobblestone, the strange change in texture registering immediately.

"Here we go," Sylas choked and I could tell he was just as nervous as I felt.

My focus followed his and found what seemed to be causing him such dread. A massive building looked to be a mixture of a hotel and office building. It possessed the intensity of Wall Street with the same lavishness of the Marriot in Midtown. Harsh whites and dark blacks climbed the spire before us. The entrance was marked by gilded dividers with velvet rope around the perimeter of a long red carpet, leading us to whatever my fate would be.

Aiden sighed and announced, "The Spire."

CHAPTER FIFTEEN

THE SPIRE

How does one describe the feeling of pure terror, of powerlessness, in the face of righteous wrath? Walking up those steps and into the mouth of the Vampire King's lair, terror and powerlessness was all I felt. My bones ached with a familiar, mortal chill that spread through my hollow bones. Time and space slowed down, at least, that was how it felt to me.

Aiden led the way with the shrouded Sylas close behind. Up the steps and into the mouth of authority, the red ropes kept us in a single-file line. Outside the entry, two large men greeted us with hands clasped at their fronts, ear pieces fixed into place to alert if any danger approached. Impulsively, I wanted to crack a joke, bring light to a dark situation, but I could feel the eyes of the tower bearing down on me like Sauron over Mordor. This place was pristine, modern and clean, but something about it felt evil beyond its glistening facade.

The shorter of the two security personnel halted us with one hand, his other pressing a small button at his earpiece. "Sir,

Aiden Pierce is here. He has... *Sylas Cole* with him." He sneered at
Sylas's grubby appearance. "Should I send them up?"

I didn't expect my two chaperones would be known instantaneously by name. I hoped to whatever god would listen that
they were on decent terms with the one who was about to
determine my outcome. With a nod of his head in understanding, the guard waved us inside.

"He's waiting for you in the penthouse. He said he was
already made aware of the situation." Aiden pushed ahead, but
the guard stopped him once again with a hand on his chest.
"Mind your manners. He's not in the mood for theatrics. No
groveling, no begging, and no *excuses*." His eyes bounced from
my face back to Aiden's. "Give his Majesty the respect he
deserves. Understood?"

I, of course, nodded like a buffoon.

"Sure thing," Aiden sniffed dryly.

A wave of relief took me as we entered through the glass
doors. The king knew about me. He knew. Maybe now he would
be more gracious than Marcus anticipated. Had Alexander come
through after all?

The lobby was pristine, and it became clear that three
undead hooligans had no place there. Gleaming metal reflected
the cool LED beaming from above us like God's holy eye. The
room's brilliance made me wince and I wondered how on earth
vampires dealt with such bright lights when our nature was to
crave darkness. Why would Carver make such a choice? Maybe
they were meant to be disorienting. Perhaps he intended to
bewilder the subject he called upon. Seemed solid enough
to me.

The lobby was as large as any belonging to the many five
star hotels in the city. Just the same, it was fitted with a front
desk, restrooms, seating areas with tables, and even a lounge

complete with a fireside couch. It was as swanky as the Met had been, but with colder tones and jagged edges.

"Jack, pay attention, kid," Sylas barked.

He and Aiden were already boarding an elevator at the far side of the vast room that reminded me of an opal face. Skipping up over my heels, I ran to catch up to the two as the metal doors began to slide shut. There was a *ping*, the cage jolted into motion, and then my heart lodged itself within my narrow throat.

I held my breath all the way up to the top floor, reminiscent of the night I met Alexander.

Aiden, Sylas, and myself all stood in silence as the flickering of lights and the whirring of machinery made the small space even smaller. The dull elevator music was just barely loud enough to drown the uncomfortable quiet. Then it hit me. I knew this song well.

Where Is My Mind by the Pixies played in tinny, piped Muzak. It was a favorite of mine growing up. I recalled listening to it on repeat in my moments of anguish and solitude. Here, however, it tinkered on a single melody line over the small speaker, and as I reminisced on past pains and sorrowful songs, the elevator raised to a height I had never been before. It must have been more than thirty stories.

The metal shaft housing us was just part of its grand design. Once out of the departure gate, the compartment itself was comprised entirely of glass. On our way up, the whole skyline was within our view, and while my companions remained unimpressed and barely budged, I pressed my nose against the glass, enamored with the glittering sea below us. The lights, the bodies, the sounds. It was like being pulled towards heaven and getting a final glimpse of Earth's beauty. Looking down over mankind, I remembered that I no longer was one of them. I was dead.

Dead to the world.

Dead to my family.

Dead my friends.

Fucking dead.

"You're a weird one, you know that, Jacko?" Aiden said with his arms folded.

Behind him, the inner wall revealed the mechanisms of the elevator within the half open shaft. He eyed the gears as they turned against each other, chewing the inside of his lip.

Sylas moved to my side to take in the view with me. The scales on his face mildly reflected the tide of lights.

"Y'know, back in my day, you'd never see anything like this," he began, his tone wistful. His eyes even looked a bit watery, but I might have imagined that part. "We didn't have this sort of technology. While old chuckle nuts back there no longer appreciates things like this, I'm right there with ya', man. It still blows my mind what humankind is capable of. Even the mundane has its magic."

I found comfort in Sylas's attempt to find common ground, yet something else gnawed at me.

"Back in your day?" I asked cautiously.

Sylas snorted and then let out a hearty guffaw, a large claw finding its way to the window to trace circles over the many buildings and billboards in the distance.

"Been on this earth three hundred years, kid... and I still haven't lost my sense of wonder. I hope, I truly do, that in the centuries to come, you keep this boyish curiosity and don't become numb to it like so many others of our kind."

"Is it common, Sylas? That so many of us just lose themselves... like..." I nudged my head in Aiden's direction hoping that my shrouded friend would pick up my meaning without being obvious.

He simply sighed. "Kid," he started, "They're all like him.

Almost every single one. It's why I love living in the Undercity. We keep things as real as possible—made the decision a long time ago to toss away the vampiric sticks up our asses. Sure, we traded the sky above for the murk of the depths, but damn it's nice to be around others who haven't become jaded."

Sylas went on to explain about how the decision to go underground wasn't a curse, it was a blessing—to avoid the laws of a failing kingdom and the ideals of a race who had lost touch with their love for the humanity they once possessed.

"We look like monsters, but that's just because we as vampires are adaptable. We evolve to the conditions we find ourselves in. We adapt. Marcus talks about it like it's some sort of curse—named our guild the *Orochi* after some Japanese scaled demon—but some of us know the truth. This ain't no curse, and we ain't no demons. Just vampires tired of the way the others do things."

I couldn't imagine it; throwing the beautiful sights of the surface, and the softness of my flesh, away for some semblance of peace. However, I could understand the longing for personal control. Not to have to answer to some king and have the entirety of your existence determined by a single fist.

Ding.

The elevator slowed to a stop. After twenty-five floors, we made it to the top, and where my fate was to be decided. The tops of buildings, and the clouds of smog hovering over the horizon haloed by lights branded in my mind as possibly the last image I would see before my true demise.

Sylas gave me one last hard clap over my shoulder, his talons digging gently into the crimson fabric of my designer hoodie. Turning from me, he drifted closer to Aiden again as they waited to exit the elevator. He made a small circle with his claw for me to follow and keep close. I obeyed, tripping over myself, nearly falling against him as they anticipated the opening of the doors.

Before they could, a strange new sound began and I just about shit my pants, if I could still even do that. I hadn't attempted to figure that out for myself, so I remained unsure.

Then came a sound like a power drill being pressed against the hard metal of the doors. The glass entry slid to the side. At the front of the narrow compartment, a strange light beamed from the face of the secondary steel door—like the second eyelid of a lizard. A harsh green beam phased from the ceiling to the floor, scanning our bodies for... something. Dangerous items, perhaps. As we stood there in rigid silence, I moved to cling to Sylas's sleeve like a small child. I couldn't help it. The light fizzled back into the small contraption that resembled a nozzle.

"Aiden Pierce: Class A. Sylas Cole: Class A+. Jack, no known surname: Class A-. Possible error."

As the strange robotic voice barked its assessment, the two men glanced over their shoulders at me, their eyes wide. Clearly, there was something I was missing. As Sylas began to say something, the doors before us gave a large mechanical crunch, the steel separating with the glass to allow us passage into the Penthouse.

Aiden began to walk forward while Sylas remained in place, squeezing my wrist tightly.

"Alright, Kid. Time to meet the Crown."

CHAPTER SIXTEEN
THE CROWN

Fear swelled in my breast and I couldn't shake the feeling that this truly might be the final end of me. Holding my breath wasn't hard to do, but it was uncomfortable.

Crossing onto the polished checkered floor of the penthouse, I clung to Sylas's side fiercely. In the short time I knew him, I had found myself feeling quite attached—not in a romantic sense like Alexander, but almost as if he were the older brother I had always wanted. My true brother forsook me and drifted far beyond my reach, and it was becoming clearer that a relationship with my blood-brother, Aiden, was never going to happen.

The second thought to hit me was: *Did vampires really turn into dust when they die? Or was that a myth?*

Either way, I hoped I wouldn't learn the truth for myself.

As I wrestled with my unease, Aiden was already waiting expectantly by a new door, his hand on the knob. He tapped his shoe, impatient.

The penthouse was laid out over a few different rooms. The first room was small, nothing spectacular. It looked like another waiting area—cold marble floors and stark gray walls. A chandelier hung low from the center of the ceiling, casting warmer, champaign-colored light so as to not blind undead eyes like the lights in the lobby did. It was lovely, even as I waited there like the peasant I was to be allowed audience with the king.

Aiden rattled the golden handle adorning an old, mahogany door, his mouth contorting with his frustration.

"Fucking Christ leaping on a pogo-stick, let us in you fucking twat," he cursed under his breath.

It was loud enough for even those with mortal ears to hear, let alone the acute hearing of the undead. I cringed. My ass cheeks clenched in panic.

Aiden noticed a small, black speaker fixed into the wall beside the door then. To my dismay, he started tapping on it in rapid succession.

Sylas gave a reassuring nod in my direction before rounding to Aiden's side. I fiddled with the zipper of my hoodie, giving myself something to fixate upon rather than my possible impending doom.

"Carver," Sylas's voice resounded in a deep baritone, intimidating even to the vampire next to him. I didn't miss the way Aiden startled. "You know why we're here. Any reason you're making us sit out here for damn near five minutes?"

What an odd way to address vampiric royalty that could demolish anyone with the snap of his claw. I chewed the inside of my cheek, tasting blood.

After a moment, another mechanical whirring began. It was then I noticed there was a camera fixed to the top of the door. Its lens barreled down at us like an angry eyeball, zooming in and out of focus. Then, from the speaker Aiden had been abusing, came a voice. It reminded me of an actor from one of the original James Bond movies—another smooth British accent, but crackled by age. It was more comforting than Aiden's cadence.

"Aiden..." the voice warned. "If you strike my property again, I'll send you a bill simply for making me wash away the stench of your hand. Do we understand one another?"

Aiden immediately ceased his wrapping and folded his hands behind himself.

"Come inside. Let's get this over with. I have many things to tend to this evening and this is on the bottom of my list."

The speaker shut off and I relinquished a breath. My shoulders detached from my earlobes, relaxing to where they usually rested. If I wasn't so high on King Carver's priority list, maybe I wouldn't be facing the chopping block so soon.

Into through the doors we went, shuffling past Aiden as he held open the entry.

This space was an even further departure from the downstairs lobby. White walls matched the ceiling above. The only dash of color was a massive black and white painting made to resemble a marble surface. It took up nearly an entire wall, no doubt won from some fancy auction. Three white leather sofas faced one another. At their center, was a glass table resting atop a black rug like a pearl housed in an oyster. Upon it was a decanter of what seemed to be scotch and an old cigar still smoking, the silver ribbon undulating into the open air.

"Boys..."

That same weathered voice steeped the air in sweet spice. It came from my left. I realized the other section of the large suite was a modern, stainless-steel kitchen, complete with a granite island and four bar stools.

This guy has to be loaded, I thought. *Of course he is. He's the King.*

From beyond the kitchen came the soft padding of old leather loafers over the tile. There he appeared, the legend himself.

I was a bit surprised, however. I had expected a robe, a

crown, maybe a scepter lodged within his fist that he would wave around, barking his royal decree. I had anticipated an upturned nose, even, and burning red eyes with bat-like features—a vampire to rule all vampires.

Instead, however, there came this unassuming, older gentleman. He looked as if he had just left the dance floor at the party depicted in the *Great Gatsby*. White slicked back hair, craters at the hollows of his cheeks, a strong nose, ashy stubble scattered across an old and rugged jaw, and unnatural silver eyes. He reminded me of what would be considered a man's man back in the roaring 20's. He was bullet-sharp. This *king* seemed to have traded his crown and royal vestments for a gray suit that cut through the stark whites and intense blacks surrounding him, as if he was subtly communicating that in a world of black and white, Carver was apparently the gray.

"So, boys, I have already been made aware of the situation and everything surrounding it." He folded his claws together— all business. "I am not happy, but I'll give you the chance to state your case and make it worth my while. Otherwise, I'm going to be bored. You know how I hate being bored."

My stomach flipped and that same gut-wrenching anxiety from earlier found its way back to my entrails like a tapeworm.

The Crown strutted his way from the kitchen and across the room, gliding across the floor like a stone over water, before sitting down on the couch facing us. Stretching out the span of his arms overtop of it, he crossed one leg over the other and gave us a cool nod to go ahead.

Aiden cleared his throat. Sylas grimaced. I wilted at the lack of those around me speaking up in my defense.

"Sir, may I speak for myself?" The words tumbled out of my mouth before I could stop them, my hands raising to catch each letter as they clattered to the floor.

What had I done?

The king blinked at me, pursing his lips as he seemed to deliberate. Aiden and Sylas both stared slack-jawed at my ungainliness.

"Hmm..." he pondered, a spotted hand raising to his chin to scrape through his whiskers. "That's an idea. It could be interesting to hear this story straight from the blunder itself. Let us see what you understand of all this. I would love to know why Alexander thought you were special enough to be an exception to my laws." A crooked smile spread across his sharp features. "Make me a believer, *Jack*."

I drew forward, coming to stop beneath that painting—the swirling, inky black entangling with the white. It inspired a metaphor for good and evil, forever enmeshed in an eternal struggle. My chest heaved, yet still, there was no true breath. It did nothing to relieve my anxious feelings, but maybe talking would.

"Sir—" I began but was cut off. The king raised his hand at me.

"Carver," he clarified. "We're friends now, Jack, and friends don't get tied up in titles. Respect is important, of course, but the undead proceed on a first name basis, be they king, criminal, or otherwise. We are kin. Aren't we?"

I frowned at him. Kin. Friends. Was there something I missed? I began again.

"C-Carver," I stammered, feeling quite stupid.

He nodded with a smile, and I supposed he was trying to be encouraging. He found the scotch on the table, and poured himself a glass before bringing it to his lips.

"Firstly, I wanted to apologize for not coming to meet you. I had no idea how the order of things were supposed to go. I wasn't informed. I was presented with a choice, and I made it. I'm sorry if that complicated anything for you. I didn't mean to rock the boat, nor do I blame my maker, but do know... I imagine

Alexander desperately wanted to introduce us sooner and he must have lost track of time, and..."

Carver interrupted me again, this time with a boisterous laughter. "Calm, boy. Calm yourself. It's okay. Proceed."

Queasiness overtook me as I spoke. I did my best to exhale and slow down.

"Furthermore," I continued. "I had ignored my maker's orders and created a sort of... *emergency*... situation with my blood brother." I gestured to Aiden behind me. "So, perhaps that interrupted Alexander's original plan. I'm aware I was created beyond the typical protocol. I disobeyed and most likely took Alexander's mind away from his tasks."

My hands shook, so I shoved them deep into my pockets.

Carver leaned forward over his knees, scotch in hand, sloshing around the glass. He seemed baffled. "Wait a moment, wait a moment. Jack. It was La Mont's responsibility to come to me *first*—to ask permission to turn you in the first place."

"I take full responsibility," I rushed to say. "Please. Don't blame him. We were both enamored—captivated by one another. It was a whirlwind. I know he would have gone to you at once. If I had only listened to his orders, he would have brought me here sooner, I swear." I hated the fact that my eyes started to sting with tears.

The room went silent. My chest ballooned up near my chin and I kept the air lodged within my lungs again like a balloon ready to be popped.

"Jack," Carver crooned, eyes of brilliant silver glinting with an amused sort of knowing. He sighed. "Do you know what will happen if I find you unworthy of the vampiric blessing—of being one of the immortals of our city, graced with our great lineage and given the honor of walking effortlessly through the night?"

I nodded. "You order me killed and I become... dust?" I had to ask.

"Dust. Yes," he admitted over a darker chuckle. For a moment, he watched his scotch swirl around his glass again.

At least I was correct about one thing. My skin prickled with cold fear, the same way it had earlier. Carver pushed himself from his seat, his gaze painting me with his judgment.

Closer he walked, taking a swig of his drink as he came to stand just before me. We were nearly the same height, though he dwarfed me by about two inches. His ethereal orbs licked my skin as they trailed me from crown to groin and back again. I could almost feel the thoughts throbbing in his skull. And then it happened...

He smiled.

"I'm impressed," he said simply. "Most vampires would throw their maker under my foot without a moment's hesitation. We are not without our honor, and you seem to hold on to yours even without a proper understanding of our ways. If you had chosen to cast blame on Alexander, I would have considered you fodder and tossed you to the flames, yet you seemed so quick to take accountability."

I might have imagined it, but I could have sworn Sylas released a relieved sigh behind me.

Carver's drooping mouth pulled to the side in an almost fatherly smile. I had proven myself, even in some small way. At least that was one Brit that seemed to like me.

"Naturally," he continued. "The way we usually do things is... different. Typically, I am introduced to a human who wishes to be turned. I make the decision for them to keep their memory of the experience or not, and then they are created in solemn ceremony... and sent to the guild most fitting for them." He prodded my shoulder with a tapered finger. "*You*, however... Well, I guess La Mont must think you're pretty special." The corners of his eyes crinkled and he almost laughed again. "He sent you to the Undercity to see if Marcus would be willing to vouch for you. Am I correct?"

I nodded in silence again, and as I did, I swore I could feel Aiden's crimson eyes barreling deep into the back of my cranium.

Carver sighed, brushing white stands back into their neatly-arranged place.

"Listen," he demanded. "The order of things has been disrupted. As such, I need penance for such a crime. I have already sent a notice to your maker. You are permitted to stay as you are just as long as you bend a knee and complete a few tasks I bestow upon you. Does this sound fair, Jack?"

The air in the room seemed to grow ten degrees colder then. The icy chill of death slid over my skin before slipping away.

"Jack?" he asked again, leaning forward ever so close as to make sure his presence could fully be felt.

He offered his hand, volunteering to seal the deal as men would. I couldn't put my finger on the uneasiness tugging at my gut, but this felt like signing a blood contract with the devil himself. There was no other choice, however. I gripped his fist, giving him the firmest shake I could muster, squeezing the way my father once taught me. I felt a knuckle pop, but to my surprise it was my own, and as I pulled away I could feel the bones dislodged in my hand from his own strength.

"So young, yet so strong," he mused. "I look forward to our business together. With that said and done, I'd normally welcome you three to stay and enjoy a drink but I have pressing matters to attend. Dawn approaches soon enough."

The skyline beyond the windows behind him caught my eye then. He was right. The clouds grew from deep indigo to a lighter lavender. The night quickly faded away. Aiden and Sylas gave a hard nod to the patriarch before turning to head for the door. They were both men of few words, even in the presence of royalty.

I went to follow, but a hand gripped my arm at the elbow and stopped me. "Oh, and Jack?"

"Yes, sir?"

"Do be careful out there. And good luck to you."

Chloe's words were echoed to me yet again. It was as if the man could read my inner thoughts and spin them upon me. Perhaps it was a warning not to step out of line. Or maybe it was just a coincidence. Either way, I would remain cautious. I did not want to become dust, after all.

"Thank you, Carver," I smiled weakly.

My hand fell over his own to grant it a few appreciative pats. He released me and I continued my journey back down to the city below our feet.

Down the elevator, through the lobby, over the red carpeted steps, the three of us found ourselves in the cab of the matte black Mercedes once again. Though it seemed out of character, the two elder vampires exploded with chatter in the front seats. They couldn't believe it! I had saved my own ass, they said. They commiserated over their mutual distaste for the man, of how they loathed his authority and his attitude.

It was a difficult thing for me to understand. Honestly, I found him quite charming. A man of age, manners, and honor. Maybe I was wrong, but my impression of him was that he was a man to revere, to fear, and that working *with* him rather than against him was in everyone's best interest.

Aiden started driving.

In the back seat, I riffled through the satchel Marcus had given me earlier. A fountain pen was placed neatly upon a stack of papers. Lucky for me, a few of them were blank.

I found inspiration once more.

Carver
Gnarled digits snap and bend
Clutched together in equal understanding
Of power, of order, of control
The scepter lays upon his lap
The crown upon his head
All ears open to his croak
All eyes watching for his next move
Royalty
Or is it a lie...
Is he a serpent in disguise?

The poem was quaint, filled with hope, but without ignoring the possibility of his duplicitous nature. Still, the visit went far better than I had anticipated and I decided to close my eyes for the rest of the car ride back to Alexander's club.

Upon arriving outside of the Prepotent, Aiden and Sylas startled with a shake on the knee. Sylas offered one more friendly smile, while Aiden simply scowled through the rearview.

I closed the car door and made my way into the lobby. My heart skipped a few unnecessary beats when I found Alexander leaning against the front desk. Apparently, he had been chatting with the security guard who had been so helpful to me before.

"Jack!" Alexander grinned, finding his way to me in seconds and sweeping me into his arms. "Your evening must have been so enthralling, so riveting, so... *shocking*! Oh, I can't wait to hear every piece of it."

I opened my mouth to speak, but he pressed a finger to my lips.

"Hush, now, my pet. Before you say anything, I have a surprise for you."

Alexander's lips found my own and my world shifted into

color and music, my eyelids fluttering with the ecstasy that was Alexander's embrace. As his kiss broke, his hand found its way to my cheek, sweeping the backs of his knuckles across my skin. His touch sent lovely little jolts through my system.

"Listen. Upstairs. Our room. Go there now. I just *know* you're going to be so excited for what I have planned. *Vous allez l'adorer!*" He uttered more french words that I didn't understand, though they sounded like the loveliest melody.

Excitement about his gift tugged at my heart. This man loved me so, and I knew whatever it was he had planned would be incredible.

Up I went. Another elevator ride, through the empty bar, higher up the carpeted staircase, and down that familiar hallway where my dreams had come true. I bypassed the door that was Alexander's office where he gave me the chance to this beautiful new life, and headed toward the doors to his room. I was relieved. I was elated.

What a man.

What a gift.

What a *love*.

I approached the doors, swung them open, stepped inside, and—

There was a woman tied to the bed frame, gagged in nothing but her underwear.

I gripped the door panel, feeling sick all over again.

At once, my world came crashing back to reality.

"Holy shit."

CHAPTER SEVENTEEN
WHERE IS MY MIND

All of my bold thoughts from earlier, the ones about what I would do when I got my hands on my first victim—those images of me coaxing some young virgin to bare her neck for me, lapping up the scents of citizens, ready to discard the remaining bits of my soul for just one bite—vanished in an instant. Those impulses fell away and instead of a free meal, all I saw before me was a poor woman bound and alone in a strange place with no understanding of why she was there and no one to help her.

"Holy fucking shit!" I cried. "Fuck! *Fuck*!"

I dashed across the room to her side. She flailed and wrenched about in pure fear as her doe eyes blinked up at me in horror. She shrieked, but it was muffled by the gag put there to silence her.

"Listen. I'm not going to hurt you, but you are absolutely not safe here. We need to get you out of this place."

I wrenched the thick ropes about her wrists, the woven strands of twine digging deep into her flesh, turning it red and raw. She looked upon me with large blue eyes in complete mortal terror.

"If you promise me you won't scream, I'll remove the gag, alright?" I went to work with nimble digits to free her from her bindings. "Yes, or no?" I prodded when the only response I received was a whimper. Bearing my fangs was probably no help, but I didn't want to think about what might happen if Alexander heard us.

The young girl gave a rapid nod of her head, tears welling her eyes. I could feel waves of fear radiate from her aura to wash over me. Any other vampire would delight in the taste of her terror, I imagined, yet there I was trying to save an innocent. This was vile and not at all what I had romanticized in my mind.

One hand free. *Thank God,* I thought to myself. At last, I successfully released the knot, the chords to falling in a heap by the bed. The girl let out a tiny gasp, but with a finger to my lips, I reminded her to keep quiet. Now it was time for the gag and then the other hand.

Undoing the neckerchief was easier work, though it had been wrapped about the sides of her mouth and drawn to circle twice about her head. How could Alexander have done this?

With a hard tug, the thing snapped and fell free, tattered fabric gliding to the foot of the bed.

"Alright," I muttered, turning my attention to her other hand. Almost there. "Keep quiet and this will be over soon—just need to free..."

My thought was cut short when something collided with my mouth. Before I could register what was happening, my new fangs dug deep into the inner of my bottom lip, producing a trickle of blood.

She hit me. She actually fucking hit me. Her hand cocked back for another strike.

"Miss, what the fuck are you doing? I'm not going to hurt you, I'm just—"

Again, I was interrupted as her lithe fist collided with the hollow of my cheek. Not just once, but again, a third, a fourth, and then a final to the bridge of my nose. I felt a snap as my nose broke upon impact. Apparently, adrenaline empowered even the smallest of humans.

"*FUCK OFF YOU FUCKING MONSTER!*" she shouted.

I felt my legs struggle to hold, my boots dancing across the floor as they skittered to keep me from falling back. I touched my face to inspect the damage, her destructive blows shaking me from my duty to save this poor girl. Instantly, I became distracted by the blood gushing down from my nostrils and onto my lips.

"Lady, what the hell are you doing?! I'm trying to save you —*agh*, fuck—that hurts," I groaned, giving up on my aim to remain quiet and undetectable by Alexander.

Some vampire I was. I had failed in my attempts to save my intended meal, and was instead subdued by her tiny, however accurate, strikes. It was embarrassing. I was a bit dazed as I watched her little fingers dig into the last binding in her endeavor to set herself free.

Oh fuck, I thought to myself, *this was about to be a bad situation.*

Screaming.

She was screaming. Horror caused this small thing to toss all caution to the wind, hoping that someone—anyone—would hear her. There was no way for her to know it, but she was in a tank of sharks and those shrill cries were as good as blood in the water.

Off she went, whizzing past me and straight for the door. I reached for her ankle, my hand just narrowly missing her as my palm swiped nothing but the breeze in her wake.

No no no, if she gets out... My head began to spin with panic. She was already across the room, steps from the door now.

"Please! Please don't!" I begged, my voice made gravely from the blood coursing into my mouth and staining my teeth.

The taste was divine. While drinking my own blood had seemed a curse earlier, it was a blessing in this moment. It sated me, keeping me focused enough without trying to tear into her jugular.

The half-naked woman finally closed the distance to the door, slamming into its mahogany face. Her shaking hands grasped the handles and rattled them desperately, a blood-curdling scream ripping through her jaw as her body shoved over and over into the wood.

"HELP ME! SOMEONE, PLEASE! I'M BEGGING YOU! I DON'T WANT TO DIE! HELP ME!"

Her voice undoubtedly carried throughout the entirety of the sixth floor, her childlike fear rattling my skull. It was interesting. I couldn't feel any of the monstrous tendencies I thought I'd have. Instead, I only felt remorse for ever thinking I could harm something so delicate.

One evening as a vampire didn't mean I had to become a murderer. There was a better way, I was certain. I had to keep trying.

"Please." I stretched my claw out to her. "If you do that, they'll hear you," I begged, pleading with all of myself as I made way towards her, both my hands raised in defense.

She continued, of course, banging against the door until her palms became pink, her supple but bruised flesh bouncing in the darkness from her desperate attempts to be free. I drew closer, my talons a good five feet from her soft skin.

"Miss," I started again, my voice lowered in my attempt to calm her as though she were a stray cat with its head stuck in a tin can. "If you make any more noise, they'll hurt you. Please, listen. I am begging you."

For a moment, she hesitated. Her hands ceased their useless banging against the hardwood and I truly thought I had gotten through to her.

"Don't—" was all I could mutter as the doors flew open.

It was too late.

There, right behind the door, stood the one, the only, Alexander La Mont. My dead heart plummeted into my stomach. If blood could still course through my veins, it all would have drained from my face.

"Alex, this girl just wants to leave," I whimpered. "Can we please help her?"

A strange new feeling tugged in my stomach as I tasted her fear on my own tongue. I wondered if being deeply empathetic was a new, vampiric trait I didn't know about.

The woman stood in the doorframe staring with the same wide-eyed expression she had given me. It told me she had seen my maker before, confirming that he was the one who had imprisoned her.

The tall, slender Frenchman hummed only a few words. "Jack..." It was like velvet being wiped across an open wound. "Make me proud."

With lightning speed, Alexander's hand swiped through the air before the girl's face. He hissed a sound like his throat was filled with waiting cobras. I wasn't immediately certain of what he had done. That is, of course, until I saw his hand held high in the air, those dangerous claws covered in thick cherry fluid.

Before I could protest, scream, or react, the girl was already hurtling towards me. She collided against my chest, her face buried within the material of my hoodie, and sending us both tumbling to the floor.

"Alexander," I choked out, staring over her head at those lavender eyes.

He glared at me from the darkness of the hallway, his mouth curved up in a wicked grin before the door shut firmly, barring our escape.

Holding her gently by the shoulders, I tried to maneuver out from under her so that we could both pull ourselves back to our feet. Dawn approached, and I knew if I could get her out of there, she would be able to escape and make it to freedom.

"Listen to me," I started, her body shivering against mine. "I know you don't trust me, but I swear I don't want to hurt you, okay?"

I could feel tears welling in my eyes from the mixture of our combined fear. The girl pulled away to stare into my hellish pits. Her own blue pools were bloodshot from sobbing.

"P-please," she stammered. To my dismay, her body was growing cold. "I don't want to die here. Please save me. I want to see my mom and dad again."

Within our close proximity, I could finally see her. All at once, I felt sick. She was only a teenage girl—a good several years younger than me, fresh out of high school.

"What's your name?" I asked as I held her there in the dismal shafts of night filtering in through the windows.

"Lina. My name is Lina Townson." Her face screwed up with dismay as tears streamed down her ruby cheeks.

"Well, Lina," I started. "My name's Jack, and I'm not going to let you die here. See those over there?" I pointed to the large, glass doors framed by the heavy curtains to keep the sun out. "Those are doors to the balcony. We're high up, but if you can get out there, maybe you can flag someone down and get help."

The girl shook her head violently, refusing over and over as she sobbed into my chest.

"He will know. Someone will find out," she cried.

I squeezed her body tight to my own, hoping that kind of support would give her the courage she needed.

"Lina, if you don't get your ass off of this floor, you're going to die."

I had a brave speech ready to go—to boost her morale and remind her of the loved ones waiting for her back home—the mother and father who were no doubt worried about where their daughter had disappeared to so early in the morning. I had my speech... and then it was gone. I opened my mouth to say something else, but I faltered, unable to unclench my jaw for some reason.

Then, against my hoodie, I could feel it. Blood trickled from the wound Lina suffered by Alexander's cold hand. My garnet eyes trailed down the girl's form to view the large gash now marring her arm. It ripped her skin deeply enough to cause her blood to fall like ribbons over her body and into my clothing, but not enough to be fatal. Suddenly, I couldn't speak—couldn't move, or anything.

I could hear the hands of a clock ticking in the distance—almost the top of the hour. It's chime would be the moment Lina's life would end.

"Jack?" she whispered up at me.

Eyes of sky landed on the muscles tensing over my jaw, my fangs gritting down against my bottom row to fight the all consuming hunger beginning to send ripples of pain through my nervous system.

Feed. I could almost hear a new voice in my head screaming at me.

Feed, now. Kill her.

It was then that a searing pain jolted from my abdomen and up my body to clamp down on my cranium—unbridled agony. It was skull-shattering levels of torment. The only cure was Lina. That much I knew.

The girl's face stared in horror as she watched the internal struggle play out on my face, my complexion muting to the color of porcelain. I fought with all of my might, forcing my jaw to unclench and growl out one single word...

"*Run.*"

The girl didn't hesitate. Scrambling to her feet, more blood from her arm splashed to the floor in her mad dash to reach the balcony doors. I prayed, begged, screamed in my mind that she would make it before this thing inside of me could take hold.

"Go," I choked, my body heaving as I began to curl inward over my knees, rivets of black spilling into my face as my hair became entangled from my violent thrashing to hold in the bloodlust.

Kill her. The voice came again, though I tried so hard to ignore it. This demon inside clutched my soul like an apple in its palm. From my place on the floor, I flipped onto my back, my body convulsing as my mind began to blink in and out of lucidity. There, above me, was that damn mural of Lucifer against the ceiling. His eyes—that horrible green glare—stared into my reds as this thing began to rip my soul apart from the inside out.

Kill. Maim. Drink...

In that moment, I lost myself. My vision grew blurry as this evil parasite dug its claws deeper, calling my vessel its own.

Lina had already made it to the doors and was beating against them, trying with all of her might to break the checkered panels of glass. We hadn't accounted for the exit to be heavier, and the lock more rigid than the way into the inner corridor. It made sense, however. Those glass panels and the curtains before it were the only things shielding us from the sun's deadly rays.

She turned about to find something, anything, that could be used to break the windows or the handles. As she scrambled within the large room, I could feel the motions of my limbs fall far beyond my control, my corpse raising effortlessly into a sitting position upon the floor.

Run, I thought to myself, but it was no use. No more words tumbled out of my lips—only the animalistic grunts of the demon taking me for a joy ride. A deep growl resonated within my broken form.

"Jack! Please! Please, no!" Lina screamed as I felt my body climb to its feet, rising to my full height. Something else was in the driver's seat. I was forced to watch from within in horror.

Though she was wounded, she was still agile. Lina moved so fast, she seemed to take flight, her bare feet sliding against the floor as she made her way to the hearth beside the bed. A miniature bronze sat atop the mantle as a decoration piece, and I knew at once it was about to become her weapon. As her little fingers wrapped about its base, the room shrank in size instantaneously, and I was behind her.

Lina, run! Please run, I begged within my mind, fighting hard to regain the control I had lost.

The girl spun, shocked to find that I was already a breath behind her. Before she could even scream, I felt my jaws open unnaturally, unhinging like a snake, as my teeth were ready to taste that sweet essence of hers. Lina raised her hands defensively, and my fangs ripped into her forearm like a pit bull and refused to let go. I growled horrible guttural noises, the sounds sending the skin around her puncture wounds into spasms as my jaw clenched down.

She screamed. A new sensation came to wash away my horror. Relief. Her sweet blood coursed onto my tongue and down my throat, my agony subsiding for a brief moment. That taste was like nothing I had ever experienced. It was elation. It was ecstasy. It made every moment of terror and hell worth it, and for a moment, I even considered killing the girl from my own place within my mind.

In my bloodlust, I had forgotten completely about the small, bronze statue. Lina raised it high into the air before smashing down over my head with force. My fangs tore through her flesh to spray her fluids against the black satin sheets and across the floor, crude scraps of skin dangling from muscle.

The force of the blow was enough to knock my sanity into submission. My mind began to claw its way back momentarily, returning to lucidity as my focus fixated on the tile beneath me.

"Lina," I choked. I wanted so badly to apologize—to say anything comforting, but it was still no use. My clarity returned with very little success.

Red fluid dripped from my muzzle, creating a small pool of scarlet over the marble. This girl I had promised to protect—to send her home to her mother and father—now had a gaping hole where her forearm should have been. Her flesh was in ribbons, some of it even strewn horribly before the hearth. My stomach wrenched, and though I was sated, I was disgusted with myself.

"Lina... I am so sorry..." I whimpered.

I reached toward her ankle in both misery and self-loathing. Over me, she struck again and again, sending the idol into my head as a fountain of blood sprayed from the crack at the top of my skull. The world began to spin. Her little voice screamed as loud as she could, echoing through the chasms of my mind, as my body found the floor. My jaw slammed against the stone before the hearth.

Off she went again, her bare feet slapping wetly as she left a trail of her own mess on her way back toward the balcony doors.

One, two, three...

Three strikes with the idol was all it took. The door handle clattered off its mount. She shoved her fingers inside the hole, desperate to force the mechanisms to unlock.

Click.

Freedom, at last, was in her reach. The doors burst outward as the young girl barreled out onto the balcony overlooking the city, and into the coming light of dawn.

From my place of shame near the hearth, I rolled onto my hip and forced myself into a sitting position. Thankful for the adjacent bed, I let my back rest against the mattress. It allowed me full view of the girl as she made her mad dash to the same railing where I had climbed off and over into Alexander's arms. It had been such a moment of romance, mystery, and eternal devotion. Now, instead of my blood between my maker's lips, it was the blood of a young, innocent girl who had been torn open for sport. Her vitality stained the balcony, and also our first moment together as lovers, repainting the memory forever.

Lina waved her arms frantically as she leaned over the railing and howled across the city, trying with all her might to catch anyone's attention. Screaming bloody murder—truly— strips of her flesh flapped in the wind. She would bleed out. I knew it. I could see it in the deep indigo crescents spreading under her eyes. Again, I looked at the damage I had done. It gaped, wide and deep, like a shark bite.

She tried.

She begged.

She failed.

No citizens in the early Manhattan morning took notice of her frantic screams over the trumpets of traffic and the discourse of life. No one would hear her from the height. No Wall Street businessman with his pockets full of opportunity, no hotdog vendor, and certainly no gangster turned their face toward the sky. No one cared about a small girl using every last ounce of her will to survive.

I was worse than every last one of them, though. I had done this to her. The sun breached the clouds, its golden rays like venom. There was no going out there to help her, and with my own blood loss, it became a struggle to move at all. I would have to sit and watch this poor girl fight through her last moments.

It took two whole minutes of attempting to call for help before the brave Lina finally slumped against the railing. Her body twisted to slide past the bars before her gaze traveled back through the open doors to meet mine for the last time. There, we stared at one another, our own brands of victim. The girl mouthed words to me, far too small for even my vampire ears to pick up. I wilted, longing to know what that final thought was. I knew the end was drawing close. Her little fingers twitched at her side for a moment as they fell to the stone. Eyes of sky blue and eyes of hellish crimson met from each corner of our two fucked up worlds that had abandoned us.

Hours passed as we sat staring at one another, but only one of us actively held the gaze. Lina had died the instant her fingers stopped twitching against the ground.

I couldn't move. More than that, I didn't want to move. I remained trapped in the room of my death and rebirth for an entire day. No Claude. No Aiden. And certainly not the maker who had forced this poor girl's blood onto my hands. Hours passed, the golden daylight eventually replaced by the muddled darkness of dusk. Once night finally fell, I found the strength to scramble to my feet, hobbling through the door and out onto the balcony to find the poor girl's corpse. Something shattered deep within me and I fell to my knees, wanting only to put her pieces back together.

Her jaw hung slack and to the side, eyes wide and still moist from tears she could no longer shed. The building's shadow fell over her upper half to keep them from drying too quickly in the sunlight. I wrapped my arms around her, my eyes welling with tears as I pressed my face against her bare shoulder, weeping without control.

I had killed this poor girl and she would never know how sorry I was.

As I pulled my face away from her skin I could see the red from my tears staining the crook of her neck. Streams of blood flowed from my eyes where liquid sorrow had once been. I truly had become a monster.

As my eyes wept tears of gore like the damned fucking thing I had become, something caught my eye near her leg. Just at her side, I saw where her small finger had traced something through the streak of blood. There, on the ground, written in the last traces of herself was a message. It was how she spent her very last moments on Earth. I stared down at it, somehow broken and numb at the same time.

4 GIV U

CHAPTER EIGHTEEN
A BROKEN WING

Night had fallen over the city. Police sirens and the blaring horns of midtown screamed across the vast, smog-covered sky. While the humans of the metropolis stepped into the darkness flooded with false light, a monster stood over a small girl whose life was just ripped away from her.

I was that monster.

Everything within me loathed what I had done down to my core. Lina's small face was now tinted with a frosty periwinkle, as if left out in the cold of winter's frost. She stared lifelessly forward, straight past where I loomed over her now to the spot where I had been sitting all day with my guilt and hollow veins.

I murdered her.

Everything I had sworn to be in my life was all at once replaced by this demon who filled my soul with only one word: *Feed*. No more timid, respectful Jamie. Nor my clumsy, mild-mannered Donovan boy. It was so easy to forget that he was dead, too. Standing in his place was this blood-hungry thing I couldn't recognize in the mirror anymore.

This poor girl—this Lina Townson—she had tried to trust me in her last moments. All of the flailing, kicking, and screaming burst behind my eyes like fireworks.

"Jack?" I could still hear her voice within my mind, like a whisper of a ghost doomed to haunt me for eternity. She had made the choice, as we laid on that floor together, to say my name—to try and reach my humanity as it tumbled around in the tides of my curse.

My chest was heavy. Whatever heart left inside felt fractured, its splinters threatening to tear through misery and soft tissue. I blinked down at her again.

Lina's youthful lips had closed forever. Their once blushing pink had turned a dull gray. The voice of my conscious had been replaced by the memory of hers, and it screamed at me for my horrible act, and for the beastly thing it turned me into. I leaned forward in anguish, my fingers leaving my side to brush small strands of blood-coated blonde from her face. My gut wrenched. Her cheek was so cold. Her mother and father would never see her face again. They would never be graced with her small smile or her tender words spoken with that harmonious tone.

Incapable of controlling my inner-animal, I had cursed myself to forever be plagued by those petrified screams. I knew they would haunt me every time I closed my eyes.

Then, a new terrible thought came crashing over me like a lightning strike; I had possibly taken someone's sister from them.

Chloe.

Not only had I abandoned my songbird, but what if my monstrous claws had stolen one just like her from a brother who would miss her forever? He would never get to feel her warmth or her joy. He would never hear her laugh.

Somehow, I always seemed to be at the center of catastrophe. I wished, just for once, I could be the onlooking bystander. Perhaps, I had always been someone's monster.

They came again—those tears stained with stolen blood. They escaped before I could stop them. I wept, cradling myself as my spine curled and my knees buckled to bring me to kneel near her body. I was unworthy to be there next to her. More of my tears slipped past my cheeks, covering the girl in even more gore and my own regret.

Images from the last few days shuffled through my mind as I sought truths in the pictures of those beautiful lies. Had I made a mistake? Or... was I tricked?

This wasn't the fantasy novel Alexander had promised—one filled with romance, passion, and love. This was a horror story, filled with monsters and the bodies of the innocent. Alexander's face at the door told me everything. To him, Lina had been nothing more than a plaything. Maybe I was his plaything too.

I choked on my tears, blood filling my mouth once again. More tears splashed over her blue cheeks. I wiped them away with the edge of my thumb, and the smear they left almost gave her a living blush. My stomach lifted only slightly, but it didn't take much to remind me of my hideous act and pull me back to reality. The flesh down her ribs, her hips, and her legs was tinged a dark purple with putrid yellow blooming around the edges of the marks like spilled watercolor.

I looked to the scribble near her hand again.

4 GIV U

I stared upon them with confusion and anger.

"I don't deserve it!" I screamed, shaking her by the shoulders. More tears slipped past my composure. "I failed you. I failed Chloe. Even in death, I just keep *failing!*" I sobbed, falling to the side, propping myself over my elbow, for the guilt was far too heavy to sit with. "I'm so sorry, Lina."

I choked over the sweet rust of my new tears. No apologies would bring the girl back from her horrible demise. No amount of crying or pleading with some invisible God would ease the remorse.

I leaned forward once more, my nose brushing against the girl's ear so only she could hear—or...at least I hoped she would.

"I'll find them. I'll tell them how much you loved them, and that this was my fault."

The promise was a valiant one, but at the back of my mind, I knew I was just a demon whispering false assurances over an empty corpse. Bringing my claws to her eyes, I attempted to close them, offering some dignity in death. Yet, as I tried to push down her eyelids so that she could finally rest, I found they were rigid. They remained frozen in place, that look of horror and hopelessness forever painted upon her face.

Something surged under my skin, then. For a moment, grief gave way to clarity and I remembered who I was and what my convictions had always been. I pushed to my feet, standing back to my height as a new gust of wind pushed raven curls messily about my face. I brushed the miasma away from my eyes, my fingertips grazing the new curves of my cheekbones. The face I was born with—my mother's face—was gone forever.

I knew the truth. I had been deceived.

I hadn't wanted any of this. Alexander's gilded words and beckoning smile were nothing more than weapons he used in order to manipulate. I didn't want to be damned as a monster, cursed to murder and maim those weaker than me. I had hate in my heart, yes, but not enough to kill. I had never been murderous, and any momentary violent impulse had always been followed by instant remorse for even the thought. No. I was forced to become a murderer, and now I would never be the same.

My world spun as I imagined the rest of my cursed days spent covered in the blood of those who had yet to live a full life. I couldn't bear the thought of that. The briefest urge pushed me to the railing. I clutched it, leaning halfway over, ready to cast myself into Hell. My hands squeezed the bar tightly, knuckles turning white as the metal gave way to my iron grip. It indented around each finger.

I couldn't be this. It was too much. If I flung myself to the city below, would I even die? If I survived, that would endanger even more people. I stared off into the sea of lights for a moment. Manhattan glared back at me in all of its defiance. She had seen my crimes and judged me with her cold eyes, the starless sky barely offering a drop of moonlight to shine upon me. Instead of heaven above, only the blackness of pollution pressed down over my shameful head. Maybe this was Hell. Perhaps, I had arrived already.

I pushed from the railing, my chest heaving from frustration at my inability to take action—to end this before it began. I turned my back on New York, the heels of my boots pivoting to push through day old blood.

Lina Townson. My unwilling victim, my escape room partner, my most recent failure.

I drifted back through the glass doors and into the room, my steel-toed boot colliding with the golden handle, sending it clattering to the side. New reminders awaited me there...

Blood still splattered the walls and bed sheets. The corners of the miniature statue were painted red now as it lay strewn on the floor near the hearth. My stomach twisted into knots as if someone attempted to wring it dry from the forbidden taste I had taken.

On the floor near the black fur rug, was the stain of blood that outlined where our bodies entangled together. It was like an art piece from some macabre gallery. We were beautifully tragic, frozen there in time, and while I didn't know her, I had never been more intimate with anyone else in my life. She was beautiful, strong-willed, brave beyond measure, and had a mean right jab. My nose was still a little off-center. She would have been a perfect friend for my poor, damaged, sister.

If I had known this girl better, perhaps I could have resisted this thing inside of me. Perhaps, I wouldn't have clamped down on her arm. Deep down inside, I knew nothing could have stopped it. The scariest part was, it could have been Chloe herself in the room with me, and I still would have reacted that way. The thirst belonged to some mindless horror, and all it took was Alexander's cruel hand to guide Lina straight into my gullet.

The stillness of destruction's aftermath squeezed my head in its vice. And I snapped.

The world seemed to pulse under my feet, and all I could feel was overwhelming rage for what he *made* me do. It was white hot under my skin. The corners of my vision blackened like I was seeing the room through a vignette. Before I knew it, I was lost to it, drowning in the deepest ends of my emotions.

"*RAGHHHHHHHHHHHHH!*" A monstrous cry exploded up from my chest, filling the room with my despair.

Squeezing my hand into a fist, I spun, striking the wood of the bed frame, detonating it into splinters. Tiny stakes stabbed into my arms and over my clavicle, but I didn't care. The only pain I felt was the knife twisting inside.

"WHY!" I screamed.

I grasped the underside of the bed, lifting the entire thing into the air before crashing it down over the floor. The antique wood crumpled, the legs breaking and buckling upon impact. The mattress came away, toppling into the bedside table, shattering the crystal fixtures to the floor.

Footsteps from down the hall approached, yet I was far too

consumed with my wrath to stop. In the blink of an eye, I was at the dresser at the front of the room, sending both fists crashing overtop. The mahogany caved, reminding me of what Lina had attempted to do to my head. *Slam, slam, slam!* My blows were a blur as the innards of the cabinet became exposed, showing Alexander's clothes folded neatly within the drawers. I was sure those articles were expensive. I tore at the fabric, yanking them free and reducing them to scraps. At last, I finished by gripping the dresser's side, and tossed the thing to the right, smashing it against the wall.

"WHY?"

The room's entry flew open. Within the shadow of the corridor, Alexander's wide lavender eyes stared upon me with horror as he took in my handiwork.

"What have you *done*? Are you insane? *Qu'est-ce que tu as fait!* *Qu'est-ce que tu as fait!*" he repeated the french words, pacing and gazing about frantically before he rushed to where I stood, hands of ivory silk cradling my face as his eyes burned into mine. "What have you done? After all I have given you, *this* is how I am repaid!"

I promptly pursed my lips and spat the blood of my victim straight into La Mont's face, the splatter pattern like a murder upon fresh winter snow.

He recoiled, shoving me away from him. My feet scrambled to catch my footing before falling to the floor.

"All of this! Why? Why? *Why! Speak!*"

Alexander wiped the blood away with the back of his hand, his lips trembling as his purple orbs scanned the room for the girl. "Where is she, Jack?"

His question sent me into another frenzy. In an instant, I was against him, my fists balling into the material of his shirt, yanking him close to my face again.

"*Dead*!" I screamed. My own words struck me like a bolt of electricity. "She is dead. *You* left me here to kill her!"

Alexander's face grew soft for a moment, eyes trailing to the broken doors, and then to the outside world to stare at the legs laying motionless just within view. I didn't miss the way the corners of his mouth twitched.

"I left her here for you. You were only meant to take from her," he mercilessly groaned, sounding vexed and disappointed. "You murdered my gift for you, Jack." His eyebrows slanted and he regarded me as though I were the wicked, pathetic one.

I howled once again, my body pressing even closer to his. "You *left* me here! You hurt her and tossed her to the floor! Do you think I'm a fool? Do you think I'm that stupid! You *wanted* me to kill her. *You trapped me in here with a corpse for an entire day*!"

Alexander finally had enough. The back of his hand careened into the hollow of my cheek. My body spiraled through the air from the force before slamming into the wall. A huge, baroque portrait crashed down over me.

"I thought you were *sleeping*!" he yowled like an angry wolf. "Not murdering this poor girl and crying about it like some sort of miserable *faible*! Why would I want her death on my head?"

"You kidnapped her, brought her here, stripped her nude, and beat her black and blue because you only wanted me to take a *sip*? Are you *insane*?" I growled.

A single one of his eyes twitched. He had failed to manipulate me, and he knew it. I pulled myself back to my feet, pulling up the dented painting in my hands. I began walking toward him again. My lip twitched in uncontrollable anger.

"No, I'm not going to buy that. You don't lock a new vampire in a room with a half naked girl and expect her to walk away with a pulse. You did this to me. You did this to *her*—"

Before my proclamation of war could be finished, Alexander

interrupted the thought with his own. "And if I did, what then? Does it matter? All of this—your new life, your hopes and dreams, our *room* over some... girl?"

I thought I felt my pulse again, but it was a lie. Taking my first victim had finally silenced my heartbeat once and for all. Nobody had to explain that to me. There was just this *knowing*. Now, the mere echoes of my humanity drummed on to encourage one last fight for my morality—for my soul. I raised the painting in my hands before turning to slam it into the wall at my left. The frame exploded into pieces.

"*HER NAME WAS LINA*! She had a family, friends—a *life*— and in an instant you chose that traumatizing me was more important than all of that!"

"A short life..." he growled, his serpent-like glare flashing in the dim light of the dismantled bedroom. "You misunderstand me, Jack. My intention was not to scar you, but to teach you a very valuable lesson." His tone grew soft again, as if trying to reel me back in.

But he couldn't. The damage was done. And I was undone. No sweet words or honeyed lies would turn my thoughts back to the way they were before.

"Jack," he gushed. "This was our room—the temple where I transformed you. Why would I wish to break your mind here and steal our future?"

I stalked closer again, my fists balled as they shook in tremendous anger.

"Tell me," I barked. "Tell me why, then. Why would you do this to me? What lesson is there in this?"

I swept my hand across the room in a grand gesture, showing the unrelenting pain he had caused and the blood stains to prove the hell I had been through. He hesitated, his body shifting as he stood in contemplation.

"WHAT LESSON?!" I screamed.

"Jack, in this world, you cannot account for every little mouse that skitters across your path. This is a hard existence. You think that this is all some Hollywood movie filled with actors and stuntmen? It isn't. This is a monstrous life, and we are damned to walk for eternity as predators to these... things." He gestured to the body rotting on the balcony.

His words cut to the bone, and my body slumped in exhaustion. Alexander placed a hand to my face while he cradled my arm.

"Amidst the pain and the blood, there can be so much beauty. You need to choose how you want to navigate this existence." He looked towards the balcony once more. "An eternity of sorrow and guilt..." His gaze shifted back to mine, the claw upon his thumb brushing against my lip. "Or an eternity of bliss."

I was tempted to bite the meat off his finger. What sort of man would play such a sick game in order to teach such a simple lesson? A sadistic choice between living in reality or living in ignorance. That was my choice. I could feel time slow, the world around me began to fade with his touch as my eyelids drooped halfway.

"Alexander," I whispered.

"Yes?" he cooed back.

"Get the fuck out and give me peace before I stake myself right in front of you."

The blonde Frenchman scoffed before releasing me, turning again to stomp toward the doors. As he stood beneath the doorframe, he spun to face me and said, "I'll give you your space—your time to... mourn. Perhaps, you weren't the man I thought you were. I guess we'll see how long this lasts."

Then, he was gone.

For the rest of the evening, I refused to leave the broken

remains of the room we, if only for a short time, called ours. The place of my making now served as the place of my unmaking. There, I remained. Sitting on the edge of the bed, my eyes strained from the blood loss, I stared half-lidded upon the annihilated New York suite.

The following week consisted of much of the same. Alexander attempted several times to pull me from the room. Each instance, I refused. Our tangents and arguments lit the walls of the Prepotent aflame. There was hardly any love between us—hardly any kindness. We were like two snarling wolves just waiting for the other to falter so the more dominant one could take control.

There also were, of course, softer moments. Claude would bring me my meal for the evening—a blood bag—enough to keep me from fading away entirely. Though I wanted to hate the taste so badly, I couldn't. Constantly, feeding reminded me of Lina, but no matter what I did, I couldn't stop myself from savoring it. I didn't deserve to savor anything. Alexander often found ways to ruin more peaceful moments, cursing Claude for the kindness he showed me. It was obvious Alexander meant to punish me by treating me as more of a prisoner, saying that if I refused to leave our room, I should have nothing. The true nature of his cruelty was on full display.

Aiden never came around. I imagined he was happier than ever, drowning in our sire's attention and glad to be rid of me in my apparent time of 'weakness'.

Then, after days of nothing but anguish and pain, after Alexander had sent a cleanup crew to remove the decomposing body from the balcony, I arose to find that somehow, the pain had dulled. Somehow, I could hardly recall the girl's face.

It was gone from me, erased. My mind had locked the memories of the evening away in its deepest depths. There were only a few things I could draw upon: that I had a horrible first taste of this unlife, that I was sore with Alexander even though I was madly and irrevocably in love with him, and a single name.

Townson.

CHAPTER NINETEEN
BACK FROM THE DEAD

A week came and went, swift in its passage, leaving in its wake the fading memories of the events that had whisked it away from me. Fragmented and fleeting, like fuzzy television static during early morning hours, snippets of memories would invade my thoughts. Yet, I struggled to pinpoint the significance of them and why they held me back from embracing my new life. Alexander had been so kind, and my ingratitude for his love and affection gnawed at my conscience. A lingering sense urged me to harbor resentment towards him, as if he had somehow earned my displeasure. Yet, introspection revealed only the persistent pull of infatuation, poised to fill the void within me.

Curiously, during that time, I found myself revisiting my earlier discussion with Sylas about the enduring humanity of vampires and how it was apparently so difficult for them to hold on to. I was afraid that I might be already succumbing to that same fate.

Emerging from the disarray of the bedroom, where I had inadvertently barricaded myself, I carefully retraced my steps down the familiar hallway and staircase. This journey led me once more to the clandestine club scene of the Prepotent. To my astonishment, this time the music overwhelmed the city's clamor, bodies now filling a space that was once desolate.

I navigated my way onto the dance floor, skillfully threading through patrons as they sensuously collided, their glistening skin reflecting the pulsating amber lights above, while the red strip lights beneath the bar cast an erotic glow on their excited spirits. Amidst this spectacle, Claude was in his element, diligently pouring shot after shot for the patrons occupying the stools. Over the past week, transformation had swept through the establishment—the floor now pristine, the lingering traces of blood wiped away, chairs returned to their accustomed spots, and the table that had suffered the bartender's crash replaced. There he stood, reinvigorated and resuming his mastery, embodying the essence of his craft.

I narrowly avoided a young mortal couple lost in their fervent embrace, their intermingled tongues a spectacle of visible saliva pooling in an explicit show. Disgusting, yet oddly captivating. The scene elicited a growl from the depths of my stomach, the inner beast almost breaking free. Its snarl echoed the desire for a taste, fueled by the unabashed passion of this couple's public display.

If one was going to indulge in such behavior, a private room seemed the more appropriate setting, for one never truly knows who or *what* might be observing.

My steps transitioned from polished wood to the soft caress of carpet. I slipped between two conversing women, their mundane chatter revolving around a man they had both dated and engaged in a dissatisfying tryst, their critiques centering on his perceived inadequacy. I couldn't help my eye-roll. I leaned in, physically inserting myself into their conversation.

"Careful!" one shrieked.

"What the fuck, bro," the other groaned as her drink almost split from her pinky-lifted grasp.

Their gazes fixated on me, anticipation of an apology evident in their expressions. Yet, I paid them no heed, my focus solely directed towards the beleaguered barkeep, Claude. Amid the chaos of the scene, his attention had barely grazed over my presence, his steely eyes flitting from one patron to another as an onslaught of drink requests bombarded him. I recognized it was his responsibility, but the overwhelmed look on his face suggested he could use an extra hand.

"Hey, Claude!" I yowled over the crowd.

Azure eyes locked onto me, a hint of surprise and recognition flickering within their depths.

"Well, well... if it isn't the prodigal son returned from the abyss. It's been quite a while. We were starting to think you'd vanished for good," he remarked, his voice lacking its former charismatic buoyancy. This time, his tones remained subdued.

"Sorry for disappearing on you. My thoughts have just been so jumbled. I'm relieved to be back on my feet now, though. Have you seen Alexander around?"

Through all the tumultuous events that had unfolded, *his* name remained the singular fixation that occupied my thoughts. It swirled persistently within the depths of my mind. My obsession. He was the man I cherished, irrespective of any baseless cause that might have sparked my irritation. I missed him so much.

In that instant, the attention of the two chattering women honed in on me, their eyes meticulously tracing each word as it escaped my lips. Their scrutiny lingered on my red hoodie, which had been reclaimed and laundered during my week of defiance. It was clean, devoid of the bloodstains from the packs I had voraciously consumed in my throes of frustration.

I paid little mind to their inquisitive stares, though I did allow myself a peek at their enticing curves adorned in sleek dresses tailored for a night in New York's vibrant club scene. Shaking off the fleeting distraction, I promptly shifted my focus back to the weathered man before me.

Claude's gave a resolute nod, his attention shifting between the two women before a single eyebrow arched in my direction. A subtle twitch played at the corner of his lip as he made his way toward the counter.

"Alexander's had this stashed away ever since you went into seclusion," he said, his voice carrying a mix of understanding and amusement. He pivoted towards me, a small object cradled in his right palm. "He said to hand this over to you the moment you decided to step out," he continued, extending his hand to me.

Nestled within his palm was a flawless new cellphone, its pristine form accentuated by a sleek red case that harmonized with my attire—a considerate detail that stirred a surge of fondness within me. Filled with emotion, I eagerly took it from Claude.

"So," I began, my voice laced with curiosity. "Is there anything else I should know?"

My fingertips glided across the glass face, coaxing a soft glow from the device amidst the ambient illumination of the bustling club. The sight was akin to a lighthouse, guiding me home after a week adrift at sea. However, before Claude could reply, the device buzzed to life, its vibrations resonating through my hands. A familiar text box materialized at the top of the screen.

> Jack, I knew you would be back with us! Oh how I've missed you! I'm away for the evening again on business, but I've left this here for you to use at your own discretion. Before you make any plans, I was told to remind you of your deal with Carver and that was a week ago. Please give him a call. His number is in the contacts section.
>
> Much love, my darling.
>
> ~ A

The world around me receded, its presence fading into insignificance. The dance floor with its writhing patrons, the bartender, the alluring vixens whose fingers were poised to explore my sweatshirt—all of it dissolved into oblivion. What remained was the stark reality encapsulated within that text box, a direct connection to the one I loved most.

My fingers moved with purpose, tapping deliberately across the digital buttons. As I completed the message, a sense of ease settled over me.

> Hey Alex, I'm just getting myself situated and I'll give him a call. Thanks for the phone and I'm sorry for how everything has been. I've had some time to think and I'm pretty sure I overreacted about...whatever it was that happened. Let's just move forward.
>
> Miss you. Love you.
>
> Your Jack.

With the brief exchange finished, and my feelings offered to Alex on a silver plate, I decided to do some exploring through the rest of the phone. Flipping from the text app, I clicked over to the contact section where Carver's name was stored. There were a few names that didn't seem familiar, but as I scrolled down, a single name seared my eyes.

CHLOE 🖤

I could hardly believe it. Was it truly her number? My fingers quivered over her name on the screen. And then I tapped it. Yes! There it was. The number for the cell phone I had given her, paid for by the job I had lost just a week prior. So much had happened since then.

The pad of my thumb found its way to the chat bubble and before I knew it, I was staring at an empty text box. Everything in me urged to send something to my darling sister. I missed her so much, the longing ached in my bones. She was probably so scared—so worried for me—no knowledge about where I was or *what* I had become. My Songbird. My sweet little Chloe.

Something tugged within my mind and I stopped typing the greeting. Was this wrong? The voice within screamed at me to remove her contact entirely—to keep her away from this night-mare world. I drew in a false breath and quickly swiped the box away and out of sight. No contact was for the best, at least for the moment.

A forceful yank tugged at the hem of my hoodie, jolting my focus away from the glowing screen. I glanced in the direction of whoever meant to steal my attention.

Seizing the fabric was the woman seated to my right, the same individual who had entertained the notion of engaging with me just moments before Claude presented me with the phone. The cougar didn't startle at the intensity of my gaze. Rather, she maintained her composure and bounced playfully in her seat. Her devious grin locked onto mine. Her olive-green stare held mine captive. Leaning in, her intentions clear, she attempted to draw my attention lower, hoping for a reaction.

Despite her provocative gestures, I refused to relent to her suppleness. Instead, my eye contact remained steadfast. A soft giggle escaped from between her pouty lips, the tension between us palpable as our gazes remained locked. Her index finger danced with the metaphorical tail it meant to tug, while the wolf within me showed no sign of yielding.

"Can I... help you?" I groaned, sounding mildly irritated.

My moment of brooding had been cut short by this club frequenter, which was irritating. I really could have used another moment or two to feel despondent.

A soft sigh emerged from my left, drawing my attention to the second woman who was casting more flirtatious glances my way, her hot-pink acrylic nail beckoning me closer. The two women exchanged glances, a colorful interplay that sent my own red gaze darting between them. My eyes, like a ping-pong ball, volleyed between their captivating allure. The blonde on the right emitted a mischievous snicker, her demeanor suggestive as she leaned in closer to me.

"You know," she began, her voice dripping with seduction, "you've got an absolutely stunning voice. Do you realize that?" She grabbed up a fistful of my designer top, a deliberate touch that exuded confidence. "And the intensity rolling off of you is just..." Her lower lip caught under her teeth, her gaze half-lidded, brimming with a smoldering allure.

"Never seen you here before. Are you maybe new in town?" her companion asked, her chest pressing into my side as she practically crawled into my lap.

Lip filler made her face appear almost duck-like. Even when she bit her lip, I couldn't stop thinking of how much she looked like she belonged in a pond.

The brunette mewled, "Sit with us, pretty please?"

What was happening? These women seemed so displeased with me moments ago, but were now fawning all over me.

Had I done something to earn such attention and not realized it?

I shook my head, wrenching my arms free from their succubus clutches. "Sorry, ladies. I have somewhere to be. I can't stay."

The two began to pout, allowing trickles of frustrated whimpers to gush all over me.

"Just one drink! Two at most!"

My gaze shifted between the two women, trailing along the contours of their figures until my garnets locked onto the throbbing pulses at the base of each of their necks.

"That's precisely my concern," I retorted, a hint of dark amusement lacing my words.

The vixens' grasp on me reluctantly loosened. With a brief nod in Claude's direction, I made my departure, my steps swift and deliberate.

"Focus," I muttered under my breath, determined to shake off the lingering distractions that clung to my senses.

The mingling scents of warm ambrosia and vitality lingered in my nose as I reclaimed the dance floor, my strides purposeful as I headed toward the elevator. It took everything in me not to spin on my heels and launch myself back at the women. The blood bag I had sucked dry earlier barely sufficed and I yearned for juice straight from the fruit. The downstairs lobby offered the ideal setting for the private call that lay ahead, free from any curious ears or... potential distractions.

I boarded the elevator's dark cage, joining the assortment of bodies that crowded the small space. Ignoring the others as best as I could, I stood amidst the collective silence, attempting to create my own bubble of solitude within the confined metal walls. Amidst the throng, my eyes inadvertently connected with those of a petite, black-haired woman. Across the sea of faces, we shared a brief yet captivating moment of mutual recognition. Her gaze held a bright, orange hue, a telltale sign of a kindred spirit—another wolf amidst the flock. Our acknowledgement of one another remained subtle to all but us.

As we held each other's attention, a small smile made her features seem brighter. Her once-tanned skin ignited across her cheeks in a delightful manner. The tangerine eye on her right side gently closed as she sent me a warm wink, acknowledging the unspoken understanding that passed between us. My heart raced as I prepared to speak, my throat constricting with a surge of anxiety. What were the odds of stumbling upon another of our kind within these walls? Was she another acquaintance of Alexander's? Were vampires in Manhattan more common than I cared to realize? Regardless, she stood before me, her presence both comforting and enigmatic, a subtle smile dancing on her lips. Amidst the unsuspecting pawns, I yearned to release the inner thoughts that had taken root in my mind.

Ding

The doors slid open, and in an instant, the bustling tide of New York club-goers flooded into the lobby, their distinctive scents permeating the stale air. The wave of humanity surged forward, sweeping over the space and obscuring the scene like a rushing tsunami. In the wake of their hasty departure, it became evident that the other vampire had been carried away by the swarm as well, pulled along in their exodus. My fleeting opportunity to serendipitously connect with another of my kind had slipped through my grasp, vanishing like a wisp of smoke. Frustration coursed through me, and I couldn't help but curse, my gaze lifting to the ceiling as a sense of disappointment settled in my chest.

"Hey, why the long face?" A quiet, but very blunt, voice came from my back, startling me.

She emerged from her hiding place behind the elevator panel, cautiously stepping into plain view. It was her—an undead woman of barely five feet, and shoulder-length hair that she messily tied back in a ponytail. Her striking orange eyes traced me from head to toe before locking with mine at last. She was a unique beauty, characterized by thick eyebrows that framed almond-shaped eyes, a delicately upturned nose resting above her deep cupid's bow. Her attire exuded an alternative flair—leather boots beneath dancer leggings, and a mesh top layered with a purple sports bra that did just enough to cover her petite frame.

Curiosity danced within her gaze, her head tilting slightly as she observed me. Another whimsical smile, similar to the first, graced her features, transforming her expression into something almost cartoonish in all its playfulness.

"Hey, buddy," she quipped, her cadence more plucky than it was smooth. "If you're going to eye-fuck me, how about buying me a drink first?"

She said it with enough gusto to capture the attention of the front desk attendant, who turned to glance in our direction with his eyebrow raised. An unnatural heat quickly bloomed under my icy cheeks, all the stolen blood I had consumed undoubtedly pooling in one place.

"No, no—I just... you're beautiful. I didn't mean to offend you," I began, and as I did, a sharp laughter sliced through the quiet and my clumsy explanation.

"You're fine." She punched me in the arm. "Just busting your gonads, Jackie boy."

Then, the curious girl twisted on her heel before heading towards a curtain concealing another corridor on the other side of the elevator. Naturally, I rushed to follow.

"Wait! How do you know my name?"

Her little hands grabbed at the red velvet of the curtain, pushing it to the side.

"I read minds," she offered over a shrug, like it was obvious and something I should have known. "So yeah... If you had a bad intention or just wanted to play *whack a mole*, I would've heard it in your thoughts. No harm done."

I ducked beneath the curtain with her, my view glued to the girl's tight back, exposed by the mesh that dipped all the way down to the base of her spine.

"Right, then," I started. If I were still capable of perspiring, I probably would have been. "So... you read minds. Does that mean you know who I am?"

The girl shook her head *no*.

"No idea who you are," she chirped. "Just your name and your intention. I don't dig too deep without knowing the person, or—in your case—*Deader* first. It can fuck me up, so I'd rather just get the basics."

She spoke like a manic pixie, her little head bobbing each time there was a lift in her voice. I attempted to keep up and to fall into pace at her side.

"Alright." I cleared my throat. "If that's the case, can I have your name?"

Her small fingers grasped at mine, and she pulled them to entwine with hers.

"Penelope. Penelope Peasly, and don't forget it!"

With an exuberant grin, she effortlessly guided me forward, her apple face radiating delight as she propelled my considerably larger form along the way. The robust boots encasing her feet made a raucous sound against the marble floors as we traversed the dark hall, until, and rather abruptly, she halted.

"Take a look around, big guy," she quipped, her snort of amusement accompanying the words.

Her jewel-bright gaze returned to mine, gleaming encouragingly. She nudged her chin toward whatever thing she wanted me to notice. Yielding to her silent directive, my gaze followed hers.

In an instant, my attention veered, and I found myself immersed in a space I had never before encountered. The plush velvet curtain had concealed a grandeur that defied my expectations. An expansive concert hall unfurled before me. I gasped. Alexander had never mentioned this to me—a grand theatre adorned in rich scarlet and opulent blacks. The open expanse of the aisle extended seamlessly toward rows of meticulously arranged seats, which in turn led my eyes to a grand stage, a hallowed space poised to showcase the arts in all their splendor. This unexpected revelation held an air of magic, evoking a sense of wonder that intertwined seamlessly with the aura of the woman who had whisked me here.

"Holy..." I started.

"Shit?" She finished.

Guided again by her infectious energy, I followed the pint-sized powerhouse through the sweep until we reached the rows of seats. They held an air of antiquity, as if remnants from a bygone, Vaudeville era. The venue, though intriguing, had undoubtedly seen more vibrant times. Its former glory appeared to have slipped through the cracks of time, leaving me with a sense of curiosity. Why had Alexander allowed such a significant part of this place to fall into disuse? The question whirled around my mind, poised to find voice, but before I could utter it aloud, my newfound companion preempted me.

Her voice rang out, intercepting my unspoken musings like a well-timed note in a symphony. "Y'know what? Not sure! I've tried to read his mind before, but he's got it sealed up tighter than Fort Knox. Can't even read the surface stuff." She dragged her fingernails along the back of one of the cushions, her claws leaving shallow trails through the dust.

I sighed.

"I'm that easy, huh?" I scoffed. "Makes me worry. Maybe I should have the power to conceal my thoughts like he can."

The idea made me anxious. If I was a failure in my human life, maybe this was an indicator I would be a failure in this life too.

"Buddy, most of your thoughts are right there on the surface, like an open book," she retorted, her words delivering a sting that I couldn't easily shake off.

Pushing aside the twinge of vulnerability, I shifted my focus back to the unveiled concert hall that had been revealed to me. The space held a specific significance, of that I was positive. Alexander was such an enigma.

Drawing a breath, I shifted my gaze back to the mysterious girl beside me. "So, Penelope," I ventured, savoring the sound of her name. "Why did you choose to share this with me?"

Her reply held a contemplative air, her finger rising to tap against her lip.

"Well, you struck me as one of those artsy types," she began, her voice a blend of playful mischief and intrigue. "And from your thoughts, it seems you're new around here. It kinda told me, 'Hey, Penelope, let's blow this guy's mind and leave him on a high,'" she concluded with a snort, a testament to her spontaneous and chaotic nature.

I shook my head, a wry smile curving at my lips as I returned my attention to the captivating stage. The opulence of the setting overwhelmed me, the splendor of the large red curtains cascading from above, a spectacle akin to a waterfall of blood— or, for a touch of refinement, wine.

"Thanks for this," I breathed, marveling.

I turned to face her again, only to find emptiness in her wake. My eyes scanned the area, futilely seeking her presence, but all that met my gaze was the rustling of entry curtains as they swayed, marking her departure.

"Penelope," I chuckled to myself.

I hadn't even noticed when she slipped from my side. I had

hoped to offer a grateful farewell, but she had vanished, leaving behind a lingering sense of chaos and intrigue.

Little did I know it, but this was to become a pivotal moment, a turning point that would mark my return from the realm of the dead...

This was the moment I was brought back to life.

CHAPTER TWENTY

RESPONSIBILITY

My exploration of the concert hall had devoured a significant chunk of my evening, but I was grateful for having informed Alex of my need to step away for a while. As the weight of impending responsibilities lingered, I found myself unable to shake off the profound impact of the hidden wonder I had stumbled upon.

This forgotten theater resonated deeply with my aspirations, the very dreams that had propelled me to this juncture. The burning desire to escape failure and ascend to stardom had driven me through so many challenges, but none quite like death.

Alexander's audition had delivered on its promise to transform me, infusing me with boundless potential for greatness. I'd never age out—never become old and ugly. I was eternal. My potential was eternal. The revelation made me shiver as it washed over my skin, the empty, cobweb-coated stage staring back at me with a dare. However, there was no denying that Alexander had yet to fully fulfill his commitment. Stumbling through the laws of the underworld was great, but I was hungry for more...and not just blood. What of the vow for art? What of the promise for glory?

My obligations for Carver were beckoning, heavy on my head. I slumped, knowing I would have to leave my new sanctuary behind for now. Uncharted territories awaited, and a realm of infinite new dangers lay in wait.

Until next time, my first and most significant paramour.

Exiting the hall, I made my way back to the lobby. Despite the bustling influx of patrons that crowded the space earlier, the room now waited cold and mostly empty. Apparently, everyone had gravitated toward the upper levels, seeking either the sophistication of fine dining or the pulsating energy of the Prepotent's club scene. Knowing I would have to soon make good on my promise to Carver, I took a moment to sink into the comfort of the couches opposite the front desk. In the solitude of the moment, I idly manipulated my phone, scanning for the one contact that held the potential to unravel my emotional composure.

My sister.

My dead heart tugged. My fingers itched. Should I extend some sort of communication—to reassure her of my well-being? Or did that choice come with more risks, potentially exposing her to the lurking horrors of this unfamiliar world?

I swept aside the thought, swiping away Chloe's information from the screen, replaced instead by an array of names I didn't recognize. I scoured down the list until my attention was drawn to a name that at once ignited uncanny nausea within my undead guts. Carver. The man made me nervous. Then again, that was his job.

Summoning my inner resolve, I initiated the call. After a single ring, Carver's voice reverberated from the other end, unmistakable in its deep baritone resonance. His presence seemed to permeate the device, his words carrying an air of familiarity laced with authority.

"Ah, there's my boy," he greeted, his tone a fusion of comfort and command serving as a stark reminder of the complex dynamics I was now enmeshed in. "I've been anticipating your call. Alexander mentioned your recent mishap and your subsequent week of solitude. But fear not, we've all experienced our moments of weakness. The allure of the blood can be an irresistible force. That's precisely why we must fortify our will and amass knowledge within this existence, lest we regress into the primitive creatures that Hollywood often depicts us as."

Again, my stomach gave a sick lurch. What had Alexander told him of my week locked away in self-imposed isolation? I was embarrassed, but I had trouble settling on *why*. I couldn't recall why I had shut myself in, why I had avoided Alex, Aiden, and everyone else. Something was missing. Details. The edges of my brain felt fuzzy. Perhaps Carver remembered more than I did...

"I know. Honestly, I still feel a little ashamed about what happened," I nudged, trying to poke him into spilling the secrets my mind had somehow locked away.

"Jack, don't beat yourself up!" he practically yelled on the other end of the line. "When I was a young fledgling, I too lost myself to my hunger. It was ages ago, yet I still hear their screams in the daylight hours. It is part of why learning to control ourselves is key to our coexistence with the mortal realm. If we all went around tearing into young women like they were pheasants, well... there would be no poultry left at the market." His words caught me and I felt that same biliousness worm around under my skin.

What had I done?

I gripped the edge of the chair with my free hand to keep myself steady. A few, short impressions of my first feeding flashed behind my eyes and caused a searing pain at the center of my forehead.

"I know. I agree. I'll try not to ever lose myself like that again. Did Alexander tell you if they're alright? My mind's a little fuzzy," I continued to goad the answers from him, even though I feared how traumatized they might leave me.

Then came the harsh clearing of his throat before an exaggerated sigh. "It happens. The thirst takes us, and when it does, the world slips away. It is a shame, though. He told me the girl was unable to be resuscitated. Blood everywhere, poor thing. Even so, these things will happen, my friend. Every night is a chance to amend the mistakes of the past and look to the future."

Carver started to drone on, but I could hardly register his words anymore. The lobby around me spun and then drifted away as more flashes of memory broke through the fog; Images of a young girl, her blonde hair matted with her own blood, my chase through Alexander's room, and then flickers of me destroying his bed. Had I gone insane from the bloodlust? I shook my mind clear of the dark visions.

"Jack? Are you alright?" the voice on the other end begged.

"I'm fine, thank you for asking Carver." I drew in a long breath through my nose, doing my best to settle myself. *Every night is a chance to amend the mistakes of the past.* He was right. "So... what can I do for you?" My voice broke. I hoped he didn't catch that.

"I need you to be an escort for a colleague of mine," he instructed, his tone sharper now. "Vincent Esposito. He has plans to go to the Gilded Rose and needs a wingman to make him look... *pleasant*... for the girls. You, of course, are someone who I imagine is very catching to the female eye, so I figured you would make excellent company for the visit."

I did my best to absorb everything he said, my mind still

barely able to cling to the present moment as more images stabbed through my consciousness. I shook my head, pushing myself to focus on the matter at hand.

"Don't worry. I'll make sure he has a fun time," I agreed, though couldn't understand why some higher-standing vampire would need a chaperone to visit a boutique. The whole request seemed odd, but I decided not to question it. "When do you need me to meet up with him?"

"Tonight," the voice commanded. "And don't worry about getting there and fumbling through the business of finding him. I've arranged for my driver to pick you up." His order was punctuated by another phlegmy release of his throat. "He'll be there within the half-hour. I suggest you be ready."

With that, the call concluded with an unceremonious click, leaving me once again in solitude within the expansive lobby of the Prepotent.

The front desk attendant provided a modicum of company, however minimal. Rising from my seat, I ventured through the room, making my way around the corner to the entrance of the men's restroom. The older, portly gentleman at the front desk regarded me with his customary smile as I passed by. I couldn't help but wonder if that smile would persist if he knew about my grisly truth. I was a murderer.

The weight of self-loathing gnawed at me, and as I stepped into the restroom, I pushed aside everything else in favor of the vague screams that would haunt me for eternity.

As I met my own reflection in the mirror, my once-brown eyes, which had previously been so warm, yet so tired, were now tinged with crimson from the transformation that both rescued and ruined me. They stared back accusingly, an image of a beast I couldn't reconcile with yet. A surge of existential questioning washed over me...

Who was this monster that stared back? The realization that

I had extinguished another's existence, cast an indelible stain upon my soul, would hang over me for the rest of my nights. How could I have committed such a heinous act and expect to continue on, bearing the weight of my own transgressions? My thoughts turned to Alexander, the trust he had placed in me, and the disappointment I feared I had inflicted upon him now. Did he seek solace in Aiden's embrace, my own inadequacies driving a wedge between us? I stumbled, losing my footing on the precarious path I did my best to navigate.

I shook my head, my hand finding the cool surface of the glass to anchor myself in reality. What was doing? I had taken a life, and here I was, fretting over keeping pace with a psychopath. I reminded myself instantly that Aiden had snuffed out *many* a life. A new thought cut through my turmoil; Was I destined to follow the same dark path?

"Mister Jack?" A voice called out, pulling me from my mental tangle. "Hey, um... there's a guy asking for you. Told him you'd be out in a minute. I was tempted to crack a joke about a mean leftover burrito, but he didn't seem like the laughing type."

It was the first time I had heard the front desk attendant speak, his *Queens* accent adding a touch of warmth to his words. Even he, who had undoubtedly witnessed countless unsettling events, appeared disconcerted by the visitor.

I slowly pushed open the restroom door, offering the older man a small smile. "I've got it. Thank you... uh..." My attempt to recall his name faltered. My tongue stumbled over words, struggling to retrieve any shred of information to mask the fact that, after a week of being here, I had neither learned nor retained his name.

"Larry!" he blurted, his mustache twitching above his lip. "My name is Larry, and don't worry about it, most don't focus on the old guy sittin' in the chair at the front."

THE VAMPIRE JACK TOWNSON 231

His laughter was kind, but I felt like an ass. "Well, Larry, I'm not going to forget your name now. We'll talk soon, alright?"

Larry batted his hand at me, his weathered features marked by deep lines that accentuated his momentary skepticism, yet a glimmer of hope lingered beneath his doubt.

"Well, get out there, Mister Jack. Something tells me you shouldn't keep a fellow like that waitin'."

I maneuvered past him and navigated back toward the building's front doors. More visitors to the establishment shuffled by, drawn to the pulsating bass emanating from the nightclub above like a heartbeat in a giant beast. As I emerged, the night air swept over me in a cooling tide, rain falling in a steady rhythm upon the pavement. The grand gargoyle-adorned building loomed over me, and before it, I spotted an important-looking SUV idling near the curb. It was black and sleek, accompanied by a man who leaned against its open door. His gaze locked onto mine, eyes radiating an otherworldly green that held an uncanny intrigue.

Dressed in a fitted suit, a white dress shirt completed by a crimson tie, and a newsboy hat that concealed his short brown hair, he exuded an air akin to a gang member from the 1920s. His face bore expertly trimmed stubble, an aesthetic that accentuated his timeless aura.

"The King sends his regards. I'll be your driver for the evening. Name's Chester."

He extended a hand toward me. His fingerless gloves came to a halt just below his wrists. Driving gloves, I recognized. I couldn't help but notice that he felt different. He wasn't like Aiden, or Carver, or even Sylas. A flicker of life still coursed beneath this man's professional exterior. My hand met his in a firm handshake, similar to the way I tested Carver in the penthouse suite. However, this time, a surprising twist occurred—

"OOF! Okay, boss, got it!"

The unexpected *crack* didn't originate from my hand, but from Chester's. He swiftly drew away and shook out his wrist in front of him. He also wriggled his fingers as though making sure none of them were broken.

"Son of a bitch, is that how they greet people where you're from?" Chester's exclamation echoed through the air, his humor evident in his voice, despite his obvious discomfort.

"You're not a..." I started and allowed the sentence to fall while watching the intimidating man dance about on his shined leather shoes upon the New York City asphalt. I closed the distance, apology overtaking me. "I thought you were... you know... like *us*!" My voice dropped to a whisper and the man responded with a laugh.

"Like you? You mean a vampire? No, man. No." Chester took a moment to scan our surroundings, ensuring our privacy in the midst of the bustling city that perpetually hummed with its own symphony of noise. "Hop in, and we can chat on the way. But seriously, ease up on the hand squeezing. I'll end up at the ER if you keep that up," he quipped, nodding toward the waiting black car. "Go ahead."

Following his instructions, I reached for the handle and slid into the passenger seat, a choice that seemed to amuse my new driver.

"Weird, dude. I can tell you're not used to this. No worries. Sit back and relax. We'll be there in no time."

I instinctively fastened my seatbelt, avoiding a repeat of the clumsy mistake that had occurred during my previous joy ride with Aiden.

As we settled in, the rain-drenched the streets as they unfurled before us. A new question gnawed at my curiosity. "So, if you're not a vampire... what are you?"

I allowed myself to relax back against the cushioned headrest. Chester fell silent for a moment, his furrowed brow revealing his confusion.

"Seriously? No one's filled you in on this stuff?" he responded, genuine concern apparent in his voice. "Look, buddy, I may be out of the loop, but even I know this much... I'm hired help. You, well, you're practically royalty, pal."

His words struck a new chord. Royalty. I thought back to revelations from Marcus and the Undercity, then, reminded that there were only three in our guild. Apparently, though, the elite circle I had entered had left me largely uninformed. Perhaps that week of isolation—of talking to no one and learning nothing new—had been more detrimental to my path than I cared to consider.

"I know it's a long story. I just... I need the abridged version. Could you help me out? I'm meeting this guy, and I don't want to seem like a complete idiot," I admitted.

My self-deprecation was met with a reprimanding finger raised by Chester. He seemed to take the Manhattan traffic as an opportunity to focus more on our conversation.

"No, we're not doing that. Don't beat yourself up. You're a vampire. Top of the food chain. You rule the night, and if sunlight weren't such an issue, you'd rule the day too. Don't talk about yourself like you're one of these... *regular* folks." He gestured to the pedestrians rushing about the sidewalks like mindless ants. "You're better—*way* better. Yeah, I'll give you what I can, just don't tell Carver I got so informal with you." He shrugged, a gesture that seemed to loosen him up and drop his walls down a bit. "That iron grip of yours from earlier caught me off guard. I'm off my game," he chuckled, and I saw the glint off a gold tooth from within the cavern of his mouth.

"So?" I began, a note of intrigue in my voice, "What are you, then?"

"I'm a six-foot-two Sagittarius who enjoys moonlit strolls in

Central Park and pizza from Mama Stefano's." His face went deadpan as he blinked at me for a moment. "No sense of humor. What's with this guy..." he muttered to himself before answering my question. "I'm a fuckin' Ghoul, ya knucklehead."

"A Ghoul?" The word conjured images of decrepit, undead creatures in my mind—zombies with outstretched arms and rotting jaws. "I don't get it," I admitted, seeking a more enlightening explanation. "You don't look like a zombie."

"Not a zombie! Holy shit. A ghoul?" Chester persisted, and I gaped dumbly in response. He sighed, clearly exasperated. "A ghoul is a blooded human bound to a vampire. We're like... vampire-lite. The drink nobody wants because you don't get blitzed from it. We get a taste of the real thing and have to work our way up to becoming full vampires. It's like an application— we're the hired help. We handle scouting, grunt work, driving, and security detail."

He delved into more details, and I found myself engrossed in his explanation. The concept of a lesser form of vampire was entirely new to me, though it seemed to make sense given all he said.

"So, I could create a ghoul?" I posed the question, envisioning the potential benefits of having a loyal assistant to share the day and night with—my very own Renfield to my Dracula. Chester's face lit up, confirming that my train of thought was on the right track.

"You could!" he exclaimed, clapping his hand against the steering wheel with enthusiasm. "But you've got to understand, there's a ton of responsibility that comes with something like that. It's not like having a new puppy. You're promising them eternal life, got it? You can't string them along for the long haul. Eventually, you've got to make good on that promise. They're not just disposable companions, they're with you until you decide to turn them or..." He hesitated for a moment.

"Or?" I prodded.

"Or until we die," he admitted, his voice softer as he conveyed the gravity of the matter. "It's not easy to kill us, though. We may not have the fancy dark gifts, but we're still five times stronger than the strongest human. It takes a lot to take us down." The way he spoke told me that he had contemplated hundreds of times that there was a possibility that he may never make it to eternal night. "We serve a purpose," he began again more seriously. His neck craned to the side, a hand leaving the steering wheel to prop his head up from his boredom amongst the traffic. "Some of us never get to see the end of our dreams. Most ghouls leave this life in body bags. We ain't stupid, but it beats being one of these sewer rats scraping by in a life where they'll never be important or become anything other than just valueless, Government livestock."

The bitterness in Chester's voice was palpable

A thought came to my mind, something gnawed at me I couldn't quite shake. "How would you describe the pay?" The question felt clumsy amidst the mortal implications of Chester's reality, but I was curious.

"The pay?" Chester's eyebrows shot up. "Like nothing you could dream of, pal. Hell... at the end of the day, the job is so good, it makes leaving your old life behind seem like a cakewalk just for the comfort alone. You got a wife, a kid? Bam, house and college tuition done and done. You got debts and scores to settle? BAM! Debt cleared and whoever you owed is either paid in interest or found a year later in a ditch." His laughter was gravelly, but his words struck me like a bolt of lightning. A growing unease settled over me. The more he spoke, the more I felt a gnawing suspicion taking root within my mind.

"Hey, Chester?" I prodded.

"What's up, Jacky boy?" He replied.

"You guys... ghouls... you're in charge of scouting, you said?"

I tilted my head, catching Chester's gaze in a similar pose, and a subtle tremor of uncertainty rippled through the air.

"... yeah. Yeah, we can be. Many of us are, y'know? For appearance's sake, we're human, and we don't have any weaknesses like the big guys, so... it makes being able to find potential progenies that much easier." He paused. "Why do you ask?"

"No reason," I lied. "Just interested in how it all works..."

The remainder of the journey stretched before me in a haze of muted voices and distant cityscape. Chester's monologue faded into a dull hum, his words lost in the tumult of my racing thoughts. My mind felt like a battlefield, each idea a soldier locked in combat against the relentless onslaught of doubts and suspicions. The revelation that ghouls were tasked with scouting and blending into human society had shaken the foundation of my understanding.

Was Chris, my lifelong friend, entwined in this elaborate tapestry of shadows? The pieces of the puzzle were falling into place, each one revealing a more complex and disconcerting picture. His sudden appearance at the coffeehouse, the seemingly coincidental conversation that led to my involvement with Alex—it was all too calculated, too perfectly orchestrated to be mere happenstance. My thoughts circled back to that fateful moment, his finger poised over the contact information, eager anticipation gleaming in his eyes. Could he truly be part of this world, orchestrating my descent into its depths?

As the rain-drenched cityscape passed by in a blur, I grappled with the weight of these suspicions. Chris had been a constant presence in my life, a friend who had shared my dreams and aspirations. The thought of him as a puppeteer, pulling the strings from the shadows, was a bitter pill to swallow. The foundation of my past had crumbled, leaving me adrift in a sea of sharp suits and sharper teeth.

The car came to a halt, and Chester's grip on my shoulder

brought me back to the present. His words, a reminder of the task at hand, echoed in my ears.

"Jacky, we're here. Vincent's waiting for you inside. And... hey, whatever's floatin' in that pretty head of yours... remember you've got a job to do, so just keep movin' forward. Besides, it could always be worse..."

I stared at him as he reached across my chest to open the passenger-side door for me. We locked eyes.

I stepped out of the vehicle, my gaze fixed on the looming entrance ahead. The path I had chosen was fraught with danger and intrigue, but there was no turning back now. I was determined to uncover the truth—to navigate this treacherous landscape and unearth the secrets that lay hidden beneath the surface.

Chester's gaze met mine again. "Could still be human," he concluded.

The rain continued to fall, a relentless cascade that mirrored the torrent of thoughts in my mind, as I ventured deeper into the heart of darkness, ready to confront the mysterious Vincent and the revelations that awaited.

CHAPTER TWENTY-ONE
WHAT'S IN A NAME

Chester's departure was swift and perfunctory, barely warranting a nod from me, for my thoughts were ensnared by the searing ache in my chest. My mind grappled with the newfound knowledge entangling me in its web.

Could my long-time companion, Chris, truly have been a Ghoul? Or was my psyche succumbing to paranoia, a result of the recent terrors that had befallen me—the obscure girl's life-less form hanging around my neck?

Stepping out into the nocturnal embrace of the city, my boots reverberated against the asphalt of New York's bustling streets. Around me, the cityscape held its familiar allure—the resplendent glow of neon lights mingling with the memories of the previous week, a poignant reminder of my inaugural encounter with Alexander at *The Gilded Rose*.

Yet, the scene before me had shifted since my last visit. The high-fashion boutique, once a solitary sentinel of silence, now bore witness to a curious spectacle. Bodies were arrayed against its windows, like curious onlookers peering into a private party, though the boutique itself seemed deserted.

"Jackie!" The voice of the Ghoul, Chester, called out from within the now-distant car. His head protruded through the open window, his tone lighthearted despite my melancholy. "Vincent's waiting by the door for you. Get in there, and remember, Carver sent you my contact if things get dicey. Have a blast, and pass my regards to Annabelle." With that, the window slid shut, and Chester merged back into the stream of Manhattan's bustling traffic, leaving behind a trail of honks and expletives.

A sigh escaped my lips, laden with a portentous weight.

"Jack? Are you... Jack?" The echoes of the now-distant SUV dissipated as a new voice pierced the air.

My head pivoted, drawing my gaze upwards to the source of the sound. Amidst the throng of revelers savoring the night's embrace, a figure emerged—a man of imposing stature. His obsidian mane was slicked back, immobilized by an excess of hair gel. Pallid skin, tinged with iridescent shades of green and red under the pulsating neon lights, enveloped his bulky frame. He towered over the crowd, his physique reminiscent of a powerlifter's, his tracksuit straining against sinew and muscle.

His gaze bore down upon me, a hooked nose casting its shadow over a lip that bore the mark of a cleft. A cigarette dangled precariously between his fingers, smoke curling upwards. "You must be Jack, right?" he muttered, his fingers deftly plucking the smoldering ember and positioning it to the side. "You've got that *Carver* look about you. Perhaps he's come through after all." His words, tinged with a note of skepticism, hung in the air, punctuated by the curling tendrils of cigarette fumes.

For a brief moment, I found myself ensnared in awed silence. His imposing presence exuded an aura of intimidation, a living fortress of strength and brawn. Snapping out of my daze, I realized my gaze had lingered too long, my hand instinctively rising to brush aside the inky locks that obscured my vision.

"Yes, that's me." I managed a forced smile, my crimson eyes locking onto his glamoured teal orbs, radiating an eerie allure. "You must be Vincent. Pleasure to make your acquaintance."

My hand extended a gesture of camaraderie, only to be enveloped by a colossal paw that swallowed it whole. A handshake of titanic proportions followed though the anticipated surge of power was conspicuously absent. It was as if a giant plush bear had taken hold of my hand, its strength incongruent with its cuddly façade.

"So, Jack, is it?" Vincent's scrutiny traveled up and down my form, his lips curling into a wry smile. "Any other monikers tucked away, or are you pulling a Cher on us?" He chuckled, the cigarette once again finding its place between his lips, conjuring plumes of dense smoke that mingled with the rain.

As his question hung in the air, our hands momentarily entwined, I grappled with the absence of a fitting surname. The name "Jack" had been bestowed upon me by Alexander, yet he had neglected to furnish me with a suitable last name—only the initial and the face to match. The silence in the dimly illuminated threshold of the boutique grew palpable, an unspoken challenge between our locked gazes, each awaiting the other's concession.

Then, like an epiphany, a name surged forth from the recesses of my subconscious, insistent and undeniable. It flowed from my lips like a silken current, both chilling and invigorating.

"Townson." I proclaimed the single word carrying the weight of significance. "Jack Townson." With those syllables, a seismic shift cascaded through my very being, heralding the birth of a new identity. The fledgling of Alexander La Mont had embraced a name that would redefine me and lay the corner-

stone of my transformative journey—a moniker that would
echo through time and herald a destiny yet to unfold.

Jack *Fucking* Townson.

And so, a singular utterance sculpted my path, setting into
motion the grand tapestry of my existence, and signaling a
dawn that would transcend all former dusks.

Vincent's brow arched, the faintest tremor coursing through
his hair lip as his head inclined in tandem. The cigarette found
its temporary freedom from the confines of his teeth. "Well, I'll
be damned," he drawled, his voice laced with a mixture of
astonishment and curiosity. "Jack Townson. Hollywood guy,
huh? That's quite a stage name."

Pride swelled within me, a spark of accomplishment ignited
by his reaction, even if the roots of the name remained veiled in
mystery. My chest puffed out subtly, a silent acknowledgment
of a job well done, even as I remained oblivious to the name's
true lineage and how I had even come up with it.

"Yeah, that's right!" I responded, a self-assured grin tugging
at the corners of my lips. "I guess you could say I've got a knack
for the Hollywood flair." Vincent's compliment, though offered
with a hint of jest, bolstered my sense of achievement. His gaze
lingered on my features, recognition mingling with a touch of
self-contempt. As he wilted, his sudden insecurity became
apparent. "Don't sell yourself short," I interjected, my hand
extending in a comforting gesture that found its mark in a
hearty pat on his arm. His muscles yielded beneath my touch.
"Awkwardness is a shared trait, my friend. Let's just focus on
enjoying ourselves."

The astonishment etched across Vincent's countenance
lingered, a brief moment of incredulity as my hand rested on his
arm. Time stretched thin before his thunderous laughter
erupted, filling the confined space with its infectious mirth.
"You're a riot!" he boomed, a broad grin cracking his features.

With an easy, new fellowship, his arm encircled my shoulders, his discarded cigarette trailing a smoggy arc before finding the pavement. Together, we ventured forth, guided by his guiding gesture, back into the embrace of *The Gilded Rose*.

The boutique's interior unfolded before us, familiar corners of high fashion welcoming us like old friends. I could almost sense my previous attire's ghostly presence wafting in the air. Yet, our journey didn't halt there. Beyond the known boundaries, past the area where the distressed front desk attendant had lingered and where Annabelle had once emerged, we continued along winding passages flanked by racks of excess inventory. There, another revelation awaited, similar to the one at the Prepotent—an elevator, its presence unbeknownst to me until this moment.

My voice quivered with a blend of intrigue and disbelief. "So... there's more shopping upstairs?" Attempting to fathom where this was all leading, I struggled to untangle the implications.

A slack-jawed Vincent stood before me, his expression mirroring my own perplexity. It was a testament to the newfound mysteries that surrounded us, each disclosure unraveling the fabric of our understanding, leaving us to navigate a world far more intricate than we had initially conceived.

"Come on, buddy," Vincent's voice carried a mix of encouragement and unease, his large finger almost comically grazing the elevator call button.

The light filtered through his skin, casting a vibrant orange hue. As the elevator arrived, we squeezed inside, his formidable frame barely accommodating the confined space, leaving me to navigate the limited area. It was a scene akin to the movie *Twins* —Vincent, an imposing monolith of stone, and me, a somber figure, our mismatched pairing a source of unintentional amusement that would have garnered a chuckle from any onlooker, had Vincent's stoic demeanor not exuded an air of latent danger.

Amidst the silence, I sensed Vincent's palpable apprehension, his movements betraying a battle against his nerves. A gesture of reassurance, similar to the one I had extended earlier, was met with his own hand, acknowledging my effort with a thankful pat.

However, as the elevator doors parted, any remnants of reassurance were shattered. My gaze pierced the veil, revealing the truth of *The Gilded Rose*—a realm far removed from the austere facade we had traversed earlier. It was a supernatural sanctuary, a gentlemen's club concealed within the boutique's depths. Golden poles extended skyward, demarcating stages that beckoned to seductive performances. Tables and couches filled the space, and patrons and dancers alike engaged in an otherworldly revelry. Neon strobes danced through the atmosphere, in rhythmic cadence with the music, conjuring an ambiance that pulsed with arcane energy.

Vincent's features once marked by apprehension, were now marred by a primal fear, his innate dread materializing before him. I instinctively held the elevator doors ajar, my gaze shifting to the towering vampire at my side. I remembered Carver's order: *be his wingman.*

"Vincent, are you okay? It's just a club. You've got this!" My attempts to infuse levity into the situation met a resistant wall, as he hesitated, seemingly paralyzed by trepidation. A nudge against his broad back served as a gentle yet insistent encouragement. "Come on, buddy! You're a big, strong, and, uh... sexy vampire. You can totally handle this!" My attempt at humor and support did little to alleviate his reluctance, his mass making the endeavor more of a struggle than I had anticipated.

His gaze met mine, fraught with a vulnerability that belied his formidable exterior. "They... they really don't like me here...

because of my looks and all," he confided, his voice a mixture of dejection and resentment. The notion was repugnant, a testament to the shallowness of judgment that plagued even the supernatural realm.

In an instant, my resolve solidified, my eyes locking onto an open seating area within the club. "Well, fuck them! We're here to have fun!" I asserted, my feet urging us forward, his weight challenging my newfound vampiric strength. A sense of determination imbued my every step, mirrored in Vincent's gradually straightening posture, a spark of hope rekindling within his eyes.

"Yeah!" Vincent's response burst forth, a newfound determination illuminating his eyes.

We moved deeper into the club, sidling up to a booth. He lowered himself onto the couch, which surrendered beneath his sheer mass, the unfortunate victim of his imposing frame. My gaze remained locked on his features, tracing the subtle interplay of emotions that washed across his countenance. Yet, his pallor had taken a turn for the worse, his complexion now resembling the very marble from which the club's architecture was carved. Following his line of sight, my own gaze alighted on a figure that commanded attention, heralding her approach with the click of stilettos against the floor.

Annabelle Cross, a vision of audacious allure, emerged from the crowd, a towering presence befitting her role as the lady of the establishment.

Her gaze, fierce emeralds aglow, remained affixed to Vincent, a magnetism that drew all attention her way. Clad in a clingy green latex dress, her svelte form was punctuated by designer implants straining against the confines of her low-cut ensemble. Ruby red hair was artfully arranged in a high bun, an ornate crown atop her regal visage. With every step, her aura radiated both command and desire, her presence casting a magnetic allure that seemed to ensnare even the most steadfast souls.

Frozen in place, we watched as she approached, her form an embodiment of raw power. Her passage propelled her past me, and with a flourish of assertive grace, she directed her focus solely on Vincent. Without a word, her stiletto-clad foot ascended, its point settling resolutely against his chest, a physical assertion of dominance that left me almost unintentionally tumbling back onto the crimson couch.

The ire in Annabelle's eyes burned with an intensity that threatened to ignite the very air around us. Her voice, a torrent of indignation, sliced through the tension. "Vincent, you have some *FUCKING* nerve showing your face here. What in the world possessed you to set foot in my domain?" Her words were a fusillade, each syllable barbed with unbridled fury. As if to accentuate her point, her hip thrust forward, propelling the pointed end of her stiletto with a menacing edge.

Before Vincent could stutter out a defense, an unanticipated surge of determination coursed within me. As though propelled by an invisible force, I pushed myself upright from the couch, my frame aligning with Annabelle's. An air of defiance enveloped me, shielding me from the trepidation that had once gripped my psyche. "Is this how you treat your patrons, *Ms. Cross*?" My voice, tempered by newfound resolve, flowed like molten steel, the weight of authority accompanying my words.

Her gaze, once locked on Vincent, pivoted to meet my own. The warmth that had been extended to me during my earlier encounter with her had dimmed considerably, replaced by a pointed iciness. "And *you*, fuck boy," she hissed, her stiletto probing deeper into Vincent's chest. "What's your angle here with this... creature? Speak up, Jack."

My outrage eclipsed my rationality, my hand instinctively curling around her calf, lifting her leg off the ground. Her balance was inextricably tethered to my grip, her initial scoff yielding to a momentary sense of vulnerability. As her weight shifted onto me, I seized the opportunity to assert myself, my voice resonating with unwavering confidence. "We're here to revel, Ms. Cross, to embrace the atmosphere and indulge in the offerings of this establishment. Carver introduced us, and we simply wish to contribute to the merriment with our patronage." The words flowed effortlessly, emboldened by an unexplainable wellspring of assurance. "Carver, the *king*, has ordered us to enjoy ourselves, that's all." With each utterance, my voice carried a thunder that echoed with an underlying power, a newfound strength that seemed to permeate my very being.

Annabelle's expression shifted, her initial rage transmuting into a more contemplative manner as she processed all I said. Her gaze flitted between us, her thoughts tracing a thoughtful pattern as she weighed our presence against Carver's involvement.

"Carver told you to come here..." Her words hung in the air, part question, part realization as if she were piecing together a puzzle.

The stiletto relinquished its grip on Vincent's chest, the weight transferring to me as I supported her leg, the encounter oscillating between tension and an unexpected moment of interest. Her directive was clear, albeit veiled beneath the cold veneer of her words. "Stay close to your friend and ensure he has a *memorable* experience," she commanded, her gaze momentarily softening as it settled on me. "You can hold onto the leg if you desire, but both of us have matters to attend to. Perhaps, another time."

With those words, I released her leg from my grasp, the stiletto resuming its connection with the floor. As if shedding her prior ire, Annabelle brushed herself off, a viper shedding its venomous demeanor. With a parting smirk and one final lingering glance, she withdrew, leaving us to revel in the provocative allure of *The Gilded Rose*.

The night unfurled before us, a canvas painted with the libidinous pursuits of the undead, our presence akin to neophytes allowed entry into a realm of newfound experiences. As dancers of diverse identities and forms converged upon our couch, their sensual performances captivated us, each movement an embodiment of supernatural grace.

Vincent sent rolls of fifty-dollar bills sailing through the air, generous offerings to the dancers who graced our presence there. The ambiance was electric, the energy crackling with an intensity that mirrored the pulsating strobes painting the scene in their vibrant hues.

Amidst the crescendo of sensations, Vincent's hand wandered to a small object concealed within his tracksuit pocket. His movements were deliberate, his fingers extracting a glass vial containing a peculiar crimson powder that glistened under the club's neon glow. A momentary exchange between us segued into an explanation—a revelation that shattered the boundaries of my understanding, fragmenting my thoughts into a kaleidoscope of bewilderment.

"Blood dust," he elucidated, the words tinged with a blend of candor and intrigue. "It's how we enjoy ourselves discreetly when feeding openly isn't an option."

The vial revealed its crystalline contents, an alchemical manifestation of high-quality blood from a donor, rendered into an unassuming yet potent form. A metallic instrument made contact with the powder, the contents adhering to its surface before being offered to me.

Staring at the vial, my heart pounded with trepidation, my mind wrestling with uncertainty. The prospect of partaking in such an act lay before me.

"You ever... uh... party before?" Vincent asked. Then, he passed the vial over to me.

Had I ever transcended the boundaries of my comfort zone? Had I ventured beyond the confines of my mundane existence, and explored the realms of experience that lay outside my familiar routine? The realization struck me with a pang—a life marked by the predictable, my existence spent toiling away for an unfulfilling job, my evenings reduced to scripted interactions with my sister, a cycle perpetuated by exhaustion and obligation.

"No," I whispered, the word a fragile admission, my voice laced with a cocktail of curiosity and a yearning for something more. The invitation to experience a world beyond my own, to tread paths previously uncharted, stirred a potent mix of emotions within me.

James Donovan was fucking dead. Literally.

Jack Townson was *undead* and thriving.

The small, crystallized vial rested in my palm, a decision teetering on the edge of a previously unexplored precipice. My thoughts swirled, mirroring the intricate dance of the blood particles within the container. In a moment that defied my prior life's caution, my hesitation evaporated, replaced by a bold resolve.

With a defiant exhale, I raised the vial to my nose, inhaling deeply. The sensation was instantaneous. An electric surge, akin to lightning coursed through my veins. Crackling sensations rippled across my senses as the crystallized blood particles traversed the bridge between my nose and brain, imbuing me with a white-hot euphoria. My vision blurred, the world transforming into an otherworldly haze, reality itself seemingly shrouded in newfound obscurity.

My body jolted against the cushion of the couch, my hand

surging to seek stabilization against Vincent's shoulder as I realized the dangers of blood lusting in a crowded place.

"Vincent!" I croaked hoarsely as I attempted to keep my voice low, even though a single scream would have easily gone unnoticed thanks to the wall-shaking bass through the speakers. "What about the humans? What about the other people here?"

Vincent's laughter rippled through the air, his head shaking in amusement at my apparent ignorance. His hand met his temple as if to quell the residual effects of the blood dust. "Buddy, this is a sanctuary," he reassured me. "Glamor magic keeps us hidden here. It takes effort, but this place is shielded from prying human eyes."

With a deft motion, he claimed the spoon and vial, replicating the action I had just taken. His reassurance resonated within me, quelling the initial surge of panic.

The night unfurled into a whirlwind of experiences— moments of revelry, indulgence, and a bond forged through stories and shared chaos. Vincent's infectious laughter and brotherhood dissolved the barriers of unfamiliarity, paving the way for a genuine connection.

Amidst our shared journey into the depths of the night, I bared my soul, recounting even the darkest corners of my past. The confession of the girl I had inadvertently taken the life of hung in the air, a heavy burden I carried around with me, and a wound that had yet to heal.

Vincent's response was a balm for my wounded soul. "Jack, that's terrible... but you can't blame yourself for every twist of fate, my friend," he reassured me, his voice carrying the weight of wisdom. "These things, these fragile moments, they're like tissue paper in the wind. You can't hold yourself accountable for a world that's made of glass and paper, where you're a hurricane. It's not your fault."

He spoke with genuine sincerity, and struck a chord within me, igniting a glimmer of self-compassion that had eluded me. Vincent's presence was a revelation—a testament to the power of empathy and the capacity for transformation, the embodiment of a good-hearted soul whose exterior belied his true nature.

His discourse continued, each word resonating with a profound sense of determination and resilience. "My dad used to say, '*Keep moving forward, don't let anything obstruct your path. Shoot for the stars, and don't stop until you crash into...* Penelope.'" The crescendo of his speech was palpable, an empowering message that echoed through the club. But I didn't understand the last part.

"Crashing into Penelope?" I queried, wrinkling up my nose in puzzlement. My gaze followed his line of sight, only to land upon a familiar figure—the very Penelope who had shown me the Prepotent's most secret treasure.

Clad in minimal attire, Penelope commanded the stage, her lithe form an embodiment of grace and magnetism. Her performance was nothing short of mesmerizing, a kinetic display of flexibility and fluidity that enthralled both the eye and the... heart.

Her movements defied gravity, a whirlwind of motion that left me in awe. The boundaries of the mundane world seemed to dissipate, replaced by a surreal dance that transcended the limitations of human capability. As her body contorted and spiraled, my perception shifted, recognizing the echoes of a past life colliding with the vibrancy of the supernatural realm.

In that moment, as Penelope danced, I found myself not just a spectator, but a participant—a witness to the interplay of human experience and supernatural allure, evidence of the indomitable spirit that united the living and the *un*dead.

I stared.

Vincent gawked.

Penelope scowled.

Before her performance concluded, Penelope's graceful descent from the stage marked a shift in the atmosphere. A new veil of melancholy shrouded her expression, her gaze laden with emotions that seemed to converge upon Vincent. Our corner of the club seemed to settle into an uncomfortable quiet as the contortionist's lips formed a pronounced frown, and it became very easy to see the turmoil brewing beneath the surface.

Her glare drifted from Vincent's towering figure to lock onto mine. In that fleeting moment of connection, a torrent of emotions surged within me—an empathetic ache for her distress, a pang of guilt for my unwitting role there. Though, I didn't understand why I should feel guilty. What history did she have with Vincent, I wondered.

With a swift and purposeful motion, Penelope's petite frame propelled itself from the stage, a determined trajectory guiding her past servers and into the enclave of her dressing room. Other patrons stared after her, seeming to mirror my own confusion. The palpable tension in the room echoed her departure, the silence growing even heavier as it permeated the air in the wake of her exit.

Vincent's gaze lingered as well, his towering form leaning over his toes in her direction, as though the top half of his body wanted to follow her path even as her form disappeared from view. An almost inaudible murmur escaped his lips, a whisper of concern and longing that barely grazed the air.

"Vincent, do you two know each other?" The question tumbled from my lips. His contemplative demeanor and the trace of anxiety that danced across his expression hinted at a story that had yet to be revealed.

His nod, accompanied by a flicker of pain in his features, confirmed the existence of a history that held some weight.

"Yeah," he began, the admission carrying hints of what seemed to be bittersweet memories. "We used to date. She was... really special to me. It's complicated, and I miss her."

The sincerity in his words resonated deeply, eliciting a surge of empathy within me. He was clearly still heartbroken. I knew just how that felt.

"Hey," he began gently. "Mind if I leave you alone for a bit? I want to talk to her." His gaze held a weighty sincerity. I offered a reassuring smile and cocked my head in the direction of the dressing room.

"Yeah, just... come back soon, alright?" I replied, a hint of lightheartedness infusing my words. "Stranger in a strange place." My laughter punctuated the sentiment, and he embarked on his journey to reconnect with the woman who had left an indelible mark.

As he receded into deeper parts of the club, my attention shifted, only to be captured by the unexpected presence of the club's provocative owner. Serpentine legs coiled themselves around my lap, a sensation that was both alien and oddly enchanting. Annabelle's arrival was accompanied by more playful energy, her proximity igniting arousal in my depths that hadn't surfaced the first time we met.

"Hey," she purred, her voice laced with mischief. "You were so quick to take control earlier. Thought I'd give you what you wanted from the start." Her alluring smile and the slyness that danced in her eyes set the stage for an encounter that defied my expectations for how this evening was supposed to go.

Her tantalizing offer hung in the air, a proposition that dared me further into a night of debauchery. As her slender figure leaned against the couch, her aura seemed to eclipse the bright lights of the dance platform, casting a spell that demanded my attention.

My hand brushed against the soft skin of her thigh, fingers

tracing the contours of her leg as a charge of electricity coursed through my veins. "Not many men can handle you, can they?" I mused, my words infused with a combination of fascination and admiration. My hands found their way to her legs, my rough palms gently brushing against her soft skin before squeezing the fat of her thigh. "You're intimidating, powerful, fucking terrifying... Who would be able to?"

Annabelle watched me, her lips gaping, some unspoken current flowing between us. Her touch started out tender as her fingers traced my jawline, each stroke sending a thrill through my senses as they became more and more possessive. The intimacy of the moment held a promise I hadn't expected would be there—an invitation to explore the depths of desire.

Our eyes remained locked, a tension building as the world around us seemed to recede into a realm of its own. With a daring closeness, Annabelle's lips hovered mere inches from mine, a promise of the intoxicating journey that awaited us.

"Do you know how many men have stood up to me on a warpath, hm?" she asked the question with a song in her tone. I imagined her tongue to be forked and rolling about in her mouth... wishing it was in mine. "Well, little fledgling?"

It was uttered as a curse, but her poisonous voice still sent shivers up my spine.

"How many?" The question vibrated across my lips, my tone a low hum that only we two could hear. I leaned my head back, pulling my face from her grasp to allow her fingers to end their insidious mission. She drew out a long hiss as I did, defiance something she clearly enjoyed.

"None. At least... none as young as you."

She leaned in closer, her shoulder pressed against my own, that gorgeous face inches from mine, allowing me a clear view down her dress to enjoy the full gift of her bosom. Ruby lips found their way to my cheek, placing a cold kiss against my pale flesh. Her legs rubbed against mine, forcing my cock to press hard against my pants and swell beneath her temptress thighs. She pulled away, her emerald stare shifting between my lips and my own red eyes.

"I see why Alex values you," she mewed. "You're really not just some dumb man toy, are you?"

I stared back with the same intensity. My grip on her legs forced them down hard against me, my hips instinctively rolling. "I'm the Vampire Jack Townson," I growled, enjoying how good the new moniker was beginning to feel. "I'm much more than I appear to be." It felt... right.

Annabelle's body reacted, her breasts heaving against my chest. In one abrupt motion, she straddled me, her full ass shifting to sit firmly in my lap, knees pressing down into the couch on either side of my hips.

"I've toppled kings, seen armies stand in fear at my wake, brought countries to their knees, and here I am... felled by some boy from New York." Her laughter was dark and luxurious like a sip of cabernet. "It feels... exciting." She pressed those thick cheeks hard against my growing member, grinding into my pelvis to see how worked up she could get me. Our eyes never unlocked. "A warlord sits in your lap and you hardly flinch. How are you so damn bold, and yet so foolish?"

"You may be some dangerous viper, but all I see is a beautiful woman hiding the real her from the world, scared to show the heart underneath the latex armor. You may have conquered kings, but have you ever allowed yourself to feel? To *really* care for someone... other than the girls you keep." I gestured to the dancers as they went about their business, tending to the patrons. "You're a goddess, but do you ever allow yourself to just be... mortal?"

The question must have struck a nerve, for her softness pulled back in anger. Those full lips quivered with whatever defense she meant to huck at me. She stared at my face before bringing her emerald jewels to rest on my mouth again, a red talon rising to play with my bottom lip.

"Oh Alex..." She gazed half-hooded at me. "Why did you get to this one before I did?"

Alexander flooded my mind for a moment. All at once, I remembered my maker and what I was there for, but before I could stand, argue, or at least pivot the conversation, my world melted away.

Annabelle's lips met mine with a hunger that sent shivers down my spine. A sharp intake of air escaped her nostrils as her chest pressed against me, blending our unique energies into an electric dance. My arms encircled her waist, the crimson of my sleeves contrasting vividly against her sleek green latex attire. Fingertips traced a delicate path along the nape of her neck before entwining in the cherry knots atop her head, a playful tug unraveling our passionate kiss.

"Get up," she hissed, her ass giving one last wiggle against my throbbing cock.

Her heels hit the floor as her other hand took hold of the hoodie and pulled me abrasively to my feet. I had no words—any thoughts of Alexander or my companion for the evening were tossed into the gutter of my mind as this Amazonian goddess dragged me through the club and to the back. Everyone's eyes were glued to us as she seemed to care little of who witnessed her sins.

Through another curtain and down the hall, she pulled me along until she finally slammed my back into the wall by what had to be her dressing room. The wall shook with the impact of my large body. Her fingers explored me thoroughly, dancing across the hoodie until she found the zipper, working to undo it. My pectorals and tight abdominal wall were now on full display for any passerby to see, my nipples fiercely erect from my arousal. Those fingers went to work, rubbing my body and making sure to feel every inch of my torso, dragging her nails, leaving red scratch marks over my defined flesh.

"Annabelle, I forgot about—" I tried to finish—anything to remind her of Carver or that evening's mission, but all that I could muster was a labored moan as her lips found my neck. My eyes fluttered closed with the ecstasy of her kiss. "Annabelle..." I tried, failed, and accepted defeat as her teeth bit into my skin as though I were a ripe apple, her fangs piercing the meat to get a taste of me.

She craned her face away for a moment, my blood upon her lips as she stared up and into my eyes. "You taste... so *fresh*. Almost human. Oh god... did you use tonight?"

As she spoke, I watched her pupils expand into saucer plates. Perhaps blood dust wasn't as common as Vincent made it seem, because at that moment, I could tell Annabelle was as high as a kite.

"Jack. Oh no..." she moaned out my name, her hands leaving my torso. One found its way to the back of my raven curls, pulling them in a death grip while the other promptly bypassed the belt I wore to forcefully breach my pants and take hold of the swollen mass, ready and waiting.

"He told me it was..." I inhaled sharply, my fangs sinking into my own lip. "...that it was normal." I tried so hard to speak, but her grip, pumping back and forth, stole the air from my lungs.

"Oh no, Jack. He drugged you. He drugged *us*," she whimpered, trying to shake off the effects of the blood dust and regain her composure.

"He's... ugh fuck... he's my friend... he wouldn't do that," I attempted to argue.

Her wild strokes sent my body into near convulsions as I tried desperately to keep my mind on task, but there was no use.

I could feel my monstrous cock lengthening with one single purpose in mind.

Annabelle finally undid my belt, my pants falling to the floor in a clumsy heap as she pumped harder and faster with less restraint. "No, Jack, he's... oh sweetheart, he's..." She could hardly finish her words as her lips danced their way up my neck, across my jaw, and found purchase upon my own, that forked tongue of hers darting at last behind my teeth, our saliva-drenched tongues twisting and turning against one another in a sick and depraved dance. Our mutual lust silenced any fight we had left.

My hand found the rubbery hem of her dress, shoving it high upon her hips, her cold, wet sex now visible to me. Those plump asscheeks jiggled freely. I wrapped my own hand around my shaft, guiding my throbbing head to press against her slit. Being undead had its benefits... Protection no longer mattered. There was no offspring to sire outside of those born by fang. I pushed hard, my other hand finding her backside and gripping it fiercely, pulling her hard against me as my cock slid inside of her.

She yelped hard, eyes of glowing green rolling back into her skull, her knuckles growing whiter than chalk as she continued to tug at my hair. I began to thrust hard into her, both of our hips slamming in furious passion like two hardened warriors on a battlefield of love and lust. In her moment of weakness, I took advantage, spinning the woman around to slam her back against the wall, pinning her there.

"Fuck! Jack!" she screamed, her other claw dragging against my back, producing trickles of blood.

I pressed my mouth against her ear, my moans replaced with guttural growls and her name again and again and again. I thrust into her with everything I had, proving myself much more than just some fledgling.

"Jack!" she screamed. "Did Vincent leave?" she asked as she tried to hold on for dear life, the intensity of the coming climax causing her to lose her footing. I clutched even tighter to her ass, hooking her legs around my waist as she remained pegged firmly against the wall.

As I grew closer, I attempted to wrack my brain as to why that question was so important, even as we threw our wet sticky bodies against each other. "Annabelle—fuck, he... I don't think so... Maybe, why?" I attempted to have something coherent leave my mouth. It wasn't a total failure.

Continuing the discourse was of no use. The room spun as our bodies tensed, her immense strength almost assuredly breaking a rib as she squeezed me tighter. My body crescendoed, electricity pulsing up my legs and into my face. We climaxed together, crying out until we were both spent and useless heaps.

Annabelle and I rested against the wall staring at one another, completely dumbfounded as to what had just taken place. Her sweat-slicked palm rested against my chest. "Jack, I think Carver sent you to meet Vincent because of the reports..."

I stopped, damp curls hanging loosely as I looked at Annabelle with concern. "What reports?"

Annabelle's brow furrowed. "Reports from the dancers that he may have... abused some of them."

The world spun and realization began to set in.

"Was Penelope one of those reports?" I quickly asked, my mind still reeling from the furious lust that had taken us and the drugs still racing through my empty capillaries.

Annabelle's features sank. "Oh no."

CHAPTER TWENTY-TWO

RATS IN THE WALL

Annabelle and I raced through the club's corridors, a blur of black and red as our hair intertwined with the rush of wind. Our swift steps raised a flutter of interest among onlookers, their curiosity piqued by our urgent passage. However, none dared to impede the Lady and her companion, sensing an aura of purpose that discouraged intrusion.

"Penelope," I urged, my hand splayed against a door.

With a swift motion of my elbow, I pushed it open, revealing a series of smaller rooms that at first appeared empty. A growing sense of frustration gnawed at me as we found nothing —no trace of Vincent or the young girl he professed a desire to reconcile with. Swearing softly, the words materialized as icy puffs in the frigid air, each dressing room I searched yielding nothing. Among the scattered makeup bags and costume racks, the telltale signs of vampiric existence remained elusive.

Annabelle's unease radiated from her, wearing her dread like an exquisite fur cloak. Her emerald eyes scanned the darkness, searching for any hint of the club's smallest dancer.

"Jack," she began, her delicate fingers finding rest on my

shoulder. "I'm going to gather my security team and head downstairs. Maybe someone saw something. Please, keep searching... We'll discuss what happened between us later." Her words turned hush, her fear palpable as it seemed to tighten around her throat like a vice. The woman who usually exuded confidence was now folding in on herself, her vulnerability laid bare.

Clearly, Carver had not given me the full story about Vincent. My own stomach twisted. Had I stumbled again by allowing myself to take my eyes off him?

Observing my vixen as she navigated her way through the club's dim interior, an unwelcome sense of guilt gnawed at my conscience. Did my negligence trigger more calamity, the ripples of chaos spreading like the unfurling petals of deadly nightshade? Perhaps Carver didn't even have the full story, we had unwittingly ushered a predator into Annabelle's sanctuary. The weight of responsibility pressed upon me. Now, it fell upon me to disentangle her from the peril that had materialized.

Minutes dragged on as I searched, each passing moment intensifying my frustration. Where could they have vanished to? Every door I opened revealed the same emptiness, an eerie still-ness that mirrored my growing unease. With each unyielding room, my dread deepened, apprehension creeping in that I might stumble upon something even worse than the silence.

During my frantic search of every nook and cranny, I found myself pausing, my hand finding solace against cool walls, another rack, a pole. Amidst the panic, a lucid thought surfaced, cutting through the chaos like a shard of clarity. I had been manipulated. The realization struck me with a force I hadn't allowed myself to feel since my transformation. I couldn't shoulder all the blame, of course, for Vincent had masterfully performed his role, dancing on the stage of his own sorrow and victimhood like any privileged white man would in the twenty-first century. And I had fallen for it, consumed by his act like a desperate dog lapping up scraps from a kitchen floor.

In his eyes, I had been nothing but a pawn—a means to an end. He had used me to access his intended target, whether it was Penelope or any other girl who had captured his twisted desires. The truth hit me like a cold shower, a stark reminder of how easily I had been misled, and the reality that I needed to confront and dismantle the dangerous game he set in motion.

He played the gentle giant well.

After a week of bewildering confusion, a week of metamorphosis that had changed not only my face but the trajectory of my life, I found it.

Finally, there she was, my revelation: *Anger*.

The culmination of emotions swirled within me—the abandonment of my sister, the elusive connection with a resistant brother, and the sire who had only shown interest in me when his hands were wrapped around my throat, attempting to squeeze the life out of me.

Anger's essence surged through me, a volatile symphony echoing within my ribcage, coursing through every vein. My features twisted, fangs unsheathed in the dim corner of the club. The pulsating lights danced across my ghoulish visage, the enchantment woven around me by glamor magic fulfilling its part of the performance and keeping my more monstrous qualities hidden from human eyes.

"Fuck!" The word exploded from my lips, the torrent of fury tearing through me like an unrelenting tempest. It erupted in a display of violent brilliance, my hand crashing through the surface it had rested against, the once-pristine white wall crumbling beneath my touch. Chips of paint and fragments of drywall cascaded to the floor, the physical manifestation of my inner turmoil.

"What the fuck was that? Shh—shut up! Quiet, you little

fucking bitch—" The words pounded into my eardrums with a piercing clarity. My senses surged to maximum, homing in on the source, originating from the other side of the wall. Extracting my fist from the crumbling hole, I felt the collective gaze of those around me, a mix of confusion and horror reflected in their eyes. Some patrons hurried to the opposite side of the floor, seeking distance, while others remained rooted, transfixed, awaiting the unfolding spectacle. And a spectacle they would assuredly witness.

Turning away from the damage, I strode along the perimeter of the wall, the voices on the other side muffled, as if a desperate effort was being silenced by brute force. Not far from the breach, an emergency staircase door beckoned, a large 'X' scrawled across it, signifying its barred access. I clenched the handle, giving it a soft jiggle. It resisted firmly, but my vampiric strength surged forth, snapping the lock with a forceful yank. The metallic crunch resonated as the metal frame yielded to my will, the safety measure breaking in two. Stepping into the dimly lit stairwell, I caught sight of the dislodged lock trapped in the doorframe as it dangled.

With my first steps, I assessed the space. The narrow staircase stretched upward to the floor above and all the way downward to what presumably lay beneath the ground level. Swinging to close the door behind me, I caught the stares of stunned onlookers. Many of them gazed at me with pure fear, but I had no time for discretion. My objective was to shield their eyes from what I was about to undertake.

Once the door was closed, I walked to the railing, leather boots thudding against the painted stone as my fingers dug into the cold metal. My senses sharpened, my focus directed toward any sound that might emerge from the concrete quiet. Inhaling deeply, I worked to steady my state of mind, coaxing a sense of calm amidst the storm within. My smoldering crimson eyes slid closed, shutting out the world. Time seemed to shift, the pace of reality around me decelerating until it almost halted, the air itself adopting the immobility of death's icy grip. He was near, and I was determined to find him.

Despite the sirens wailing in the city beyond the club, I pushed past their clamor. A woman berated her boyfriend at the top of her lungs for fucking a girl in the bathroom stall in his drunken stupor, wet sticky bodies slamming against each other on the dance floor—all of that ceased as I zeroed in on one direction. It led me down the stairwell. Frustration pulled down my brow. The destination became clear, yet one question remained: Where was he?

Coming to a standstill, I allowed a few more illusory breaths to fill my useless lungs, my mind quieting to grant my vampiric abilities space to flourish. Silence enveloped me, punctuated by the faint scuttling of a mouse within the walls. Then, a floor below, a woman's muffled attempts to speak, her voice stifled by a hand, and the squeak of shoes against hardwood. As I honed in on what I believed to be Vincent and Penelope, my tranquility wavered. The rage within my heart ignited like a can of gasoline, Vincent the spark that ignited it.

Once again, reality faded, and the energies swirling in the atmosphere merged with my being. My eyes absorbed the mingling forces, my body trembling as my very essence synchronized with the oscillations of the airwaves. I became a blur, like Hermes himself, the god of speed. Momentum surged through me as I hurtled toward the source of the sound, instinct propelling me toward my target—to uncover a traitor.

The stairwell was gone in an instant, my body crashing through the doorway entrance to the floor below, the metal face caving inwards from the supernatural blow. To my luck, I found myself on a floor uninhabited by the sex-fueled patrons and staff from the *Gilded Rose*. There was not a single living soul in that area, in fact.

The door clattered to the floor before me, revealing a new, mirrored room: a dark dance hall that was meant for the girls to practice their routines, no doubt. The thin layer of dust across the floor made it clear, however, that the space hadn't been utilized in quite some time. Perhaps that was the reason the stairwell's entry was closed off.

The floor beneath me was an expanse of cold wood, stretching toward the surrounding walls. Translucent tinting coated the window panels, casting a shade that barred the sun's eager intrusion. Dim lighting played upon the metal elevator doors at the side, causing them to shimmer faintly. Positioned across from me, the mirror on the opposite wall reflected my entrance. I observed myself briefly, my gaze then slipping beyond the mirror's frame, past it to the hallway adjacent, leading to another unseen space. There, in the shadows, was where I needed to be.

With cautious steps, I navigated the darkness. The muffled sounds of whimpers reached my ears, stifled by a heavy hand that clamped down on cherubic cheeks, suppressing any hint of noise.

"Vincent!" My growl filled the air, a guttural warning that echoed through the space.

As I moved, the mirror once again caught my eye, reflecting back my form with unsettling crimson hues emanating from my eye sockets. The depths of the darkness no longer obstructed my vision; instead, it was as if I had merged with the night itself, my perception unimpeded by the absence of light. A reassurance, indeed, given the nature of my newfound existence.

My footsteps resonated on the polished floor as I approached the hallway, my focus directed toward the source of the whimpering. The sounds grew clearer, a beacon guiding me closer. Step by step, I advanced, drawn to the door at the side. Its surface was shrouded in darkness, and a sense of energy seemed to emanate from it, a sensation I could almost taste on my tongue.

"JACK!" The cry of a smaller woman ripped through the area.

I rushed towards her, another voice responding. "Shut up. Shut *up, you* fucking bitch!"

Then came the sick sound of heavy knuckles meeting flesh. My pace hastened with the horrific realization of what was taking place. My gaze landed on the restroom sign as I ended my approach, the simplistic image of a woman standing just above.

With a swift, twisting motion, my body coiled like a tightly wound spring. My fist clenched, and the nascent talons emerging from my fingertips dug into my palm, eliciting pain that kept me anchored in the moment. The agony was necessary. Blood welled over my palm where the talons breached the skin, a testament to my growing ferocity.

My arm snapped forward like the lash of a whip, fist meeting the door's wooden surface with an impact that reverberated through the air. The entry yielded under the onslaught, splitting down the middle. Splinters erupted like shrapnel, littering the bathroom tiles below. Half of the door plummeted to the ground with a resounding crash, a noise that surely drew the attention of the patrons above. Their alarmed screams filtered through the building, intermingling with the chaos that was about to unfold.

I welcomed the bedlam, embraced it as a necessary cover for the mess that was about to transpire. In this moment, it was just me, Penelope, and the treacherous bastard, Vincent Esposito.

As I entered the room, my glare drank in the darkness,

unveiling a sight I wished I could unsee. It was a tableau of horror, etched into my vision with painful clarity. There, shrouded in the obscurity of heavy shadow, was a scene that elicited a sickening churn within me.

Vincent's monstrous grip closed around Penelope's delicate throat, the stark contrast between his massive hand and her smaller frame almost surreal. Her face was a canvas of violence, marred by blood and bruises. Her split lip mirrored the jagged wound that marred Vincent's own birth as if fate had conspired to align their suffering. Blood tears streamed down her face, mingling with the traces of her ordeal.

Her orange eyes, once vibrant, now swelled and bloodshot, bore testament to the agony she had endured. Against her near-nude form, Vincent loomed, his intent evident in the crude forcefulness of his presence. Yet, he seemed to have met resistance. Penelope fought with a ferocity born of desperation, her smaller frame pitted against his monstrous advances. His features bore the scratches and gashes of her struggle, his teal eyes wild and untamed, exuding a feral madness far beyond what I had witnessed before. The colors of his eyes seemed to smolder in the dim light, reflecting back at me with an eerie intensity.

The air was heavy with tension, a malevolent dance of power and vulnerability playing out before me. At that moment, my resolve solidified. Vincent's reign of terror would end here, and Penelope would be free from his clutches.

Mangled lips pulled across his face, that hair lip twisting with his distaste for my involvement. "Jackie, little buddy... What are you doin' here?" As his bellowing New York accent invaded the room, his demeanor softened. He still tried to play the friend card he had worked so hard to pull from the deck. "This, it isn't what it looks like..."

Her small voice interrupted his, muffled by the hand around

her throat squeezing her windpipe to restrict her from speaking. "Help."

Enough was enough; I refused to be a pawn in his games any longer. With an explosion of fury, I propelled myself forward, my body slicing through the air like a projectile, colliding with him much as I had with the door. The force of the impact sent him reeling, stumbling away from his position and releasing Penelope from his clutches. Her freedom was hard-won, her form tumbling against the sink in a chaotic ballet of escape.

Vincent's body crashed into a bathroom stall, the door giving way under his bulk, folding inward as he struggled to regain his composure from the shock of my sudden burst of speed.

"Jackie, you're a fast one—I'll admit, I didn't see that coming!" His veneer of casualness overlaid the tumult beneath. He extended his massive hands, arms converging in a bid to entrap me, to neutralize the perceived threat I posed. But his fatal miscalculation lay in underestimating my capabilities. He thought of me as a mere pest, an annoyance to be swatted away. In truth, I was a venomous wasp, capable of delivering a lethal sting.

Beneath his raised arms, I maneuvered, my fist driving into the soft midsection of his tracksuit, just above the zipper. The impact struck his lower ribs, the bones giving easily to the force before snapping with a sickening crack. A primal howl of anguish erupted from him, the sound a raw symphony of pain that reverberated through the cramped space. Feet stomped overhead. Our pandemonium caused an instinctual response from the patrons above to flee from the violence unfolding in the hidden depths below.

Vincent attempted to retaliate, arms descending upon me with renewed desperation. His strength met my resolve as his limbs collided with my back, sending my body careening against the peach and white checkered floor.

"You little *FUCK*! This is how you repay me?" His fist seized a handful of my hoodie, his grip unyielding as he exerted all his strength.

With a swift motion, he tugged with a force that threatened to tear the fabric from my body. His arm twisted, the motion calculated to send my body hurtling into the air before veering off, aiming to propel me directly into the wall.

The collision was fierce, the force of the impact causing expensive fixtures to crash to the floor, revealing the wall's skeletal structure as its hidden layers were laid bare.

In response, Vincent's laughter growled forth, a twisted amusement that filled the air. "Tiny little bastard, you really thought you were something? Nah, kid, I've got at least fifty years on you. No way you're gonna overpower *me*," he taunted, heavy footsteps resounding as he bore down on my prone form.

His approach was swift, a relentless charge as he closed the distance between us like a bull. In a surge of motion, Vincent lunged forward, his grip finding the dusty expanse of my shirt's back. He lifted me from the ground, elevating me with an uncanny strength. His hands adjusted, fingers encircling my throat with an ironclad grip. Darkness began to encroach on my vision, a shroud that blurred my surroundings, rendering them almost unrecognizable.

His hold was unrelenting. It throttled my windpipe and sent my mind racing. Pain and desperation converged, urging what remained of my nerves to fire with frantic energy. In response, I writhed and contorted like a fish out of water, my body attempting to wrest free from the vice-like hold that threatened to extinguish me.

"*VINCENT STOP!*" Amidst the struggle, Penelope's voice

pierced the air with a guttural scream, her desperation tangible as she reached out.

Her fingers clung to the fabric of Vincent's track pants, an attempt to pry him away from his ruthless assault on me. His attention wavered, torn between his savage determination to harm me and the girl fighting for her life at his feet. His gaze shifted, no longer fixated solely on me, his distorted grimace shifting to take in her figure sprawled against the bathroom cabinets.

"What, you soft for this one, now? I'm never enough, am I?" His voice dripped with bitterness, accusation laced through his words.

He acted with swift brutality, wrenching his leg back to free himself from her clutch, and then launching his boot forward. The impact of his kick struck Penelope's chest, propelling her backward until she collided with the cabinet, the force of the blow audible in the resounding crunch that followed.

Seizing the opening his distraction granted me, I acted. My fists clenched anew, and I brought them down like hammers on either side of his face, my strikes connecting with his battered countenance. The blows landed with a vengeance, the rhythmic thuds echoing over all the porcelain and glass. At first, the impact of my strikes seemed to leave him unaffected, his attention returning to me, his twisted laughter resuming its eerie cadence.

"Is that it? All you've got are those tiny things?" His taunt rang out, mocking my efforts.

But within me, a fiery resolve blazed. The anger that had smoldered within my chest ignited, becoming a force that rushed through my veins, fueling my determination to push back against the monster before me.

I will protect her.

The rhythmic impacts transformed into a relentless

onslaught, each wet slap upon his face akin to a wrecking ball, his flesh absorbing the force of my blows. His features, once twisted with sadistic amusement, now broke under each strike as his head whipped violently from side to side. His feet stumbled in reverse, the urgency to distance himself from my ferocity palpable in his every movement.

My fangs bared in response to the adrenaline swelling in my veins, the sensation of my gums burning as they extended my ivory weapons to their full length. A guttural scream escaped my lips, a primal sound that echoed through the bathroom's confines, reverberating off the walls. The crimson hues of my eyes cast an eerie glow upon his face, painting his features in the same vivid colors that filled my view.

Despite his desperate attempts to crush the unlife from me, my survival didn't hinge on the intake of breath. His weakening grip faltered, the strength he had sought to exert dwindling in the face of my unwavering determination. In the moments of his disarray, and his confusion, I shifted tactics. My brutal fists morphed into outstretched fingers, bony claws of ivory extending to their razor-sharp potential.

With a fervor fueled by anger and vengeance, I launched myself at him anew, each slashing motion designed to cleave flesh from bone. Chunks of his face were torn away under the force of my onslaught, an unrestrained brutality that seemed to hail from the depths of a nightmare. It was as if a demonic specter had been summoned from the crossroads, demanding its pound of flesh from a fumbled deal.

Vincent's movements were uncoordinated, a mix of agony and fear propelling his clumsy retreat. He collided with the frame of the bathroom stall, the impact resounding with a thunder.

"That's enough of that!" he bellowed, his fingers tightening around my throat once more. He lifted me over his head, his immense strength evident as he propelled my body forward with a force that defied reason. I was sent hurtling through the doorframe, the same one I had splintered upon my entrance, and I crashed into the adjacent wall.

The back of my head struck with a jarring intensity, stars bursting in my vision as the impact reverberated through my skull. Blood seeped within my ears, a sinister echo of the ensuing war. My sight was tinged in red, a haze that shrouded my surroundings. Through that haze, I witnessed the lumbering giant's approach, his massive form barreling toward where I lay discarded.

Penelope's body rested on the floor nearby, a testament to her endurance, her unlife preserved despite the brutality she had encountered. It struck me then: I had drawn Vincent away from her, diverted his attention, and now, as he closed in on me, I felt the shackles of restraint fall away. The fury, the anger, the unquenchable thirst for justice surged through me, igniting a fire that would not be extinguished easily. I was prepared to let loose, to unleash the storm.

"Carver sent you to keep an eye on me. I figured it out the moment I saw you... empty-headed pretty boy with barely any bite—had to be a setup. Get me to do somethin' stupid with my guard down. And you know what? I did. And I don't regret it."

Vincent's fingers closed around tufts of my hair, gripping them with an ironclad hold that radiated pain through my scalp. His hand poised menacingly, ready to deliver yet another brutal blow to my already battered face. He regarded me with a twisted sort of scrutiny, his teal eyes glinting in the subdued illumination of the bathroom.

"Little things like you don't deserve the gifts of your beauty. It should be *ME*," he spat, his voice a venomous snarl that seethed with envy.

His fist exploded forward, colliding with my cheek in a sickening impact. Pain radiated through my face, the force of his blow sending my head reeling to the side. Blood pooled in my mouth, and I choked on its sweet, rusty taste, my fangs digging into my lip as if in a desperate bid to draw out the torment.

His words continued to spill forth, a twisted tapestry woven from his bitterness and resentment. "Instead, I repel every female in town—laughed at, mocked. They won't touch me with a ten-foot pole... unless I force 'em to." His admission was a disturbing revelation, a window into the darkness that pervaded his existence.

As my vision swirled in disarray, I braced for the impending onslaught. My body was battered, my strength waning, but within me, an ember of defiance still glowed. Despite the pain and the chaos, I clung to that ember, determined to use it as a spark to fight back against the relentless storm that Vincent embodied.

A moment of disorientation dissolved as I locked eyes with the giant vampire, and the ephemeral shimmering of his features gave way to a newfound clarity. The specter of my father loomed before me, an incarnation of the cruelty and torment I had dealt with in my past. In that moment, all I saw was my opportunity to finally fight back.

"You know what, old man?" I growled, my words a gritty challenge that resonated with the weight of my history. I savored the taste of my own vitae in my mouth, a reminder of my otherworldly existence. "It's not about the looks, it's about personality... and yours is shit. You're just a poor excuse for a man. You hurt women to raise yourself up, because deep down inside... you know it isn't about the size of your micro penis, it's about how filthy your heart is. That's why they won't touch you, Vincent, it's because you're a monster in more ways than one."

My words cut deep, each syllable a scathing indictment of his character. His eyes widened in the darkness, a wild glare that mirrored the headlights of an oncoming eighteen-wheeler barreling down a highway. His teeth ground against each other, his thick cheeks jiggling with the force of his pent-up rage. A primal war cry erupted from his lips, spittle flying into the air as the lines etched across his face deepened in his fury. A singular lid twitched with his frustration, a twitch that betrayed his unraveling composure.

With a ferocity akin to a hurricane, his balled fist hurtled toward me. The air itself seemed to warp around the broken and cracked knuckles as they bore the force of his attack. His meaty appendage raced forward, a juggernaut of fury aimed directly at my face.

At the precipice of desperation, my resolve hardened to its peak. As Vincent's massive fist hurtled toward me, I summoned every ounce of strength and agility I possessed. With a violent wrench, I contorted my neck with a ferocity that ripped the strands of hair he gripped. The strands tore from my scalp, leaving nothing but tatters within his clenched fingers. This brief moment of liberation granted me the space I needed to evade his strike, to move my head back and away from the trajectory of his attack—a sudden twist that caught him off guard.

"What?!" His exclamation was a breathless mixture of disbelief and surprise, his words escaping in a stunned rush. But I wasn't done yet.

With a speed that seemed to defy the laws of nature, I gunned forward, my movements a blur that outpaced his comprehension. The world around us seemed to slow, the temporal manipulation of my vampiric gift granting me a moment of clarity in the midst of chaos.

My jaw unhinged with a serpentine grace, mimicking the predatory action of a snake striking its prey. In one fluid motion, I brought the full force of my elongated fangs down upon his flesh, puncturing and tearing into the tender meat of his clenched fingers. The sensation was a visceral one, the taste of his blood flooding my mouth as I drank him in, savoring the metallic tang of his life force.

Vincent's scream shattered the air, a cacophony of agony that reverberated in the confined space. He struggled, his shoulder rolling back in a desperate attempt to dislodge me from his hand. But I was unyielding, my grip steady as I bore down with the force of my assault. His fingers twitched and writhed, his efforts to remove me growing increasingly frantic.

The fingers that had once tangled in my hair now clawed at my face, a futile attempt to free himself from my relentless grip. His palm and then the back of his hand slapped against my cheekbones in a frantic rhythm, a physical plea for release that was underpinned by the grim knowledge of the inevitable outcome of my assault. I was akin to a pit bull, my jaw locked rigorously onto its prey. The truth was inescapable: the only way to extricate me was to kill me.

With another wrench of my head and a fierce clenching of my jaw, I sensed the core of his knuckles give way. The taste was divine against my secluded tongue, its fluids spreading to saturate my throat in a cascade of crimson. Vincent staggered in retreat, his grip on me unraveling as he gazed upon the wreckage of his hand in disbelief. His focus fixated on the macabre sight before him: the ends of some of his fingers dangling from the rest of his hand by mere threads, while others lay discarded and twitching upon the floor.

"*YOU FUCKER! YOU SON OF A GOD DAMNED WHORE!*" he screamed. "This will take months to heal! *MONTHS!*"

Distracted by the sight of his mangled fingers, Vincent's attention was drawn away, giving rise to an entirely novel sensation, one I had yet to experience. Vampire blood coursed through my veins, infusing me with an entirely different kind of potency, unlike anything I had encountered before. Waves of raw power surged within me, the undead sanguine energy providing not just strength but an intoxicating vitality surpassing the satisfaction derived from human blood.

In an instant, a torrent of memories flooded my consciousness, each one originating from Vincent's perspective. Vivid recollections unfurled before my inner sight—the moments he had shared with Penelope, his emotions leading up to my arrival downstairs, and the repugnant scene where he had imposed himself on her, his unwelcome hands violating her nearly bare form. The resonance of murder reverberated through my thoughts, its anguished notes resonating deeply within me.

Vincent's awkward movements drew my gaze as he swayed unsteadily, the once imposing figure now hunched over, desperate to locate what had been severed from the base of his knuckles. His remaining hand fumbled over the mutilated digits, a mourning touch for what had been lost.

"You prey on the weak because it makes you feel powerful, when deep down inside you're just a shamble of a man crying for what you feel is owed to you. You're pathetic, and to think... I pitied you, I was so ready to believe you were some misunderstood creature—a phantom in the belly of some opera house wishing for love. No, you're just a dog, and you'll die like one. Rapists belong in one place and one alone; in the gutter choking on their own blood. I'll make sure that's where you end up, when you've screamed your last scream I'll see to it that your ashes are scattered somewhere befitting a lowly maggot like yourself." My words hummed through the darkness as I towered over his fallen form.

It was a foreign sensation. *Power*. I liked it.

Vincent stared up at me, his vibrant orbs reflecting both agony and bewilderment, his features contorted in pain. "What the fuck are you, kid?" he managed to rasp out amidst his suffering.

I loomed above him, a relentless force. "I am the Vampire Jack Townson," I declared with certain authority.

With those words, a surge of newfound strength propelled me into action, each of my fists becoming a blur as they rained down upon him. Empowered by the dark gift I was gradually mastering, my speed doubled, transforming my blows into a relentless barrage, just as Aiden had with Claude.

Desperation led Vincent to raise his hands in a futile attempt at defense, but it proved futile. The damage inflicted was too severe, his tracksuit succumbing to the onslaught as fabric tore and shredded, debris swirling through the air as my ferocious assault continued unabated.

"Stop! *STOP*! I give! I fucked up, I'm just—"

"You're what? *SAY IT*! Convince me—tell me everything you want me to hear while that poor girl lays crumpled on the bathroom floor!" I cried.

My voice was unrecognizable to even myself, more of a snarling beast than any trace of the humanity I possessed only moments earlier. Vincent's feet slid back as my blows sent his body across the floor and into the wall, the power of each hit causing cracks to chip and spread like veins across its face.

"I will never let men like you go unpunished, do you hear me?" I cocked my arm back and I could feel it shaking from its raised position, my fist covered in the older vampire's blood as he lay crumpled against the wall. His own fluids slicked his lumpy flesh as he sputtered blood in his attempts to speak.

"J-Jackie... s-stop—" Vincent attempted, his throat and mouth swollen. "We-we're pals... d-..." he tried and failed.

I held back my fist for a moment. "Go on. Say what you wanted to say," I growled, my eyes mad with frenzy.

"Don't-... make me... like that poor girl... you fuckin' murdered..."

His face contorted into a sinister grin, a cacophony of laughter erupting from his massive belly. That was the breaking point for me. Without hesitation, my fist collided with his sternum with a finite crunch, the hard bone giving way and caving inward. A wheeze escaped him, his body teetering on the edge of collapse, but I was far from finished.

My claws extended eagerly, sinking into the flesh of his shoulders. His jaw dropped slack, his eyes widening as a fresh wave of agony coursed through him. Feeble hands weakly clung to my wrists, a futile attempt to alleviate the excruciating pressure, but even that was in vain. He was about to embark on a one-way trip, and I was fast-tracking him there. With a swift twist of my hip and a decisive pivot of my body, I unleashed a primal cry, channeling all the newfound power coursing through me. My talons clenched fiercely, hurtling the man with unbridled force towards the mirror positioned on the opposite side of the bathroom.

The impact was thunderous, a resounding crash and shatter as the mirror exploded into a barrage of gleaming shards. They impaled his body in a hail of glittering death before he plummeted to the floor in a crumpled heap. His face was now a grotesque distortion of its former self. I approached his fallen form, my talons coated in his blood, their macabre sheen contrasting eerily with the dim, tinted light seeping through the windows. The time for closure had come, and I was resolute in fulfilling my vow. This was the fate he had earned, the fate he deserved.

"JACK!"

A voice echoed from the shattered entrance, and my focus swiftly darted to discern the source. There stood Annabelle, her expression a canvas of horror as she beheld the monstrous tableau I had wrought. With each click of her heels against the ground, she hurried toward me, emerald eyes pulsating through the dimness as she navigated the shadows.

"Jack, oh fuck, what have you done..." Her gaze remained locked on the mutilated form of the once formidable Vincent Esposito, her wide eyes reflecting a mix of disbelief and revulsion. "Jack!"

My response was silence, my senses a whirlwind from the amalgamation of my adversary's potent blood and my own.

"Where is Penelope? Jack..." Annabelle pressed urgently.

Her hand settled on my shoulder, a touch meant to anchor me amidst the storm of my own making. This time, her attempt at connection bore greater weight, my gaze gradually trailing toward the entrance of the female restroom at the rear. Her slender fingers released my blood-stained hoodie as she dashed to investigate, her heels resuming their sharp rhythm against the floor.

A scream, her soft voice ripping into the air as she found the poor girl in a mess on the tile.

I turned to walk over to the door that was in splinters, my talons still extended at my side. "I tried."

Annabelle clung to Penelope with fierce determination, her fingers brushing aside disheveled black strands from the girl's face. Her once-neat ponytail had been undone in the harrowing struggle for her undead survival. Tears, like softly flowing rivers of blood, cascaded down onto Penelope's face and neck. The pain of her friend's ordeal mingled with Annabelle's own frustration at not having been the one to confront Vincent as I had. With both hands, she carefully lowered Penelope's head to rest upon her lap, leaving traces of crimson upon the muted shine of the latex.

I lingered over them, a silent observer, steadfastly watching the poignant scene unfold. I remained until the security detail arrived, not wanting to leave either of them alone until assurance could be found in the form of capable hands to handle Vincent's aftermath. It wasn't that Annabelle couldn't handle the situation herself, but rather that I wanted to shield her from having to do so.

Men in impeccably tailored suits flooded the room. I winced as revelation hit me. They had been absent from their posts when we first arrived. I noted their conspicuous absence and the enigma of their sudden vanishing act upon Vincent's arrival. It was a question that would demand attention at another time, after the immediate crisis had been addressed.

Leaving Annabelle to her staff, I exited through the obliterated door and found myself back in the stairwell. It was a chance for both me and my red-headed *'friend'* to find the space we might need in the wake of the ordeal. I retrieved the gifted cell phone from my pocket, and finally took a moment to check my messages.

As I distanced myself, I activated the screen, revealing a series of missed texts from the previous evening. They were all from a concerned Alexander, a mix of curses and uppercase letters, many of them in French. I couldn't help but wonder what he might have known or discovered to warrant such frustration. With a swipe, I dismissed the notifications. I wasn't ready to let him know that I had read them.

Among the messages, I noticed a text from Carver.

I imagine things went well this evening.

I paused, my smoldering glare shifting from the phone to the wreckage I left behind—the destroyed door and the room painted in blood. After a moment of contemplation, I typed out a response.

> You knew this was going to go out of hand, didn't you?

The phone immediately went to symbols of Carver's swift hand typing...

> Did you discover anything important?

> Yeah, I did. Vincent isn't just a pig, he's a serial abuser, but you probably knew that.

I had my suspicions. The reports... I couldn't decide if they were true. No one would go with Vincent, and Annabelle surely didn't want him there alone. I couldn't just allow a coeval to walk unpunished if the accusations were true. I had to get a trusted pair of eyes on him.

What better way than a beautiful new fledgling on his arm to pull in the ladies?

> And he would feel confident... because I was so new?

> Precisely. Did it go accordingly?

Vincent almost murdered one of the dancers and tried to do the same to me.

There was a pause in our conversation. Carver's dots stopped and started over and over again.

> Jack, are you alright? I hope you aren't hurt.

> I'm fine... a bit beat up but I've had worse. He won't be...

We'll talk soon, I want to be fully
brought up to speed.

I powered down the phone and slid it back into the home against my leg. This world was strange and confusing... a web of games that I didn't quite understand, but I knew only one thing... a monster had been taught a valuable lesson, and I had done my part to keep a friend safe. Poor Penelope.

Amidst the pain and horror, amidst the wreckage and chaos, one undeniable truth stood clear—I hadn't failed her. In the wake of this transformation, this rebirth of identity, the curse that had haunted me for so long seemed to shatter at last. I was no longer shackled by the specter of failure.

As I began to turn, intending to ascend the stairs, the distinctive sound of Annabelle's spiked heels echoed against the floor. My blood-smeared face shifted, capturing the sight of her alluring figure as she drew near. There, in the shadows just beyond the doorframe, she cradled her arms around her form-fitting dress. Her face was marked by trails of blood tears, her vulnerability exposed, while her security detail lingered behind, providing solace to Penelope.

"Is she... going to be alright?" I asked, a hesitance straining my voice.

A false pulse still beat violently behind my eyes from the effects of the adrenaline and the harsh fluorescent lighting of the emergency stairwell. Fear gripped me, and a haunting question remained locked within my mind: Would the girl truly recover from this ordeal?

"She's a resilient soul, but I fear it will be quite some time before she finds a sense of safety again," the lady of the club admitted, exhaling a breath that seemed to carry a weight of its own. Her hand lifted, sweeping across her cheeks to clear away the trails of blood. "Your intervention saved a dear friend," she added, her voice a mixture of gratitude and relief.

Annabelle's emerald eyes moved from where they had fallen on the railing to lock onto mine, an unspoken connection forming between us. My gaze, somewhat awkwardly, averted from the intensity of her stare.

"Jack," her voice broke the silence, carrying a sincere earnestness. "About what I said earlier before everything happened... I want you to know I'm sorry. My resentment wasn't directed at you. I'm immensely grateful you were here."

With the urgency of her feelings, she closed the distance between us, enveloping me in her embrace once more, drawing me close against her bosom.

Our eyes locked, igniting a familiar sensation, reminiscent of that heated encounter in the hallway where our bodies had collided. It was a magnetic pull, a tantalizing temptation to press my lips against hers once more. Yet, this time, her arms acted as a barrier, pushing me away gently. Her soft features twisted into a grimace, a mix of emotions playing across her expression.

"It's late, and dawn is approaching. Your sire is probably worried about you. You should... leave," she urged.

A sigh escaped me, acknowledging the truth in her words. With a resigned nod, I turned to depart, feeling her hand grip mine for a brief moment before her lips met my cheek in a fleeting kiss.

"We do need to talk eventually... about all of this. But now isn't the time or place. Goodnight, Jack Townson," her words lingered in the air as I made my way back up the stairs and into the club.

The scene was now abandoned, patrons scattered as if a bomb had gone off.

Pausing for a moment, a heavy feeling settled upon me. I

had to return to the place that had become my home, yet an intense longing tugged at me to break away, to embrace this newfound existence and revel in the mastery of the night. What if I didn't want to go back to Alexander? Shaking my head, I pivoted on my heel and headed toward the elevator. This time, there was ample space within the carriage, given my oafish companion's absence now. His fate was well deserved.

As the night drew closer to its end, the first rays of sunlight creeping beyond the horizon, I recognized the time had come to conclude my mission and return to the Prepotent. The situation with Alexander remained shrouded in uncertainty, and a sense of foreboding accompanied my thoughts of homecoming. Amidst the chaos I had found myself amidst, a new perspective began to crystallize—I wasn't merely the catalyst or instigator of these events. Rather, I had become a tool, an instrument wielded for a grander purpose. Though that purpose remained enigmatic, it was this understanding that allowed me to see my role in vanquishing an actual monster's reign of terror and restoring some semblance of tranquility to a friend's life.

With a simulated exhale of breath and the casual sweep of my hand to push back a few ebony strands, I brought my phone into view. My fingers navigated to find Chester's number, a contact I hadn't recognized earlier but now considered a potential ally. My text messages were succinct, emphasizing the urgency of my immediate extraction from the scene. Almost as if by premonition, his car was already stationed at the front, poised and ready.

It seemed Carver had briefed the Ghoul, furnishing him with the details necessary to prompt his swift arrival at the *Rose*. As I exited the elevator with a burst of energy, I spotted the passenger door wide open, beckoning me through the plate glass windows.

From the boutique's front door, I erupted, the splashes of

highly saturated red and green neon dousing me in their colors before fading with my dive into the large black SUV. Chester snorted, his hands gripping the wheel as he watched me hurry to fasten my seatbelt.

"'Ey, man, we need to scoot so move faster next time," he growled, his frustration palpable.

His fingers drummed impatiently against the surface of the steering wheel, his attention consumed by the traffic. I cast a quick inspection over myself, my crimson eyes sweeping across my disheveled form. I was indeed a sight to behold, looking as though I had emerged from a war zone—blood splatters adorned my face, my hair was in disarray, and the powder from debris clung to the designer hoodie that I practically lived in. However, despite my appearance, the driver showed no inclination to inquire about my well-being or the state I was in. His gaze remained fixed ahead, waiting for the unending wall of cars to disperse so he could navigate onto the road.

"Not going to ask if I'm alright?" I questioned, a tinge of hurt seeping into my tone.

My innocence, my hope for empathy, was still evident. Chester's response was a simple, resolute shake of his head. The tires squealed as he accelerated onto the road, the force causing my body to jostle within the seat. Grateful for my foresight in fastening my seatbelt, I braced myself against the movement, reflecting on the lack of concern from the one individual I had assumed might show some semblance of care.

"Woah," I shouted, my hands clutching the '*Oh shit*' handle attached to the ceiling of the car. "What's going on? Why the intensity?!"

Chester seemed altogether different than he did during our earlier ride to the club.

"Jackie, I need to focus. We need to get you back home and I need to get away from you pronto." He cleared his throat, brows furrowed in concentration as his gaze remained fixed on the road ahead, navigating skillfully through the traffic that didn't meet his preferred speed. Meanwhile, I offered a slight shake of my tangled curls, my attempt to regain clarity amidst the whirlwind that had defined the night.

"Give me something, anything, come on..." I found myself practically whining, the undercurrent of worry palpable in the air, its weight hanging like a noose around my neck. The Ghoul beside me seemed to sense the tension, responding to my unease.

"Fine—fine! Carver said *NOTHIN'* about what you were going to do in there. I thought you were a—well, y'know, a soft guy! Pretty boy with velvet for hands or some shit. I didn't know you were going to almost merc a made man!" Chester's words struck me, a term I had heard before—'*made man*.' It sparked a recognition within me.

"*Made* man, like in those old Mafia movies?" I ventured, seeking clarification. Chester's response was immediate, a firm shake of his head followed by a sharp slap of his palm against the steering wheel.

"No, you putz! Like the real deal, but worse... like the *Family*" he muttered.

My brow raised with my intrigue. "The *Family*? Okay, clear that up a bit for me. How bad is this?"

Chester practically snarled as he responded, the gravity of the situation evident in his tone. "Jackie, it's bad—REALLY bad. They have this uh... what are they called," he struggled to recall for a moment, his fingers snapping near his head in a futile attempt to jog his memory, "Dark Gifts. They have this Dark Gift that allows them to do this remote viewing thing. It's almost like a hive mind. Imagine the mob, but everyone under the big boss can turn on their television at home to see what sort of trouble the others are in. It all stems from Papa Alessio, their sire. He's old—somethin' around four hundred years. Guy came over during the early 20th century and started moving immediately."

The revelation hit me like a tidal wave, a torrent of information crashing over my senses. I sat in my seat, endeavoring to absorb the jumbled words of fear that Chester conveyed. As his voice washed over me, I couldn't help but feel a creeping sensation—was I about to face the dire consequences of my actions? The city lights outside seemed to blur as I began to disconnect from the present, the savage struggle to save a friend from a monstrous fiend juxtaposed against the potential peril I now faced. Despite the apprehension that clawed at my heart, one truth remained steadfast: I didn't regret what I had done.

My fingers threaded their way up through my hair, claws raking through the thick strands in a display of pent-up tension. My palm settled over my eyes, temporarily smothering their fiery glow in the midst of my panic. "What do we do?"

Chester's head snapped to the side, his gaze fixing on me with a quizzical, cockeyed expression. "Sorry, boss, there's no 'we' in this. You've got your own shit to take care of, and I'm goin' home! We don't know each other like that," the Ghoul grumbled, his attention briefly shifting to the road before returning to me. He continued, a hint of gruff advice seeping into his tone, "If I were you, I'd get in touch with Carver and lay low for the time being. Maybe your sire can reach out to Alessio and smooth things over. I'm sure you had your reasons for what you did... for your sakes, I hope there were some damn good reasons."

With his words echoing in my mind, I found myself grappling with the magnitude of the situation. The options laid out before me were uncertain, and the consequences of my actions had woven a complex web of potential outcomes. Yet, amid the turmoil and uncertainty, one thing remained clear: I had made a stand, I had taken action, and even in the face of potential danger, I couldn't find it in me to regret my choices.

I stared blankly at the sputtering half-dead as he went off. "He was molesting the girls in the club," I murmured.

Chester's brows raised as his head bobbed from side to side, "Alright, shit... that's a good reason. That's... well fuck, good on you. But still. Let's hope that the Family understands your reasoning."

All I could do was stare out the window, my gaze fixed on the streams of burning yellow, blues, and reds that painted the cityscape. As the city rushed by, thoughts of the evening's events whirled within my mind, the weight of the night's actions pressing heavily upon my crimson-clad shoulders. The certainty of having done the right thing clashed with the realization that these mafiosos wouldn't perceive it that way. They had witnessed me pummeling their comrade within an inch of his unlife—though I hadn't succeeded in killing him, the intent was unmistakable.

My thoughts spun like inner cogs attempting to interlock, but instead, they stripped the mental gears bare. My mind was a whirlpool of uncertainty, and I found myself ensnared within it. There seemed to be no way out of this situation, my fate precariously balanced on the actions of my ghoulish driver. With mounting anticipation, I clung to one thought: that Alexander would intervene, that he would protect me.

My fingers delved into my pockets, retrieving my phone once more. My fingers deftly navigated the interface to locate Alexander's number. Pressing the call button, I held the phone to my head, the sound of ringing echoing in my ears as I waited for him to answer, my heart pounding in anticipation.

Ring-ring. Ring-ring. Ring-ring. "You've reached the cellphone of the one, the only, Alexander La Mont, please leave a message after the tone."

He would be a savant, yet have the most unceremonious and cliché voicemail I'd ever heard. I began to speak, my voice trembling, as I was ill-prepared for the news I had just received. "Alexander, it's Jack. I'm in some trouble, and I could use your help... I'm kind of scar—"

Before I could complete my sentence, the car jerked violently to the side with a metallic crunch. Chester and I were flung about the SUV like ragdolls. Something had struck us. My head became a ping-pong ball, colliding with the dashboard and side window repeatedly, the force shattering the glass. As the car tumbled across the street, the asphalt dangerously close to my face as we flipped, I couldn't help but think of the earlier incident with Aiden that had prompted me to fasten my seatbelt. Thankfully, my foresight paid off. However, a quick glance told me that Chester hadn't learned that lesson, as his body careened wildly within the cabin.

"CHESTER! CHESTER, HOLD ON! GRAB MY HAND!" I screamed, my voice lost amidst the chaotic symphony of destruction that enveloped us. I reached out desperately, my fingers extending, hoping he would take them. My seatbelt anchored me, saving me from a similar fate.

"*CHESTER!*" I shouted again, his eyes meeting mine momentarily in the midst of his disoriented tumbling.

His face twisted into an expression of terror. Amidst the chaos, my own Dark Gifts activated, briefly slowing down the world around me. But despite my powers, there was little I could do. The windshield shattered from the outside, fiberglass fragments suspended in the air like frozen raindrops. Chester's expression of dread remained etched in my vision.

Fumbling with the seatbelt, my hands moved with blurring speed, fighting to undo it. My grip tightened around the belt, and I tore it from its base. As the world began to catch up to me, I found myself flailing from the momentum, barely missing

Chester as his body was sucked out through the shattered wind-shield, disappearing into the blurred light beyond my reach. My screams turned into a high-pitched whistle in my ears, the world around me blurring further.

He was gone. As quickly as the thought formed, the car's deathly spin abruptly ceased as it slammed into something. My neck jerked, and my head collided violently with an object. Darkness enveloped me, the world fading into blackness.

CHAPTER TWENTY-THREE
THE FAMILY

D arkness enveloped me. Within my unconscious state, there were no dreams—just a void... and Alexander. Always Alexander.

Dream Alexander stood before me in the abyss, his clawed hand outstretched just as mine had been when I tried to save Chester from his fate. In this surreal limbo, our fingers brushed past each other, a desperate attempt to find something, anything to hold onto. It was a futile endeavor, but in the midst of my failures, his velvety voice flowed through the confines of my mind.

"Try harder. Come to me..." His words reverberated within my mental space.

I stretched forward, my arm somehow elongating as I strained to grasp his hand. Yet, once again, I fell short.

"Come to me..." he crooned once more.

"Alexander, I can't! I can't do it!" I whimpered, my voice trembling with fear, unable to muster the strength to bridge the distance that separated us. My words faltered, breaking under the weight of oncoming tears.

"Jack... I can't lose you..."

The words dissipated, and my world shifted from the darkness of dreams, back to a very real and tangible darkness that enveloped me... wherever I was. Where was I? Something obstructed my sight—a bag over my head. How cliché. I gained awareness of the rest of my undead body. My semi-barren nerves sparked with sensation, guiding me as my hands and feet tingled back into my control.

My hands flexed at the wrists, the ache of the recent crash coursing through them and extending to my fingertips. Electric pain shot through the bones encased in harder, supernatural flesh. I could feel that my hands were bound together, restrained by metal chains of some sort. They constricted tightly, pressing against my muscles and the emerging bruises just beneath my skin, evidence of their unforgiving grip.

I wondered if I should try and escape., but I figured moving with haste might result in getting decapitated. I was clueless about what I was up against, of course. It seemed wiser to settle my nerves a bit more before making any decisions.

Gradually, I regained sensation in my legs and feet. It became evident that my ankles were also bound and crossed by chains. What puzzled me most, however, was the absence of my shoes. The bottoms of my feet scraped over rough concrete and the sensation of what felt like broken glass threatened to slice into my skin if I attempted to get away. However, it wasn't the pain or the looming threat of it that occupied my thoughts. It was the realization that the perpetrators had stolen my awesome new boots.

In the oppressive darkness, I could hear muffled words, too faint for me to discern, deliberately kept just out of earshot. They concealed their ghoulish plans, tailor-made for little old me. I remained silent, teeth gritted, my eyes squeezed shut, straining with all my will to reach out to Alexander with my mind.

Nothing came—no words, no hope.

A singular set of heavy footsteps approached my position, the echoing clack of heels on stone growing louder with each agonizing breath I took. We must have been inside now, shielded from the breeziness of the city. The atmosphere around me was muggy and uncomfortable as it clung to my skin. The dry autumn air had been replaced by a suffocating humidity, the result of too many bodies confined in too small a space. The stench was unbearable, a putrid odor reminiscent of a week-old corpse left out in the hot sun, or the place where the highway crew dumped roadkill from the congested city streets.

"You know, I had a son named Jackie once, but that was... a very long time ago. It pains me deeply to have to do this to another young man bearing the same name as my long-departed flesh and blood," a voice emerged, croaking like the grinding of old machinery in a factory long forgotten.

The voice drew nearer, the shroud covering my head impeding my ability to make out any features. I felt something pressing firmly against my clavicle, the sharp tip of an object. A hand descended to my shoulder, an old and fragile hand that trembled as it gripped just beneath my hair. I inhaled deeply through my nose, attempting to glean any information from the proximity of this person. The scent of stale cigars and the metallic tang of blood clung heavily to the intruder, shrouded in mystery.

With a clearing of his throat, the man continued, "I must say, I am impressed. You did quite the number on my boy. It will take a while for him to return to normal. You're vicious... foolish... but vicious. It's admirable." As he spoke, I couldn't help but take the insult personally, my fists clenching and relaxing within their bound state at my back.

"Yeah, I'm the stupid one, alright," I retorted, my words tinged with a hint of anger. "Your *boy*, or whatever he is, was putting his hands on people without their consent. I'd say if anything—"

"Don't finish that thought, if you know what's good for you," the old voice warned, croaking ominously from somewhere near my head.

I fell silent, realizing that this was not the time for my attitude or anger.

I couldn't restrain myself any longer. Fueled by anger and spite, I roared, "—That your damned boy was the stupid one, and he got what he deserved for attempting to rape some poor girl! What? Are there no rules against sexual abuse among the leeches of the world?"

My vehement words were like a catalyst. The shroud was violently torn from my head, and my messy curls spilled onto my shoulders where his hand had previously rested. The liver-spotted paw withdrew as its owner briefly turned away, clutching the black sack with old and weathered claws. I could see him now, and to my surprise, he was far smaller than his voice had projected. His form was hunched in an old gray three-piece suit, a long black tie disappearing behind his vest. He clutched the sack with an almost rigor mortis-like grip, his fingers twitching and shaking, the rings adorning his knuckles shimmering in the dim light.

I seized the opportunity to survey my surroundings. My mind raced as I tried to piece together where I might be. It appeared that I had been brought to an old warehouse, possibly located just outside the city—an isolated place where no one would hear my screams.

As the man returned, his face finally came into view. His old, wrinkled features were before me, his lips permanently pulled into an eternally disapproving frown that met the loose jowls

THE VAMPIRE JACK TOWNSON

that hung on the edge of his face. His bulbous nose bore a resemblance to De Niro in his later years, with craters and pock-marks to match. The unmistakable marks of a constantly furrowed, bushy gray brow were etched deep into his skin as well. He was surprisingly worn for a vampire, bearing the scars of time.

He tossed the black sack to the side. His now free hand moved to smooth out unruly strands of shorter, slicked-back white hair. He was a man of age, but not one who exuded the grace of a gentleman, like Carver. He had a rougher edge to him.

"Alright, I'll give you that. my progeny, he's... a bit of an issue at times. He doesn't really understand the boundaries with the ladies. But did you have to take his fingers? I mean... you did quite a number on him, but the guy has work to do for *me*. How's he supposed to handle business with a gimp hand? Tell me that, Jack. The face, the chest, the ribs... I could forgive that, but let me tell you, there is no greater tool for a working man than his hands. You take those from him... well, he may as well be dead. That's what you almost did, Jackie. You almost killed my boy. So, it's got to be an eye for an eye. There has to be some sort of... *justice* for this. You know?" As he spoke, his eyes filled with a hint of regret. Those pulsating teal orbs held a hesi-tation as he continued speaking. As his body shifted, I could see the object that had been pressed against my neck a moment ago —a long dagger clutched in his other hand.

"Sir," I began, but the man pulled his lips to the side, as if not wanting me to finish, as if he didn't want to humanize me before he enacted whatever he had in mind.

"I had to do something," I continued, determined to make my point. "What would you have rathered me do? Just sit there and take the hits he was giving, just let him destroy my face and break me. I think we both know that your progeny, Vincent, is a piece of shit and had it coming. You seem like a family man... I have a sister. She means the world to me. And when I saw that poor girl he abused, my sister was all I could think of. I'm sure that if you were there, maybe you would have similar feelings." My words hung in the pungent air of the warehouse, challenging him.

The man rushed toward me, the dagger singing as it came dangerously close to my throat. He closed in rapidly, surprising me with his agility, especially for someone who appeared so aged.

"And what?" he growled. "Am I supposed to just let this go because you were playing the white knight? We would have handled it, we would have done something... Carver sent you to give him a good night, keep an eye on him so he didn't do anything stupid, and you failed. You took your eyes off him!" *His* eyes became wild. "You did this! It's your fault that girl got into that mess, and it's *your* damn fault my biggest hitter is down for the count—"

"NO!" I snarled, my voice unyielding. "Not this time. I did the right thing, and I'm not letting anyone take that from me— not you, and not that bastard! You had the opportunity to stop him. Hell, you're his sire, right?" My words exploded with the heat of anger, melting the older Italian's expression into a mild realization.

"Yeah, *YEAH*!" I continued, my frustration mounting. "You had all the power in the situation, and I'm sure you were well aware of the accusations, maybe even saw some of the acts yourself. Yet you did nothing. *Hear me*? You did NOTHING, Alessio. That poor girl's blood is on your hands because of your own inability to act and rein in your subordinate!"

A hard palm met my cheek, and the world spun as a brutal slap erupted from Alessio's right hand. His dagger remained pressed against my throat, and I felt the stinging pain in my cheek where he had struck me.

"You talk a big talk, but have you ever taken care of anything outside of your sniveling little sister?" Alessio sneered. "Nah, I thought not. You couldn't imagine the weight of the responsibilities I have. One of which is keeping my family safe above all else. I've been around for hundreds of years, and I know one thing—if my boy has an issue, we handle it! That wasn't for you to do, nor anyone else! Hell, even Carver, the fuckin' *king* knew to stay out of it, yet you took shit into your own hands. You acted like some sort of... cowboy. Who the fuck do you think you are?"

I stared back into his eyes, my fangs bared, and my own vision pulsating an unsettling miasma of multi-toned reds. "I'm a nobody," I retorted, my voice dripping with defiance. "And even a nobody knows that if you put your hands on a woman, you deserve whatever is coming to you. The fact that you can't see that... *damn*, maybe those centuries didn't really do you any favors, because you're just as ignorant and bloated as any human thug on these streets."

Alessio's demeanor shifted. His eyebrows drooped and the line of his mouth straightened. He seemed to come to a decision. He straightened up and moved away from my chained body. I watched him warily, uncertain of what he was planning next.

"Well, Jack," he said with a sigh, "that's a real shame that we couldn't see eye to eye on this, that you couldn't understand how this works. You seem like a good kid, like you've got some promise for the future, but sadly... it'll have to be through a muddy dirt road instead of shining golden streets. Can't say I didn't try to help you understand, and I can't say I'll enjoy watching this, but I know someone who will."

Alessio waved a hand over my shoulder, and I realized that we weren't alone in this dark place. With a strained effort, I craned my neck back to see who else might be there with us, my curiosity mixed with a growing sense of dread.

"Jackie," a familiar voice boomed, and I felt a shiver run down my spine. A large, imposing figure limped into my line of sight, just next to Alessio.

It was Vincent, the vampire I had confronted earlier, his face stitched and his hand wrapped in bandages, the aftermath of our brutal fight. His teal eyes matched his maker's in their unsettling glow as he joined Alessio at his side.

"Hey, pops, sorry for all the trouble. I can take care of this from here," Vincent said, attempting to usher the elder vampire away. But he shook his head adamantly.

"Absolutely not, after the trouble you've caused us, *fottuto idiota*," Alessio replied, his tone stern. "I'm staying here while you boys handle this. Make sure this... *Mister Nobody* learns his lesson."

My heart sank as I realized just how trapped I was.

"The fingers?"

Alessio stopped to glance at me again, his glowing eyes growing soft for a moment. He shook his head, "Nah, use the stick. Need to give him some credit, he almost put you out and he's pretty young, not to mention the massive balls it took to talk to me the way he did..." He gripped my strands with a squeeze, wringing them before releasing in an almost grandfatherly way. "Maybe, when this is all said and done, we can patch this up. But for now... let's enlighten you to the power of the Family." Alessio gave one last slap to my shoulder before passing behind me.

Two men swiftly filled the void left by his exit, while two others slid in from the opposite direction. I found myself encircled by five vampires, their piercing teal eyes fixed on me, arms casually folded over their vibrant, mismatched tracksuits.

Vincent broke the silence with a wry smile. His gaze flicked to one of his companions, and he extended his good hand, palm up. "Well, Jackie," he drawled, "we could've been pals. It's a shame the night's taken this turn." With a fluid motion, the vampire at his side handed him a matte black device, its edges gleaming with sinister intent.

Vincent continued, "You see, Alessio had different ideas about our future together, but I believe I've gained some insight into your true nature." He casually flicked his wrist, and the device sprung to life, crackling with malevolent energy. "This is no ordinary toy, pally. It's a high-voltage taser. You might think it has no effect on us, *the undead*, but you'd be mistaken."

As he inched closer, he jabbed the instrument toward me, and I braced for the impact. The prongs found their mark, stabbing into my exposed skin, sending surges of electricity coursing through my body. The pain was unlike anything I'd ever experienced. I clenched my toes against the unforgiving glass floor, feeling it cut into my flesh, blood trickling across the various gleaming fragments.

The world became a blinding white abyss as my muscles convulsed, my neck tensing and relaxing with each cruel shock. In that agonizing moment, I realized the true extent of my vulnerability.

"S-stop! STOP!" I gasped between ragged breaths, my voice trembling as the relentless shocks coursed through me. Each jolt seemed to sear into my very core, making my fangs sink into my quivering bottom lip. A warm, metallic taste flooded my mouth as a stream of blood trickled down my chin and onto my chest.

Vincent's assault momentarily stopped, and I slumped against the unforgiving chair, my body trembling uncontrollably. His malicious grin returned, a triumphant glint in his teal eyes. I wanted to say something, to beg for mercy, but the words refused to form. They were drowned in involuntary gasps and agonized whimpers.

In that torturous moment, as the world spun around me in a blur of pain and despair, I couldn't help but wonder how I had ended up in this nightmarish situation—a desperate waiter who fell in love, died, and was now surrounded by a vampire mafia in an undisclosed warehouse, getting tortured like some classic Stallone movie.

"Jackie, you've got a whole world of pain coming; this is just the start," Vincent sneered, waving a dismissive hand at one of his vampire comrades, Mitch, who eagerly stepped forward. "Jackie, meet Mitch. Mitch is going to have some fun now," Vincent grinned sinisterly, casting an expectant glance at his companion.

Mitch, lanky and menacing, cradled the long, cylindrical device in his hands now. He bounced it with a sadistic rhythm, his grin widening.

"Pleasure to meet you, Jackie," Mitch said with mock courtesy, his voice dripping with malice. He playfully warned, "Just don't accidentally bite your tongue off, alright?" With a cruel flourish, he swung the device toward my head, my neck snapping to one side and then jerking back as the baton returned on its descent. The electricity surged through me, my body convulsing uncontrollably as I remained pinned against the chair.

Mitch's assault continued relentlessly, one blow after another. My body throbbed with pain, my ribs aching from the earlier fight and the force of the relentless strikes. Blood filled my mouth as I bit down on my lips, trying to maintain some semblance of composure. My vision blurred, and my mind reeled as Mitch laughed with a perverse delight.

"Hey," I coughed, a wisp of smoke escaping my dead lungs into the air. Mitch paused briefly, allowing me to continue. "Why don't you... let the big guy have another go at it? You hit like a thirteen-year-old girl. Do you need me to buy you some... tampons?" I spat the blood that had collected in my cheek, and it splattered dangerously close to Mitch's eyes.

"You little fuck!" Mitch howled in frustration, pressing the top of the weapon firmly against my forehead.

The shocks sent a searing jolt through my body, causing my eyes to roll back in agony. My fingers danced involuntarily within their restraints. Vampires and electricity, a deadly combination. I couldn't help but wonder what other surprises awaited us, although I had no desire to explore further. This torment was more than enough.

As the volts surged through my cortex, sparking painful memories and sensations, my mind sought refuge in a distant recollection—a simpler time, a memory long buried in the recesses of my undead existence.

In the recesses of my mind, I was transported back to a moment in time when Chloe and I sought refuge from our troubled home lives. I was in high school, Chloe in junior, and our daily escape from the harsh realities of our father's neglect led us to the nearby town center. After school, we'd frequent our favorite coffee house, where we stood side by side against the worn steps, our hands tightly clasped—a gesture of the unbreakable bond between an older brother and his younger sister.

I had always looked out for Chloe, even back then, as our father became no more than a mere sperm donor instead of a parent. In public, I kept her close, a silent promise to protect her if needed. To outsiders, our closeness was perceived as odd, even sickening. Our peers, those we were forced to share our teenage years with, couldn't resist the temptation to mock and jeer at our unique connection. They hurled cruel words—freak, psycho, and worse—at both of us.

On that fateful day, one asshole went too far. He insinuated the unthinkable, that Chloe and I shared an incestuous relationship. I couldn't tolerate it any longer. Without hesitation, I jabbed him in the face, sending him sprawling to the ground.

Blood gushed from the broken bridge of his nose, a crimson waterfall of consequences for his thoughtless words. Yes, I had struck first, and it was this initial act that triggered the onslaught.

Four more of them descended upon me, fists raining down upon my young body, driving me to my knees. Chloe tried valiantly to intervene, but her small frame couldn't halt the storm of aggression. Helplessly, she watched her brother bear the brunt of their blows, my face quickly becoming a grotesque canvas of black and blue.

I remembered the words I whispered to her in that moment of anguish: "Don't worry," I reassured her, even as tears streamed down her face. Her little knees were red and raw from kneeling on the ground, peering through the legs of the boys. "I'll be fine, just don't watch." I forced a smile to mask the agony coursing through me, every wild blow a searing torment. And then, as if summoned by some dark force, it happened—I burst into uproarious laughter.

My hands instinctively cradled my head, providing a flimsy shield against their attacks as my eerie cackling echoed through the chaos. The taunts and curses of the boys quickly dwindled into silence, their aggression replaced by bewildered stares. I continued to laugh, tears mingling with my sister's sobs against the unforgiving sidewalk.

"What is wrong with you... you fucking freak?" one of them muttered, unable to comprehend the unstable behavior I had unleashed. It worked. They retreated, leaving Chloe and me with our bruised flesh and battered bones, but at least we were safe.

My focus returned to the nightmarish scene, the beanpole of a man—Mitch—relentlessly beating me with the electric baton. Each shock sent my heart racing, a stark reminder that it still had the capacity to pound in my chest, even when I had believed it to be utterly dead. I gazed upon the five men surrounding me, just like the tormentors from my school days. But this time, there was no Chloe by my side, no one to shield me from their brutality. It was a cruel twist of fate how history seemed destined to repeat itself.

As that bitter irony settled in, a familiar sound emerged, as it always did during my moments of overwhelming despair— maniacal laughter. It burst forth from my throat, the walls of the foundry echoing the chilling sound as it flowed past the bewildered men. Mitch's relentless beating halted, if only for a moment.

"Jesus fuck... Hey, Alessio, you seein' this?" Mitch redirected his attention to the large, deformed figure of Vincent, whose expression had transformed from one of cruel delight to one of concern. Alessio's gaze locked onto the source of the laughter, and he too appeared perplexed by the sudden shift.

"He's a fucking psychopath. You should've seen him earli- er... I don't think this one is mentally all there, just wearing a mask of sanity... dangerous little fucker," Mitch muttered, his words carrying a gruff exterior but laced with an unmistakable undercurrent of fear.

My battered body shuddered from the relentless damage it had sustained, patches of blackened skin testament to the ruth- less electronic assault. My fingers and toes felt numb, twitching involuntarily. I could only imagine the gruesome state of my face, but the thought faded beneath the relentless laughter that poured forth, a symphony of madness that was unsettlingly effective.

The echoing footsteps returned, the sound of leather shoes traipsing ominously against the floor. Alessio reentered my field of vision, though I struggled to maintain focus amid the over- whelming agony.

As Alessio approached, a chilling silence settled over the

scene, broken only by more sporadic fits of laughter—a stark reminder that even in the face of brutality, there was a defiance, a flicker of the indomitable spirit that refused to be broken.

"What's so fuckin' funny... Jack," Alessio hissed, his gaze dark with unease. The unnerving laughter had transformed me from a mere nuisance into a perceived threat, and his patience had worn thin. He brandished the dagger tightly in his hand, a cruel reminder of our earlier conversation about the fate of my own fingers.

I laughed, each burst of mirth punctuated by hacking coughs that spewed smoke like some demonic spirit being exorcised from its host. My voice emerged as a low, crackling rasp. "You're all fucking dead men... all of you." With a sudden, violent motion, my head whipped back against the chair, my long, sweat-slicked curls lashing against the wood. Laughter and screams intermingled, echoing through the warehouse. "YOU'RE ALL FUCKING DEAD MEN!"

Alessio's knife came to my throat again. He pressed the blade into the soft, dead flesh, a trickle of blood climbing over the shining surface to replace the silver with a sinister shade of crimson. His voice was harsh and dripping with frustration.

"You've got nothing, you're all talk and no action—just laughing your ass off like some lunatic on their last rites. What the fuck do you have, huh? Shut the fuck up unless you've got something valuable to say. I've had enough of this."

Alessio began to drag the knife across my neck, the world around me blurring as my eyes fluttered. The cold blade sawed through my flesh, slitting my throat with each agonizing motion. My laughter became a wheezed, frantic struggle as I fought to hold on, the fear of it all coming to a brutal end coursing through my mind.

Then, a voice from the back of the room shattered the dreadful silence, accompanied by the thunderous rush of heavy boots. Another man emerged into view, and I tried my best to cling to consciousness, my blood oozing down my chest as I stared forward, searching desperately for something, anything, to anchor me as the room spun.

"The fuck do you want, huh? We're busy wrapping this up!" Alessio snarled as he pulled the dagger away, leaving my throat slashed but my head still intact.

"Boss... the drivers outside are dead. They're fucking dead..." the newcomer stammered, trembling in his boots, his eyes wide with terror.

Alessio pulled his focus from me then. "Th'fuck did you just say? They're dead? No alarm? No nothin'?"

The man nodded vigorously, his clenched teeth revealing fangs that peeked out from his bottom row. "Dead. Heads are just... fucking gone... They ain't even there!" He gestured urgently to a phone in his hand, prompting Alessio to look.

The old patriarch of the Family left me in my own blood for a moment, moving to get a better view of the screen. His face paled, an astonishing sight for one already as pale as death itself. In an instant, Alessio was back on me, his dagger pressing against my cheek as his glare burned with fury.

"Who the fuck followed you, huh? Who did you call?" Alessio's voice trembled with panic. The notion that someone had effortlessly eliminated his men without raising an alarm quite obviously sent chills down his centuries-old spine.

I shook my head, my voice barely able to escape as bubbles of blood formed at the opening in my jugular.

For a moment, he paused, his brows furrowing as he drew closer to my battered face. "Who made you? Who's your maker, kid?" he whispered, his voice dripping with intensity.

My smile returned, and I realized the power of the revelation I held. My voice crawled from my battered throat, finally finding enough strength to make an impact. "Alex-...ander..." I began, and Alessio's eyes widened in shock, while Vincent and the others exchanged uncertain glances. "La-... Mont."

Vincent's face fell, mirroring the expressions of the rest of the group. It became evident that they had no prior knowledge of Alexander's connection to me; I hadn't even mentioned it back at the club. Panic etched itself across Alessio's features, and I began to suspect that there was much more to Alexander La Mont than I had initially believed. The sheer terror that washed over these seasoned vampires in response to that single utterance spoke volumes.

Alessio abruptly pushed away from me, causing the chair to teeter dangerously on its hind legs. My weary eyes struggled to stay open, intent on witnessing the unfolding drama.

"Leave him, leave him now! We are getting the fuck out of here, you understand!" Alessio barked, his voice quivering with urgency.

Vincent's face displayed a mixture of confusion and apprehension as he hastened to his sire's side, a hand resting on Alessio's arm. "Pops, it's just one guy. I know he's got a reputation, but we've got at least ten of us here, five inside and five guarding the doors, even without the driver and familiars... no one will miss 'em."

A brutal hand struck Vincent's bandaged face, the fabric peeling off to reveal the still-healing, raw patches of flesh I had torn away earlier. Alessio's voice thundered with rage, "One guy, ONE fucking guy? We have one rule in this damn city, and that's no one pisses off Alexander La Mont!"

Vincent let out a pained groan, his head shaking from side to side. "I didn't know you two were friends..."

Alessio's hands clenched around Vincent's mutilated face, his voice a venomous hiss. "No, numb nuts, we ain't friends. I once witnessed Alexander dust a man with a mere swipe of his hand for saying he was having a bad hair day. He's a fucking monster! How could you not ask about him earlier, you brain-less MORON!"

Alessio's hand rose into the air, poised to strike his progeny once more, but in an instant, it vanished, severed cleanly down to the bone, leaving only a grotesque nub hanging in the air. His blood followed suit, spraying crimson fluid in the direction of the missing appendage. The elder vampire's face contorted in agony as he lowered the stump into his view, ruby droplets dousing his features. A primal scream of terror tore from his lips, his old jowls quivering as his body convulsed.

"*MY HAND! MY FUCKING HAND!*" he howled, his cries of anguish echoing through the building.

Vincent rushed to search for the missing appendage, but there was nothing, not even a trace or droplets of blood upon the ground.

A chilling voice resonated from the rafters, spreading an eerie silence throughout the open space. "Ah, what a dreadful decision you've made tonight, to steal from me what is mine, to defile what I have created... you are pitiful creatures, insignificant bugs to be crushed beneath my booted heel. And now, you shall watch your very corpses ignite in flames at the touch of my righteous hand."

Vincent reached back and retrieved a handgun from the waistband of his blood-soaked tracksuit. Alessio leaned against him, his eyes fixed in shock on the nub that had once been his hand. I watched in awe, my senses overwhelmed by the unfolding chaos.

The mobsters gripped their weapons tightly, and two of them hurried to grab shotguns from a nearby crate. They pointed their firearms wildly, scanning the area for any sign of the unseen threat that plagued them. A piercing, high-pitched whistle cut through the air, and one of the men suddenly froze, his eyes widening in terror. His sibling, equally alarmed, turned to look at him.

"Tommy...?" he uttered, his hand reaching out to nudge his brother. But as he did, Tommy's head rolled from his shoulders. The top of Tommy's cranium hit the ground and erupted into ash, his body disintegrating into cinders that fell onto the cold stone floor of the warehouse.

The remaining mobster panicked instantly, clutching his shotgun and making a frantic dash for the exit, his face filled with terror.

"Where the fuck do you think you're going, Gio!" Vincent screamed, his gun aimed at his own blood brother. "Stop! Get back here— we don't abandon Pop!" Vincent fired a warning shot, and for a moment, it seemed like Gio might reconsider. He halted in his tracks, hesitating.

But then, a sharp, feigned inhale filled Gio's lungs as he helplessly watched. His legs abruptly ceased their flight, and his torso slid from its base, landing in a gruesome heap on the ground with his innards scattered below. A horrifying vocal fry echoed from just beyond Gio's severed legs. Then, it stopped— just beyond the forlorn pair of shoes, a rolling severed head stared back at us in horror before exploding into dust, taking the legs and torso with it.

"I've killed your men swiftly, but because you dared to take my love away from me, you shall not have the same mercy," the haunting voice echoed from the shadows, sending shivers down our spines.

Even I, an undead creature myself, felt fear coursing through my undead veins.

"The only thing I truly cherish in this entire world, and you tried to steal him from *ME*!"

Alessio called out to the darkness, his voice quivering with desperation, "We didn't know, Alexander! We had no idea! Just let this go, and we can find a way to move forward without needless violence..."

Alexander's voice surged from the shadows, dripping with menace. "I'd say violence is quite necessary. You should have been more vigilant, paid closer attention to his scent and every nuance of his being—everything about Jack is infused with me. For your ignorance, there can be no other consequence than to see your head severed from your shoulders."

Alessio cried out, fear tightening its grip on him. "For Christ's sake, we've worked together. We go way back, Alex!" His voice shook with raw emotion as he pleaded with the empty darkness, his throat strained.

Vincent and Mitch refocused their attention on another area where the voice seemed to emanate, both firing their handguns wildly into the shadows, their desperation driving them to defend against an unseen but horrifying enemy.

"I'm right here," the voice resounded with an eerie flash as Alexander materialized seemingly from nothingness. His form was adorned in the same glorious white coat as before, now expertly designed with splashes of blood and gore that rendered it an unsettling masterpiece.

The men swiftly turned their guns toward the seasoned murderer, firing their weapons wildly. Bullets appeared to strike their intended target, but their effects were far from the expected outcome. No blood spilled, and no carnage followed. Instead, his form shimmered, the bullets passing through him as if he were nothing more than a shimmering specter. A radiant translucence enveloped him, revealing a dark gift I had not yet witnessed. Alexander stood there like a golden deity, untouchable and ethereal, his near-white strands of hair flowing as if moved by a supernatural wind that remained imperceptible to us all. He was beyond their reach, a manifestation of power they could never hope to touch.

Mitch cast his gun aside. "Fuck this shit!" He snatched the taser baton back into his grip, swiftly activating it with a snap of his arm.

With determination burning in his eyes, he charged past Vincent, who had exhausted his bullets and was now supporting his sire. Mitch closed the distance, wildly swinging the electrified baton at Alexander, each strike missing its mark as the head of House Epine maintained an almost impassive expression, effortlessly evading the onslaught.

Then, one blow landed, sending electricity coursing through Alexander's form, causing him to briefly solidify. He stood there, seemingly unfazed, allowing the teal-eyed younger vampire to believe he had achieved victory.

"YEAH! I got you, fucker! I got you!" Mitch exclaimed triumphantly, pressing the baton harder and forcing Alexander back for a brief moment.

Alessio murmured to Vincent as they regained their footing, "Help him. Help your brother. I'll be fine."

With Alessio's permission granted, Vincent nodded at his father and drew his own taser, joining Mitch's side. The two men stood together, both jabbing their tasers forward and appearing to electrocute my maker in a desperate bid to gain the upper hand.

A lump formed in my throat, and fear gripped me like a vice. Thoughts raced through my mind, contemplating the conse- quences if Alexander were somehow subdued. Was this the moment I would meet my true death? My voice trembled, but as I attempted to protest, it emerged as nothing more than a raspy whisper.

Panic surged within me, and my head slumped forward, my vision fading in and out. My vitae had nearly depleted, leaving a cold, hollow feeling in my chest. The uncertainty of what lay ahead weighed heavily on my undead heart.

"GGYAHHHH!" A piercing scream shattered the air, jolting my attention back to the gruesome scene.

In the blink of an eye, Alexander's hand had pierced through Mitch's chest, the very tormentor who had subjected me to such pain. Vincent's scream mingled with mine, his desperation evident as he attempted to electrocute the older vampire, to do anything to stop the horror unfolding before us. His other fist raised, striking Alexander's marble jaw with a futile, frantic determination.

My violet eyes remained fixed on Vincent, watching as he fought with all his might. But it was too late for Mitch. Alexander withdrew his claw from its macabre residence, and Mitch erupted into a burst of cinders, his flesh melting away, and his bones crashing to the floor in a cloud of dust. Vincent's attack faltered, his words reduced to incoherent blathering as he bore witness to the gruesome end of his comrade.

"Now, it's your turn," Alexander declared, and Vincent attempted another blow, but La Mont had grown tired of the game. In a swift, brutal motion, he batted Vincent's hand away with such force that it shattered the bones, leaving what was left of Vincent's fingers gnarled and twisted—useless, just like the rest of him.

Vincent stared at the mangled hand for a brief moment. Sorrow etched deep lines into his features, and his expression crumbled.

"Both hands, *BOTH HANDS!*" His scream wrenched from him, ending in a guttural sound. But before he could react further, Alexander's hand shot upwards, sliding beneath Vincent's jaw. Terrible claws tore through flesh as Alexander's hand wrapped around the bone, fingers cradling Vincent's teeth from the front.

Alexander finally smiled, his violet eyes burning with a malevolent intensity. "I won't kill you," he hissed, "that's for my

Jack to do." With a twist of his hip, there came a sickening pop. Vincent's jaw was ripped from its base, a gruesome fountain of gore spraying out. The ivory-tinted, pink thing clattered to the floor, and Vincent's tongue hung loosely, blood dripping from its tip and staining the cold stone. He fell to his knees, defeated and broken, his bandages scraped and hanging in disarray.

Alessio, witnessing the gruesome display and the stark power difference between himself and Alexander, began to back away, trembling.

"Alexander..." Alessio began, his shoes skittering across the blood-covered stone of the warehouse floor, his voice trembling with fear, "I didn't know... I didn't know he was yours..."

Alexander's monstrous steps reverberated through the space, the dust of Mitch's remains scattering as he closed in on Alessio.

"How sad for you," he retorted, his tone laced with venom. "I would make sure to write such a pitiful excuse on your grave... sadly, you won't have one. And if you do, I will desecrate it and kill any who dare glorify you from now until the end of time. I will dedicate myself to it, believe me." Alexander's claws raised, the blood of the others dripping down his talons momentarily before he snapped the hand to his side, ejecting the blood in a disrespectful manner. "I will also say, I never liked you... all of your power relies on others. You and your... *family*... are just ants, breeding with no true purpose outside of your own little schemes and games. Someone had to be the boot, but I hadn't had a reason until now."

His claws snatched Alessio's face, mirroring what he had done to Vincent. Alexander's purple eyes blazed in the dim light, reminiscent of a monster in an old horror movie.

"Why be an ant when you can be a god?" he growled.

Before Alessio could respond, Alexander's other hand gripped the opposite side of his face. Both palms pushed inward, and the old mobster's voice erupted into a labored scream of terror, piercing the air. Alexander continued to exert pressure, pushing and pushing until what was inside sprayed to become the outside. With a final, sickening twisting motion, the body of the elder exploded into a cloud of ash, showering Alexander in his remains.

I stood there, silent and immobilized, unable to comprehend the sheer insanity of the scene. However, Alexander had more in store. His narrow hips swung his legs, landing gentle steps towards me. His claws slashed through the chains binding my hands and feet, freeing me from my bonds. I nearly collapsed, but Alexander's arms caught me.

"Jack, there is one last thing we must do before we can go... You must enact your vengeance."

At my feet lay Vincent Esposito, his jawless face reflecting a mix of desperation and pleading in his bloodshot eyes. Until this moment, I had felt no power or ability within me. Yet, watching my once-friend turned foe, his helplessness spurred me to stand, rising to near my full height. His eyes widened, head shaking from side to side. His throat emitted wet, unintelligible gurgles that were hardly understood but easily deciphered as begging—for mercy, for something, anything. He knew.

Over him, I raised my bare foot, and his begging grew more frantic.

"For Penelope," I wheezed, and with a force that cracked the stone beneath, I sent my foot crashing down onto his head.

The blow was so violent that it separated hair, flesh, and bone, turning him into a pile of ashes and gore that scattered into the air. My body was littered with the remnants of Vincent Esposito. Alexander watched, his violet eyes gleaming with satisfaction at my brutal act. My chest rose and fell as I gazed down at the heap of dust, my artificial breath pulling in the debris of long-dead bones and skin.

It was over.

Alexander extended a bloodstained claw in my direction, his soft smile drawing me to place my hand within his own. The familiar feeling of home enveloped me once more.

"Let's get you home, my love."

CHAPTER TWENTY-FOUR
THE ROAD TO HELL

As dawn approached, we left the scene behind, and my earlier suspicions proved correct. They had taken me to a place where no mortal would find me, but Alexander was no ordinary man. Upon our exit, with the dim light of the sun barely peering above the horizon, I saw an unexpected face. Just beyond the doors, standing on the loading bay's ledge... was Aiden.

He wasn't alone, though. Beneath his booted heel lay the last surviving member of the Family that had been present. The vampire's throat was pressed down upon, and my blood brother aimed a massive handgun at his head from his prone position.

"Ah, Jacko! You're in one piece, I see. I was wondering if you'd make it out of this little situation unscathed. Well, I see that you've managed to survive, at least," Aiden said, scanning me up and down. The man beneath his foot squirmed for a moment, but Aiden's leg came down hard to keep him from escaping. Aiden's red eyes shifted from me to Alexander, and his scowl turned into a more pleasant expression. "Ah, my darling, shall I put an end to this one? I figured with their gift, the entire family knows what happened. We may as well add more ashes to the furnace."

Alexander waved a dismissive hand and walked over to Aiden's side, staring down at the fallen mafioso. "No, it's not necessary. Alessio is dead. However..." He trailed off, took a knee, and grabbed the short tufts of hair on the pinned man's head. His violet gaze locked onto the man's teal one. "Listen closely. This is a warning to your entire Family. No doubt you've seen that Alessio is no more, that your little colony is in pieces. If you come near my boys in any way, I will destroy the last of you and anyone you've ever come into contact with. Do you understand?"

The man attempted to nod but failed due to the weight on his esophagus, his body shivering.

"Well then, Aiden," Alex continued, standing up, a claw briefly clasping my brother's shoulder before he made his way back to me. "You may finish the job now."

The man began to protest as Alexander and I walked down the ramp, leaving him behind. Aiden pulled the trigger, and a gunshot rang out, the bullet slamming into the man's head and sending pieces of it scattering in all directions. Chunks of flesh and blood sprayed into the air before disintegrating into even more ash.

"Well! This was fun!" Aiden smiled, his fanged grin contrasting with his crimson-splattered face. He returned the handgun to his breast pocket and joined us. "I've got to say, Jack-o, I half expected you to come out of here with very little of you left, but here you are... standing on two feet. I have to admit I'm impressed." He reached for a cigarette and placed it between his teeth. "When Alexander told me what was going on, I refused to come. As I said earlier, I don't tolerate failure lightly.

But with the circumstances and this prime opportunity, I just couldn't pass it up."

I turned my head towards Aiden, my anger hardly contained. The wound on my throat had barely healed, and my own vitae had spilled onto my chest. "Aiden, shut the fuck up. I get that I don't mean anything to you, but just... close that fucking asshole on your face and let me have some peace. I'm not in the mood." My words came out like a violent accident on a street corner, with Alexander as the passerby, watching in horror and excitement at the circumstances and hoping to see the damage.

"Is that what I get?" Aiden plucked the cigarette from between his lips, waving the unlit thing in the air as he spoke with mild upset. "I take time from my work to save your pathetic ass, and you treat me like this? Shame on you. I should cut you down here and now."

As his nasal British tone filled the air, I snapped back. "We both know Alexander would never let you, and let's be honest... I sort of freak you out. We both know you don't want a round two... You just want your daddy to yourself."

Aiden's hand flew into my face. The white cigarette held between two claws stabbed almost against my cheek from his position. I opted not to even look as I turned my face from him.

"Careful, little runt... You started a mess we had to clean up. Don't get all uppity on me," he growled, his hand leaving my cheek to place the cigarette back between his teeth. His eyes, crimson with anger, focused forward again.

I wanted to argue, to scream and defend why I did what I did, but I could feel the cold of the wound on my neck and the blood loss starting to set in. I was so hungry. That gnawing feeling returned to my stomach, and I knew I was in a dangerous place. I had to keep my mind as focused as possible on holding it together as the rays of dawn pierced the sky in blazing yellow.

"As much as I'm enjoying this little tit-for-tat, let's not forget what time it is. We're all the way across town, and morning's light is about to break. Let's focus on the proper priorities, boys," Alexander calmly interjected.

His words made it clear that continuing to dally and fight could lead us all to meet the same fate as the portion of the Family that had crossed paths with the Epine. Both Aiden and I ceased our argument and got into the matte black car from that first night.

Our ride was silent, the tinted windows of the sports car protecting us from the damaging sunlight as morning broke. Aiden took the front seat next to Alexander, and I chose to sit in the back. My decision seemed to confuse my sire, but I rested my head against the cushioned headrest and closed my eyes. My inky curls were still stained with my own blood, giving them a coppery tint. Exhaustion weighed heavily on me, and as I drifted during the short car ride, I found myself reflecting on many important things.

Alexander had given me this new life, but it was far from the mystical or magical existence he made it out to be. There was a dark side, and I had witnessed so much of it in such a short period of time. I wondered whether Alexander was the saving angel who had rescued me from mediocrity or the one-winged Lucifer who fed me lies and lured me further into the darkness. Something familiar gnawed at the back of my mind as if these thoughts weren't new, but I couldn't place where they had come from or why they felt so right. As my mind swam, I lost myself for a moment, and the beautiful face of Annabelle returned to my mind's eye.

Her ruby lips were plump and inviting, and I recalled the

sensation of kissing them. Memories of our passionate encounters flooded my thoughts—her hips grinding against mine as we
pressed into each other against the club's backroom wall, her
breathy, sin-kissed moans repeatedly whispering my name.

Jack... Jack...

"Jack?" Alexander's voice snapped me back to reality, and
my eyes fluttered open. I had lost track of time, my hand
instinctively reaching to graze my throat, where Alessio's knife
had left its mark in a manner similar to my sire's fangs.

"Jack, we are home," Alexander continued, his gaze filled
with concern. "I want you to get upstairs, undress, and get into
bed. I'll have Claude send in a few bags of our best blood—no
donors, as we wouldn't want a mess like last time." His words
stung, but I knew he was right.

"In the evening, we'll have Doctor Cadaver come to the
Prepotent. I don't want you traveling until I'm certain you're
well and won't fall apart." I nodded in agreement, my hands
trembling as I undid my seatbelt.

"And Jack?" Alexander's voice softened, and he peered
deeply into my eyes. "We need to eventually talk about what
happened. I want to know everything—Carver, Annabelle,
Vincent, Alessio, and the driver. It's important."

A cold chill ran through me at the mention of Annabelle.
What would Alexander do if he knew? How would he handle the
news that I had been with a woman, especially after she asked
why he had found me before she did? A wave of nausea washed
over me, but there wasn't a hint of regret. Who would regret
such an experience?

I retreated for the morning, the three of us taking a route
through the garage and a more complicated path to avoid the
sunlight. Within minutes, I was upstairs and in our bed, nestled
in those black satin sheets. As I lay in my coffin of silk with my

thoughts, I couldn't help but look up at the ceiling, where the last face of my death, Lucifer, seemed to stare back at me knowingly. He saw my sins and knew of my betrayal. It was only a matter of time before I had to face the road to hell I had paved with my good intentions and accept the consequences my choices would bring.

CHAPTER TWENTY-FIVE
BLOODY TEARS

I had slept as if I were dead to the world, my body clinging to the sheets as I hardly encountered any dreams or images of my sire. Instead, the blackness of the void matched the dark hues of the sheets, nurturing my body back to some semblance of health. There were moments, of course, when I would awaken to see the image of Claude standing over me, quite literally feeding a tube into my mouth from a blood pack, like a mother to her babe, ensuring I didn't lose control or fade completely into nothingness. Then, I would sink right back into the oblivion that had been granted to me by my sire's loving hand.

But now, with a start, I awoke again. This time, it was prompted by a large thump coming from the side table next to the bed. My naked body lurched forward, palms flat against the sheets, muscles tightening in fear, half-expecting a knife-wielding Alessio to be looming over me once more. However, this intruder was not some weathered mafioso. It was an older gentleman with short, stark white hair, dressed in a white coat as if he had just emerged from an abandoned laboratory. His cracked and broken fingers sifted through the contents of a large leather bag that had landed on the table. He grumbled in frustration, clearly searching for something of grave importance. His yellow, jaundiced gaze was aided by coke-bottle spectacles, darting every which way to find what he needed.

"Son of a rotten whore on a Tuesday," he cursed under his breath, his fingers rummaging through the bag. As the doctor continued his frenzied search, his bulging eyes found me from just across the way. "Well! Hello there, mister..." he greeted me, his voice filled with a strange mix of irritation and curiosity.

"Townson," I confirmed the name I had given myself.

"Townson! Right, wonderful. Hello there, mister Townson, I am Doctor Amelius Corpus, but you can call me Doctor Cadaver..." he introduced himself, "everyone does!"

As my vision cleared further from my slumber, I had a chance to take in the stranger's appearance more thoroughly. The moniker "Doctor Cadaver" made perfect sense. He appeared nothing like me, being a shorter man with chalk-white skin, snowy hair, and eyes of a sickly yellow as if the whites had been soaked in formaldehyde. His face, neck, and hands bore small scars, as though he had tried to stitch himself together at some point. I couldn't help but stare at this peculiar figure, but to my surprise, he didn't seem bothered by my scrutiny. In fact, it was as if he expected it.

"Go on, ask what you want to ask," he sighed, finally finding a small mirror in his bag and examining it closely, his broken nails tracing its edges.

I stammered, my voice barely a whisper. "What are you?"

The man smiled, his hand adjusting the spectacles perched on his nose. "I'm a vampire, like you, but... a child of Alchemy, of magic turned science. In my quest for knowledge, I experimented upon myself, uncovering secrets that I now offer to our kind here in this city. Across the sea, there are the original families who are also educated in the secrets of the philosopher, but here, I am the only one with the knowledge to aid our kind, and to help you adapt and evolve."

His words flowed effortlessly, and I sensed sincerity in his every gesture. Thinking again about Alexander, I couldn't resist the opportunity to ask, "Sir, I was told magic changed my face. Can you... change it back?"

Corpus studied me, leaning in close, his yellow eyes fixated on the mask of flesh that concealed my true visage. His fingers, calloused and precise, explored every contour, every seam, without missing a detail. The room hummed with anticipation as he probed, the tension palpable.

"Fascinating," he began, his gloved hand returning the small mirror to his coat pocket. "You seem to be stuck with this one, my friend. Whatever magic was used here was quite powerful, and I hate to say that not even my tools could sculpt a new face for you. I could embark on some research, attempt to unravel the enchantment, but it appears this mask is the mark of an elder... a power not easily shaken, young sir Townson."

My stomach plummeted, a heavy realization settling in like an anchor in my chest. The thought that I could only glimpse the man I once was in a fading picture of the past, never in my own reflection, brought a deep ache. I was trapped in the flesh cage he had built me, permanent evidence of his control. He owned not only my soul but my image as well. I was his Jack, inescapably marked by his influence, forever.

"Mister Townson?" The voice pulled me back to the present, my crimson eyes fluttering as I felt the blood tears longing to spill upon my manufactured face. I did my best to rejoin the conversation, giving the scarred creature a helpless nod.

He cleared his throat, inching closer as he settled down on the edge of the bed near my shoulder. "Mister Townson, during your physical altercations of the prior evening, did you happen to notice any foreign objects piercing your body? Unusual pains in unexpected places?"

I shook my head silently, my thoughts still ensnared by the inescapable reality I faced. The doctor continued, "I ask because such objects, if left inside, could become troublesome. They might hinder your nightly routines and business. It's crucial to remove any obstructions, should they exist."

Once again, I offered a wordless shake of my head, my gaze fixed on the man's disfigured face. He let out a feigned sigh before pressing on, "During the car accident, did you experience a head injury? Did you sense any fractures or breaks in any part of your body?"

I remembered the accident, my body bouncing about and the world going black. "I did have a few moments that felt like breaks or bruises, and I did lose consciousness..."

The doctor nodded before retrieving a small instrument from his bag, a lopsided contraption that he brought to my ribs to tap gently, his fingers rubbing in a small circle, and then to my head, repeating the motion.

"Hmmm..." he mused aloud, his brow furrowing as he pondered over the damage that could be felt. "Well, my fine friend, you seem to have mostly healed. As for floaters, I'm not entirely sure yet. We'll need a deeper examination at some point to determine and remove what we need to. But for now, you seem... healed! Which is a lovely thing," he added with enthusiasm, placing the tool back inside his bag.

Suddenly, the image of Chester being torn through the windshield and disappearing rushed back into my mind, and a surge of dread coursed through my veins. I reached out to gently grasp Corpus's sleeve.

"Doctor," I began, my voice trembling, "did a friend of mine come to you? His name is Chester, he's a driver for Carver Wellington, a Ghoul—"

The doctor's face fell immediately, and he took my hand in his.

"Jack, I... yes, a Chester Montague was sent to me, but by the time he arrived, he was already too far gone for me to do anything of substance. It's a tragedy, and I am sorry for the loss of your friend."

The world spun, and the weight of guilt and grief pressed down on me. I realized that my actions had directly led to Chester's death, the man who had gone out of his way to teach me about his kind and offer encouragement. Tears, long held back, now streamed down my face, and I gave a hard nod of acceptance, letting them fall onto the sheets around my head.

"Thank you. Please... would you happen to know... did he have family?" I asked, even more guilt weighing on my mind.

The doctor simply shook his head, his unsettling yellow eyes narrowing as my blood-colored cheeks betrayed my emotions. A hard inhale through my nose followed.

His fingers darted forward to brush against my face to inspect the crimson tears. "Fascinating," he murmured, his eyes gleaming with an unsettling curiosity. "You smell... *very* unusual indeed." He brought the drops to his lips, drawing them in with a flick of his tongue.

"Hey! What the hell, doc!" I snapped at his rude sampling of my sorrow. I leaned up on my elbows, but Corpus raised a hand to signal me to wait. I reluctantly gave him the chance to explain.

"Blood dust and... is that... how truly interesting." His eyes locked onto mine, a sense of intrigue in his voice. "I should take a sample with me to ensure you're truly alright. Drugs are... nothing to play with, Mister Townson." He reached into his bag with lightning speed, placing a small vial beneath my cheek to collect the remaining blood tears. "Oh, I forgot to ask, is this permissible?"

"It's fine," I snarled, still flustered.

"Lovely. I also need to ask, when I tasted your... tears... I was met with certain images. Very slight, nothing... too revealing," his words dropped to a hushed tone, his brows knitting lower in some sort of concern.

"What do you want to know?"

Corpus glanced around the room and then back to me, his hand resting on my shoulder. "Mister Townson, were you sexually active this evening? Between us, doctor-patient confidentiality." He matched my anxious expression.

I felt the room begin to close in on me.

"Whatever happened," he reassured, "I assure you it is something to be expected, especially when under the effects of blood dust. It is an aphrodisiac, after all, and a potent one."

I cast a nervous glance around the room, my chest rising and falling rapidly as I considered how to keep this from Alexander, if possible. My gaze returned to Corpus. "Will this stay between us, doctor?" I asked, my voice trembling.

He nodded, leaning in closer.

"Yes, I was... active, I mean." The admission created a sour stab in my chest.

"Whom with, Mister Townson?" he inquired gently, and I couldn't help but dart my gaze around the room again.

"Annabelle Cross," I whispered her name, trying my best to keep my voice as quiet as possible.

He smiled, his hand leaving my shoulder to adjust the bridge of his spectacles on his narrow nose. "Miss Cross is quite beautiful," Doctor Corpus began, "we saw to that nearly a century ago when she came to us for assistance. Although... to be fair... she was always beautiful; she just needed to match how she felt inside." His words left me puzzled, my mind racing with different interpretations of what he meant. Seeing my confusion, he continued, "Perhaps you two should speak. It is not my business to share, as it would be quite unprofessional of me. Just try to be understanding, Mister Townson, when the conversation does occur."

I couldn't fathom what he was implying, nothing seemed to make sense. Annabelle was a captivating enigma, powerful and graceful, like a goddess among mortals.

"You don't know?" a voice from the doorway interrupted, and our eyes shifted to find Alexander looming in the shadows like a wolf in the woods. "Annabelle Cross used to be a man, nearly a century ago... isn't that right, *Doctor Cadaver*?"

La Mont's blunt revelation shattered my world into fragments as I struggled to process the news. With his body leaned against the doorframe, Alexander wrapped his arms across his chest, a sardonic smirk on his lips.

"Mister La Mont! That is... quite discourteous of you! It was not your business to tell!" Doctor Corpus exclaimed.

The small room's previous atmosphere of safety was obliterated in an instant.

As Doctor Corpus defended Annabelle, Alexander waved a dismissive hand toward the door. "Get out, now. Or suffer the consequences."

Cadaver didn't need a second warning. He lifted his leather bag and stormed toward the doorway without sparing me a second look.

As he reached Alexander, they exchanged a tense glance before Cadaver spoke again, "Mister La Mont, your progeny is well and unharmed. Even so, I would still send him in soon for a more thorough look..."

Alexander retorted, "Don't worry... I intend to."

The doctor hastily exited. Alexander placed a hand on the door, firmly locking it behind him.

"So..." he began, his lavender eyes softly glowing in the room's gray shadow.

The air seemed to shift from serenity to a much more palpable danger. Arms folded against his chest, he advanced slowly toward me, his dress shoes squeaking on the floor as he crept closer.

"You went on a mission for Carver that I allowed you to partake in, and yes... I *did* allow it. You are mine, after all. And on that mission, not only did you get into an altercation... which led to me having to save you and kill members of a well-connected vampire guild, with whom I have business ties, but you also..." He halted right before the foot of the bed. "*FUCKED MY GREATEST RIVAL IN THE ENTIRE CITY. YOU RUINED OUR CHANCES AT HAPPINESS AND THREW MY LOVE IN MY FACE AS IF I WERE SOME UNWORTHY DOG FOR YOU TO KICK INTO THE GUTTER!* You bit my hand as I tried to feed you, forgetting my generous gift!"

Alexander reached down, his hands closing around my ankles on the ebon sheets. With a forceful yank, he pulled me toward him, my back colliding with the mattress as the coverings smothered me. Panic surged through me, and I flailed, feeling my body pressed against his.

"Tell me," he demanded, his clawed hand tearing away the fabric from my face.

I gasped for air, my body instinctively reacting as if I were suffocating, even though I wasn't. His hand returned, wrapping around my throat, and he pulled me up to his eye level, reminiscent of our initial moments together as lovers and my final moments as a human.

"Was I not good to you?" he screamed, his claws digging into my flesh. "Was I not altruistic and generous, caring... loving! Why, why, *WHY*, Jack!"

Finally, I fought back, our faces mere inches apart. I wrapped my hands around his wrist, desperately trying to free myself from his grasp, my fangs bared.

"Because you haven't fulfilled a single promise yet, Alexander!" I shouted. "You promised me a life better than my own, and instead, you've led me down a rabbit hole of chaos and death! My instincts are screaming at me to run from you because deep down inside, I know something is wrong... that you're not the man you claimed to be!"

I continued to struggle against his hold, my body wriggling as I hovered over the bed, the sheets still clinging to my skin. The room seemed to close in around us as the tension reached its peak.

He roared defiantly, spittle flying into my face, "*WAS IT NOT I WHO WHISPERED THE DARK WORDS INTO YOUR EAR? WAS IT NOT I WHO EARNED YOUR HEART AND YOUR LOVE? WAS IT NOT I WHO BESTOWED UPON YOU THE GIFT OF IMMORTALITY?*" He screamed, and so did I.

"Alex! ALEX!" I yelled, desperate to penetrate his thick-headedness. "YOU'RE NEVER HERE! I've faced so much turmoil, pain, and loss without you! I've seen horrors, all the while you're with Aiden—who, by the way, you didn't tell me about when you turned me, or *God knows* who else!" I continued to struggle, trying to wrench free, but his grip remained unyielding.

"THAT IS WHAT THIS IS! JEALOUSY!" he screamed, his voice filled with venom. "Jealousy for the progeny I made a hundred years ago, who acts more like my pet than my lover. Oh, my little *JAMES*! MY JACK! You're a twisted beast to say such things just to hurt me!" He pulled me even closer, our faces inches apart. "How was he... Jack? How was *Mister* Cross? Did he fulfill your every desire while he was wrapped around your cock like the filthy whore he is?"

The spiteful question was too much to bear. My arm raised at my side, my palm sliced through the air and crashed violently into Alexander's face. Tufts of long blonde hair scattered as his head whipped to the side.

"*SHE* was incredible, and is no whore—you fucking monster!" I shouted, my violent assault causing a gash to appear across his cheek. The crimson line produced red liquid that trickled down to his concrete jaw.

His head slowly turned to face me again, pain evident in his eyes for the unexpected strike I had landed against him. He whispered, "A monster am I? After all I have done for you? After I allowed you into my home, fed you of my flesh and of my blood —made you all that you are..." His words were an attempt to confuse and guilt me, but I could feel the heat of anger rising in my chest.

I screamed, drawing myself closer. "You changed my face— without my consent! You tossed away my old identity, my old life... You ENSLAVED ME!" Tears welled in my eyes, my lip trembling as I began to realize the enormity of all that I had lost in that one defining choice. The man I once was had vanished.

"*YOU ARE MINE!*" Alexander bared his fangs, his eyes wild with fury. His grip upon my throat tightened, bringing me back to the night of my death. "You are mine and mine alone. It is my will to do with you as I please, to change you and torment you until I am proud of the work I have done! I OWN YOU, JAMES! THAT MAN YOU WERE IS DEAD AND BURIED. THE VERY SHEETS BENEATH YOU ARE HIS TOMB. There is no one but the *Jack* I have created!"

The hand I had used to strike him curled its bony fingers inward until the claws drew blood from my palm. The familiar rage surged within me, growing more frequent. "I AM NOT A FUCKING SLAVE!" I roared, the force of my words practically shaking the walls. My fist struck his angelic face repeatedly, blood gushing from his nose and lip. Alexander stared into my eyes, the pain etched across his features like a painting.

"I am no puppet, no art piece for you to change and manipulate," I continued, my voice trembling with rage. "I am a person... I am a fucking *person!*"

"NO!" he snarled, his hips twisting as he pinned me against the wall. I wriggled, struggling like an alley cat trying to escape a trap. His grip cut off the blood flow to my brain. "You are a *monster*... just like me. Your nature is dark. You are hungry, lowly, and selfish. You take what you want... just like you took that filthy slut. I will know everything, I WILL!"

His fangs slid to their full length as he lurched onto me, those massive things piercing the flesh at the base of my neck. My clavicle sprayed with my own blood as the pain he had removed from me during my transformation returned in full force. I realized he must have kept me from feeling it that night of lust and romance, for in this moment, anguish was all I could think of.

Hot, burning pain, reminiscent of Alessio's knife against my throat, flooded my senses. My blood flowed into Alexander's mouth instead of down my chest. He pulled away from the entry point, my vitae masking his chin and dripping onto the floor. All at once, he resembled a creature from my darkest nightmares. His face underwent a ghastly transformation, the strands of blonde hair and the once-pink complexion replaced with gossamer white and fine china-like pallor. The veins under his eyes swelled, matching the hues of his iris—a horrific visage from a horror movie. In his break, a ribbon of more dead blood trickled down his chin and onto his chest.

"Alexander..." I begged, my voice reduced to a low whimper as I desperately clung to his hands. He paid no heed to my pleading tones, his mind awash with the bleach that were my recent memories. His violet eyes darted from side to side, fixated on nothing in particular as he watched the scene from the *Gilded Rose* unfold within his mind.

"So, this is what you really look like. It was all a... a lie?" I managed to maintain some semblance of composure, my lips trembling as tears threatened to spill once more. I could now see the man I had loved for what he truly was, not the boyish facade he wore, but the monster that lurked beneath the surface, now fully revealed.

He glowered down at me, his pain from earlier gone and replaced with vengeance. "Yes," he growled, "this is what I am, and I was happy to keep it at bay for your comfort and your safety, but you had to make the choice that you did. You chose to break my heart for some tranny cunt." As he uttered those blasphemous words, the hand that hadn't yet found my throat rose to swipe its claws against the healing scar across my neck, allowing it to gush onto his fingers before he brought them to his mouth. My heart raced with fear and revulsion.

"Ah," he moaned, his tongue lashing out to lick up the stolen blood from his fingers. "You taste so divine, unique, like nothing I have ever tasted..." His eyes fluttered, and a shiver of horror ran down my spine.

"I hope you fucking DROWN!" I screamed, my voice barely more than a crackle from his death grip on my windpipe. My sire's face twitched in response to my words, his eyes rolling back as waves of memories consumed him.

"Jack..." he smiled down at me, his voice cold and taunting. "Your sister... is adorable. Those sweet cherub cheeks, that short black hair, and those eyes... they're so pitiful. Was she damaged in her youth? Only trauma can cause that sort of... innocence in one her age."

That was the breaking point. Rage surged through me once more, white-hot fire, my fists hardening as I swung them with newfound strength. Each knuckle found its mark on his hideous face, and even he stumbled back in surprise, his grasp faltering as I found my footing on the floor.

"*YOU NEVER SPEAK ABOUT HER!*" I roared with each strike. "EVER!" Another blow landed. "Or I'll FUCKING MURDER YOU!"

Alexander staggered backward, his stance failing, and he almost clattered to the floor. Blood sprayed from the strikes against his nose and lips, his own fangs tearing into them as his blood mingled with mine.

"Yes!" Alexander growled, his eyes wild with madness. "Show me your anger, show me your fury! Give me that monster that killed that poor girl in cold blood, show me what you did to her—JAMES!" He regained his composure and returned to his stance, meeting my violent blows. He did his damnedest to dodge them, even using his speed to counter, but wherever he went, I followed, my fists connecting with his face, sending him rebounding back each time. His face became a grotesque canvas of our mingled blood.

"I've had enough!" he snarled, and as my last fist returned, it passed through his body. His form shimmered, as it had in the warehouse, and just as it solidified again, his body collided with mine. His hands returned to my throat, and a swift thrust of his elbow sent me sprawling to the floor, the impact cracking the surface beneath me. Pain rippled through my bruised and healing bones, and I struggled frantically beneath his grasp.

From the doorway, the sound of the handle jiggling offered a glimmer of hope, like a chorus of angels coming to save me from this demon. However, instead of an angel, another devil emerged.

"Alexander..." Aiden's voice came from the other side of the door, his silky English inflection singing our sire's name. "I heard commotion. Do you need me?" His question hung in the air, laden with uncertainty.

Alexander responded swiftly, his hand still clamped around my throat while the other brushed stark strands of white hair from his view of the door. "No, darling," he cooed. His sultry voice a horrifying contrast to his phantom appearance. "Jack and I are... having a little bit of a conversation. It's best you let us continue it in peace." His words painted us as if we were a dysfunctional mother and father talking to their child, except in this situation, Daddy was really beating Mommy to death behind closed doors.

I whimpered, struggling to free my voice from the suffocating grip. "Aiden... please... *please*... help me." Tears streamed down my face, my body pinned to the floor. "Brother... please... oh god, please!" I begged, pleaded, my voice barely a whisper but I knew he heard it.

Aiden remained hidden behind the door, his silence the only response. His presence, however, was palpable. "Aiden, I told you to *leave*," Alexander's voice boomed, his slender progeny's claws sliding against the door as he departed.

Abandoned. My blood brother, who most likely knew what was happening, left me to the ferocity of our sire. In that moment, I saw our relationship for what it was. We weren't brothers, we weren't a family at all. We were prisoners to a monster from which there was no escape.

Alexander growled down at me, the darkness of his shadow distorting his visage further, making him even more ghoulish in appearance as those violet eyes sparked. "I can see it all, Jack... your hands on her body, your lips upon her skin... *your sins*!" His neck wrenched to the side, eyes fluttering to focus on more of my stolen memories. "And of your family, your friends... of your human life. Should I find them? Should I make my way to your little town and gut them all as penance?" His voice was hardly recognizable at that point.

"No—please!" I begged, my body lurching out of instinct, but Alexander's hand forced me down harder onto the floor.

Clawed fingers found their way to my cheek, caressing my

jaw as my blood tears trickled down onto them. I half-expected him to lap them up again, but this time he just stared, his expression softening.

"Then it's simple," he started. "You belong to me. I am the only one you lay with." He sighed, the corners of his lips tightening as he regarded me as if I were some unruly child. "Perhaps I wasn't clear enough... perhaps it was my fault for not explaining in detail."

I wriggled beneath him, my eyes darting from side to side as I sought an escape. "All you need to do is say that you won't ever touch that *man* again, that you won't... even sniff in *his* direction." I could feel his grip loosen, his victory seeming inevitable.

But as Alexander spoke, I worked up a thick ball of phlegm in the back of my throat. I chose to send it exactly where it belonged. The loogie shot straight into his eye, his body jerking back as his grip faltered.

"She's a woman, a beautiful woman, and you're just jealous that she was brave enough to be who she was inside while you hide this fucking monster under a *mask*!" I screamed, my body vibrating as my inherited dark gifts kicked into gear. The undead form I called my own erupted as I sped toward the door, my salvation tantalizingly close. *So close*, I thought, my fingers outstretched toward the handle, almost about to grasp it as the world blurred from my speed. *So close.*

But my body jerked violently, a searing pain swelling in my neck. My hands hovered just before the door, my fingers twitching in desperation but not quite close enough. Alexander had wrapped his claws into my hair to keep me just far enough from my freedom. A single hand of my own reached back to clutch his grip on my strands, a desperate attempt to force him to release me. My naked body was mere inches from salvation.

"No. No, you won't be getting out of this that easily," Alexander hissed, his voice a venomous whisper against my ear.

"I give you my word... my solemn oath that if you leave me, I will harm them. It would pain me to cause you so much agony... but I will." He leaned in close, his words a seductive lure. "Just... be my Jack... that is all I ask."

I stopped.

If I left, Chloe was in danger, everyone I knew would be at risk. I had a responsibility now, one I couldn't escape. I had made this bed, and I would have to sleep in it. It was, after all, my tomb. This decision had cost me my freedom. What was I fighting for anyway? My life had been reduced to ruins, my world destroyed. At least there was a twisted comfort in this horrible place.

"Yes," his voice whispered, pulling me back against him, my tightly set backside pushing against his groin. My head began to spin, the world turning fuzzy as his words seemed to manipulate my thoughts, drowning me in feelings for him. "Yes, little Jack... yes, come back to me. Stop your fighting. Just... be mine."

"I don't want this, Alexander," I begged, my voice quivering. My mind struggled, alternating between resisting and succumbing to his influence.

He snapped, his tone harsh. "Jack, you're mine, and you need to remember this... now shut up."

Reality split. Pain erupted through me as he forced himself upon me. There was no tenderness, no love—only dominance and a cruel reminder that I was nothing more than his property. He pushed hard. My fingers finally found the door, but I was promptly pushed roughly against it. The possibility of escape taunted me, but the dreaded realization came: I was his property.

He owned my body.

He owned my soul.

He even owned my name, and the face I wore.

And in doing so, secured my inability to ever return home again.

Alexander took advantage of my surrender for nearly two hours, electing after he was finished to leave me a crumpled mess just before the door as the time had flown, his own pleasure all that would be the result of his attempts.

"I'm glad you saw it my way" he glowered down at me, standing to his full height as he began to walk towards the door, his pants pulled back at the end of his... work. "Do remember this little lesson. I'm sure we'll... talk about it later," he muttered hurriedly, seemingly aware of the damage he had done.

I lay there in my own mess, defeated and destroyed, used and discarded like a broken doll.

"I love you, Jack..." he whispered, but I responded only with silence, just as Aiden had. Alexander leaned down to place a gentle kiss upon my cheek, and then, with a casual twist of the doorknob, he left me alone in the cold room.

After his departure, I remained where I was, a vacant shell. No thoughts, no feelings, just a dissociation, drowning in the trauma of it all. Tears continued to stream down my face, unchecked. There was no sorrow, no anger, not even the physical pain of the damage Alexander had inflicted.

Eventually, I rose from my place on the floor, shaky and unsteady. My naked body bore the marks of our encounter—blood, sweat, and bruises. I shuffled toward the dresser near the door, using it to support myself as I stared at the reflection that was no longer mine.

My fist clenched, and tears welled up again. I released a silent, body-shaking scream and struck the glass mirror. Shards shattered, reflecting my crimson eyes back at me. But now, there was something different.

The blood tears from my assault had carved a new pattern on my face, unique and striking. Red smeared points down my angular features, and most notably, contouring the sides of my nose. I traced the lines and contours, finessing the ichor to perfect the image. Both edges resembling haunting dagger-like fangs of scarlet. If James was gone forever, maybe someone new could rise to avenge him. The bloodied marks now created a mask for me to live in—a reminder of that night, of what I had endured, but most importantly, who I was to become now.

It was mine. Something I would never allow Alexander to take away.

Despite the pain and torment, Alexander's assault hadn't broken me; it had forged a new identity. James was dead, buried beneath the bedroom floor of his monster forever.

However, Jack, *my* Jack, was born.

CHAPTER TWENTY-SIX

CLAUDE

A night passed. I chose to sleep where I was discarded, refusing to rest on the bed in the room where I had been violated and lied to. Instead, I huddled against the unforgiving floor, my mind swirling with thoughts of my own despair. Memories and images cascaded like a relentless storm.

I recalled the cruel hands of Alexander gripping my hips, the gruesome fates of Alessio and Vincent, Chester being torn from the vehicle, my passionate encounter with Annabelle, Penelope's sorrowful eyes, Carver's welcoming smile, Claude's white-whiskered face, Sylas leading me through the sewers, Marcus's kindness, Aiden's snark, Chris's painful betrayal, the fiery-haired girl jogging through the rain, and the faces of Chloe, Bradly, and my mother.

My face had been altered, my identity stripped away, and I was thrown into the darkness of this new existence. Yet, amid my contemplations, an image pierced my mind—the shattered mirror. Its shards were strewn across the dresser, a powerful symbol of my fractured self. And there, in the broken glass, I saw a reflection of something new—Jack Townson, *the Vampire Bohemian of New York*. No longer Alexander's progeny but a survivor forging a path toward an uncertain light.

A night passed, followed by a day that crept along slowly, and as night fell once more, Alexander boldly summoned me. He had promised to take me to Dr. Corpus's place of work, and the two of us silently piled into the car. There was no sign of Aiden. The ride was shrouded in silence, with only the bustling New York traffic and the soft, persistent drumming of fresh rain against the car's roof breaking the quiet. Neither of us dared to speak, for we both understood the depths of what had transpired. We held titles of Sire and Progeny, but the reality was clear—we were master and property.

During those painful hours alone, I realized the true nature of our relationship. I was little more than a plaything for Alexander's amusement, a pawn to be used and discarded at his whim. In essence, I might as well have been adorned with an invisible collar, the words "Alexander's pet" etched into it.

Our meeting with Dr. Corpus was brief. The aptly named Doctor Cadaver quickly assessed me, his trained eye catching the fresh marks that had yet to heal from the previous night. He knew the truth, but he wisely kept his opinions to himself, offering only small, reassuring smiles.

When all was said and done, I left with a clean bill of health —no broken bones, nothing out of place. With that, we returned to the Prepotent in a rather unceremonious manner. No arguments, no violence, no intimacy—just a typical rainy New York evening shared with the man who had desecrated me.

Alexander left me alone in our room, the same room where so much had happened—my death, my rebirth, and my unraveling. He spoke of important matters that demanded his attention, his words dripping with insincere promises of a future together. But I knew better; these were empty words that would never materialize into reality.

His lips pressed against mine before he departed, and I couldn't help but feel a wave of revulsion surge within me. The man disgusted me, but I was bound to him, trapped in the gilded cage of his making. When he sensed my reluctance to return his kiss with enthusiasm, he pulled me closer forcefully, demanding my submission before breaking away with a deceitful smile. And then, as swiftly as he had arrived, he left me to my solitude.

Back in the room that held so many memories—both painful and transformative—I found a glimmer of hope in the wreckage. The shattered mirror reflected a distorted version of who I was meant to become. With no makeup at my disposal and an unwillingness to resort to the methods that had provided the blood I needed for the design, I ventured out into the world on my own once more.

I practically stumbled down the hallway with my limited speed, finally reaching the stairs and descending to the club's dance floor. Claude, the ever-diligent tender, was already at work, cleaning up in preparation for the approaching evening crowd. The atmosphere was calmer now, with the patrons of the night not yet making their way to the Prepotent.

As I watched Claude, I contemplated my newfound determination—a desire to discover who I was meant to be in this world of darkness and deception.

"Hey, Jack!" Claude's warm greeting cut through the fog of my thoughts like a lifeline in the darkness. "Feel like it's been ages since we talked, or since you took a seat. Why don't you pop down on one of the stools and I can get you something before you head out to wherever you're headed" His Southern drawl held genuine concern, a stark contrast to the turmoil brewing within me.

His offer to have a drink and chat was tempting. I hesitated, my instincts urging me to leave, but I decided to follow his suggestion, recognizing the need for both nourishment and a friendly conversation. As I approached the bar and took a seat, my weariness washed over me like a heavy shroud, and my eyes struggled to stay open.

Claude prepared a glass of the coveted crimson liquid. "Thanks," I muttered as he passed it off to me. The glass felt cool in my hand as I raised it to my lips and took a long, deep sip. The rich, sticky vitae flowed over my tongue and down my throat, satisfying that unrelenting craving that had become my constant companion.

However, this time, something was different. As I drank, I felt a gnawing presence deep within me, an insatiable hunger that clawed at my insides. It was as if a malevolent beast lurked within my gut, demanding more than just blood. This inner demon threatened to consume me, and I couldn't help but think of the parallels between my own existence and Renfield's servitude to Dracula.

Claude watched as I rapidly consumed my drink, as if he sensed my urgency to sever ties and embark on my adventure through the rain-soaked city streets. With every gulp, I aimed to break free from the stale air of the bar, yearning for the exhilarating promise of the night beyond.

"Jack," his voice sliced through the club's dim ambiance, his eyes locking onto mine with a predatory gleam. "You're looking rather drained. Have you been neglecting to feed properly?" I lowered my drink to the bartop, meeting his intense gaze but offering no confirmation or denial of his assumptions. "You do understand the consequences of that, don't you?" he inquired.

I responded with a slight shake of my head, my voice soft and tinged with uncertainty, "Nope, no one has taken the time to teach me these intricacies... so."

He exhaled in frustration. "Well, let me rectify that. You remember that girl? That's what happens. You lose yourself, and your body goes rabid. You'll get what you need either way. And if you think that starving yourself is the answer to protecting people like some sort of shining white knight? Buddy, let me tell you, you'll only end up hurting more people in the process." With his words, I could feel a burning in my chest, and I knew in that moment he could see me - my guilt, my hesitations. Instead of opening up, I did something far worse. I yelled.

"I killed a girl in cold blood, and I can hardly even remember it. I can't... I won't hurt another innocent person. I'd rather lock myself away than take that chance. Or die from starvation..." My pain stung him, my intensity hardly landing. It came off more as that of a cornered dog than that of someone rabid.

"Listen," he leaned in closely, "I lost myself a time or two before, too... hell, we all have. It's part of this whole messed-up existence. Actually, it's how Alexander found me." I stared at him for a moment in shock, wishing to ask more but finding my answers without the questions I had longed to make known. "I was pretty young, a few years in, and my own guild had abandoned me. It wasn't because I was some sort of issue..."

I couldn't contain my curiosity any longer and finally asked, "Then why?"

Claude chuckled, his whiskers twitching as he cocked his head to the side. "I ended up sleeping with my guild leader's wife, Astartes. She was... simply gorgeous. When he found out, the entire guild left me for dead, branding me a traitor. I deserved it, so I was left to fend for myself. I realized I couldn't get what I needed. I had depended on my higher-ups to provide for me, and as a result, I didn't know how to hunt or keep things discreet." As he spoke, I saw his eyes darting around, as if reliving the past in that very moment. "It drove me to the brink of hunger, and eventually, I lost control, ending up taking out a family in their home in Queens, the whole gruesome ordeal."

As Claude's face fell, I couldn't help but ask another question, even if it seemed foolish, "What about that 'being invited inside' stuff? Did you trick them or...?"

The bartender laughed, shaking his head from side to side. "No, that's utter nonsense, a complete myth... in fact, I think it's one we vampires might have invented," he sighed. "Anyhow, Alexander found me covered in blood; luckily, he was in the area. He helped me dispose of the bodies and the house in the correct way, then offered to take me in. He gave me a new purpose, and since then, I haven't lost control even once."

"That poor family..." I exclaimed in horror, bewildered by how he viewed the moment as a victory rather than a massive failure. "Doesn't it ever weigh on you?" I asked.

"We're predators, buddy. It's inevitable; you can't torment yourself like this. Just restrict yourself to one person every once in a while, and the rest of the time, stick to bagged blood. That's how we stay under the radar... unless you're like your sire and brother. They have their ways, and well... just don't emulate them." His words left me momentarily perplexed, shifting my thoughts away from the unsettling memories and back to La Mont and his pet.

"What do you mean...?" I asked. Claude visibly panicked, his steely eyes widening as if he'd said something he shouldn't have. He nodded sharply, causing his ashy hair to bounce, and quickly returned to his work.

"Just find someone who makes sense, be smart about it, and, most importantly, make it quick. Don't hesitate, and never underestimate humans. Got it?" The change in topic was apparent, but I was too focused on escaping the Prepotent and beginning my journey to dwell on it.

"I understand," I mumbled, pushing myself off the stool. I

slid my empty glass of crimson forward with a simple gesture of my palm. "I really needed this. It's been challenging without Alexander or Aiden here to guide me. So... thank you," I said, acknowledging the most candid conversation the older vampire had ever offered me.

Claude's face seemed to brighten for a moment, his cheeks puffing up as his eyes squinted in sheer joy. He cleared his throat, reverting to his more gruff demeanor. "Hey, it's no problem. Just, uh... remember what I said, all right?" With that, he turned his back to me, resuming his task of cleaning the counters in preparation for the approaching night's chaos.

"Thanks, buddy..." I whispered as I pushed myself away from the bar, the echoing clicks of my boots resonating throughout the now-empty club.

CHAPTER TWENTY-SEVEN
FANGS

O nce more, I ventured out onto the city streets, the rain pelting down onto my red hoodie, drenching the fabric and me to the bone. Yet, I felt nothing—no cold, no discomfort. Rain was no obstacle for me, and I could dance in it all night if I wished. But that wasn't my intention for the evening. I sought the colors I had glimpsed on my own face, the blood tears that had slicked my skin, creating that sinister contour—a symbol of my pain and my oath. I needed it, to feel the power surging within me again.

So, I stumbled along the walkways and gutters, hoping to find something to satisfy my craving. However, most stores appeared closed at this hour. I had wasted time talking to Claude and dawdling, or so I thought, and it had cost me the opportunity I so desperately desired, aside from the fluids coursing through the patrons who surrounded me.

I could hear them all—the passersby and living, mortal vessels. The drumming of their heartbeats resonated in my ears like a chorus of impending death, filling my mind with thoughts of murder and images of throats tightly clenched between my jaws, my fangs glistening with the elixir of their lives. I tried to ignore it, to push the relentless hunger aside, but with every step, it waged war against my resolve, my mind and primal instincts locked in a fierce battle for control.

Come on, the voice returned again. *Take one of them, rip them open, pour their sweet blood into your mouth and sate what you know you must, be the monster we know you are.*

"No," I thought aloud, my tones hushed to avoid eavesdroppers. "I won't be what you want me to be, I won't..."

Come on, Jack... you know I'm catching up. You can't escape me for long.

"Shut up..." I hissed, my feet quickening their pace along the cluttered sidewalks, trying to avoid any possible collateral damage I might cause. The relentless hunger was becoming unbearable, a tangled mess of rolling pain churning in my stomach. The demon inside me didn't beg; it demanded. It knew only how to demand.

I stumbled for a moment, my footing giving way, and I found myself on the verge of collapse. To my surprise, a hand caught me, preventing my fall. I looked up to see a young woman, her arm cradling mine as she held me just inches from the wet pavement. Her hazel eyes peeked out from beneath soaked chocolate hair, her sun-kissed skin attesting to days spent basking in sunlight.

"Careful! Are you alright?" She offered kindness, her voice carrying an accent I couldn't quite place. It should have sounded beautiful, but all I could hear was the relentless voice in my stomach screaming at me to kill her. Her scent, reminiscent of a warm gazpacho on a cool autumn evening, filled my nostrils. The aroma of garlic, tomato, and onion overwhelmed me, forcing my knees to momentarily buckle.

I pulled free from her grasp, unwilling to succumb to the darkness that threatened to spill her insides onto the sidewalk as payment for her kindness. My boots found their grip once more, and I continued on, heading in the opposite direction of her. She didn't follow, but her eyes lingered on me, their gaze drilling into the back of my inky curls slicked against my skull. In that moment, she had no idea how fortunate she was. With just a drop of her blood, I would have been upon her. Perhaps it was lucky for both of us that it didn't come to that.

I eventually reached a convenience store with a sign that read "24/7" and hurried inside. They had to have what I needed; it wasn't a high ask. Despite the pain gnawing at me, it took some time to navigate the aisles, but I eventually found the item I sought—a simple eyeshadow palette. It was nothing fancy or unique, but it would be mine. I had never worn makeup before; where I came from, it wasn't very progressive. Even in my ravenous undead state, I felt a twinge of fear about the judgment that would come. What would people say? What would Alexander think? Would they see me as a freak, or would they allow me to live as I wished? There was only one way to find out: purchase this small makeup palette and put it to use.

However, there was an issue—I had no money. I had forgotten that life without my Vampire Daddy meant I had to be self-sufficient, even if my freedom was only for a few hours this evening. I attempted to walk past the register and exit through the theft detector, but it beeped loudly as I passed through. The heavier-set man behind the counter leaned his head back to watch me, maintaining his silence, only casting a skeptical glance in my direction as I awkwardly hobbled back to the front.

"Hi there, I just—"

"Are you paying for that?" he grumbled, clearly not being in the mood for any nonsense.

I took a moment, considering all I had learned over the past weeks, my eyes locked onto his without wavering. "No... I'm not going to pay for it. You're going to let me have it for free." It was a bold move, I admit, but it was worth a try. The older man stared at me, his back hunched and his stomach spilling over the belt of his pants, his expression a mix of disbelief and irritation.

"No," he retorted firmly, "you're going to pay for it, or I'm going to call the cops." My free hand frantically checked my pockets to see if I had any money, but I found nothing. "If you can't pay, you need to leave until you can..."

I cursed under my breath, my eyes darting around as I tried to figure out how to handle the situation. Then, it occurred to me that maybe I wasn't putting my full intent into it. My mind had been preoccupied with thoughts of gore, not on the task at hand. Perhaps I needed to clear my head and try again. I took a deep breath, false breaths stinging my insides as I centered myself, my jeweled eyes fluttering open to meet the man's own. "No. I'm not," I stated flatly. "I'm taking this with me."

To my surprise, I watched as the cashier's pupils dilated into saucer plates, and he seemed to be drawn toward me. "Yeah... just... take it," he mumbled, his head drooping forward as if he were under some sort of spell.

"And... I get anything I want for free from here on, understand?" I decided to push my luck. Why not try?

He nodded his head in compliance, and I had successfully compelled him. I reached my makeup kit forward to scan it, the cashier sluggishly pushing some keys on the register's screen to enter some sort of code.

"Thanks," I muttered as I wandered back through the store's exit, hoping the alarm wouldn't go off again. Fortunately, it didn't. I had what I needed and had also learned a new skill in the process. It was an interesting sensation, like being a snake with a small mouse wrapped in your tail, ready to devour it. It was challenging to describe without the right mindset, but that's precisely how it felt to me at that moment.

If I wanted to, I could have sunk my teeth into the cashier's chubby neck and drained him, leaving behind a bloody stain on the floor. But he wasn't my type, and it would have been unwise with the presence of security cameras and potential witnesses. I needed to press on, find someone worthy of death, someone deserving of my cold touch and swift execution.

Outside the store, I stared at my reflection in a mirrored window and got to work. I opened the makeup kit I had purchased and smudged my clawed fingers into the saturated red eyeshadow. I brought two fingers to my face, applying the makeup to my eyelids and nose. I attempted the same look I had worn before, but with the rain and the pain coursing through my core, it was far from perfect. It was, at best, a messy first attempt, but it would have to do. As I gazed at my reflection, the face that Alexander had created was once again mine. A smile curled at my lips, and I knew that I was finally finding myself again.

With my newly adopted look and a sense of determination, I ventured into the darkness of the city, searching for someone whose sacrifice could quell the relentless pain inside me. I didn't want to be a killer, but a disturbing realization was starting to dawn on me, and Claude's words echoed in my mind. This was what we were, and denying it would only lead to more casualties in the long run. Claude's own story was a chilling reminder of what could happen if I let my guard down. The memory of that family he had taken haunted my thoughts, their faces becoming vivid in my imagination. I couldn't afford to make the same mistake; I had to find my own way to survive.

As I walked the familiar streets, hunting for someone to satisfy the insatiable thirst that tormented me, I couldn't help but chuckle at the irony of potentially dying from thirst in the middle of a rainstorm. The absurdity of it all briefly lightened my mood, but the underlying darkness and the voice in my head soon took over again.

Any of them will do, just pick one it hissed.

"No, we're not harming any innocents," I snarled in return, feeling crazy.

Who is really innocent though? Hasn't everyone committed some terrible act they hide? Aren't all closets meant for clothes and skeletons?

"Shut... the fuck... up." Damn, the voice was starting to make sense and I didn't want to admit it.

The voice in my head taunted me with more disturbing questions: How *many dictators could have been stopped if someone had taken them out before they rose to power? How many lives could have been spared?* It challenged my belief that I was somehow different, some kind of angelic figure sent to save lives. The voice insisted that there was no heaven, only hell, and it was here among us. I had to make a choice, to be either the tormented or the demon.

The words weighed heavily on my mind as I continued my search through the rainy streets. The moral dilemma consumed me, and I couldn't help but wonder if there was a middle ground, a way to survive without becoming a monster. But in a world where I was no longer a human and my existence was bound by the thirst for blood, finding that middle ground seemed increasingly elusive.

"Stop. Stop talking," I couldn't help but emit a low growl, and it drew some attention from the nearby crowd. In the bustling streets of New York City, however, strange occurrences were not uncommon, and a few raised middle fingers were the usual response. They found my behavior odd but continued on their way without missing a beat. In that moment, I realized how perfectly suited Manhattan was for a vampire like me.

That's the spirit, the voice sizzled. *You're getting it now.*

I found myself inexplicably drawn by a scent, an aroma of warm Spanish soup that sent a tingling sensation through my gums and made my fangs ache. It filled my senses and reinvigorated me, guiding my footsteps with a purpose I couldn't fully comprehend. Following this scent, I walked ten blocks down, navigating through the city's changing atmosphere from friendly and bustling to shrouded in mystery and uncertainty.

Despite the crowd, her scent was unmistakable and irresistible. My mind conjured an image of her with her chocolate-colored hair, and I couldn't help but wonder if she tasted as delicious as the soup of her heritage. As I got closer, the warmth of her fragrance caused drool to form in my parched mouth and spill onto my cracked lips. I had no intention of killing her. Instead, I planned to take only what I needed and leave her in a place where she could be found and receive medical attention.

Liar, the voice returned, *We both know you're going to drain her dry and leave her for dead.*

"Shut the fuck up!" I finally screamed, the voice in my mind cackling violently in my own tones.

Lie to yourself all you want, you're too far gone to avoid this now.

I pressed forward, the rain drenching my skin and turning my makeshift makeup into a grotesque display. Passersby had stopped to stare, avoiding eye contact with me as if I appeared unhinged. But I didn't care about their judgment; I was so close that I could practically taste her. Soon, I would once again know the flavors of the past.

Just one bite

I refused to argue any longer. The voice was right... just one bite.

I turned the corner and, to my surprise, found the woman who had foolishly helped me. However, she wasn't alone. A masked man in dark clothing held a knife aimed at her, and she was slumped against the wall, her body weakened. The assailant fumbled with her wallet, and her fearful eyes met mine, silently begging for help in her moment of distress. That's when I realized why her scent had drawn me; she had been stabbed in the side, blood trickling down into the dirty alley. I was the only witness to this gruesome scene.

Kill them!

The voice inside me came back, and I found myself doubled over in pain, my steps faltering as I fell into the dim light of the alley. My palms scraped against the rain-slicked pavement, but the pain in my gut was overwhelming.

"This is my lucky day, holy shit..." the masked man turned in my direction, his blood-coated knife aimed at me. "Wallet, keys, cards, everything, or I'll slit your throat before I slit hers," he threatened with a sinister smile, inching closer.

I took a deep, false breath, my mind racing. His scent, like old Slim Jims and stale beer, assaulted my senses, and I knew he would do. I mustered a wicked smile, ready to reveal my true nature.

"Oh... is that right..." I pushed myself to my feet, the darkness seemingly wrapping around me as the alley grew even darker. The dim light above us flickered, creating an eerie atmosphere. "You can't kill what is already dead," I proclaimed, my words a blend of my own voice and the demon's inside me. In that moment, I decided to remove my glamour, revealing my true form to the thief.

The man jumped back in shock, his eyes widening as he stared into my blazing red pits. The knife in his trembling hand betrayed his fear as he began to back away.

"What the fuck are you... hey! HEY!" The thief screamed in terror as he realized I couldn't possibly be human. But instead of running away, he shouted to his comrades at the other end of the alley. Two more men dressed similarly to him rushed forward, looking at the woman against the wall and then back at me.

"Holy shit..." one of them muttered in disbelief, while the other one laughed nervously. "Is it Halloween yet? Nice makeup, bro." The first man pointed at my eyes, which were now an inferno of crimson, revealing the monster within me.

"Shoot this motherfucker!" The man to the side raised a handgun and attempted to fire. But in an instant, I moved faster than their eyes could follow. My hand closed around the barrel of the pistol, crushing it before it could discharge a bullet. The thief shrieked in terror as I loomed over him, my monstrous presence dominating the alley.

I couldn't resist the urge any longer. The demon within me demanded its fill. My hands shot forward, gripping the thief's throat and lifting him into the air, right before his stunned friends. Bone-like claws extended from my fingers, digging into his soft flesh, crushing his windpipe, and silencing his screams. His mouth opened wide in a silent plea for mercy as he choked for air.

The other two thieves watched in horror, their fear and confusion paralyzing them as they witnessed the gruesome scene unfolding before them.

"Was it worth it, being such pathetic cowards, harming innocents to get another fix?" I felt the hunger take me then, my jaw dislocating as my fangs slid to their full lengths for all to see, my head surging forward violently as I pulled the man's neck to my mouth.

The pulsating blood flowed into my maw like a river of sweet, crimson nectar, and I drank deeply, the warm life force of the thief coursing through me, filling me with power and satisfaction. His screams faded into the background as I feasted, the euphoria of the kill taking hold.

The other thief, still in shock, raised his hand with a trembling grip on the pistol. He fired round after round into me, but the bullets had no effect. With a swift and effortless motion, I tossed the drained thief's lifeless body against the alley wall. His head collided with the stone, his skull erupting on impact, leaving him to slide down its face, his lifeless eyes gazing into the gutter.

One down. My crimson eyes locked onto the other thief, my fangs still extended, dripping with gore. I stalked toward him, the hunger still ablaze within me.

"You fucking FREAK!" The man continued to waste all of his ammunition, firing into me over and over as my favorite hoodie became riddled with holes.

Click, click, click. The weapon emptied beyond capacity the man continued to pull the trigger, praying to some god that the monster at his front would go away if he just believed that the weapon would do the work.

"Pitiful, little thing. You're nothing but a meal, your life utterly wasted... I'll make sure you're put to good use."

The thief's screams were muffled by the vice-like grip of my claws on his cheeks as I slammed him to the ground, his desperate struggles futile against my supernatural strength. His arms flailed wildly as I forcefully dragged him into the inky darkness of the alley, leaving a gruesome smear of blood in our wake. With a swift motion, I slammed the back of his cranium onto the unforgiving ground with a crack, pinning him in place.

The hunger that had consumed me drove me to sink my fangs into his chest, right above his heart. The taste of his blood was intoxicating, and I drank deeply, feeling his life force drain away with each swallow. He convulsed briefly before going limp, his heartbeat fading to nothing.

His friend, the original thief, stood frozen in terror, his eyes locked onto the gruesome scene before him. I released the lifeless body and stared back at him from the shadows, my crimson eyes glowing with the remnants of my bloodlust.

"No, no- please!" The man's panicked footsteps echoed in the alley as he fled from the gruesome scene behind him. His fear-fueled sprint seemed to make him clumsy, and he stumbled over his own feet, glancing back repeatedly to see if I was pursuing him. But I walked with deliberate intent, my supernatural abilities allowing me to maintain a relentless pace.

As he continued to flee, he dropped the wallet he had stolen, a futile attempt to gain some speed. The discarded wallet fell to the ground, forgotten in his desperate escape.

I knew that it was only a matter of time before I caught up to him. His fear had clouded his judgment, and he was no match for the inhuman speed and strength that I possessed.

In his mad dash to escape, he lost his footing, his head meeting the stone beneath in a violent collision. His feeble arms struggled to break his fall, but the relentless force of gravity overpowered them. A gory trail of blood escaped his wounded mouth, staining the ground beneath him.

"Fuck, please! Please! GOD!" he screamed, and I answered.

"God?" I whispered in response, for I was there even before his head left the ground, looming before him in wait. "What do you think your god would say now, hm? Praise you for a life of shit and crime, for the possible murder you've committed? What do you think? Will heaven allow you through its pearly gates?"

Tears welled up in the man's eyes, glistening as they spilled down his cheeks, his frantic movements causing him to scramble backward on his backside. His pitiful whimpers echoed through the Downtown streets, falling upon indifferent ears of passersby who chose not to involve themselves. I advanced slowly, savoring the palpable fear that radiated from him like a noxious perfume.

Drawing closer, I lowered myself to his level, crouching down with my arms resting upon my knees. I locked eyes with him, my face contorted in a grotesque grimace that unveiled the lurking monster within.

"What do you think?" I asked once more.

"I... I don't want to die..." he begged, the stench of urine filling the air as the thug pissed himself from utter fright. "Please just let me go... I won't tell anyone... I promise, I swear!"

His words may have been true, but discretion no longer mattered. He was a dead man the moment he turned his cruelty on that poor woman.

"No," I growled. "Say hello to your god for me."

My mouth stretched wide as the thief's anguished screams filled the air, his trembling hands desperately attempting to halt my inexorable approach. My jaws clamped down on either side of his neck, my fangs biting into his flesh like a vise. He struggled to escape, his pleas and cries fading into incoherent murmurs as his very essence flowed into me.

His futile attempts to push me away and his wildly flailing arms slowly ceased, surrendering to limpness as life ebbed away. I withdrew with all my might, tearing his throat open with my teeth, allowing streams of his crimson life force to splatter across my face and clavicle.

Gore covered my mouth and face as I shifted my gaze towards the woman who had aided me earlier. She leaned against the wall, her breaths coming heavy, and bloodshot tears staining her eyes. In her weakened state, she would have fled, but the loss of blood rendered her immobile. Her own life's essence mingled with her attacker's, forming a chilling tableau on the ground below.

Approaching her, my eyes locked onto her tearful face as she silently begged for mercy. I could sense her yearning to return to the life she once knew. Temptation tugged at me, urging me to claim her life, to extinguish what remained of her existence. Yet, I resisted. I didn't want to become her monster, only theirs.

"Jack, you have to do it..." A voice emerged from the shadows, and I turned my head to gaze upon the approaching figure. There she stood, Annabelle Cross, the woman I had longed to see once more, the one who had occupied my thoughts and stirred desire within my breast. In that blood-drenched alley, she materialized like an angel of death, a vision of otherworldly allure.

Her presence was bewitching, and her attire defied her usual style. She adorned herself in a long, crimson satin dress that clung to her every curve, a black fur shawl draped elegantly across her shoulders. Her lustrous, cherry-red hair cascaded in loose waves down her back, a stark contrast against the macabre surroundings. She looked every bit like a seductive siren, a temptress born of the night.

"Annabelle... what are you doing here?" I asked, my surprise apparent even through the dense layer of blood caking my face, neck, and chest.

A gentle sigh escaped Annabelle's lips, her countenance softer and more compassionate than I had ever seen before. Her sympathy extended first to me and then to the unfortunate human who had willingly offered her arm. "If you don't, she'll either die from her blood loss, go on to live a short and grueling life, or someone else will have to kill her."

I stared in disbelief, my eyes leaving Annabelle to stare pleadingly with the woman at my front as she returned the sorrowful gaze.

"Why? Why would they have to?" I practically whimpered.

"Because she's seen too much. She knows far too much... and I'm afraid she's too far along to just have it glamoured away. Finish it. Do the humane thing. Finish it" Her words resonated with genuine compassion, a stark departure from the embittered vixen I had known at the *Gilded Rose*. She had evolved into a woman who genuinely cared for me and sought to bring an end to this ordeal as painlessly as possible for the girl.

I locked eyes with the woman, her tear-filled gaze mirroring the sheer terror of this nightmarish evening. She shook her head from side to side, as if desperately wishing to awaken from this gruesome ordeal.

"I'm so sorry," I began, my voice heavy with remorse, my own eyes welling up with crimson tears. I knew all too well the unspeakable horror that this poor girl must have endured.

Annabelle approached us with a purposeful stride, the sharp staccato of her stilettos echoing against the cold concrete. Just before her arrival, one of the men I had drained started to twitch, only to meet the swift and lethal kick of her stiletto heel, which plunged into his head before she effortlessly withdrew it.

"Bastards... good riddance," she spat with contempt upon the lifeless body, her gaze unwavering. She then made her way to where the two of us stood. With a blood-splattered hand, she gently cupped my cheek, her emerald eyes locking onto mine.

"You don't have to bear this burden alone," she stated, her lips tracing the taste of the spilled vitae I had taken from the wicked men. It was a cherished kiss, a reminder of the tenderness I had missed so dearly. "We can face this together."

I met her gaze, offering a subtle nod of agreement as our attention shifted toward the woman who had unwittingly become the star of this fateful evening.

"We're so sorry," she started.

"We don't want to do this..." I added.

"This is simply a really bad case of *wrong place wrong time*," Annabelle sighed.

"I tried to help you... I tried."

It was the truth. I *had* tried, but I also lied. In reality, I had ventured here with a singular purpose—to bring us to this very moment. Whether my heart could muster the resolve to end her existence, or if it would be the dormant monster within me that completed the task, this was the precise destination I had intended for us all along. The irony lay in the fact that it was the other men who had stumbled into the wrong place at the wrong time. Karma had a peculiar way of dealing its hand to those who truly deserved it.

Annabelle rested a comforting hand on the woman's shoulder, pulling down her sleeve to reveal the vulnerable flesh beneath. She lowered herself to gently place her lips upon the sturdy flesh, puncturing it and grazing against the bone below. I followed her lead, nuzzling the girl's cheek before delicately sinking my fangs into her throat. We both drew as gently as possible, allowing the sweet release to guide the poor girl to a more peaceful realm, letting her drift away in our embrace until she was gone.

The weight of grief began to settle upon me, a crushing realization that I had been the instrument of death for all these people. The woman, who had only sought to help me to my feet, now rested lifeless in our arms. Tears welled up and streamed down my cheeks, mingling with the blood of all four of us, a haunting testament to the choices we had made.

"Jack, there was nothing you could have done," Annabelle whispered soothingly before leaning in to place a gentle kiss upon my lips. Our embrace parted, allowing our eyes to meet, and in that close proximity, it felt like an eternity since our electric encounter at the club. I had questioned whether our connection had been merely a byproduct of the intoxicating blood dust of Vincent, but as I gazed into her eyes, I could sense the profound love I held for this woman, undeniable and genuine. It was real, and it consumed me utterly.

She sighed, breaking the silence. "Jack, come with me. I'll

call my cleaners to handle this little mess, but someone must tend to you as well. Let's return to the *Rose*. I truly want to discuss what's happening between us."

I nodded and followed her like a lost puppy in the pouring rain, my hoodie soaked with both the city's tears and the blood of my meal. In that moment, there was only one thing I knew for certain:

I was in deep trouble, and yet... I didn't care.

CHAPTER TWENTY-EIGHT

BITE MARKS AND BATTLE SCARS

Annabelle and I didn't linger in the alley for the cleaners to show up. By the time they arrived to dispose of the bodies, we had vanished into the heart of the city, seeking refuge in the welcoming embrace of the *Gilded Rose*. The place held an odd sense of familiarity, a home away from home. Though I hadn't frequented its pulsing lights and stripper poles often, it was a haven where I discovered a newfound sense of freedom and an unexpected love.

Upon our arrival, Annabelle swiftly informed her staff that we would be occupied for the night, granting her girls a well-deserved break and clearing the establishment just for us. I had never experienced someone so completely fixated on me, so unwaveringly focused, that they would shut down their own business to provide me with an intimate setting. In fact, I had never had a partner who would even take a single day off from work for me, let alone offer it willingly. Yet, there she stood, ushering her employees away to give us unrestricted access.

With the place emptied, I felt compelled to explore. I took my time, drinking in the surroundings, and allowing the smaller details of Annabelle's touch on the club to seep into my consciousness. Portraits of found family adorned the walls, alongside abstract paintings from various artists. I ventured towards the back, curious about the dressing rooms, gaining a sense of the lives that unfolded there and the genuine care Annabelle bestowed upon her troupe.

Amidst my exploration, I stumbled upon a peculiar painting. It depicted a tall man with a fiery red beard and piercing green eyes, his ginger hair knotted and intertwined as he wielded a modestly sized axe. The axe head rested at his feet, and he was dressed as a true Viking warrior. A fur cloak enveloped his broad shoulders, nearly swallowing his stark blue tunic. His arms were sheathed in dark leather gauntlets that allowed only his fingers to breathe. The portrait bore the marks of time, with some parts faded and smudged, suggesting it had been retouched over the years. Yet, there was something about it, something strangely familiar and captivating that eluded my grasp.

"So, you like him?" Annabelle discovered me gazing at the portrait, my rain-soaked clothes still clinging to my cold, lifeless form, while my curls had gradually dried, springing back to life around my face. I shifted my attention to her with a start, her footsteps so subtle that they nearly sent me jumping out of my shoes. Glancing downward, I noticed she had removed her stilettos, and she now moved barefoot, leaving a trail of small puddles as she approached. Her eyes remained locked on the portrait, mirroring my own fascination from moments before.

I looked at the portrait once more, my gaze mirroring the same fascination I had felt moments ago. "Yeah, there's something strangely familiar about this picture," I admitted, the fragments of realization slowly falling into place. My crimson eyes flicked to Annabelle and then back to the aged painting, a growing sense of understanding washing over me.

She smiled, her eyes briefly closing as a soft laugh escaped her throat, her slender hand rising to conceal it. "Jack," she said, her gaze locking onto mine, a single brow arching higher as a sly smirk played on her lips. "I know you know. Cadaver told me everything about Alexander... We have a very close relationship, as you can imagine." She exhaled softly. "We should talk."

I nodded in agreement, tearing my gaze away from the portrait and following her as we made our way back to the main floor. There it was—the red leather couch where she had first begun to seduce me, where she had asked what if she had found me first. My fingers instinctively intertwined with hers as she led me to the seat of our initial encounter. She gracefully settled herself, giving a gentle tug to bring me down beside her. As our eyes locked, it became apparent that, for the first time, we were simply two individuals uncertain of how to proceed, engaging in the most human interaction either of us had experienced in years.

With the vulnerability of a schoolgirl with a crush, she playfully poked me, attempting to break the silence but showing signs of nervousness. "So, Jack... were you upset when you found out? I just want to make sure you're okay." Her voice, which had earlier been strong and confident, now carried the trepidation of a young woman terrified of my judgment, of the possibility of rejection. Waves of her fear washed over me.

I paused, breaking our eye contact to recall the moment when I had learned of the news, a memory clouded with anger and betrayal. "It was definitely a shock," I began, causing her brows to knit together in concern. The weight of anticipation and dread hung in the air; I could only imagine what she had gone through when she heard about Alexander's actions. "But I understand why it would be difficult to tell me. It's a significant revelation... a monumental choice. All I could think of was how brave you were for being true to yourself and making such a profound decision. I wasn't angry, at least not with you. My fury was directed solely at Alexander for disclosing news that wasn't his to share. And then..." My words trailed off as I revisited the painful memories of what he had done to me.

"Jack... you can tell me what happened," Annabelle implored, her hand finding its way to my leg as she stared into my eyes. They were eyes of emerald concern, locked onto the makeup smudged across my face. "I want to know, I want to be here for you... I want to tell you everything, but I need to know that you're okay." Her voice trembled with genuine worry.

I raised my own hand to my barely dried skin, fingers gripping my temples as I began to pull down on them, smudging the wet eyeshadow I had used to accentuate my marks, making them appear even more pronounced. "I'm all right," I replied, my words strained and unconvincing. I shifted against the squeaking leather of the couch, the red hoodie beneath me soaked through and causing an uncomfortable series of sounds.

My eyes, filled with crimson pain, fell to the floor as I struggled to articulate what had transpired. "He forced himself onto me. I tried to resist, but he... he says he owns me, that I belong to him, and that I can't see you anymore." As the words tumbled from my mouth, the gravity of the danger I had placed myself and possibly Annabelle in became painfully clear. My hand returned to my face as I slumped back against the seat, my voice tinged with exhaustion. "Fuck... he's going to kill us."

Annabelle's initial concern morphed into sheer horror, her features contorting mildly as her fingers dug into my leg. "He did what?" Her words dripped with venom, her struggle to suppress the anger that churned within her chest evident. After a moment of composed breaths, her heaving bosom gently rose and fell beneath her dress as she redirected her focus. "For as long as I've known Alexander, he's always been a cruel man— nothing more. We occasionally collaborated on specific tasks or when our goals aligned, but we were never friends. He always regarded me as a rival, as opposition, and I had no interest in engaging in a pissing match with him. This is..." Her words trailed off as she leaned forward, her arms enveloping my drenched body to draw me closer, her narrow chin resting upon my shoulder just beside my drying curls. "I'm so sorry, I'm so damn sorry... I never thought he could sink lower than what he did to my girls, but this—this is unspeakable. We need to get you away from him, Jack."

I welcomed her embrace and held her back, finding solace in the simple act of being able to hold her against me. It allowed the terrifying memories to momentarily fade into the background, overshadowed by the warmth and familiarity of her presence. "How?" I asked, my eyes locked onto hers through the smudged red marks, my gaze briefly dipping to her lips before returning to meet her eyes. "Alexander is powerful, cunning, and vicious. I watched him tear through those Family guys like tissue paper, and I... I didn't stand a chance. He won't just let me go."

My companion rose from her seat once more, reaching for my hand to pull me along. "I have some ideas, though you might not like them... but it's time someone put La Mont in his place," she declared as she led me, my footsteps echoing in her wake. We navigated through the club, retracing our steps toward her room.

As we arrived, my gaze settled on the spot where we had consummated our unholy union, where the memories of her moist flesh parting only for me and her fangs in my skin still lingered. "Jack, come on..." She tugged me forward, her hand pressing against her door as she pushed it open to unveil a deceptively spacious room—her own. A massive king-sized bed adorned with red silk sheets dominated the space, an alluring contrast to Alexander's bed. A mirror hung above it, inviting those with playful imaginations. A large closet sat at the back, just past a dresser filled with clothes and makeup. "The walk-in is more than it seems. Let me show you..."

I followed her cautiously, my curiosity piqued by what she was about to reveal. She disappeared into the closet for a moment, the sounds of clicking and whirring filling the air of the modestly sized loft. "Come on."

I entered behind her, passing by rows of dancers' garments and lavish clothing she had collected over time. Then, I witnessed something that left me perplexed. At the back of the closet was a hidden door that she had opened. The room on the other side was bathed in dim crimson lighting, reminiscent of the Prepotent's nightclub. Intrigued, I stepped forward. Annabelle held the door open for me, and I entered a room that seemed to be a portal to history itself.

In the center, a mannequin sported old medieval armor from a time period I couldn't quite place. Its arms brandished the very same axe I had fixated on earlier in the portrait. The walls were adorned with compartments, plated glass drawers, each housing relics from ages past.

"Annabelle, what is all of this?" I asked in hushed tones, feeling as if I had stepped into a place I wasn't meant to see. My gaze rose higher to take in the weaponry hanging on the walls —handguns, automatic rifles, swords, machetes, instruments of death collected and possibly ready for use. It was an arsenal, and a lump formed in my throat as I wondered why a boutique and club owner possessed such an extensive armory.

Annabelle's words were soft, hesitant, as if she feared my reaction, feared I might flee like a startled deer in the forest. "Jack, I haven't been entirely honest about who I was," she confessed, "so... this was the only way I could truly reveal myself to you, to expose my past in the hope that you'll accept me and trust me to help you get out of this."

I listened intently as she spoke, my eyes widening in astonishment as she ventured further into the red room, her fingers gliding over the ancient armor at the center, her nails tracing each rivet and dent. "My name wasn't always Annabelle; it was once Ulf, son of Erik, the Red Wolf." Her admission hung in the air, leaving me stunned.

"How long ago was this, Annabelle?" I finally managed to choke out.

"Almost a thousand years ago," she replied with a sigh. "Yes, I'm older than I've let on. It's something I've kept... very quiet. You are one of the few who know this, along with your sire..."

The realization hit me like a tidal wave. A thousand years— an ancient vampire, and she wanted my love, my trust, and my attention. I remained silent, my interest and curiosity growing with each passing moment.

Annabelle continued to share her past, her words carrying the weight of centuries. "When we invaded England, we were so certain of victory, whether you call it foolishness or bravery. But we were wrong. Almost all of us perished in that battle. I was among the few who survived, saved by my own Sire, Phoebe. She saw me on that battlefield and saw something in me, something beyond the hardened warrior and the epitome of masculinity. She sensed the woman trapped inside me, struggling to break free. Phoebe could truly feel me, and she chose me as a way to allow my femininity to flourish. She became my lover, my teacher, and showed me the world from a female perspective, allowing me to become what my father could never accept—a woman."

Annabelle gently took both of my hands in hers, guiding me to sit on the floor in the war room she had revealed. Her words began to make more sense with every passing moment. "Despite accepting my femininity, my true love remained the art of battle. It's the expression of the body and the strategy of the mind that I've always cherished. Over the ages, I secretly took part in many wars, adopting various names and aliases. My maker always stood by my side, watching from a hidden place, enjoying the local flavors while I spilled blood on the battlefield. She allowed me to embrace both who I had been in the past and who I knew I was inside. She helped me release the girl who longed to be herself in a world dominated by men and in societies that could never truly understand."

As Annabelle's story unfolded, I couldn't help but feel a deep sense of empathy and connection with her, understanding the struggles she had endured over the centuries.

I sat there, slack-jawed, as I absorbed Annabelle's remarkable story, my mind throbbing with the possibilities of everything she had witnessed over her long life and unlife. Finally, I cleared my throat and asked, "So, you weren't kidding when you said a warlord sat before me, were you?"

A bashful giggle escaped Annabelle's lips, her soft, pale cheeks flushed for a moment as she shook her cherry-red mane. "No, Jack, I was being entirely honest."

Nodding, I couldn't help but feel an overwhelming curiosity about her past. "Okay, so how did you end up here?"

Annabelle paused for a moment, her lips pursed in thought as she ventured back in time. "Well, eventually, I fought my way to the Americas during the Revolutionary War, and I found a home that I truly enjoyed. I decided to stay with my maker here. By then, I had had my fill of combat and chose to rest with her, finally taking the time to embrace my maker for all that she was and allowing myself to fully embrace who I was inside. It was a challenge, being trapped inside a large man's body. Even in many of my interactions with our own kind, I had to hide my truth because they just didn't understand. That is, until the nineteen hundreds when a certain Doctor Amelius Corpus arrived in New York City—a grand alchemist, a master of magic turned science, with the ability to heal our undead forms faster than with just blood. He even ventured into the realm of changing anatomy. It was one of his earliest attempts at gender reassignment, and Phoebe stood by my side throughout the entire transformation."

Annabelle's story was like nothing I had ever heard before, a testament to her resilience and the remarkable journey that had brought her to this point in time.

I blinked rapidly, my mind struggling to process all the information I had just been given. Cadaver was much more than he seemed. Reaching forward, I took Annabelle's hand in mine, squeezing it tightly as I asked, "What happened then?" I wanted to know more, to understand the rest of her incredible journey.

Annabelle's expression changed, her face falling as she withdrew her hand to fidget with her own fingers. Her teeth pressed into her bottom lip, and she began to speak with a touch of sadness. "My own kind didn't really understand— those who knew me judged me harshly. Phoebe was seen as a poor sire, and we were forced into seclusion for a brief period of time. During our seclusion, Phoebe and I spent a few years with only each other. She taught me my final lessons."

"Final lessons?" I asked, it sounded grim.

Annabelle nodded, her crimson tears glistening in her tear ducts. "Yes, final lessons... on what it meant to be a vampire and embracing myself unapologetically. Afterwards, she said she was truly pleased with my journey, left everything she owned to me, and..." Her face twitched as a blood tear slid down her cheek. "Walked into the sun."

"Annabelle, I'm so sorry," I whispered, refusing to let her endure this moment alone. I reached for her hands again, pulling her into a warm embrace with her head resting against my shoulder. "Why would she make that decision?"

Tears flowed freely as she allowed herself to be vulnerable, her long fingers gripping my clothing and tugging. "She said she had seen enough of the world, that watching my journey and evolution was the greatest adventure she could have asked for. She was far older than any of us, her time going back to the Greeks. She felt her time was over... that she was so tired, but so proud. And I let her go..."

I gently cupped her face in my hands, my lips finding hers as I kissed her through the blood tears that dripped down her face and onto her barely dried red dress. She broke the kiss after allowing a few more tears to land, looking at me pleadingly. "That's why I'm telling you to trust me with this, to understand that I can do this for you... but it means you're mine, that I become your sire. I promise, I will never—ever treat you the way he has. Do you accept me?" Her eyes searched my face, awaiting my response.

"Yes. I choose you. My loyalty is yours," I declared without hesitation. From the moment I had met her, it was clear that she was the one I was meant to be with. Our lips met once again, and we clung to each other, smudging the red markings on my face against her cheeks and nose. We were a storm of red glitter and gore, a fitting reflection of everything we stood for together.

Breaking the kiss, I gazed into her eyes, a rising fear constricting my chest. My crimson garnets softened as the muscles in my face relaxed. "Annabelle, what are we going to do?"

She returned to kissing my face, tasting the stale blood of the men I had murdered that the rain hadn't fully washed away. "Don't worry about that," she whispered between kisses, her cold breath caressing my wet lips. "Just let me handle it, and when I tell you what to do, be ready." I nodded, resting my head against her as her lips continued to trace my face. "It's all going to be okay."

Then, a thought struck me, a startling realization. "Are you going to kill him...?"

Annabelle pulled back, her wide eyes locked onto mine. "Jack... he hurt you, he's hurt so many people, including the girls I promised to keep safe. And besides..." She hesitated for a moment. "No one actually likes Alexander. They're all afraid of him. He's powerful, frighteningly so, and his influence extends deep into every seedy corner of this city."

Her words left me deeply perplexed. Was Alexander truly at that level of malevolence? I needed to know more, so I asked, "You've mentioned your girls since the night I met you, and I still don't understand what happened. What did he do?"

Annabelle's expression turned somber as she wrapped her arms around me, seeking comfort for the painful truth she was about to reveal. "Most of the girls here are either runaways, homeless, or supernaturals without a family or a place to call their own, so I take them in. I give them a safe place and a sense of family. But that also means that no one really... misses these girls, except for me, and Alexander knew that."

My mind raced with thoughts of what this could mean, what terrible acts he might have committed. I ventured cautiously, "Did he kill them?"

She shook her head slowly, her cherry-red hair brushing against my chest. "No," her words were barely audible, "much worse... Alexander is a monster, worse than you realize, and he deals with some dangerous vampires. There's... a blood trade. That's where he gets all of his bagged blood for the club. Many vampires in the city get their bagged blood from him. It's not from hospitals or blood drives; it's more like human trafficking. He sent my poor girls into the lion's den to be bled dry, and I'll never see them again."

My heart sank, realizing that my maker was not just an unapologetic jerk but indeed a monster.

"So... we kill him. We move forward and never look back." My lips found hers once again, my teeth gently biting her bottom lip as she gasped. My fangs pierced her lip, drawing her blood into my mouth as we kissed, sealing our deadly pact. Our fluids mingled as our tongues danced, tasting each other's blood-tinged saliva, and we were bound together in our resolve.

We would kill Alexander, and if Aiden had to be a part of that list then so be it.

On the floor of Annabelle's arsenal, surrounded by weapons of death and a history of violence, we found solace in each other for the rest of the evening and through into the daylight hours. We shared our life stories, recounting our losses and victories, tales of our families and those we had lost. Annabelle proved to be different from the image I had initially painted of her. Her tenderness was something I had desperately needed all my life. Whenever she sensed my emotional turmoil in our conversations, she responded with a kiss, a gentle smoothing of my hair, or a playful twist of my curl with her lithe fingers. We stayed that way until exhaustion overcame us, falling asleep in each other's arms. The impending murder weighed heavily on my mind, a sinister shadow lurking in the background of our newfound intimacy.

CHAPTER TWENTY-NINE
DOUBLE CROSS

The sun rose and fell, casting its ethereal glow upon Annabelle and me. Our embrace was not driven by lust, but by an enduring love that transcended time. In the midst of this intimate connection, I slipped into a dreamlike state, as I had countless times before.

Within the shadowy recesses of my mind, haunting visions of Alexander tormented my thoughts. His figure emerged from the darkness, and I yearned to reach out to him. This time, however, as our hands stretched towards each other, I hesitated. With a swift withdrawal, I narrowly avoided the grasp of his clawed fingers, determined to break free from his relentless pursuit.

Alexander continued to haunt my slumber, an ever-present specter, emerging from the depths of my subconscious. Each time, his hand extended urgently, compelling me to return to him. With every attempt, I resisted, my desperation growing with each passing moment. He seemed omnipresent, an inescapable nightmare.

Then, unexpectedly, his voice pierced the eerie silence of my dreamscape. '*Why do you reject me, Jack?*' His words were as silky as spun webs, filled with confusion that pierced my very soul. '*Why do you forget my love, my promises... my gifts?*' he implored once more.

I turned away, refusing to meet his gaze. In a hushed tone, I whispered, '*I am staying with Annabelle...*'

His face contorted, his lithe form transforming into a demonic presence. '*What does she have to do with us, Jack? We are bonded, you and I. She has no place in our story,*' he insisted, attempting to sway me back into his dark embrace.

'*No,*' I snapped, my voice filled with resolve. '*No more. I see you for what you are, and I know the truth. You're a monster.*' My fists clenched, and I screamed in the surreal realm, Alexander's undulating form barely holding together.

'*Then I'll take her from you...*' the vile entity hissed in response."

My finger unwrapped, my claws hanging with purpose. I raised them high at my side.

'*If you hurt her, you hurt me,*' I declared fiercely, my resolve unwavering. '*Annabelle is my choice... You're nothing but a nightmare, and I want to be rid of you!*' With a rageful scream, I thrust my talons into the form before me. My bony fingers tore through the image of Alexander, shredding it to tatters. The vaporous remnants of what had appeared to be a man softly dissipated, flowing away into the recesses of my dark mind.

As I felt myself beginning to stir, I heard one last message echoing in my consciousness. Whether it was my own anxious thoughts reawakening, memories buried deep within my subconscious, or a sinister message from the monster himself, one thing was certain—it haunted me. '*My dear Jack, you will never be free of me...*' And then, it was gone. My eyelids fluttered open, welcoming the crimson hues of the war room where I had fallen asleep. Annabelle lay beside me, her slender form wrapped tightly in my arms. Even as we lay there, I couldn't shake the image of my maker dissipating and his haunting last words. It was almost as if he knew our plans and would be ready to reclaim me at the first opportunity.

But it was a foolish notion. There was no way Alexander could invade my dreams. I was letting my fear get the best of me, allowing that lump in my throat to crawl to the tip of my tongue. We would carry out our plan, and I would finally be free.

Annabelle began to stir against me as she woke as well, her soft emerald eyes trailing up my neck, then along my jawline, locking onto my own orbs.

"Hello, my darling Jack," she purred, her voice as gentle and enticing as cream. Her words were a sickeningly sweet dessert meant for me alone, revealing a side of her that no one else would ever be graced with. I gazed back at her, my mind still buzzing with concern, but I brushed those thoughts away in favor of her exquisite face and the promise of a future with her.

"Good morning... evening? Is that still the norm, or do I need to change it up?" I quipped, my charm winning her over instantly. A playful giggle escaped from her throat as she buried her face into my collar, nuzzling her nose against my cold flesh. In response, I rested my head against hers, my sharp chin parting the thick cherry strands of hair where they lay. "This is going to be a hard night, isn't it?" I asked rhetorically, fully aware of the answer to my own question.

My female companion, my potential surrogate sire, bit a fang into her bottom lip, her breath cascading over me where she nestled. I could feel the weight of what lay ahead pressing upon her. "I wish there was another way, I wish we could just be together... but he will never let you go without a fight."

"No, you don't," I called her bluff, her emerald eyes rising to meet mine, filled with confusion. "You don't really want this to go peacefully. You hate the man... you want him dead, don't lie." Annabelle glanced up at the ceiling. An arsenal of weapons she had collected over the years adorned the walls of the room. The gears in her mind turned, reflecting on the ages of blood-lust and battle. With a hard exhale, she turned her gaze back to me.

"You're right," she exclaimed. "I don't want this to be peace-ful. I don't want this to be simple. I want him to suffer for what he did—to my girls, to you, to me. The number of humans, vampires, and supernaturals he has tormented is countless, and he has to pay." I shook my head, gently pulling away from her slender fingers as they adjusted their grip on my sleeves.

"Jack, this isn't about vengeance; it's about justice. He needs to pay, and Carver would agree with that sentiment."

My eyebrow arched, a silent question etched across my fore-head. "Carver?" I asked. "What does he have to do with this?"

Annabelle appeared sheepish, my inquisitiveness and forth-rightness catching her off guard. "Jack, we all despise Alexan-der. Even the King," she explained. "Someone has to do it... I can do this for us, please just let me."

Anger and concern churned within me, my love for Annabelle fueling my apprehension about her putting herself in such danger. My dream still lingered in my thoughts, amplifying my distress. "If Carver hates him so much, why doesn't he just take him out?" My question had merit; why didn't the King simply command his followers, or whatever they were called, to apprehend La Mont and execute him?

Annabelle sighed, her head tilting to the side as she studied my face. "Jack," she groaned, "that's not how it works. Carver wields significant power, but Alexander remains... untouchable. He's a cunning bastard, but he also contributes a lot to this city. In fact, if it weren't for Carver, La Mont might have ascended to the throne himself. Many vampires consider Alexander the rightful ruler, which is a part of why Carver despises him so intensely."

"Great," I huffed, feeling like a moody teenager. "So we can't rely on anyone, can we?" I disengaged from her loving touch and rose to my feet, my boots discarded nearby. My bare feet met the cool, tiled floor as I stood deep in thought, contemplating my next move. I couldn't leave the Rose; he would undoubtedly find me if I did.

Annabelle gazed up at me from the floor, her hands pressed flat against the cold surface, her unruly crimson hair cascading to the side. "Jack, I need to see your phone," she half-ordered. I had forgotten about it amidst the intensity of our shared plans. I reached into my pocket to retrieve it, a cell phone gifted to me by Alexander. I extended it to her, the digital screen lighting up with numerous missed calls and texts from him. Yet, as I briefly glanced, I also noticed missed messages from Aiden, Claude, and Sylas. It seemed that no one knew my current location, my last known presence being at the club where Claude and I had discussed the nature of our existence and the necessity of confronting the monster that dwelled within us.

Annabelle accepted the phone into her grasp, her delicate fingers gently curling around it as she rose from the floor. Her red dress, disheveled and stained from the previous night's tumultuous events and our restless slumber, clung to her form. She fixed her gaze on the screen, her fingertip gliding over the notifications until it came to rest on a particular name.

"Who's James?"

The question from Annabelle halted me in my tracks, the world seemingly shrinking into a suffocating little box as panic began to consume me. My mouth hung open in disbelief, and I silently pleaded with her through desperate gestures to return the device to my trembling hand. There, amidst the names illuminated in the dim room, my sister's contact stood out. My body quivered with a mixture of fear and hope as I clutched the phone tightly, swiping the screen to reveal the messages I had missed.

> James? Is this your number? I had someone contact the house with it and say it was your new phone. I haven't seen you in weeks, Brad and Dad were just as worried as I was. We thought maybe you got hurt in the city, we even filled out a missing persons case but they said they couldn't find anything, even with the information we gave them.

I scrolled down, my hands shaking.

> I'm not mad, Jamey. I'm just... if you didn't want to come home you could have told us, at least me? I knew you hated it here, but I never thought you would just vanish. I miss you...
> 🩶

The last message I missed had come just as I awoke, ironically. And my heart sank.

I really hope your audition went well, I hope your star is shining so bright. Just... don't forget me, please. I love you. Bye big brother.

Blood tears welled in my eyes as I handed the phone back to her, my head shaking as I fought to compose myself. I knew exactly what this was.

Annabelle moved swiftly, enveloping me in her arms and cradling my head with a soft hand. "Jack, oh no... Jack, what happened?" she implored, her voice filled with concern as I stood there in silence. Her expression softened as she tried to comfort me.

"We need to kill him," I whispered, a quick acceptance that seemed out of character, even to me.

"I don't understand, help me understand... Who is James? Who was that?" Annabelle pressed for more information.

"That's my sister... she knew me as James before Alexander renamed me, and... I never gave her this number," I explained, my hands balling into fists, the hooked talons on each finger digging into my palms, drawing blood.

"Jack... holy shit," Annabelle exclaimed, her chest heaving with panic as she grasped the implications of what had just happened. "You don't think..."

"I don't care. A threat is a threat. He has to die. I can't lose her. Tell me what to do, and we'll do it," I insisted.

Annabelle shook her head, attempting to pull away and take the phone back to begin the necessary actions. My hands clamped onto her arms, preventing her from leaving. "No, let me do this. A progeny should never take part in the death of their sire; it isn't right," she argued, her determination evident.

"No! I am doing this; no one goes near my sister... he dies, and when I'm free, I can explain all of this myself to her," I insisted, stumbling over my own words as I tried to formulate a plan. However, Annabelle quickly snapped me back to reality.

"Jack..." her brow furrowed in concern, "you know you can never see her again, even with him dead... you'll just put her in danger." Her words were a harsh reminder of the harsher reality that I didn't want to accept, though I knew she was right.

"It doesn't matter, either way... we end this, and then I make sure this phone is destroyed, and that no one ever knows who I used to be," I replied, finally releasing her.

Annabelle wasted no time, pacing around the room as her slender fingers danced across the screen, transforming the corner of the red walls into a flurry of white light. Her glowing green eyes added to the vivid display against the crimson backdrop. "Where did they take you? The Family, I mean," she asked, her gaze remaining fixed on the screen.

I took a moment to retrieve the memories of my torment at the hands of Alessio's sons and the deformed Vincent. "It was a warehouse, a really secluded place off the south end. Why?" I inquired, curious about her line of thought.

Annabelle returned with the phone and placed it back into my hand. "There, it's done," she said. "Whatever you do, don't let him think anything is off. Answer as sweetly as you can. Just keep milking his spot until he's good and ready, and when he shows up... we will be, too." Her words were unconventional, but I had grown accustomed to her unique way of speaking. I scrolled through the brief conversation that had taken place, and it seemed to have gone well.

I nodded, understanding the plan. "Thank you, Annabelle. I couldn't have done this without you," I said sincerely, my grati-tude for her unwavering support and assistance clear in my eyes.

With our plan in motion, we had a glimmer of hope in the face of an imminent threat. As I prepared to face my sire, the woman I had come to love stood beside me, her loyalty and determination matching my own.

> Jack?! Where ARE you?! I have everyone searching for you, and no one has found a thing! Jack? JACK!

> I'm here, Alexander! Sorry, I got stuck for the night in a girl's apartment, I'm trying to take this more seriously and found my first.

As I reviewed the text message exchange, I couldn't help but feel a pang of guilt. It wasn't a complete lie; I had indeed encountered a girl, albeit in a situation rife with danger. Several muggers had been involved, and while I had intervened, Annabelle's response had a point. My description of the mercy killing did make it sound more malevolent than an act of kindness.

I knew that this deception was necessary to lure Alexander into our trap, but it weighed heavily on my conscience. As we awaited his response and our impending confrontation, the lines between truth and deceit blurred in the shadowy world of vampires and secrets.

You did? How did it go?

You were right. It's just what I am and I have to stop pretending. I'm really grateful, actually, I feel much better. More myself.

That's WONDERFUL! XOXOXO I'm so proud of you, look at the vampire you're becoming! Incroyable!

Actually I was wondering if you could come to where those mobsters had me? I want some alone time with you, and I couldn't shake the image of you dismembering those bastards for me. It was... so heroic.

Anything for you, I'm so glad you thought so! I can't wait to have my hands on you again, I'll head there when I'm free in a few hours.

How about closer to midnight, I want to make sure I look my best for you.

Of course! Oh, and Jack?

Yes?

> Please don't scare me like that again, you're my entire world... keep me in the loop?

> Of course, my love.

> See you soon. 🖤

As I scrolled through the text conversation on my phone, I was taken aback by Annabelle's sharp memory. She had remembered the details I had only briefly mentioned during our time cuddled on the floor—what had transpired after I left the club. After closing the phone and returning it to my pocket, I voiced my thoughts, seeking clarity on our plan.

"So, that's the plan? Lure him to the warehouse, making him think he's going to have a romantic evening, and then..." I trailed off, the implications of our plan hanging in the air.

Annabelle nodded, already selecting weapons and preparing herself for the upcoming encounter. "I'm not an idiot. Alexander will either show up expecting a romantic evening, fueled by his own narcissism, or he'll come fully prepared for a trap. So, I'm going to make sure we're ready for either scenario. He said he'd be there just after midnight, and we'll be heading over now. We can't risk any security or any of the girls being involved in this. It's dirty business killing a vampire of such high status, especially one as dangerous as him," she explained while loading ammunition into a bag she had retrieved from beneath one of the drawers against the wall.

"What are you bringing? How is this going to go?" I inquired, but Annabelle barely broke eye contact with the bag as she continued her preparations.

"You're not involved. I don't want to risk you getting hurt," she declared firmly, causing me to react strongly.

"Bullshit!" I protested vehemently. "I'm involved whether you like it or not. Just show me what I need."

Annabelle sighed, her footsteps echoing on the floor as she moved to another part of the room. Mounted on the wall was another weapon, an unusual dagger with a rose etched onto the hilt. She handed it to me, emphasizing that it was for defense in case Alexander came after me, but she wanted me to avoid the fight as much as possible. I accepted the weapon, my fingers briefly entwining with hers. I pulled her close, our lips meeting in a brief, passionate kiss as our eyes locked in an intimate gaze.

"I understand," I whispered, our lips almost touching as we spoke. "I'll try my best."

Annabelle lingered for a moment before breaking away, making her way toward the secret door leading to the war room. She tried to lighten the mood with a comment about her dress, and her determination lifted my spirits.

"I'll be right there. Just need a moment to myself," I told her as she disappeared into her room.

Alone, I contemplated our plan to double-cross my maker, the dreadful possibilities it held, and the undeniable truth: Chloe had my number, and I hadn't given it to her. Someone who knew both of us had made sure she received it, putting her life in grave danger. It served as a stark reminder that even if Alexander couldn't get to me directly, he could still cause immense harm.

I stared at the phone for a moment, an overwhelming desire to send Chloe a message surging through me. But I knew now that I could never do that. He had stolen my chance to ever reconnect with my Songbird, and for that, he would pay.

CHAPTER THIRTY

BATTLE FOR MY SOUL
PART 1

I t was time. Exiting the battle room through the walk-in closet, I couldn't help but notice that Annabelle had changed into a sleeker outfit. She wore black leggings that hugged the curves of her backside and a tight red athletic tank that strained against her curves. This outfit was chosen for mobility and combat readiness, ensuring she could maneuver effectively in the coming storm. Her cherry-red hair was tied up in a ponytail, and her intense scowl was focused on gathering her weapons and gear. She was even more striking to me in this outfit. While I had admired her in club attire and elegant dresses, there was something undeniably sexy about her donning clothes meant for the battle that lay ahead. She was my warrior queen, and I was her damsel in distress.

With a bag filled to the brim with an assortment of weapons, we began to make our way to the boutique to get a move on. Annabelle had already informed her security detail that she would be taking a personal evening if anyone asked, and my whereabouts remained unknown to the broader New York vampire populace. We would head to Annabelle's car parked in the nearby garage, making sure to park it in full view of the public in front of the boutique to avoid arousing suspicion about her involvement in what was about to transpire. Annabelle hailed a cab by snapping her fingers in the air, the yellow and black vehicle stopping as soon as the leggy redhead flagged it down. I was honestly more surprised that the rest of the traffic didn't come to a screeching halt as well.

As the cab pulled up, the driver couldn't resist eyeing Annabelle from head to toe, completely unaware that indulging in his gaze would be his last mistake. We climbed into the cab, sitting close together, and began discussing our plans for the upcoming confrontation as vaguely as possible.

Annabelle spoke to me, her voice filled with a mixture of caution and concern. "Jack," she began, "I know you're committed to this, but... you have to understand, there's a pull that a maker has on their progeny. You might feel compelled to save Alexander or get in the way when things start." She gripped my hand tightly, then placed it in her lap. "You have to fight it. This needs to happen, and you can't get in my way."

I wanted to argue, to insist that I was stronger, that my feelings for her outweighed any pull Alexander might have. But she silenced me with her words. "You don't need to argue or claim that you or your feelings are more powerful than the pull. You just need to do what I tell you to do," her finger gently touched my lips. "Let me do this."

As she spoke, I noticed that the cab driver was still listening to our conversation, his raised eyebrow reflecting his curiosity about our unusual discourse. I wondered how Annabelle planned to handle him. Would she end his life to ensure our secrets remained safe? The intensity of the situation began to take its toll on me, and I felt a rising nausea in the pit of my stomach.

"Jack," she snapped through whispered words, and my gaze

snapped to meet hers. "Stay out of the way, okay?" I nodded quickly, my mind and body feeling conflicted and unsettled.

"I get it," I finally managed to say. "I'll stay back. But if you need me, I'm there. I would do anything for you." I tilted my head to rest it against hers, our bodies pressed close together. In the midst of the impending danger, the bond between us grew stronger, a testament to our unwavering commitment to each other.

The rest of the cab ride was quiet as we neared our destination. Annabelle had given the cab driver an address close to the warehouse to avoid drawing attention. We would continue on foot for the remainder of the journey. It left us vulnerable, with no vehicle to escape in if something went wrong. If we had to confront Alexander, it would be on our own terms.

As we arrived at the specified location, the cab driver asked for his payment, extending his hand as if expecting cash. However, to his surprise, Annabelle didn't reach for her purse. Instead, she took hold of his hand in her slender grip and spoke in a hollow, almost mesmerizing tone. "Everything you've seen, you haven't seen. Everything you've heard, you haven't heard. You don't know how you got here, and you never saw us." Her green eyes flared brightly, and to my astonishment, so did the cab driver's. His brown eyes widened, and his jaw went slack as if he were under some kind of spell. It was baffling.

Then, to my further surprise, he repeated her words in a dazed manner before resuming his normal posture and looking forward. My lady and I exited the cab, stepping onto the gritty streets of the southern island. The cab driver raced away in confusion, narrowly missing my toes in his haste.

"What was that?" I asked, still trying to wrap my mind around what I had witnessed. Annabelle raised her wrist to her mouth to stifle a giggle, her eyes dancing with amusement. She seemed to relish these moments when I didn't fully understand things or when I displayed a certain level of naivety.

Annabelle took my hand and gave it a firm tug, her other hand clutching the large duffle bag concealed weapons of death. "Come on," she urged, her voice filled with urgency. "We don't have time to go into it now. We'll discuss it later, my little Jack, later." Her fingers slid across my face, guiding me forward toward the warehouse where I had been held captive and tortured by Alessio's demented Family. The place had been cleared out, devoid of any signs of life, with only the lingering, stale scent of the blood Alexander and I had spilled.

"What do we do now?" I asked as we walked up the ramp through the loading dock. Memories of Aiden's large handgun erupting to scatter the mobster's head into pieces as we entered flashed through my mind. I couldn't help but wonder how he would react to Alexander's untimely death. I imagined him mourning and vowing some form of vengeance, but I didn't fear it. After all, Annabelle was ancient, and I doubted Aiden could ever harm anyone as old as her.

Annabelle halted, her hand pressing flat against my chest. Her eyes, like fields of summer, bore into mine with an intense, burning gaze. The crimson hue of her irises reflected in my own red-tinted orbs.

"Your only role in this is to coax him in, make him feel safe," she explained with determination. "Then I'll take it from there. I'll also need to know what happened when he fought Alessio and Vincent, briefly, of course."

I nodded in agreement, hurrying to lead her inside. I recounted everything I had witnessed, from the strange voice in the darkness of the rafters to the incredible speed and peculiar abilities that seemed to allow him to phase in and out of reality. Our plan was set, and now it was a matter of executing it with precision.

"Alexander is feared across the entire city and most vampiric circles because of what he can do and that he won't hesitate to do it," Annabelle explained as she began to work on setting up small explosive devices. My curiosity got the better of me, and I couldn't help but ask, "What are those?"

Her eyes remained fixed on her task as she continued to place the devices in carefully chosen locations. She ignored my question at first and simply said, "The less you know, love, the better. Just trust me and stay here."

I obeyed her instructions and watched as she climbed hand over hand up one of the support beams, disappearing high into the ceiling. For a fleeting moment, I wondered if I was simply trading one captor for another, but the thought quickly left my mind.

Annabelle continued her preparations, placing devices and incendiaries throughout the entire warehouse, in places I couldn't see. As she finished, she dropped the bag onto the ground at our feet and revealed a large handheld axe, the same one I had seen in her war room.

"This should help," she hissed with a grin. "We just need his head. It's one of the only ways to do this, aside from sunlight. What time is it?" she asked, prompting me to check my phone. The dull pulsing screen displayed 11:38.

"We have an hour. We're ahead of schedule," I replied, my anxiety evident as I fidgeted with the cellular device before returning it to my pocket. The weight of the impending confrontation with Alexander pressed down on us as we waited for the inevitable.

"Jack, what's wrong?" Annabelle asked with concern, her hand resting on her war weapon's handle, her eyes fixed on me. "You're not having any doubts, are you?"

I shook my head, my gaze still fixed on the large axe slung across her slender frame. "No, I'm just... this is scary. Alexander made short work of those men, and I hardly did any damage when I laid a hand on him. What if this doesn't work? What do we do?" Despair washed over me, and fear gnawed at my heart.

Annabelle crossed over to me, placing her free hand on my cheek, her vibrant green eyes locking onto mine, attempting to soothe me. "Sweetheart," her voice was gentle and alluring, "if this doesn't work, then we'll find a way out. We'll regroup. We won't stop fighting."

I couldn't help but ask the question that haunted me, the one that had been nagging at the back of my mind. "And if he kills you...?"

Annabelle chuckled, her laughter rich and confident. "Kills me? Jack, we're nearly the same age, and hell, I have more experience. I'd bet on us, not that arrogant little pissant. We're going to make it through this, and then... maybe we'll get away from the city, see the world, just you and I for a bit until everything cools down. Have you ever been to Czech? It's beautiful. I could introduce you to a few friends, and we could talk about wars fought and won."

Her words offered a glimmer of hope, and I couldn't help but smile despite the impending danger. Annabelle had a way of making even the darkest situations seem bearable, and I clung to her optimism like a lifeline. We were in this together, and we would face whatever came our way, side by side.

I shook my head, frustration bubbling up inside me as Annabelle seemed to dismiss my concerns. My hands shot out to grip her wrist, pulling her closer to me. "Annabelle, take this seriously," I urged, my stomach churning with worry. "If anything ever happened to you, I could never forgive myself. I would do anything to keep you safe."

She laughed, brushing off my words and concerns with a gentle touch. "Jack, I'm supposed to keep you safe, remember?" Her brow furrowed as she leaned in closer, playfully mimicking my fears. "This isn't because you're a big strong man and I'm the lady, is it?"

I snapped, my frustration getting the better of me. "NO, ANNABELLE! IT'S BECAUSE—" But my words were cut short as our eyes locked, and her facade crumbled. "It's because..." My chest heaved, and I struggled to find the right words.

Her lips parted, and her expression softened into a gentle smile. "I love you, too," she whispered, her voice filled with sincerity. My world froze, and we exchanged meaningful glances as the world around us seemed to come to a standstill.

"I really do, Jack," she continued, her voice a tender murmur. "But we can never be together if this doesn't happen, and he will never rest if we run." Annabelle pulled her hand free from my grasp and raised it to cradle my cheek gently. "If you love me, you'll take that dagger I gave you and hide when things happen. And when it's time to end this, you let me and trust that I can do it."

I nodded, my eyes briefly leaving hers before she gripped my chin, forcing me to refocus. "Jack, I may get wounded. This may be bloody. But you have to trust that I can do this." Her words hung in the air between us, heavy with the weight of our shared determination. We were in this together, and we would see it through, no matter the cost.

With those solemn words, our fate was sealed. The night ahead held the promise of danger and uncertainty, but it also held the hope of a future free from the shadows of my past. As Annabelle and I stood there, bound by love and purpose, we prepared to face the ultimate challenge. It was a battle not just for our own survival but for our love, our freedom, and our future together.

The warehouse loomed before us, a dark and foreboding fortress that held the key to our destiny. We were determined to confront the monster that had haunted our lives for far too long, to put an end to the reign of terror that Alexander had imposed upon us.

As the minutes ticked away and the midnight hour drew near, we readied ourselves for the confrontation that would test our resolve and our strength. It was a night that would determine the course of our eternity, and we were willing to face it together, no matter the cost.

"It ends tonight," I echoed Annabelle's words, my voice filled with determination. It was a battle that had been a long time coming, and we were ready to face it head-on.

CHAPTER THIRTY-ONE
BATTLE FOR MY SOUL
PART 2

12:34 AM

The screen of my phone flashed with numbers, and a sensation of dread gripped me. My unbeating heart threatened to leap from my chest into the open air, while a sour fear churned in my stomach, its acidic tendrils clawing up my throat. Alexander was late. Annabelle had disappeared to find a concealed spot, ensuring she left no trace, even going as far as to wash away the lingering scent of her perfume, allowing it to vanish down the shower drain. We'd been inseparable for the past twenty-four hours, yet now, I had no idea where she hid.

Four minutes might sound insignificant, but in this excruciating wait, each second stretched into an eternity. What was causing the delay? Maybe it was the infernal traffic of New York City, or perhaps his duties as a blood trader held him up. But a nagging thought gnawed at me—did he suspect my plan? No. Could he? I attempted to shake off the paranoia, but the image of Alexander advancing toward the warehouse with Aiden in tow sent shivers down my spine. He was my sire, an ancient and malevolent presence in my mind, and his primal fear had become mine.

Then, in the distance, I caught the faint rumble of tires against rain-soaked asphalt. It had to be him. I forced myself to slow my breathing, to appear normal. I struggled to quiet my false breaths, but panic clung to me like a second skin, and I feared he'd see through my act.

Footsteps followed by the subtle thud of a car door echoed in the night. I knew it was him, and his heels clicked on the path we'd taken earlier, growing louder and nearer. His energy, magnetic and irresistible, tugged at me, pulling me in his direction.

This was it.

We stood at the precipice of the final battle, my first true stand, and an overwhelming dread surged within me, rising like an impending tidal wave, threatening to crash down and engulf me where I stood.

"My *DARLING*!" The voice shattered through the mostly empty warehouse, reverberating like the shards of a broken mirror against my clenched fist. I forced a fake smile as my eyes locked onto the figure of my maker. Alexander had dressed impeccably for what he believed was a romantic evening—a brilliantly fitting ruffled poet shirt, snug black slacks that clung to his legs, and his hair styled with casual elegance, as though he'd recently stepped out of a shower. The sight of him took my breath away, for he had bought into my charade entirely, oblivious to the treachery lurking just beneath the surface. Oblivious to the dagger I planned to bury in his throat the moment Annabelle signaled readiness.

"Alex!" I boomed, my voice exuding authenticity as my feet carried me toward the man who had forcibly thrust me into this undead existence. "Oh, how I've missed you! I'm so grateful

THE VAMPIRE JACK TOWNSON 411

you've come, and I'm deeply sorry for the fright I caused you last night." My words felt convincing, even to my own ears, as I concealed the truth that they were a carefully crafted facade, designed to lure a beast roaming freely in the wilderness, unsuspecting of its impending execution.

La Mont shook his head, his golden mane of hair cascading around his clavicles as he lifted both hands to run nimble fingers through his locks, ensuring they appeared loose and alluring to me.

"Jack, mon doux garçon, never doubt for a moment—I'm incredibly proud of what you've revealed to me!" His words were buoyant, laced with genuine admiration. "You see, I always knew there was a predator within you, yearning to break free and stretch its legs." He chuckled at his analogy, likening me to a young lion cub claiming its first gazelle.

But his smile faltered as he drew nearer, closing the gap until only a few feet separated us. His soft lavender eyes grew distant, and a previously unseen sorrow etched across his features, an expression that had never graced the marble countenance of the Frenchman.

"Alexander, what's troubling you?" In an instant, I lost my composure, reverting to the young human who once trailed in his footsteps, desperately trying to keep pace with the dark angel who had once promised to rescue me from a life of mediocrity. I took a hesitant step forward, my world shrinking until there was only him.

He sighed, his hand still resting on his forehead, sharp talons scratching gently at his golden mane just above. "I owe you an apology," he began, and my heart plummeted at his words.

"Alex, you don't have to... Can't we just enjoy this beautiful evening together, please?" I pleaded, attempting to deflect the impending revelation, but it proved futile.

"Love, I pledged to bestow upon you the world, a life filled with bliss and adventure, fame, and affluence. Yet, I delivered subjugation and terror. Instead of parting the sky to shower you with glitter, I let it rain blood... That was never my intention." He closed the gap between us, his hand leaving his head to rest on the crimson fabric of my shoulder. My instincts urged me to run, to recoil, or even to strike him, but his touch had a peculiar effect—melting my resolve.

"I never meant to harm you, to subject you to abuse. I've contemplated a way to make amends." He admitted, his eyes filled with sincerity.

I raised an eyebrow, fully aware that Annabelle would chastise me later for indulging him. "What's your idea?" I inquired to keep him engaged, though I couldn't deny a flicker of curiosity.

Alexander's eyes sparkled with enthusiasm, his other talon gripping my opposite shoulder. "The old venue downstairs, the opera house. I had no use for it, but then it dawned on me—an opportunity to deliver on my promises." I felt a pang of apprehension as he continued, "It's yours now. You have complete control. We can restore it as a working area for the Prepotent, give it a name of your choosing, assemble a cast of young hopefuls for you to employ and feed upon when needed, and grant the city, the world, a glimpse of your brilliance and talents."

I let out a sigh, my façade crumbling. "Alexander..."

"What, you don't like it? Come on, my love, give it a chance!" His smile was infectious, exuding a boyish and charming quality that made it impossible to resist.

"Alex... oh, damn it... I don't know the first thing about running a show, let alone acting in one." I clenched my hand into my hair, grappling with the overwhelming realization of what was about to unfold. I pulled away from his grasp, pacing back and forth, my smile mirroring his but tinged with anxiety rather than joy.

"I'd teach you everything, just as I promised. I'll share the tools I've acquired over the long years, transform you into not only a savant but a master of your craft! Imagine it, Alexander La Mont and his protege—" Alex draped an arm around my shoulders and gestured dramatically with his free hand, as if presenting our names on an imaginary marquee, "—the renowned Jack Townson, and your name will shine in bright red lights!"

I allowed myself to envision the scenario, my smile still present but faltering. "It's a tempting idea, but we've been through so much, Alex... is it truly enough to forgive you for what you did to me? You... you violated me, Alexander."

He took a step back to my side, his expression filled with remorse. "You're right. You're absolutely right. I would never force myself upon you again, ever. I would... fight for your love, instead of trying to imprison it."

I halted in my tracks, locking my gaze with his purple eyes.

"Alex," I whispered.

"Yes, my Jack?" he replied, his voice filled with genuine longing.

"Did I ever tell you the name I chose...?" I uttered, and the world seemed to freeze as realization washed over me. Alex stood there, perplexed by my question.

"Of course you did. You... mentioned it during the car ride to the good Doctor's," he replied, his fangs digging into his lower lip as he spoke.

"Alex... I never told you. I never breathed a word of it. How did you know...?" I inquired again, my words stumbling as I tried to maintain my composure. Something was gravely amiss.

La Mont's expression soured, his head tilting slightly as he contemplated how he had known the name I had chosen for myself.

Then, his visage shifted from boyish jubilance to one of determination. "I promised to fight for your love, and I wasn't lying. That's precisely why I'm here."

"No..." I whispered, panic seizing my body as I began to realize the horrifying truth.

Alexander leaned in close, his words whispered so only we could hear. "I may have lost your love, and that was my doing, and hers," he pointedly mentioned. "She's manipulated your mind, making you see me as the villain in this tale. But did she ever disclose her true abilities to you? How she can twist and rewrite minds, fabricate new intentions that aren't your own, or compel you to walk off a cliff and believe it's your choice? I'm offering you a chance to step back from the edge before it's too late." His eyes bore into mine, unwavering. "If I have to take drastic measures, I will."

I recoiled from his closeness, my feet stumbling as I moved away from him. My boots scraped against the warehouse floor, near the very spot where those men had once tortured me. "How... how..." I muttered, my voice caught in a loop of disbelief, realizing that Alexander knew everything.

He simply shook his head, his fingers tracing up his sharp cheekbones to tap gently against his temples. "When you dream, I am connected to you. I can witness your experiences and the true depths of your feelings for me. I saw it all, Jack, I saw you pull away from the illusion of me and pledge your love and loyalty to Annabelle. Instead of desiring retribution, I understood that she must have been manipulating you against me. So, I gave you a chance... and I did some introspection of my own. I meant every word, my love, when I said I was sorry for everything. I want the opportunity to make amends, to make it right, as long as you stay by my side."

A voice emerged from behind him, and neither of us had noticed her approach. Annabelle stood there, a shotgun leveled at him, her finger poised on the trigger. "He's no longer yours. You lost him... justly."

I shook my head defiantly, my voice resolute. "I'm in this with you. I won't let you face this alone!"

With my intentions laid bare and my allegiance firmly declared, Alexander gave me one last glance before turning to face the woman who had stolen my heart. His head shook in resignation.

"Ah, *Ulf*," Alexander spat with a tinge of blasphemy, "where is your honor? A sneak attack? How... Viking of you." The lithe ancient in white began to pace, preparing himself for what was to come. "How could you two do this to me, after everything we've been through—Annabelle," he turned his gaze briefly in my direction, "after I made you what you are."

Annabelle raised her weapon even higher, her eye twitching with anger. "Endless disrespect and, most importantly, you had gold and treated it like lead. You not only harmed your progeny but raped him, Alexander? Even the ones you create don't want you."

Alexander erupted, his voice piercing the air as his talons clenched in fury. "I gave him a new life, made him what he is. We're bound by a contract! I OWN him. Do you think your brief sexual escapade qualifies as love? Enough to come between the blood bond we share? Not even in the slightest. You're a failure, a failed vampire, and failed progeny," he grinned maliciously, "and a failed guardian to the girls you claim to love so dearly."

The tension continued to mount, voices escalating to new levels of aggression. It was clear that this confrontation was on the brink of disaster.

"Listen, it doesn't have to be like this!" I cried out, adding my voice to the cacophony of heated exchanges between my two elders. "We can all just walk away. I can go with Annabelle, and you can continue your life. We just want happiness, to exist... Please, just let us go. You admitted it yourself—you failed me, you abused me. Let me go." My voice wavered from its initial intensity, ending on a note of sorrow, filled with fear of what would happen next....

Annabelle and Alexander almost spoke in unison, "No."

She held her gaze steady on my sire, her gun pointed at him. "We're well beyond that point, Jack. There's only one way out for him, and he knows it, even if he were to say the words."

Shock rippled through me, my legs growing weak with confusion. "Annabelle! You said this wasn't about revenge, you said—"

My words were abruptly cut off by her resolute voice. "I said this was about setting you free, and it is. But I lied... it's also about revenge. Revenge for the vampires he's harmed, for the girls he's murdered and sold into slavery, for his constant disrespect and unwavering arrogance. He dies tonight, whether he intended to let you go with me or not."

I felt my voice tear at my vocal cords in desperation. "ANNABELLE!"

"Face it, Jack," she declared, her aim unwavering. "He came here fully aware of the consequences."

Alexander turned to face me, his voice filled with earnestness. "She's right. I knew what I was doing because I love you, and I won't let you go without a fight." La Mont shifted to fully address the one to whom I had professed my loyalty, his purple gaze locked onto her emerald eyes. "He's mine, and you know you can't defeat me. You know you're outmatched."

Annabelle's eyes locked onto my face once more, her head nodding slightly. "You know what to do—RUN, NOW!" She turned her fierce gaze toward Alexander. "There's only one way this ends—either you die... or I do."

With those chilling words, she pulled the trigger, igniting the morning with a deafening explosion of pellets erupting from the barrel. I darted away, my body vibrating with the familiar speed that carried me out of harm's reach. I didn't know what bullets could do against a monster like La Mont, but I had no intention of remaining in the crossfire between two ancient vampires battling over their claim on me.

The tiny metal shards slammed into his body, puncturing his flesh and creating small holes in the poet's shirt he had so romantically worn during our time together. The white fabric instantly darkened with red spots as he stumbled backward. "Is that all you have—a mere toy invented by small men? It means nothing to me, just a distraction."

As he spoke, he seemed to shimmer, moving so swiftly that the dust from the warehouse floor swirled into the air in his wake. Annabelle swiftly turned and fired again at an empty spot in the room. In the exact spot she aimed, Alexander reappeared and staggered once more, his surprise evident in the confusion etched onto his marble features. Blood began to saturate the remnants of his once-white shirt, falling to the ground like confetti from what had previously been called a shirt.

Once more, Alexander vanished from sight, and I observed Annabelle repeating her tactic, tracking him down out of thin air and unleashing another round of buckshot into his unyielding flesh. The tiny pellets caused sparks to fly as they struck his armor-like skin. This time, the closer proximity caused him to stagger and nearly lose his footing. He clutched his chest, black powder marks forming beneath the tattered remnants of his shirt. The fabric disintegrated, joining its siblings in tatters on the floor. To my astonishment, my sire's blood sprayed into the air, but his chest remained miraculously intact. He was stronger, faster, and more durable, but Annabelle was a master tactician. She had spent centuries studying the art of war, making her the perfect counter to my tormentor.

"You bitch, how—" Alexander groaned, forcing his body to rise to a full stance once more, defying Annabelle's skill. His talon reached to grasp the last remnants of white fabric on his barrel chest and tossed them to the floor. His blood dripped down with them in droplets, the scent of singed flesh mingling with the rising steam. The fiend curled against himself, his knees briefly buckling as he struggled to regain his composure and brace for another assault. His lavender eyes burned like boiling pools through his soft vanilla strands, yearning to drown the crimson vixen in her own blood.

Annabelle laughed, a hand rising to her lips as she had done before, her heavily lashed eyes batting closed. "Oh, Alex... While you may have forsaken your humanity for power, I spent my time honing my skills and studies, learning everything I could about countering an elder like you. I've dreamed of this day for over a century." Her lithe hand gripped the pump of the firearm, ensuring the round was ready.

La Mont wobbled but managed to regain his composure, his nose pointed upward as he glared down the bridge at Annabelle. "All of this... over some human girls and some harsh words. You're frail, fragile, with no spine for this life. Your maker failed you, and now you're stuck in a strip club because all you know how to do is be a whore. And now you've stolen my progeny... I'll tear the flesh from your bones for this."

Annabelle shrieked in response, her voice laced with rage. "THEY WERE MY CHILDREN! I was entrusted with their care, they trusted me, and you sold them to be murdered!" Her anger caused spittle to fly into the open air. Her eyes were wide and swollen with sorrow. "You have no idea how hard my journey has been, how much I fought to become who I am and live my life. You might think they're just words, but each one is a

DAGGER in my back, each deserving of death! You will never do it to me again or to anyone else!" Her lips trembled as she screamed, her chest heaving wildly as she kept the barrel of the firearm aimed at him.

Alexander's countenance softened as he took her words into consideration, realizing the extent of the harm they had caused her and the profound pain of the loss of human life. "For what it's worth," he began, "I apologize. I was raised as a Catholic, and to me... what you've done is an abomination. Still, my words were wrong."

Annabelle shook her head, her teeth gritting tightly. "No! Absolutely not! I will -not- be manipulated by you! If anything, that just means you're a hypocrite to your own upbringing, using it against me to be a fucking bastard! And that's more than enough for me to keep my focus, and not only that..." Her eyes found me, and I stood there slack-jawed behind the doorway. "You assaulted that beautiful man. You *broke* him, Alex... *look at him*!"

My sire slowly turned his head to the side, his eyes catching where I was standing, the crimson markings still adorning my face. He hadn't noticed them until now. "I am making him strong," he whispered, his face contorting into a painful grimace. "You have no idea how my sire treated me, what I had to do to get to where I am now, what I've sacrificed. What I've done. What I've lost."

Annabelle's finger tightened on the trigger of the shotgun, her gaze locked onto the blood splattered hypocrite. "You're convincing yourself of that, and nothing more. We see through you—your infatuation. You changed his name, his face, and then took advantage of him. You promised this boy the world and then tore it apart. You're a sick bastard, and tonight it ends." She pulled the trigger, and another round of buckshot exploded into the air. Alexander seemed to vanish from his spot,

his body gone as the pellets slammed into the ground and rico-
cheted into the doorframe where I remained, hidden as best I
could. Annabelle's emerald eyes searched the surroundings,
trying to locate where he had gone, but with no success. She
stared at the shotgun, muttering frustrated words as she realized how few shells she had left.

As she did, a miasma began to form where she stood.
Alexander materialized behind her.

"ANNABELLE, BEHIND YOU!" I screamed, my hand flying to
the dagger at my side, my feet preparing to move. Yet, hesitation
crept in, confusion clouding my thoughts. Was it possible I was
trading one captor for another? She had lied to me. Every step
she took seemed to indicate that she wanted to take matters
into her own hands, prioritizing revenge over freeing me from
my perceived monster. Was I merely swapping one evil for
another?

Annabelle heard my desperate plea and swiftly spun on her
heel, swinging the shotgun behind her. However, it proved of
little use as Alexander's clawed hand closed around the barrel,
tossing it aside and seizing her throat. He lifted her off the
ground, her toes barely grazing the floor, their faces mere inches
apart.

"Did you really think that could stop me? Did you believe a
weapon meant for large game could defeat one of the strongest
vampires in the known world?" He grinned triumphantly, his
jaws opening wide as if preparing to sink his fangs into her neck
to drain her essence. Fear lodged in my throat, and I searched
desperately for a way to intervene.

"Wait!" I screamed. "Alexander, please!" His attention
momentarily shifted to me, while my female companion's face
bore a furious expression.

"Jack, stay out of this!" she hissed. As his head turned to
focus on me, her hand dipped into her pocket, retrieving a

hidden item she had stowed away in the large duffle bag we had bought—a syringe. With a forceful jab, it pierced the skin on his neck, just a few inches beneath his ear. A dark red fluid, with an odor resembling festering roadkill, filled the syringe. Alexander winced as the needle punctured his flesh, his tightening grip causing Annabelle to groan, but she remained steadfast. With a determined push of the plunger, the fluid found its way into La Mont's neck. He sputtered and released her, falling back onto his backside, his eyes widening in fear.

"What did you—what?!" he hissed, his fangs bared as he began to stumble and fall. With her newfound advantage, my love merely tiptoed her way to where the heels of his shoes rested on the ground, staring down at him with a wicked grin.

"Can you feel it, Alex?" Annabelle taunted. "I doubt anyone has ever had the courage or ability to get this close to you. I was skeptical about using my 'hail mary,' as I aptly named it, but you gave me the perfect opportunity, and Jack helped me exploit your vulnerability."

I watched in horror as the man who had made me, the man I inherently loved, began to cough up torrents of his own blood. He hacked and sputtered, his blonde hair becoming matted with crimson. "Annabelle... holy shit," I muttered as I left my hiding place, my dagger still clutched tightly in my hand. "Is he dying?"

She simply shook her head, her eyes fixated on what remained of his soul with a mix of anxious excitement and vindication. "No, I've injected him with dead man's blood. It's one of the few weaknesses the books got right. We need living blood to survive and stay strong. If we feed from the dead... well, we begin to revert to a death-like state for a short period of time. He's struggling with a complete shutdown. The room is spinning, and even he can't resist it for too long."

My maker, my sire, my love, began to crawl away, while

Annabelle laughed sadistically. "Don't run. This is so much more boring than I expected." She tossed the syringe to the ground and turned her back momentarily.

Alexander and I locked eyes, his face marred by scattered purple veins, his hair shriveling and decaying until it turned white once more. I could see him clearly now. He was a monster. Yet, he was also mine. His mouth hung open, struggling to speak, his lips stained deep crimson as he desperately tried to shake off the effects. A single hand reached out toward me, a desperate plea in silence.

"Jack," Annabelle called as she returned, "in the bag, there's a wooden stake. Get it ready, just in case." She strutted back to the gruesome scene, dragging the large axe of her heritage behind her. "To think, Alexander La Mont will be on my list of kills. It's a shame I can't keep your head as a trophy, Alex." She was reveling in this moment, driven by equal parts pleasure and vengeance, and I began to feel like her lackey.

"Jack!" she snapped, jolting me from my thoughts. I darted from behind the door, my boots clomping loudly against the stone floor as I made my way to the bag on the ground. My hands deftly searched through the contents, most of which had already been used.

There, neatly resting at the bottom, was a beautifully crafted wooden stake, its end wrapped in silver and its tip stained in red. I whispered as I held it in my hands, my crimson eyes tracing the surface to find small runes carved into the metal.

"Will this kill him, Annabelle..." I murmured.

"No, no..." she sighed as she approached him. "It's just for decoration. It won't kill him—only paralyze him if he gets the upper hand and tries to turn the tables." She explained, the head of the axe raising and slamming onto the ground, sending sparks near Alexander's feet.

Alexander laughed through his own blood, turning his head

to gaze at Annabelle and shifting his body as well. "You know," he coughed out, flecks of blood spraying onto his chest, "this is far, far from over." With those ominous words, he began to phase, and Annabelle's eyes widened with realization.

"NO! NO, YOU DON'T!" Annabelle raised the axe with lightning speed, bringing it crashing down where Alexander had been. His body phased away just before the blow could land, leaving the axe head to carve a deep dent into the asphalt where he had once lain. Annabelle's frustration boiled over as she shouted, "Alexander, you can't run from me!"

I followed her gaze, scanning the surroundings in an attempt to catch a glimpse of him myself, desperately hoping that maybe there was a way he had managed to escape.

CRACK-THOOM

An explosion from above wrang out, a rafter down the way crumbling and falling, and Alexander falling with it, blackened scorchmarks and tiny flames tiger-stripping across his upper half. She really had all of this figured out—*everything*. It was then I realized just how terrifying this woman truly was.

With a sinister smile she bounded her way towards the rubble, leaping over the landing to raise her axe high, ready to slam it down onto his fallen form. "It's *over*, La Mont! It's FINISHED!"

Down it went and I closed my eyes.

"No..." he coughed.

My eyes opened just in time to see what had taken place. Annabelle's axe rested in Alexander's cold grasp, the head placed right against his palm as a ribbon of his blood flowed down his forearm to his elbow. Annabelle's face changed from victory to horror.

Alexander's sinister smile remained, even as Annabelle struggled to retrieve the axe from his grip. His voice rasped as he explained, "No, you've not won... this is only the start. I had to see what you had planned for me. It was Jack's mind that led me to know that you were planning something undoubtedly, and I knew there were few options you could go with. To close the gap, to keep me from phasing, and to poison me... how else would you take my head if not for sunlight? Which, I'm guessing, is why you made the hour so late... to stall for the dawn just in case that didn't work out, am I right?"

Annabelle's face contorted with shock and disbelief as she continued to struggle in vain. "How?! How aren't you poisoned?!"

Alexander's laughter echoed through the warehouse, a haunting sound that sent shivers down my spine. "Annabelle, my dear, you forget that I've had centuries to build up an immunity to such things. You underestimated me."

Annabelle's expression shifted from horror to desperation as she realized her plan had backfired. Alexander had outsmarted her, and now she was trapped with her own weapon in his hands.

The malevolent figure raised his hand high into the air, clenching it into a formidable fist that came crashing down onto the ancient waraxe, shattering it at the handle and reducing its formidable length. "You misunderstand," he sneered, "I am indeed poisoned, but it's far easier to combat when you anticipate it. Besides, my dear, this isn't some cinematic tale. You won't catch me off guard so easily... little girl."

With a resounding clang, the axe fell to the ground, taking Annabelle with it. Her body spun from the abrupt impact, and she scrambled to regain her footing, her palms pressed firmly against the floor. Her long fingers instinctively reached for the broken weapon, clutching it tightly as she stared at it in disbelief. "This was my father's, you wretched creature..."

"Good," he growled, slowly rising from the rubble. "I'm certain he would be disappointed in you, as I am. Why not add one more disappointment to the list?" With a sudden surge of strength, he was back on his feet, scorch marks marring his porcelain skin, covering his shoulders, chest, and even part of his jaw. He twisted his head to the side, producing a loud popping sound from his neck. "I, too, was a warrior, Annabelle. Death is a familiar companion for both of us, but I've chosen to bury that part of my history."

His polished dress shoes moved silently over the debris-strewn floor, stalking his prey with the same eerie calmness as a great white shark prowling the ocean depths. "I can feel it," he coughed, his eye wincing as his knuckles folded inward, claws clenching to fend off the effects of the poison. "The blood of the dead man... I presume Corpus provided it to you as a contingency. Excellent. I'll be sure to visit him once this is over. And as for your club, I'll decimate your staff and the girls you protect. I'll drain every last one of them for this transgression. *Je vais tous les tuer*, every last one!"

Annabelle's meticulously tied hair came undone, strands cascading over her face as she desperately clung to the shortened axe, determination fueling her every move. "No! You'll meet your end before you lay a hand on them. You're finished!" With a bone-chilling battle cry, she surged to her feet, moving at supernatural speeds to confront Alexander amidst the scattered debris. The axe whizzed overhead, but her unbridled rage made her strikes erratic and uncoordinated.

"Is this the extent of your prowess?" Alexander taunted, his laughter echoing in the dimly lit warehouse. "I expected more, *Loup rouge*. Show me the fury your sire tempered from before she turned you!" He skillfully evaded each swing, his body gracefully weaving backward as Annabelle relentlessly closed the distance. Their feet moved in an eerie synchrony, a deadly dance masked as a macabre duel. Blood tears streamed down

Annabelle's face, the axe singing through the air, missing its mark with each pass.

Then, an opportune moment arrived. Alexander's foot slipped on a fallen stone, diverting his focus from his evasive maneuvers. "I've got you!" Annabelle declared triumphantly, embodying the spirit of a timeless warrior. The axe plunged into his chest with a sickening thud, a crimson spray painting the air and staining her face. "How does it feel to know you're defeated? To realize you'll meet your end in this wretched warehouse while I return to those who cherish me? But not before your progeny and I make passionate love atop your ashes!"

"It's like a dream, one you've been imagining since the moment you laid eyes on him!" Alexander remained surprisingly coherent, his fist clenching into a vice that hammered into Annabelle's jaw, each blow snapping her head back as her crimson mane came loose, swirling wildly around her. With a swift move, Alexander seized the axe handle, intertwining his fingers with hers, his claws digging into her hand to maintain control as he violently thrashed the fiery-haired warrior backward.

Until this moment, my encounters with vampires had been brief and lightning-fast, hardly ever on equal footing. But when elders clashed, it was like witnessing titans in a battle that shook the very foundations of the city, causing cars and buildings to crumble in their inability to yield to the raw mastery over the powers of death. All I could do was watch, the wooden stake in my hand trembling, a potential game-changer in this clash of supernatural heavyweights.

Annabelle locked her gaze with Alexander's piercing purple orbs, both sets of fangs bared in a supernatural display of fury. Her face bore the marks of brutal blows, blood staining her features. "I won't die here, and you'll never—never—harm that man again." She struggled to halt Alexander's relentless advance, her feet sliding against the ground as he pushed her back. "You think I brought this axe because it's made of iron and oak? No, not at all!" Alexander's brow furrowed as he listened, his brutal punches momentarily halting.

Without warning, the weapon came to life, emanating sudden pale blue streams of electricity from the head lodged in Alexander's chest. He released the weapon with a deafening roar of agony. "It's because this axe was blessed by the mystics of my village, my father's weapon enchanted by the gods. He gifted it to me for one purpose—to slay monsters like you!"

The tension in the room reached a fever pitch as I watched Alexander sink to his knees, wisps of smoke curling from his body, casting an eerie blue illumination.

"What in the world..." I mouthed in disbelief, witnessing the undeniable presence of magic unfold right before my eyes. My world expanded exponentially in that moment, leaving me little time to comprehend the imminent destruction of my maker.

"There are... no gods," Alexander murmured, his fingers tightly gripping the axe head embedded in his chest, the searing heat of the ancient iron beginning to cauterize the wound. "I'll prove it to you." With grim determination, he commenced pulling and tugging at the weapon lodged within him.

Annabelle summoned the ancestral power once more, electricity crackling and climbing up Alexander's body as he struggled to free himself. "Just die!" she screamed, her visage alight with the electric fury of a tempestuous sky. "Let this end!"

Their eyes locked in a battle of wills. "*Never!*" Alexander declared as the axe head finally dislodged with a final, violent tug. It sputtered and sparked between them, sending currents surging through both vampires as they fought for dominance over the weapon.

CRASH!

The room erupted in a blinding flash of white, forcing me to shield my eyes. When I dared to look again, I understood what had occurred—Alexander had wrested control and, with an immense display of power, sent the thunderous weapon hurtling into the ground, shattering it into countless pieces. He stood there, shirtless and formidable, bearing the scars of the fire and the gaping wound from the axe head, resembling a villain from a horror movie. Annabelle, defeated, sank to her knees, her hands frantically sweeping across the ground to gather the shattered remnants, blood tears staining her face.

"My... you..." she stammered, her gaze fixed upward at him, her thoughts in disarray.

"Let's just say that whatever I possess is mightier than your ancient, feeble gods, or perhaps they have forsaken you," Alexander mused, leaning down to seize Annabelle by the face, lifting her head and using his other hand to grip her throat. "It's over now."

Hovering in her vulnerable position, Annabelle thrust her hand into the gaping hole in Alexander's chest, reaching for his heart. "If I die, we both die. I'll ensure it. Then you won't harm anyone ever again."

My voice erupted in a desperate scream as I watched her clutch at my maker's heart, daring to rip it from his chest. "Annabelle, you'll die! You don't even know if that can kill him!" I finally found my courage, my body moving closer to the two warring elders, determined to halt the madness. "What about everything we shared, what about our love?"

"Jack," her flickering green eyes briefly glanced my way, "this is about loving you... I can't let him..." Her words were strained, and Alexander's grip on her tightened, as if he intended to sever her head from her shoulders.

Alexander posed the ultimate dilemma, and I found myself trapped in an impossible choice. I had to act, to make a decision that would change everything. My fate, and the fates of everyone I loved hung in the balance.

"What will you do, Jack?" Alexander's words echoed through the warehouse. "How will you resolve this? Will you save the woman you love, the sister you cherish, and leave with me? Or will you watch us both perish?"

My thoughts raced, and I knew there was only one choice left. Doing nothing would mean losing the woman I loved to the man who had both created and torn me apart. I would be his slave for all eternity. There was only one choice.

Rushing towards them, I raised my hand with lightning speed, calling forward my inherited dark gifts. I sent it slicing down upon my intended target, right at the crook of Annabelle's arm. The impact severed the soft flesh through her elbow, causing her to scream in agony. The sounds of her pain harrowed up to the rafters, shaking the building, her body frozen as her pleading, glistening green eyes searched desperately for me.

"JACK!" she wailed, her feet scrambling for purchase on the ground. "*WHAT ARE YOU DOING? NO! WE'RE SO CLOSE!*"

Her words tore at my heart, but I couldn't falter now. I had to save her, no matter the cost. As the arm holding Alexander's heart fell away, it disintegrated into dust within the cavity of his chest, scattering across the ground. A sense of relief washed over him, and a smile touched his features. "Yes, good... a wise decision. You've chosen well," he conceded, lowering Annabelle to her feet and releasing her.

But Annabelle, consumed by blind fury, turned on me. With quickness born of desperation, she grabbed the dagger from my belt and lunged at Alexander, her remaining hand driving the blade into his chest repeatedly. She narrowly missed his heart, the blade sinking into flesh again and again. Her fury deafened our ears as she screamed for his death—the most fractured and disturbing agony I had ever heard.

"Jack, remember what I said!" Alexander cried out, fumbling once more as his dress shoes skidded across the blood-slicked stone. "I will kill her, I will kill them all!"

I roared, my voice echoing through the chamber, "Only if you promise to leave the Gilded Rose alone, only if you swear —SWEAR—to keep your word! Spare her life, grant them peace! Put an end to this madness, and I'll be yours!"

Annabelle's anguished scream pierced the air, a heart-wrenching plea, "JACK, NO!"

Alexander, his sinister grin never fading, replied, "It's a deal."

With those fateful words hanging in the air, my fingers twitched, and my hand slipped as I thrust the wooden stake forward, driving it through her back. The edge found its mark, penetrating deep enough to reach the organ I had promised to protect—her heart. In an instant, her body stiffened and became rigid, her movements faltering and then ceasing alto-gether as blood tears trickled down her cheeks. She gasped for breath, her voice choked, "Ja-Jack... I lo-loved you... I love you... please, please don't—cckkkk... don't do this..."

As I withdrew the stake, Alexander stepped away from the scene, retrieving the dagger and pulling it free from where it had lodged. "I'll leave you two alone for a moment," he announced, his purple eyes glancing back at Annabelle with a strange mix of sympathy and nostalgia. Through strands of bloodied blonde hair, he regarded the girl who had once been his rival and friend. "Goodbye, Annabelle... may our paths never cross again... worthy opponent." With that, Alexander left, stumbling over the warzone and retracing his steps, allowing me a private moment with the woman I loved.

"Jack—J-jack! Why—why did you—" she began to falter,

her body giving way. I caught her in my arms, crumpling with her on top of my own. Red hair mingled with the fabric of my hoodie, our hearts beating as one. I held her close, bypassing the stake still lodged in her back. "Let me—l—*ckkkkk*... let me f-fight for you. Please... I love you... I love you."

Tears blurred my vision as I nestled against the back of her cherry-red mane, my own vitae disappearing into the strands as if they were returning to their rightful home. "He's just going to win, and I can't... do this. I can't. I love you... I truly do... but losing you isn't worth my freedom. Let me bear this burden, damn it."

Annabelle's face contorted as the rigidity of death set in, her once-gleaming green eyes now fixed on the ceiling above. "You... you... you coward..."

She lay there against me, my arms cradling her tightly, knowing that this would be the last time I held her this way, the last time she would want me to. This was my destiny—a slave to a master who would never again be her monster. I could bear that burden for her, I could do this. I understood it would destroy me, transforming me into something worse than I could imagine, but for her sake? I would let that last flicker of humanity die if it meant she would live.

"Goodbye, my warrior queen..." I whispered, placing one last kiss upon the back of her head before parting from her, leaving her frozen on the ground, a breathtaking statue, a poignant symbol of my sacrifice, and the most beautiful effigy I had ever seen.

INTO THE UNKNOWN

"Alexander and I departed the warehouse just as dawn threatened to break, the battle for my escape lasting until the clouds softened, and the sky resembled the deep sea. Annabelle lay on the warehouse floor, her beauty frozen in time but marred by the blood tears of my betrayal. Alexander granted me permission to contact Penelope, alerting her to the danger. The poor girl, still healing from emotional wounds, rushed to the south end, accompanied by Annabelle's security. She would never trust me again, but as we sped through the traffic to evade the approaching sunlight, I knew I had done the right thing. Annabelle was a remarkable woman, a vision with a heart of gold. I would rather shatter it than witness its destruction. Broken pieces can be mended over time, but obliteration leaves no chance for redemption. It was better to endure her hatred and resentment than to witness her reduced to ashes.

"As we drove, Alexander gently gripped my hand. A new side of him emerged, one I hadn't seen since our first encounter, a tenderness that he had buried in my early weeks as a vampire.

His demeanor and caution gave me hope that he would make a sincere effort this time or at least treat me better.

"Upon arriving at the Prepotent, Claude had already concluded his work for the morning. Only one figure remained in the bar: Aiden. He sipped from a martini glass filled with blood, barely acknowledging me as Alexander walked past. I approached Aiden, my legs heavy from the recent battles. It was only fair to ask where he had been. When I did, he glanced at me, his lips curling from the rim of the glass.

""You understand now, don't you?" he said more as a statement than a question. "This is your home, and he'll never let you go. It's best to accept that. If there's ever a next time, know that I won't stay out of it. I'd relish the opportunity to have him to myself again."

"The night ended unceremoniously. Alexander tended to his wounds and ensured I received the necessary fluids. He revealed that the bedroom now included a cozy cot on the floor. He offered me the bed, but I declined politely, opting for the small mattress. He didn't take offense and genuinely seemed to understand. We slept through the daylight hours.

"Weeks passed, and occasionally, Annabelle's name appeared on my phone. She called or texted, trying to reach me, but I chose to ignore her. I knew she must have been worried and heartbroken, but I needed time to clear my mind and shake off the love I felt for her. Eventually, I succeeded, as did she, but our connection was forever altered, as was Penelope's, the young girl I had saved.

"Amidst the heartache, Alexander made strides in the following weeks, hiring more staff and reviving the Prepotent's reputation. He asked for my input on what to name the revital-ized theatre, and I suggested *The Paramount*. The area was cleaned, seats and curtains replaced, and a new sign hung outside, proudly displaying my name in red light.

Jack Townson Presents
The Paramount
Coming Soon!

The name, which had once carried so much pain, now stood at the center of my rebirth. I feared it might attract too much attention, but Alexander was showing me that his words held some truth.

"Alexander fulfilled his promise of educating me in the ways of the savant, providing me with lessons and hiring experts to fill any gaps that remained. I had grand plans for the opening, and when the day arrived, I took the stage as the star of our first show, *Monster and Man*, which I had written myself. It told the story of a man tormented by an unending desire to kill, a tragic love story in which the love interest is frozen in time as a living statue. The audience's thunderous applause confirmed that I was meant for this.

"However, as I gazed into the audience, I noticed the absence of those I loved most: Chloe, Brad, Dad, Penelope, and Annabelle. I had traded my freedom for her safety and gained fame in return. The streets of New York were paved with supernatural and human citizens praising my name. Alexander's repeated words had come true: "*One day, the world will say that the Vampire Jack Townson is the most famous and influential vampire in New York, or even the world.*"

"In my quiet moments, when the theater was empty, and Alexander had retired for the day, I sat there with the book Marcus had given me, and I continued to write, a certain muse springing to mind more often than I cared to admit.

The Cross
Petals caressed with care
My fingers, do touch and entice

With promise of love and laughter
Of new life and awakening
Of kindred unity and understanding
Yet, I release the delicate thing
And allow it to shatter upon my feet
Left in the cold, I taught it pain
And the meaning of resentment

"In those moments when writing couldn't console me, when the pen on paper couldn't offer the comfort I craved as a slave to the man who had assaulted and transformed me, I often found myself scrolling through my phone, staring at the texts I never answered. I would picture her face, my Songbird, and how I missed her large eyes and her black, choppy hair. Her softness, love, and care. One day, I told myself, I would find a way to make it work, to bring her back to me, but deep down, I knew it was too dangerous. One day.

"You might be sitting there, across from me, wondering how I got to where I am, how everything turned upside down. Well, my friend, while I may have thought myself docile and complacent, with the world at my feet and my craft finally realized, the truth was that the heart is much stronger than the mind. In time, the call to find love again would come, and I would find myself in a new world of trouble. But that's a story for another time. The world outside awaits, fresh and full of possibility. What do you say? Shall we take a break from the pain of the past and see what it has to offer in this place where I've chosen to rest my crown?"

Across from the large vampire sits a shorter man, his dark skin and wide eyes fixed on all he had divulged as the mental pictures seem to dissipate in the air.

The man called Algernon stands, calloused hands

THE VAMPIRE JACK TOWNSON

smoothing out his suit pants. "You know, Jack... you really know how to keep an audience on the edge of their seat."

"Don't leave us on a cliffhanger!" says a small witch to Algernon's left. Verona folds her arms in frustration, her heart-shaped mouth twisting to the side.

Others had piled into the library to listen to the recount as well. A werelion named Grendal towers over every other head in the room, his tail shifting side to side, nearly slamming into a haphazard stack of books. Several other vampires also huddle together in the more shadowed corners, waiting for the next chapter of the story, and just as well, a few pairs of glowing yellow goblin eyes blink eagerly from various places for the vampire to continue.

With a hearty laugh, the Vampire Jack Townson stands to his full height, setting his glass of the famed red substance on a side table. He leaves the fire and the conversation, his large boots echoing across the floor, just past his eager attendant.

"Algernon," he growls, "we have much to do. The past is the past, and our time is now." Jack walks down the corridor, passing old landscape paintings and forgotten family portraits. Shadows creep with his every step, undulating and swirling about his form as his power courses.

His long crimson coat nearly drags across the floor behind him. More glowing eyes watch from the darkness within each door frame he passes, the manor's inhabitants always hungry for his attention. Jack stops just before a massive set of double doors, their cracked and ancient wood giving them an air of timeless existence. His claws caress the surface.

"Are you coming?" he asks.

Algernon, his seemingly human companion, sighs, his neck craning to the side as his tight curls bounce atop his head with the motion. "I think I'll sit this one out," he grumbles, an eye squinting in exhaustion. "The manor needs someone to watch over it, and you graciously gave me this position. Have fun for me, and say hello to David."

Jack's fists begin to pry open the massive doors, Algernon's voice breaking through the darkness just before he can disappear inside.

"And Jack," Algernon calls out, "please, just... keep the chaos to a minimum, for me, and don't get into trouble?"

Jack turns to acknowledge him, his red eyes dancing in the darkness.

"No promises," he grins with a deep growl.

His bejeweled claws pull the doors open to their fullest, revealing Draconia—a sprawling, nightmarish land with twisted, bony trees and massive mountains on the horizon. The skyline fills with soaring creatures of a truly damnable nature.

Jack Townson smiles. "Good morning, Neverland."

ACKNOWLEDGMENTS

I would like to thank the entire Fangfam for believing in this story and in this journey, to my partner, Shayne, for the encouragement and the glitter, and to every storyteller who came before me who paved the road with blood, magic, and other impossible things.

ABOUT THE AUTHOR

Jack Townson, a multi-talented artist, is the heart and soul of the thriving FangFam community across various social media platforms, including TikTok, Instagram, and Twitch. With an ever-expanding following that now exceeds four hundred thousand devoted fans, he's left an indelible mark on the digital landscape, garnering an impressive 4.2 million likes under the #Fangfam hashtag.

Beyond his online presence, Jack is a versatile artist, encompassing the roles of actor, singer, and writer. His most celebrated work to date is "The Vampire Jack Townson," an original story that first captivated audiences on TikTok. This immersive narrative plunges into the hidden world of a supernatural being and the profound journey towards rediscovering one's humanity.

Jack extends an invitation to his followers, beckoning them to peer into the psyche of an undead bohemian—an artist and a creature of the night, eternally ensnared in a world of nightmares. It's a life devoid of sunlight's warmth and the enduring embrace of true love, offering a unique glimpse into the enigmatic existence he portrays through his creative endeavors.

ALSO BY JACK TOWNSON

Blood and Roses

Death and Lilies